MW01611066

TWELVE TORTOISE TUSSLES

Claire zeroed in on Butch. "The mother of *your* child is up to something."

"Up to what?"

"I don't know exactly, but it's something that is making her face twitch again."

Butch rubbed his jaw. "What conspired prior to this twitch?"

"*Twitches*," she clarified. "Several over a short period of time. But I can't tell you anything more than that."

"Why not?" Mac asked before Butch could.

She glanced back and forth between them. "Because Kate made me pinky swear not to say anything to anyone. She forced me into the deal by threatening to hurt my Jeep. And then she added that if she hears of my tattling, she'd hurt my Jeep some more."

"You mean she's going to shoot it again?" Mac asked with a solid dose of sarcasm. "Or smear more pies around inside it?"

"She didn't specify and I didn't want to ask and risk putting ideas into her head. I simply backed away slowly and left before she started foaming at the mouth."

"Can you at least tell me if there is another person that spurred the return of her twitching?" A muscle pulsed in Butch's cheek. "Jesus, she's not going after Grady's deputy again, is she?"

Claire mimicked zipping her lips.

"Damn it, Claire," Butch growled.

"Listen, all I can tell you is that you need to stay hot on her tracks day and night so that Ronnie or Penny or I don't end up in jail again."

Also by Ann Charles

Deadwood Mystery Series (Book #)

Nearly Departed in Deadwood (1)

Optical Delusions in Deadwood (2)

Dead Case in Deadwood (3)

Better Off Dead in Deadwood (4)

An Ex to Grind in Deadwood (5)

Meanwhile, Back in Deadwood (6)

A Wild Fright in Deadwood (7)

Rattling the Heat in Deadwood (8)

Gone Haunting in Deadwood (9)

Don't Let It Snow in Deadwood (10)

Devil Days in Deadwood (11)

Never Say Sever in Deadwood (12)

Short Stories from the Deadwood Mystery Series

Deadwood Shorts: Seeing Trouble (Book 1.5)

Deadwood Shorts: Boot Points (Book 4.5)

Deadwood Shorts: Cold Flame (Book 6.5)

Deadwood Shorts: Tequila & Time (Book 8.5)

Deadwood Shorts: Fatal Traditions (Book 10.5)

Deadwood Undertaker Series
(co-written with Sam Lucky)

Life at the Coffin Joint (1)

A Long Way from Ordinary (2)

Can't Ride Around It (3)

Catawampus Christmas Carol (3.5)

The Backside of Hades (4) (Fall 2022)

Jackrabbit Junction Mystery Series

Dance of the Winnebagos (1)

Jackrabbit Junction Jitters (2)

The Great Jackalope Stampede (3)

The Rowdy Coyote Rumble (4)

The Wild Turkey Tango (4.5)

Jackrabbit Jingle Balls (4.7)

In Cahoots with the Prickly Pear Posse (5)

Twisty Tortoise Tussles (6)

Dig Site Mystery Series
Look What the Wind Blew In (1)
Make No Bones About It (2)

AC Silly Circus Mystery Series
Feral-LY Funny Freakshow (Novella 1)
A Bunch of Monkey Malarkey (Novella 2)

Goldwash Mystery Series (a future series)
The Old Man's Back in Town (Short Story)

TWISTY
TORTOISE
TUSSLES

Book 6

USA Today Bestselling Author

Ann Charles

Illustrations by C.S. Kunkle

This book is for Doris P.

Your love for the Morgan sisters' adventures inspired me to keep writing even when the going got tough.

Thank you!

Twisty Tortoise Tussles
Copyright © 2022 by Ann Charles
Prescott AZ, USA

Cover Art by C.S. Kunkle
Cover Design by B Biddles
Editing by Elizabeth Flynn
Formatting by B Biddles

E-book ISBN-:13: 978-1-940364-84-1
Print ISBN-:13: 978-1-940364-85-8

Dear Reader,

I love watching dust devils. I find it fascinating how they twirl and twist, playing out in the open desert like little kids, spinning and spinning, growing dizzy, making a mess in their wake.

For those of you who aren't familiar with dust devils, Wikipedia describes them as "strong, well-formed, and relatively short-lived whirlwinds" that "form as a swirling updraft under sunny conditions during fair weather." Some dust devils are skinny and bendy, a piece of licorice reaching for the sky. Others grow big and fat, eating up everything in their way and tossing debris high into the sky in their wake. No matter the size, they are visible examples of chaos, following a twisting path, carrying the potential to create mayhem—much like the Morgan sisters.

In this story, I tried my hand at weaving together five different character plots. This turned out to be a handful, especially with Kate misfiring and twitching along the way. I felt like each of the five plots were out in the desert, spinning here and there. Some were thin and tall, bending to and fro as they danced across the pages; others grew massive as the story spiraled higher and faster.

By the end of the book (which took longer than I'd planned due to life repeatedly smacking me with a flyswatter during the writing process), each of the dust devils had finished spinning out their tales. Bits of chaos floated through the air around me as I read back through the tussles and spun along with the characters, weaving frayed plot threads and double-checking crisscrossed timelines. Finally, the story was ready for my editor and beta team—and eventually fun-loving and wonderful readers like you.

Now it's your turn to twist with the dust devils and enjoy the tussles on the pages. I hope this installment of the Morgan sisters' adventures give you some smiles, laughs, and a few shared cringes!

"Outside of a dog, a book is man's best friend.
Inside of a dog, it's too dark to read."
~Groucho Marx

Ann Charles   www.anncharles.com

Acknowledgments

Writing a book can be a solitary endeavor for some authors, but not for me. I have many people who helped me turn this story into a book for you to read. Thank you to the following:

Doris Pearce for motivating me to keep writing and shipping off those chapters to you. (And Jan Lawrence for helping your mom and me communicate more easily.)

Sam Lucky for brainstorming, plotting, reading, editing, formatting, graphic designing, uploading, cheering, and everything in between.

My kids for all of the shoulder massages and hugs and positive words.

My first-draft crew for your patience and help: Kristy McCaffrey, Diane Garland, Michelle Davis, Mary Ida Kunkle, Marcia Britton, Margo Taylor, Paul Franklin, Lucinda Nelson, Stephanie Kunkle, Wendy Gildersleeve, Vickie Huskey

My awesome editor who kept waiting and waiting and waiting for me to finish: Elizabeth M.S. Flynn

My good friend, Diane Garland (from Your Worldkeeper), for answering my series-related questions at any hour of the day or night.

Michelle Davis for helping double-check on the timelines and talking about yummy pies along the way.

My Beta Team for help making the story clean as a whistle.

My brother, C.S. Kunkle, for drawing illustrations and the cover art to help bring this story to life.

You incredible readers for your support both online and in person. Sharing laughs with you is better than ice cream!

Clint, my brother, for being a funny wimp when it comes to reading love scenes.

And the late James Caan for his inspiring portrayal of "Mississippi" in the movie, *El Dorado*.

"Would you mind telling me why you have such a great passion for my company?"

~Alan Bourdillion Traherne (aka Mississippi)

Cast

Claire Alice Morgan (1–6)—Main heroine of the series, middle Morgan sister, Mac's girlfriend

Kathryn "Kate" Morgan (2–6)—Youngest Morgan sister, Butch's girlfriend

Veronica "Ronnie" Morgan (3–6)—Oldest Morgan sister, Grady's girlfriend

MacDonald "Mac" Garner (1–6)—Main hero of the series, Claire's boyfriend

Valentine "Butch" Carter (1–6)—Current owner of The Shaft (the only bar in Jackrabbit Junction), Kate's boyfriend

Sheriff Grady Harrison (1–6)—Sheriff of Cholla County, Ronnie's boyfriend.

Penelope Harrison (5,6)—Sheriff Grady Harrison's sister; owner of The Mule Train Diner

Mississippi Brown (3,4,5,6)—FBI agent responsible for keeping an eye on Ronnie

Chester Thomas (1–6)—Harley's old Army vet buddy

Harley "Gramps" Ford (1–6)—Claire's maternal grandfather, Ruby's husband

Ruby Ford (previously Ruby Wayne-Martino) (1–6)—Mac's aunt, owner of the Dancing Winnebagos RV Park, Harley's new wife

Jessica Wayne (1–6)—Ruby's teenage daughter, Harley's stepdaughter

Manuel "Manny" Carrera (1–6)—Harley's old Army vet buddy, Deborah's husband, the Morgan sisters' stepfather

Deborah Ford Carrera (2–6)—Claire's mother, Harley's daughter, Manny's wife

Henry Ford (1–6)—Harley's beagle/dog

Joe Martino (1–6)—Deceased; Ruby's first husband, previous owner of the Dancing Winnebagos RV Park

Aunt Millie (3,4,4.5,5,6)—Sheriff Harrison's aunt, leader of the library (Geritol) gang

Ruth and Greta (3,4)—Members of Aunt Millie's library gang

Luke Beals (6)—Cousin of the Morgan sisters, Harley's grandson

Gary (2–6)—Bartender at The Shaft

Deputy Ernie "Dipshit" (1–6)—One of the sheriff's deputies

Elizabeth Harrison (3–6)—Grady Harrison's ex-wife

Mindy Lou Harrison (3,6)—Sheriff Harrison's niece

Sophy Wheeler (previously Wheeler-Martino) (1,2,4,5,6)—Claire's old nemesis, Joe Martino's first wife

Hailey (6)—Jessica's new younger friend from school

Sadie (6)—Ronnie's new acquaintance

Lyle Jefferson (3–6)—Ronnie's ex-husband

Randy Morgan (4.7,6)—Father of Ronnie, Claire, and Kate

Steve Horner (3,4)—Jessica Wayne's father, Ruby's ex-lover, Mindy Lou's ex-lover

"Dead men don't bite."

~Robert Louis Stevenson/ ***Treasure Island***

Chapter One

❖━━◆━━❖

Monday, January 28th
Yuccaville, Arizona

I, Kathryn Morgan, current president in chief, officially call to order today's emergency meeting of the Prickly Pear Posse to discuss how best to rid this dusty, sunburnt corner of Cholla County, Arizona, of one Deputy Dipshit, aka Ernie the dingleberry bully, who likes to harass innocent young pregnant women and wrongly throw them in jail."

Claire Morgan frowned at her younger sister, who stood at the head of the table in The Mule Train Diner with her chin raised high and her smile wide. Actually, Kate's smile was too wide. Deranged clowns looked less creepy.

"Hold on there, Cuckoo Kate." Claire held up her hand to stop this screwball train before it reached bullet speed. She'd been back in Jackrabbit Junction only a day after spending a few weeks in Tucson. She needed some time to catch her breath, for crissake. "Why are *you* president in chief?"

Kate jammed her hands on her hips, which made her pregnant belly more pronounced under her pink tunic. Her left eye twitched. "Dammit, Claire, I warned you about calling me chubby or cra—"

"I didn't say *crazy*," Claire cut in, motioning for Kate to lower her voice before half of the town of Yuccaville came to see what all the commotion was. As it was, they had the attention of several of the lunch eaters scattered around them, in spite of the late, great Johnny Nash singing loudly through the overhead speakers about how he could see clearly now the rain was gone.

"I said 'cuckoo,' as in one of those cute *slender* birds that were sacred to Hera, the Greek goddess of women and childbirth and family," she explained. "Which, I would like to add, are all things you *should* be focusing on at this precious time in your pregnancy."

Rather than a beady-eyed, crooked sheriff's deputy. Claire kept that last line to herself, having been a witness multiple times to the wild effects of her sister's flip-flopping pregnancy hormones. All it took was one wrong word—or look—and Dr. Jekyll morphed into Mr. Hyde. Or rather *Ms.* Hyde. Then sanity took the first flight south, and Kate started foaming at the mouth.

The wrinkles lining Kate's mob-boss glare deepened as she loomed over Claire. "You are a teller of untruths, Count Fibula, and your trousers have combusted."

Claire held up her wadded paper napkin. "Come any closer, window licker, and I'll plug that hole in the middle of your face."

"Criminy, you two knuckleheads." Their older sister, Ronnie, who sat across the table from Claire, waved her hand between them, playing referee. With the black-and-white striped sweater she was wearing over her black stretch pants, she looked even more the part. "Knock it off. We're in public."

Some things never changed no matter how much time passed, like Claire leaping before she looked, Kate not quite telling the *whole* truth, and Ronnie trying to be perfect—as in the perfect daughter, sister, wife, girlfriend, citizen, diner patron, etc., ad nauseam.

Ronnie frowned up at the pink-cheeked watermelon farmer still presiding over the lunch table. "There is no such thing as a president in chief, Katie. It's commander-in-chief. Now sit back down. You're making a scene."

"Claire started it." Kate sounded as if she were six years old with her blond hair pulled back in pigtails again, instead of cruising toward thirty-two with her wavy curls styled in an elaborately coiffed bun.

Ronnie turned her brown-eyed scowl on Claire. "And you promised you'd stop calling her crazy."

"I didn't—" Claire started, but then gave up with a sigh. "Fine. Whatever. But if anyone is the posse's president, it should be you, Ronnie."

"Why Ronnie?" Kate asked as she returned to the chair next

to Claire.

"Because she's the oldest."

Ronnie had Claire by two years and almost two months. Unlike Kate, who took after their mother with her blond hair and blue eyes, Claire and her older sister shared their father's darker complexion. Only Ronnie was taller, and these days she weighed at least a whole bone-in ham less, especially after months of stress and anxiety repeatedly kicking her in the gut. Where Claire tended to eat carbs and drink beer to escape her problems, Ronnie used yoga, jogging, and gin to find the gumption needed to face the sun each morning.

Huffing, Kate picked up her half-eaten turkey and cranberry pita sandwich. "Officially, Natalie is the oldest."

Claire shrugged and then stole one of Kate's pita chips, since she'd already chowed down her meatloaf sub and cheese-stuffed mashed potato balls. "Yeah, well our cousin isn't in Arizona at the moment, so Ronnie reigns." She bit the chip in half.

"Maybe Penny should be in charge." Kate's gaze shifted to the seat across the table, settling on the brunette with the heart-shaped face sipping from a glass of iced tea. "How old are you, anyway?"

Penelope Harrison was the owner of The Mule Train Diner and the county sheriff's sister—as in the same Sheriff Harrison who was doing the horizontal hokeypokey with Ronnie when he wasn't chasing down bad guys or nosing into Claire's dirty laundry.

A smirk twisted Penny's face as she set her glass down on the table. "I turned thirty-five last fall, and according to my mother, my baby-making clock is ticking so loudly it's scaring away the single guys clear over in New Mexico."

Claire pointed what remained of her chip at her younger sister. "There you have it. Ronnie turns thirty-six next week, so she's the oldest by far."

"That doesn't mean she's the wisest," Kate shot back.

Ronnie threw a pickle slice at Claire. "I told you to shush about my birthday." Another slice hit Kate in the cheek, making her gasp. "And I am by far the wisest over you two nincompoops."

"Nice, Ronnie." Claire plucked the pickle off her faded *Calamity Jane for Territorial Governor* T-shirt. "Keep it up and I'll tell the owner and get you kicked out of here. I hear she's a real hardass, same as the sheriff."

Penny chuckled at the play on her last name and grabbed
another slice of pickle from Ronnie's plate, tossing it at Claire, who
caught it midair and dropped it next to the first one on her plate.

"Good catch." Penny turned to Ronnie. "So, you're an
Aquarius? It's no wonder my brother is ga-ga about you. He's a
Gemini."

"What does that mean?" Claire asked, noticing that an older
lady with shoulder-length silver hair sitting at the diner's counter
kept glancing their way. Her eyes were dark, her face smooth,
contrasting with her silver bangs in a striking way that made Claire
stare back. The lady turned away quickly when she ran into Claire's
gaze.

"Ronnie and Grady are both air signs. They're super
compatible and good at communicating." Penny elbowed Ronnie,
grinning. "Aquarius females are also super sexually attracted to
Gemini."

Kate giggled around a mouthful of sandwich, mumbling
"Hubba hubba" at Ronnie with an exaggerated wink. Or maybe
that was another twitch.

"That would explain her inability to keep her pants on around
your brother when they are in *my* Jeep," Claire said, joining in the
teasing.

"I told you we didn't have sex in there," Ronnie growled under
her breath. "There wasn't enough room to finish the deed," she
added, shifting in her chair as if reliving the cramped scene. "They
need to make the cab space larger for bigger guys."

Claire wrinkled her nose, trying not to picture the scene
Ronnie was painting. "Well, I for one am thankful for that lack of
foresight by the Jeep company's engineering team."

Ronnie raised her cup of coffee, frowning across the table at
both of her sisters. "Okay, enough about Grady and me." She took
a sip. "Let's get back to why we're here—Katie apparently has had
another run-in with Grady's deputy and we need to talk her down
out of her tree."

Kate shook her head. "I didn't have a run-in with Deputy
Dipshit." She took another bite of the sandwich, moaning in
appreciation. "This is so good," she said to Penny around the bite.
"Sweet, tart, rich, chewy, and delicious."

"Thanks," Penny said while typing something into her cell

phone. "I make the mayonnaise fresh each morning and add a few special ingredients to offset the tartness of the cranberries. It's one of the many things I learned in culinary school in San Francisco."

"If you didn't have another altercation with Deputy Dipshit," Claire said to Kate, "then why did you insist we have this meeting?"

Kate swallowed before answering, taking a moment to wipe away the glob of mayonnaise on the corner of her mouth with her napkin. "Because we need to take him down a notch or two before his britches get any bigger."

Ronnie shook her head, groaning. "Katie, we've gone over this before. It's not your job to put Deputy Dip—I mean, Grady's deputy—in his place."

"According to one of my favorite astrology sites," Penny cut in, reading from her phone's screen, "Aquarius females often seem rebellious. They are known for their tempers, so you don't want to piss them off. While they don't get mad easily, all hell breaks loose when they do and someone might lose a limb."

Kate snorted. "That is so you, Ronnie."

"That is not like me at all, Katie."

Claire grinned. "It sort of is. Remember what you did to that waitress who clocked me outside The Shaft last fall?"

"That was different. She was a well-known killer threatening to kidnap and torture you for information."

"True, but still, you didn't know she had a deadly reputation at the time."

Penny was still focused on her phone. "Here's your horoscope for today, Ronnie." She cleared her throat and read, "You will meet a new purpose that will lead you down a different path if you choose to follow it. Only those who take chances succeed."

"That sounds like something from a fortune cookie," Ronnie said, scowling.

"Sort of," Penny said. "But fortune cookies are typically more vague with wisdom like, 'Now is a good time to travel,' or 'A stranger will provide the answer to your problems.'"

Claire snickered, adding, "Or something like, 'Today is a good day to wear underwear,' which is something we all agree upon for Captain Commando here."

"All but Grady," Kate blurted, following it with a giggle.

Ronnie rolled her eyes. "I told you two bozos to zip it about my underwear."

"That horoscope is spot-on for why I called this posse meeting." Kate took a sip of her lemonade. "Ronnie, you need to help me take down Deputy Dipshit. Teamed up with Claire and Penny, the four of us will make a killer posse."

"And do what?" Ronnie leaned forward, whispering now. "Invite him to a lone-tree necktie party and dress him up in a piñata suit?"

Kate cringed. "Sheesh. Violent much? We're not some vigilante hemp committee here. I was thinking more along the lines of convincing Ernie to climb into his stupid monster truck and leave town for good."

Claire glanced toward the counter. The old woman sitting there was watching them again, this time via the reflection in the chrome napkin holder, in between perusing a newspaper and eating fruit from the bowl in front of her. Claire watched as she stabbed the fork into the bowl, snaring first a grape and then a piece of cantaloupe.

Something about the lady had Claire feeling fidgety, but what? The voyeur's worn flannel coat, baggy faded jeans, and muddy combat boots seemed a typical clothing style for many of the locals here in Yuccaville. She shrugged. It was probably nothing more than curiosity after overhearing snippets of the conversation coming from their table. With Claire's notorious history for paranoia, she decided to keep her unease to herself and returned her attention to Kate's posse nonsense.

"Kate, what's your sign?" Penny asked, holding up her phone.

"I'm a happy little Cancer crab," she said, popping a chip in her mouth.

"Cancer, of course." Penny laughed lightly.

"Why is that funny?" Claire asked.

"Well, Cancers are super devoted to their loved ones."

"Yep, that's me. Family is everything."

"So devoted, in fact," Penny continued, "that they will go to amazing, unhealthy lengths to protect and defend them, no matter the cost physically or mentally."

Ronnie nodded. "Such as chasing down a serial killer through the side streets of Yuccaville while she's four months pregnant and armed with only a taser gun."

"That's not entirely true." Claire stole another chip from Kate. "She had Deputy Dipshit's handgun when she faced off with the killer in the alley."

Ronnie groaned. "Don't remind me."

"They are also known for their cheerful disposition," Penny said, "and ability to sniff out a fake. And they won't hesitate to poke a bear repeatedly when they perceive a problem."

"Which is a great reason to stay far away from Deputy Dipshit," Ronnie said, leveling her gaze on Kate. "Right?"

"Wrong," Kate shot back. "He's a fake and I know it. My mother's intuition is cranked up on high now, you know. You guys need to trust me on this. He's behind those anonymous threatening letters left on Gramps's Winnebago last month, and he's out to hurt Grady's career."

"Kate will make a great mom." Penny's attention turned to Claire. "What about you? What's your sign?"

"She's an Aries," Kate said.

Penny typed on the phone's screen, then looked across at Claire. "Fiery, hardworking, clever, independent, and stubborn."

Kate clapped her hands. "Nailed it."

"I'm not fiery," Claire grumbled.

Although the independent part was accurate. That very independence was what had made committing to a relationship so hard for most of her adult life. Hell, until Mac had shown up and won her over, she'd had a bad habit of running far and fast from any form of commitment. Now she was buying a bar with Mac. Even more surprising, after spending the last few weeks planning their future together while he finished up at his job in Tucson, she couldn't wait to get started on what came next for them.

"You're not really clever either," Ronnie said, and then dodged when Claire reached across to pinch her forearm.

"Nobody works harder than this girl, that's for sure," Kate said, patting Claire on the head like she was a good egg. "And she's like a dog on the hunt when it comes to sniffing out assholes."

Claire pulled away from Kate, grimacing. "I don't think that came out as the compliment you intended."

"Or maybe it did," Ronnie said, chuckling. She pushed her chair back, standing. "I need to run to the little girls' room. Be right back."

The old lady at the counter glanced at Ronnie as she passed on the way to the restrooms at the back of the diner. Claire tried to decide if it was merely curiosity on the lady's part or something more.

Ronnie's ex-husband had caused a lot of problems lately from his cozy cell in the country club–style prison for the rich and criminal up in South Dakota. He'd rolled over on some nasty kingpins who liked to take out their revenge by shipping loved ones' body parts via the postal service. A finger here, an earlobe there, maybe a kneecap as a bonus. While Ronnie and her ex were completely split up with no love left between them, Lyle's enemies didn't seem to know or care about that, which made Ronnie a prime target for revenge.

"You said your birthday was last fall," Kate said to Penny, who nodded. "What's your sign?"

Penny's smile had a hard edge to it. "November 5th, which makes me a Scorpio."

"As in the scorpion," Claire added. "Unpredictable and deadly."

Penny let out a deep, evil-sounding laugh, touching the tips of her fingers together. "Don't forget cold-blooded. We make excellent assassins."

"Great!" Kate said, shoving her empty plate away. "We could use a sniper and a ruthless kidnapper for the Deputy Dipshit job."

Claire did a double take. "Now, hold on for a damned minute, Kate. I know you aren't a fan of Ernie's, but you need to bring this revenge business down to a sane level or you're going to wind up in jail again with the bail set so high that your sugar daddy can't cover it."

"I'm not going to shoot him," Kate said, as if Claire was the nutter at the table.

"Well, that's a relief."

"At least not with an actual gun."

Penny aimed a set of raised eyebrows Claire's way. "Uh, Kate," she said, placing her phone on the table. "Have you talked to Butch about any of this?"

"Of course not. Why would I? He's the father of my child, not my keeper."

"Aren't you engaged?" Penny asked.

Kate crossed her arms. "No."

"But not because of a lack of asking on his part," Claire explained to Penny.

"His proposals have been half-assed at best." Kate frowned down at the table. "Besides, I'm not ready to be shackled just yet."

"I don't think he plans to shackle you," Claire said. "Unless that's some kind of kinky sex game you two are into these days."

Kate shot her a sideways glare. "We're not like Ronnie and Grady with their handcuffs and spiky leather collars."

Claire cringed. "Spiky leather collars?"

A gagging sound came from Penny. "Come on, Kate. That's my brother we're talking about. I don't even like to watch him kiss your sister."

"I don't know for sure on the collars, but I found one in the back seat of Grady's pickup once."

"What were you doing in Grady's back seat?" Claire asked.

Kate's left eye twitched. She looked toward the counter. "Uh, just looking for a map."

Claire glanced at Penny. "Did that site about astrology signs say anything about Cancers being big fat fibbers, too?"

"They do tend to swing from one emotional extreme to the next." Penny held up her index finger. "Oh, that reminds me, Aunt Millie wanted me to give something to you, Kate." She hopped up and jogged to the end of the counter, reaching over it and coming back to the table with a small gift bag tied closed with a pink ribbon. "She said it's for the baby and that you'd know what to do with it."

Claire stared at Kate, whose cheeks had suddenly turned dark pink. "Why is Grady's and Penny's aunt Millie giving you a gift? You two don't like each other."

Kate avoided looking at her, peeking inside the edge of the bag. "That's not true. We reached a peace accord over the holidays. We're cozy as bugs in a rug now."

Claire crossed her arms. "I don't believe that."

"Why not? You don't think I can bury the hatchet?"

"Sure you can, especially in the back of your enemies, and a short time ago Millie was just that." Claire reached for the bag. "What's in there?"

Kate jerked away, holding the bag out of reach. "None of your bus—"

A pounding noise over at the counter snagged their attention.

The old woman who'd been playing voyeur was bent over, her shoulders hitching as she slammed her fist on the counter.

"Hey, is she …" Claire started, standing so fast her chair fell over.

Ronnie came running from the back of the diner, sliding to a stop next to the old woman. "Are you choking?" she asked, grasping the woman's shoulder.

Claire couldn't see if she responded, but Ronnie slid around behind the woman, performing the Heimlich maneuver on her. Claire had taken a step toward them when something popped out of the old woman's mouth and dropped onto the floor.

A grape rolled to a stop next to the base of the neighboring bar stool.

The older woman gasped and then coughed, holding onto the counter as she re-entered the world of the breathing.

Penny joined Ronnie at the counter. "Are you okay, ma'am? Can I get you anything?"

"Water," she answered, her voice husky. She took the glass Penny held out to her, drinking several gulps and then setting it down. "Thanks," she said to Penny, then turned to Ronnie, who was still hovering at her shoulder. "I owe you a life. Thank you."

Ronnie's frown probably matched Claire's. *A life?* That sounded like something from a video game.

"You don't owe me anything, ma'am. I'm glad I could help."

The lady pulled a fanny pack from under her flannel jacket and unzipped it, pulling out a wad of bills. "Take this as a thanks."

"That's a big wad," Kate whispered in Claire's ear.

Ronnie pushed the money away, shaking her head. "Really, you don't owe me anything. I'm glad I could help."

"I'd like to repay you somehow," the lady pressed.

"I won't accept your money. Your thanks is enough."

The old woman's dark eyes narrowed slightly. "We'll see." She tossed several bills on the counter to cover her lunch costs before stuffing the wad of cash back in her fanny pack. After a nod at Penny, she headed for the door, leaning heavily on her cane, which creaked with every step.

The door had barely closed when it was pushed open again,

the bells overhead jingling doubly.

A petite blonde in a bright red curve-hugging coat and rhinestone-studded sunglasses strutted into the diner. Her sneer started when her gaze landed on Penny and changed into an all-out snarl when it settled on Ronnie.

"Well, well, well," the blonde said. "Look who we have here patronizing my sister-in-law's diner."

Is that ...

"Elizabeth," Kate whispered the answer to Claire's unspoken question. She leaned closer to Claire. "What a suspicious coincidence, don't you think?"

"What do you mean?"

As the blonde made a point of slowly taking off her black leather gloves, Kate filled Claire's ear with a breathy explanation. "What are the chances of Grady's skanky ex-wife being here in Penny's diner at the same time as us? Deputy Dipshit is probably using her as a spy."

Claire pulled away and scowled at her sister. "You need to get a new hobby, Nancy Drew. Maybe have your new best friend, Millie, teach you how to knit some baby booties."

Elizabeth pocketed her gloves, speaking loud and clear for all in the diner to hear. "I have a proposition for you, Penny."

"I'll let you two catch up," Ronnie said, taking a step toward the table.

A rustling sound came from Kate's direction as she stuffed the gift bag from Aunt Millie under her chair.

"Oh, you can stay right where you are, trollop," Elizabeth told Ronnie. "This is about *you*, after all."

"Did she just call Ronnie a dollop?" Kate had returned to Claire's side.

"Not dollop, you doof. Trollop."

Something jabbed Claire in the ribs, making her grunt.

"Don't call me a doof, you boob."

"Shhhh."

"What do you want, Liz?" Penny asked, a muscle pulsing in her jaw. Her gaze was razor sharp and pointed.

"Ohhh, there's the scorpion," Kate said in Claire's ear.

"I'll make this simple enough for you to understand, *Pen*." She pointed at Ronnie. "Either she exits from Grady's life or you do."

"Me?" Penny touched her chest. "Where am I going?"

"To the poorhouse after I destroy your reputation in this town and your diner business dries up, sending you rolling toward the horizon like a tumbleweed." Elizabeth pushed her hair back from her face, her smile ghoulishly toothy. "I'll give you some time to consider my proposition, but you know as well as I do whose family runs this town. If you want to keep your little business here intact, along with your brother's reputation and badge, you'll pick the side of the right woman for Grady's future."

After shooting a glare in Kate and Claire's direction, Elizabeth turned and flounced back out the door.

"Christ," Ronnie muttered, returning to the table and falling into her chair. "I really don't like that bitch."

Penny joined them. "She's always been like that. Head high school cheerleader with a rich granddaddy who was a superintendent at the mine. Her uppity grandmother owns the country club at the edge of town. I don't know what Grady ever saw in her." She scowled toward the door. "Actually, I don't think he had much choice after she set her sights on him and sank her claws in good and deep."

"She's like an Alabama tick," Claire muttered, not liking the tension lining Ronnie's face now, or how she was twisting her napkin as if it were a certain blonde's neck.

Penny smirked. "You sound like Aunt Millie. She's wanted to take Elizabeth down a notch or two since she screwed Grady over years ago."

Oh, really? Claire wondered if Millie was serious or just swaggering for show.

Kate tapped her finger on the table. "Well, bloodsucker or not, she should know better than to mess with the Prickly Pear Posse." The whole left side of Kate's face spasmed for a second or two.

"Oh, hell," Claire muttered, exchanging a worried look with Ronnie.

Ms. Hyde was back.

Chapter Two

Later that evening ...

T he Shaft was filled with shadows and silence. No classic rock or old-time country music cranked out from the jukebox. No beer poured from the taps. No pool balls clacked in the back corner. No Morgan sisters flitted here and there taking orders. After being open for six days straight, Jackrabbit Junction's only eating and drinking joint was taking Monday night off. Butch had decided a break once a week through the winter would be good for the staff so everyone could catch their breath.

Mac Garner could relate. He sat at the bar flipping through a brewing supply catalogue after three tiring weeks filled with long days on the job. Finally, after more than a decade and a half of working for the same company in Tucson, he was free of his obligations there and able to settle in Jackrabbit Junction with Claire.

Make that with Claire *and* her family. He chuckled to himself, flipping a page. Even paradise came at a price.

Grabbing an order pad, he jotted down notes and costs for the equipment needed to build a small brewery behind The Shaft. With the paperwork for the purchase of the business and surrounding lot well underway, he and Claire would soon be taking over the daily operations of the bar.

He flipped through several more catalogue pages, making sure he had noted all the equipment he'd need per his research over the last few days. Then, after a quick totaling of the numbers, along with the cost estimate Claire had come up with for the addition's building materials, he stared down at the final figure.

That couldn't be right. He added again.

Shit.

He tossed the pencil on the bar and rubbed his eyes.

Buying The Shaft itself wasn't cheap, even though they were getting a hell of a deal on it. Building the brewery on back was going to add another third to the overall cost, and that was with Claire and him doing the construction themselves.

He needed more cash. He could dig into his retirement savings, but the tax penalty for that was high. There was one other way, but …

A clanking sound rang out through the order window behind the bar. Mac looked over, catching a glimpse of Butch Carter in the kitchen. The aroma of grilled hamburger drifted out, spurring a rumble in his stomach.

He focused back on the list of dollar amounts on the order pad and rested his chin on his hand. Was he doing the right thing? Quitting a good paying job as a geotechnician in a well-known Tucson firm to take up bar ownership? He'd been following a solid career track for years, his future all planned, his home paid off, his retirement funds diversified appropriately for his age. Then Claire had slammed into his life, sending him reeling.

The batwing doors leading to the kitchen, supply room, and office eased open. Butch pushed through backward, carrying two plates loaded up with burgers and fries. He came around to the customer side of the bar, setting the plates down, and took the stool next to Mac.

"So, what's the verdict?" Butch asked, reaching over the counter and coming back with a stack of napkins.

"Building a microbrewery is expensive." Mac grabbed a fry and dipped it in the small bowl of orange sauce next to his burger.

Butch nodded. "I looked into it years back when I first bought this place. It was pricey even then. So, I chose to put money into remodeling the joint, figuring I might add the brewery later." He lifted his burger, sizing it up. "Then I got the bug to start rebuilding classic cars and growing baby cacti, and the brewery suddenly seemed like too much work. That's when I found a guy over in Yuccaville who likes to brew and set up a deal to sell his beer instead."

"Makes sense." Mac took a bite of the french fry. "What's this sauce?" It was tangy and sweet. "It's really good."

Butch swallowed his bite of burger. "It's a secret recipe."

"Does the recipe come with the bar?"

"I'll consider throwing it in if you promise to let Kate continue working here until she's ready to have our kid."

Mac ate another fry. "Is this something she requested or are you trying to keep her too busy to get into any more trouble?"

Butch shrugged. "A bit of both."

"Speaking for myself, Kate's help and expertise would be much appreciated." Mac considered adding a caveat about her staying home when the squirrels in her noggin got rowdy and started bouncing off the walls, but instead shoved a fry in his mouth.

"Thanks, man." Butch took another bite, adding after he swallowed, "She's already made it clear that helping me in the garage isn't going to happen."

"She's not into old cars?"

Grinning, Butch grabbed a napkin from the stack. "When I suggested that she could detail and polish the cars, she threatened to crush my *huevos* in a vice."

Mac cringed. "Damn."

"I feel sorry for the next guy who crosses her when she's feeling rambunctious."

"You're not making me feel too good about my earlier agreement to keep her on here."

Butch laughed and clapped Mac on the back. "She'll be fine. She mellowed while you and Claire were gone."

"Would that statement hold up if you were hooked up to a polygraph?"

"Most psychologists agree that lie detectors aren't legit." Butch's smile dipped at the corners. "Just don't mention anything around Kate about her growing baby bump, her wavier hair, her swollen toes, or her tendency to morph into Taz the Tasmanian Devil when she goes too long between meals."

Mac picked up his burger. "Maybe I'll learn some sign language and stick to that." He took a big bite.

"Good idea."

Butch must have brushed the burger with the secret sauce, too. Mac closed his eyes for a moment, enjoying the perfectly grilled meat and juicy flavors. Damn, Carter was going to be a hard act to follow in the kitchen.

"So, Kate's mellowed, huh?" He glanced at Butch. "Does that mean she's done with her conspiracy theories about Grady's deputy?"

"I certainly hope." Butch grabbed a fry, his brow wrinkling as he ate. "But I'm going to keep an eye on her just in case."

A few bites later, Mac shared his list of equipment needed for the brewery with Butch. They were discussing the difference between IPAs and pale ales when they heard the rumble of an engine outside and tires crunching through the gravel parking lot.

Claire joined them a minute later, cursing as she hung up her jacket on the pegs next to the front door. Her work boots thudded over the worn, wood plank floor. Instead of joining them on the stools, she stormed behind the bar and started pouring a glass of beer.

Mac pushed his plate with a few remaining fries in her direction. "Hey, Slugger. Hungry?"

White paint streaked across her brown Dancing Winnebagos RV Park sweatshirt and up her neck. A couple of tendrils of her dark brown hair appeared to be paint-dipped, as well. She must have come straight from his aunt's RV campground, where Claire worked helping out around the place.

Mac's focus drifted north. Claire's cheeks were extra pink and blotchy, which might have been thanks to the stiff breeze blowing through Jackrabbit Junction this evening. She met his gaze straight on as she raised the glass to her lips. Her eyes were practically sparking, and not in the hot and sexy way he liked best.

Nope, she was just pissed.

"What's wrong?" he asked.

Normally, she only got this pissed off when her mother was around to pick at her. But Deborah was still in Tucson with Manny, her husband, going through a six-week alcohol rehab program. Mac and Claire had driven past the place before returning to Jackrabbit Junction. It had looked more like a fancy resort than a rehabilitation center, but since the place was keeping Deborah far away from her daughter and him, Mac didn't care if it were the Taj Mahal filled with palm frond–waving servants painted in gold.

"Gramps needs to head north for a few months," Claire said, wiping the foam from her upper lip with the back of her hand. She held the glass toward Mac. "You want some?"

He could stand to wet his whistle. At his nod, she handed it off and grabbed another glass.

"What did Harley do now?" Butch asked, shaking his head when she offered to pour him a glass.

"He wants me to build a bird viewing platform behind the tool shed."

"Back in the ravine?" Mac frowned. There wasn't much else back there.

"Yep. About thirty feet back from the banks of Jackrabbit Creek so that the platform will be safe when it floods during monsoons. He has it all staked out already."

"He wants this done before monsoon season?" The rains typically kicked into gear in July. That meant she had about six months. How long was it going to take to build the brewery addition?

"No. He wants the platform built *yesterday*." She took another swig of beer. "Gramps says that the reservation list for March is already full with incoming bird watchers, and we need to spruce up the park so that it gets good online reviews this year."

Butch scoffed. "Since when has your grandfather given a rat's ass about online reviews?"

"Since Jess built the damned website for the RV park."

Mac's cousin, Jessica, had a project before Christmas in one of her high school classes that required learning how to build a website. So, she'd made one for the Dancing Winnebagos RV Park as a gift for Ruby, her mom. On a high note, the website seemed to be bringing in more business. But Claire had been unhappy with it from the get-go.

Initially, the problem with the site had to do with a killer hunting down Claire and Ronnie due to some stolen diamonds they'd stumbled upon. Now, though, the website was causing heartburn thanks to their grandfather's newfound obsession with five-star ratings. Mac had witnessed this firsthand last night during supper when Ruby and Harley had argued about repainting the laundry room white, all because Harley said it looked too dingy in the website pictures.

The results of that argument explained the white paint splattered on Claire this evening, he realized.

"A viewing platform, huh?" Mac lifted his drink. "How are people going to get back there? You're going to have to grade a path and throw down some gravel."

"Oh no, gravel is not good enough for Mr. Five-Stars. He wants me to also build a boardwalk out to it." She finished her beer in several loud gulps and slammed the glass down. "I asked Gramps, 'Do you know how much time that's going to take me? I'm just one person and that's a full-time job.' To which the smartass replied, 'There will be two of you.' "

"Does he mean you and Garner?" Butch asked, shooting a frown Mac's way.

"No, he means me and Jess, after she's done with school each day. Do you have any idea how much that girl can talk? How little work she actually does? I mean, I love the girl, but she gets me so distracted half of the time that I nail my own shirt to boards."

What in the hell was Claire's grandfather thinking? He knew she needed to build the brewery.

"Harley needs to hire that job out," Mac said. "You're going to be busy here."

"What about the permits?" Claire asked.

Mac thumbed in his burger buddy's direction.

"I pulled in a few favors," Butch told her. "The paperwork for the sale and the architectural plans for the addition were put on the fast track with the title company and county."

"Good, I guess." Her frown said otherwise. "Mac, when is the lumber we ordered going to be dropped off?"

"In a few days."

"So, you and I can start with the footers by next weekend."

"Well, about that." Mac cringed in anticipation of telling her about his earlier idea on how to add more cash to their pockets.

Her mouth tightened. "What about it?"

He raised his hands. "Just hear me out, Slugger."

"I'm listening." But she crossed her arms, essentially barring the gate.

Butch stood and grabbed their empty plates. "I'll let you two have a moment alone to discuss this."

After he disappeared through the batwing doors, Mac clasped his hands on the bar. "I've been pricing out what we need yet for the brewery and it's going to be more than I'd figured."

Her forehead lined. "How much more?"

Mac thought about trying to candy coat the truth, but then remembered with whom he was dealing. One of the things he loved about Claire was her no-nonsense take on life. Her full lips and dark eyes were a bonus. Along with her hips. Especially when she wore her toolbelt and not much else.

He blinked out of fantasyland. "Enough to drain a good-size chunk of the amount we set aside to build a house."

"Ah, hell." She rubbed the back of her neck. "What about Gramps? He offered more than we needed. Maybe we increase what we borrow from him."

"I'd rather not." Mac didn't want to be indebted to Claire's grandfather any more than necessary. That opened up more opportunity for Harley to have a vote in their business decisions, and three would be a crowd, especially since two of them were related by blood.

"So, what's your solution for us, Mac?" She leaned onto the bar across from him, covering his clasped hands with hers. Her hands were warm, same as her gaze. "Borrow from a bank? Use the proceeds from the sale of your house in Tucson?"

"Our house," he corrected.

"Your name is on the deed, not mine."

"We've had this argument before."

"I know." Her grin was flirty, yet had a hard edge. "And if memory serves, I didn't give an inch that time either." She leaned forward and gave him a quick kiss.

He held her in place, tasting the beer on her lips before pulling back to whisper, "You're too stubborn for your own good."

"Maybe." She reached up and tweaked his chin. "But you like your women big-brained and hard-headed."

He chuckled. "I never should've told you that."

She rested her elbows on the bar. "So, what's the solution?"

"You remember me telling you last week that they offered me a consulting position if I wanted it?"

"Yes, *and* I remember we agreed that you were going to decline it."

"Yeah, but I didn't get around to telling them 'no' yet."

Her head tipped slightly. "Where are you going with this, Mr. Garner?"

"There's a job they're working on down in Bisbee, and the lead is out for a few weeks after falling off a ladder and breaking his hip. He needs to go through therapy before he can return, and I was offered the option to take his place until then."

"Bisbee? That's almost as far as going back to your place in Tucson."

"Actually, it's farther. The worksite is close to the Mexican border near an old open-pit copper mine."

She growled.

"They offered me triple-overtime pay," he added to sweeten the deal.

She tapped on the pad with the brewery figures next to the catalogue. "That still won't be enough to cover all this."

She was right. It would take several more consulting jobs to make a significant dent in the total. "But it will be a good start, and if I fill in a few more times here and there over the next several months …"

"And in the meantime, what?" She glanced toward the swinging doors as Butch rejoined them. "I build the brewery addition *and* run the bar on my own while you're gone?"

"I can help out for a bit longer in the evenings," Butch offered, settling onto a bar stool. "After all the work you've done to help out in a pinch, Claire, it's the least I can do."

She nodded, but her tight lips made it clear she still wasn't on board.

Mac squeezed one of her clenched fists. "I'll be home on the weekends to help."

"How do we know that for sure? Usually they have you working seven days a week on these bigger projects."

He let go of her and reached for his beer. "They mentioned it last week when they offered me the consulting job."

Claire cursed under her breath. "Why didn't you tell me about all this before now?"

"Because I didn't think it had any consequence in relation to our situation." He peeked at her over the rim of his beer. "Have I told you lately how gorgeous you are when you're mad? The way your eyes light up and your cheeks flush deep pink really—"

"Flattery will not help your cause, MacDonald Abraham Garner."

He cringed at the sound of his full name. He couldn't help it. It was a long-worn reflex from childhood.

Claire drummed her fingers on the bar as she stared him down. "I thought we agreed there'd be no more secrets, especially when it came to the RV park and this place."

"The job offer wasn't a secret. Like I said, at the time it seemed irrelevant to our plans. But then I started doing some math tonight and … well, you know the rest."

"Right. So, I'm supposed to build a brewery addition *and* a viewing platform in the next couple of months?" She snorted. "I think you and Gramps have me confused for a robot."

"Well, remember, officially Jess is supposed to help you with the viewing platform when she's not at school *or* working for Butch in his cacti nursery." His joke went over like a bloated hippopotamus.

She ran her index finger around the rim of her glass. "You're going to have to make this up to me, McStudly."

He winked. "Name the place and your price."

"I'll see if Kate can help me more in the nursery while Jess helps you," Butch said.

Claire pursed her lips. "I'd probably get better help from my sister than Jess, which reminds me." She zeroed in on Butch. "The mother of *your* child is up to something."

"Up to what?"

"I don't know exactly, but it's something that is making her face twitch again."

"Shit." Butch rubbed his jaw. "What conspired prior to this twitch?"

"*Twitches*," she clarified. "Several over a short period of time. But I can't tell you anything more than that."

"Why not?" Mac asked before Butch could.

She glanced back and forth between them. "Because Kate made me pinky swear not to say anything to anyone. She forced me into the deal by threatening to hurt my Jeep. And then she added that if she hears of my tattling, she'd hurt my Jeep some more."

"You mean she's going to shoot it again?" Mac asked with a solid dose of sarcasm. "Or smear more pies around inside it?"

"She didn't specify and I didn't want to ask and risk putting ideas into her head. I simply backed away slowly and left before she started foaming at the mouth."

"Can you at least tell me if there is another person that spurred the return of her twitching?" A muscle pulsed in Butch's cheek. "Jesus, she's not going after Grady's deputy again, is she?"

Claire mimicked zipping her lips.

"Damn it, Claire," Butch growled.

"Listen, all I can tell you is that you need to stay hot on her tracks day and night so that Ronnie or Penny or I don't end up in jail again."

"Penny?" Butch repeated. "You mean Grady's sister?"

Claire nodded.

"Has Grady put his sister in jail before?" Mac asked Butch, who shrugged.

"Oh, there's another thing," Claire continued, turning to place her empty beer glass in the sink behind the bar. "I think Grady's ex-wife is now on Kate's hitlist, too."

"More like her 'shit' list," Mac said.

Butch scrubbed both hands down his face.

"Grady's ex is the one that Kate nailed with the water nozzle over there, right?" Mac nudged his chin toward the spray gun next to the beer tap handles.

"Yep, that's her." Butch scowled at Claire's back. "Why is Elizabeth on the radar now? Kate told me she had no interest in Grady's ex because she'd won the battle."

"Yeah, well that may have been true before today, but now there's a new fight on the horizon. This time Elizabeth is trying to pound on both Ronnie *and* Penny, using her family's clout in Yuccaville as her hammer."

Butch shook his head. "Damn it, why does Kate have to get in the middle of this? It's not her fight."

Claire grabbed a dish towel, smirking in their direction. "Because Kate is a Cancer."

Chuckling, Mac said, "That's one way of putting it."

"A cancer? You mean to society in this corner of Arizona?" Butch asked.

"No. I'm talking about her astrological sign. She always has and always will take on anyone who tries to hurt those she loves." Claire hung the towel on the hook next to the sink. "Most of the time that's a good trait. But with my sister knocked up with *your* child and the crazy Carter DNA wreaking havoc in her body, this is an impending doom type of situation that could really make Grady pull out his hair."

"Not just Grady," Butch grumbled.

Claire shrugged. "Elizabeth picked the wrong family with which to fuck. That's the problem, plain and simple."

"You should sic your mother on Grady's ex when she gets back from rehab," Mac said, sort of kidding. But yet not, knowing from experience how sharp Deborah's teeth were.

"And on top of it all," Claire said, reaching into her sweatshirt pocket, "I think we have yet another problem."

Butch cursed and rose from the bar stool. "I think I need a drink after all."

"What now?" Mac went to the worst thing he could think of first. "Is this about Ronnie and the bullshit her ex-husband pulled when he rolled over on those arms dealers?"

"Nope." Claire held out a plastic baggie half-filled with used cigar butts. "I found these in the ravine behind the RV park this afternoon when I was out there sizing up the work to do for that stupid birding platform."

Mac took the bag from Claire, grimacing at the chewed and burnt pieces. "Gross. Please tell me Jess isn't sneaking out back to smoke cigars." On top of the fact that it wasn't good for her lungs and her mother would be mad as hell, Jess could start a grass fire during the dry months.

"I don't think it's your cousin."

"Manny or Chester?" Butch tossed out, joining Claire on the other side of the bar.

"Your grandfather smokes cigars, too," Mac added.

Claire shook her head. "None of the above. I suspect that the sharp-clawed bitch who tried to blast a hole through my chest last spring with a shotgun might be onto something."

Butch frowned at Mac. "Sophy Wheeler?"

"Joe's ex-wife?" Mac handed the bag back to Claire.

"The one and only." She poked one of the butts through the plastic. "Boys, I'm afraid Joe Martino could still be alive … somehow."

Chapter Three

Tuesday, January 29th

W hat on Earth makes you think Joe Martino could possibly still be alive?" Kate hollered ahead at Claire, who was leading the way over the hardpan, gravelly dirt broken up by islands of sand.

Her sister carted a shovel and a pickaxe over one shoulder along with a backpack, leaving Kate to carry the tote filled with bottles of water, chips, energy bars, and a bag of homemade, caramel gingerbread cookies, thanks to Ruby.

The cool morning breeze rattled the scraggly dead weeds that stuck up here and there on the landscape, reminding Kate of raggedy tufts of hair on an old, half-burnt doll's head. Claire appeared to be following a narrow trail that had started behind the RV park's tool shed and meandered deeper into the ravine while skirting Jackrabbit Creek. A critter trail, most likely. Kate grimaced about what kind of critters they might come across, hurrying to catch up with her sister.

She tucked deeper into the pink knitted scarf that Penny's aunt Millie had included in the gift bag yesterday, catching a whiff of her own coconut-scented shampoo.

Along with the scarf, "Mad Dog" Millie had snuck in a folded piece of paper—a printout of an article about a Maya knife missing from a museum down near Mexico City. Kate wasn't sure it was the exact same knife she currently had squirreled away under the sink in her bathroom, but it certainly looked similar.

The write-up was in Spanish, but translated notes were scribbled on the page, including some next to the caption under a grainy picture of the knife. Kate figured the translation was probably thanks to one of Millie's bruisers, since the writing was different from the note at the top, which stated how much Kate owed Grady's aunt for her detective services.

She scowled up at the clear blue sky. Millie wasn't cheap either, dammit, which was why Kate planned on wearing this scarf until she'd gotten her money's worth out of it. She knew better than to complain to ol' Mad Dog about the cost for information, though, after learning her lesson the hard way last summer when she'd tried to use the library's resources without first consulting Millie and what Kate had started calling the "Geritol Gangsters." Just plain "gang" didn't sound nearly as cantankerous and scrappy as these older babes were each time she had to deal with them.

Unfortunately, Grady's aunt was about the only one around with whom Kate could work when it came to the knife, because Millie wouldn't crawl up Kate's backside for stealing it from Deborah in the first place. It wasn't officially stealing, though, since her mother had found it in a small, velvet-lined case down in Ruby's basement office and swiped it for herself first.

If one were to look at it sideways, Kate was just borrowing the knife and keeping it safe while she tried to figure out where it had come from originally. Her sisters didn't need to get tangled up in this mystery, what with Ronnie's worries about more hitmen coming for her thanks to her ex's bullshit; and Claire trying to work two jobs, building not just an addition onto The Shaft, but also some sort of bird lovers' platform for Gramps.

Speaking of something being for the birds ...

"Did you hear me, Claire?" Kate yelled over the racket of winged critters that were busy chirping, cheeping, and screeching in the trees and bushes around them.

"Of course I heard you." Claire turned, walking backward for a few steps. "Hell, half of Yuccaville can hear you with the way sound travels back here, so keep it down, megaphone mouth. You're scaring the wildlife."

"Whatever," Kate grumbled. She waited for Claire to face forward again before giving her sister a middle-finger salute.

"So, what makes you think Joe is back from the dead?" she asked after several steps. "And don't tell me it's only because of a bunch of cigar butts you found back here. You and I both know there are three Army vets shacking up at the RV park who could be responsible for those."

A low, gurgling croak made Kate pause and look behind her. A raven watched them from its perch high on a cottonwood tree branch overlooking Jackrabbit Creek. "Quoth the Raven, 'Nevermore,' " she said quietly.

"Are you quoting Edgar Allan Poe?" her sister asked.

Claire was right. The acoustics in the ravine were really good. Even the trickle of flowing water sounded like the creek was only a few feet away instead of thirty or so.

"Just answer my question." Kate dodged a small barrel cactus.

"It's a combination of things, really," Claire said as she continued toward where Gramps had supposedly set out some sort of markers for his bird watching deck.

Kate waved good-bye to the raven and then followed after her sister, only to stop again a tad farther along. "Eww!"

She frowned down at what looked like an impressive pile of rabbit droppings. Either that was one big bunny or it came from something else, and knowing what she did now after months of living in the Sonoran Desert, it was probably prickly and pokey instead of cute and furry.

"Watch for the mule deer scat," Claire warned.

"A little late." Kate stepped over the pile, keeping her eyes peeled for more. Her hand-made leather boots were supposed to make an impression, but not *in* a pile of crap.

As she dodged another group of poop pellets, a spindly creosote branch snagged the sleeve of her lightweight wool coat, tugging a couple of threads loose near the cuff.

Darn it! When Claire had called this morning and said she needed help at the RV park, Kate had figured she meant spending time behind the counter in the General Store. This traipsing around through the rough and tumbleweed-choked wilderness was beyond Kate's pay grade, especially since she worked for free most of the time to help out Ruby and Gramps.

She skirted yet another pile of poop. That one looked pretty fresh. She glanced around, half-expecting to be trampled by a whole herd of the long-legged turdmeisters any minute now.

"How can you tell it's a mule deer?"

"The telltale hoof prints near the piles." Claire shot a frown back Kate's way before starting up a small rise. "Listen, if you're going to try to be some kind of ace junior detective, you need to learn how to scope out a crime scene better."

"I'm not trying to be some *junior* detective," Kate snapped. "Remind me, who was it who found the diamond killer a few weeks ago? Was it you? Was it Ronnie?" Kate sidestepped an extra-bristly teddy bear cholla cactus. "That's a big fat nope to both, because it was me, that's who. Kate the ace detective."

Claire's scoff echoed off the ravine's walls. "Let's get real here, Ace, since your imaginary fan club members are busy painting their toenails and it's just the two of us right now. You didn't 'find' anyone. You *stumbled* on the diamond killer while on an ice cream run."

That was true, but … "And then I chased him and caught him."

"That's your version of it. But according to a key witness, you basically tried to perform a hit-and-run on the guy with your car."

That could also be arguably true, but those details ran together like a Jackson Pollock painting thanks to the rush of adrenaline that had flooded Kate's brain by that point in the whole ordeal. But had she actually tried to hit …

Wait a darned second!

"If this so-called key witness of yours is Deputy Dipshit, then that's a bunch of poppycock. That doughnut glaze–fingered buffoon doesn't know his ass from his elbow."

"And," Claire continued, ignoring Kate's objections. "Our cousin actually chased the guy, not you. According to what Ronnie said you put in the sheriff's report, you claimed to have had a side pain and had to return to your car mid-chase."

Kate gasped, pointing at her baby bump. "Because I'm pregnant."

"It's funny how your pregnancy comes up only when you need an excuse." Claire scaled the rise and then dropped the shovel and pickaxe on the ground, along with her pack, so she didn't notice Kate sticking her tongue out at her.

"I beg to differ." Kate took the hand Claire offered to help her up the crest of the small hill. "Don't forget, I'm the one who rendered him immobile so the cops could catch him without anyone else getting hurt."

Claire guffawed, scaring a bunch of tiny brown birds from a

nearby bush. "That's a tray full of pork pies and fat lies. You shot him in the leg, Ms. Hyde, because he called you 'crazy,' and you know it."

Yanking her hand free, Kate glared at her sister. "Listen, I saw him. I chased him down. I handed him over to the cops practically wrapped in a big red bow. Therefore, I saved both Ronnie's and your asses. End of story."

"Wow." Claire took the tote bag from Kate and pulled out a bottle of water. "That's one hell of a load of crappleberries you're trying to spread around here." Her wide smile took the sting out of her words.

While Claire took a drink of water, Kate stared over at a square of land marked with stakes and lined with yellow string. This was it? The site for Gramps's viewing platform?

She looked back toward Jackrabbit Creek and followed the line of vegetation along the ravine. It was a nice view, that was for sure. There was a fair sprinkling of trees, shrubs, and other hangouts for the tiny, winged dinosaur-ish leftovers that drew the masses to this corner of the state in the spring, as well as some hiding places for mule deer, javelina, and jackrabbits. Of course, that meant there'd be coyotes, rattlesnakes, and some other desert predators sneaking around, too.

She turned to the east, trying to see the Tres Dedos mountain range over the wall of the ravine. Did mountain lions make it this far down into the desert? She'd have to ask Butch. He'd been around these parts long enough to know all about the wildlife's habits—especially when it came to the local human wildlife.

She returned to Claire. "I still don't get why I'm here."

"Is that some sort of metaphorical question? As in why you were put on this Earth besides the obvious reason—to annoy your older sisters?"

"Keep it up, sasspot, and I'm going to hogtie you and leave you here for the vultures to nibble on."

Chuckling, her sister held her hands out, palms up. "Can you feel the magic in the air?"

The air felt the same as it had when she'd arrived at the General Store an hour ago—cool and dry. She sniffed, noticing a hint of yet another desert animal. "What magic? This place stinks like skunk and everything is trying to poke holes in me. There's nothing magical about that."

"Exactly." Claire scowled at the square staked in the ground. "Not to mention that it gets pretty dang hot when the sun swings around here in the afternoon, especially if there's no breeze blowing and summer is just around the corner."

"If you think this is such a bad idea, why don't you tell Gramps that?"

"I did, but he says I'm just bucking him on this job because I have a brewery to build."

"Are you?"

Claire shrugged. "Maybe a little." She picked up the shovel and walked over to one of the stakes. "And now that Mac is going to be heading out of town again, I don't think I'm going to get much of anything done over at The Shaft besides serving drinks."

Kate had heard an earful about Mac deciding to take a short-term job rather than borrowing more money from Gramps during her ride with Claire to the tool shed in the new two-seater UTV. The old golf cart was still around somewhere, but Gramps had decided something with more horsepower and better traction was needed to haul building materials throughout the RV park.

Her sister had also mentioned something about the possibility of Joe still being alive when they'd arrived at the tool shed, but not much more on the subject after dropping that bomb.

Claire stabbed the shovel into the ground next to a stake. "With Mac leaving, you're going to have to help me."

"Why me?" Kate tried to keep the whine out of her voice but failed, judging from Claire's eye roll. "What? I can't work clear back here. I'm pregnant."

"And we're back to that excuse."

"It's not an excuse, it's a fact. I need a bathroom close by and you know it."

"There are bathrooms all over out here." She thumbed toward the creek. "Just go behind one of those cottonwood trees. Nobody will see you. Besides, you're not peeing that often yet, and we're not *that* far from one of the campground restrooms. It's just up the trail a piece."

"How do you know?"

"Because I built that particular bathroom last year."

"I mean about how often I'm peeing. Are you keeping track of my bathroom trips?"

"Maybe."

"Claire Alice, that's a violation of my privacy." Kate pulled the other bottle of water from the tote and uncapped it. "I will not go pee behind a tree. It's too hard now with this added weight up front. I can't get my balance right."

Claire gave her a narrow-eyed look. "That sounds as if you've been practicing peeing out in the open. Could that be during one of your stakeouts while spying on a particular lawman?"

Pretending she didn't hear that question, Kate continued with, "On top of that, I get leg cramps when I stand too long. And my ankles swell up."

"Okay, princess." Claire returned to shoveling. "I'll bring out a chair for you to park your whiny ass on, along with a bucket so you can put your feet up. What else will your highness require?"

"When I bend over too much, I get heartburn." Kate took a sip of water. "And I really don't think an almost twenty-week pregnant woman should be doing manual labor."

"Sheesh, I'm not asking you to haul boards on your back or harness up to lead a mule train." Claire paused, leaning on the shovel, glaring at Kate.

Something in her face reminded Kate of Ronnie. Her sisters had always shared brunette traits, but the mischievous glint in Claire's dark eyes and rounder cheeks usually set them apart. This look right now was more of a bossy older sister.

"Then why me?"

She blew a wisp of hair out of her face. "The truth of the matter is, I need a helper for this job, and you are pretty much the only one available."

The only one ... "What are you talking about? There are plenty of other people who can help you out, and I have a bar to open every day. Drinks to serve. Tips to collect."

Claire smirked. "I thought a pregnant woman such as yourself shouldn't be doing manual labor, like walking around carrying heavy trays of beer pitchers for hours on end."

Kate lifted her chin. "I plan to be supervising mostly."

"Great. And you still can—in the afternoon. This is a morning job."

"I always open the bar in the morning."

"You usually open it, but not anymore. Butch and Ronnie will take over that role. And Chester has agreed to help out in the kitchen and behind the bar when needed."

"They're going to need more help than that." Ever since Butch added gourmet sandwiches to the menu and upped his marketing game, business had doubled. Actually, more like tripled.

"Well, I'll still be working there in the evenings after I finish here."

"That's not enough."

"And Butch and Mac talked about opening a little later and closing earlier during the week through the winter. It will help make the ownership transition smoother. Not to mention the new waitress we all agreed to hire," Claire added as she returned to shoveling, grunting as she worked.

New waitress? Since when? Why didn't Butch mention anything about that?

"What new waitress?"

"Grady's niece. Ronnie recommended her."

Kate gaped. "*What?!* Mindy Lou is going to start working at The Shaft? Why wasn't I told about this before now?"

"You would know all about it if you'd come to the mini-meeting last night at the bar when Butch texted you, but you were too busy doing something else, apparently." Claire dumped a half-shovel's worth of dirt, casting Kate an eyeful of suspicion. "And by the way, where were you? Butch and I thought you were with Ruby helping out at the General Store and had probably left your phone in the car, but when Mac and I got back to the RV park, she said you weren't there at all yesterday."

Kate looked down at the tote, pretending to search for something inside of it.

"*And* you didn't reply to any of Butch's texts to join us at the bar, either."

"Uh, I had an errand to run in Yuccaville," she fibbed, but only a smidgeon. She was on an errand—one that would help save Ronnie's ass if Kate found what she was looking for to prove her suspicion.

"All evening?"

"It wasn't all evening. I was in bed by the time Butch came home." No fibbing there. When Butch had joined her under the covers and started asking questions about her whereabouts, she'd distracted him with the same old naked trick that had put a bun in her oven.

After she'd finished diverting his attention, she'd claimed a need to run to the bathroom and added a side trip to the kitchen for some pretzels and a few bites of the jumbo chicken burrito she'd picked up in Yuccaville after driving around town chasing trouble for an hour or two. Butch was asleep when she'd eased back into bed. Then this morning, she'd escaped to the RV park while he was in the shower, leaving him a note that Claire had called, needing her help.

"What was this errand that required you to sneak away to Yuccaville?" Claire pressed, pausing to look at her after dumping another partial load of dirt.

"I was not sneaking," Kate snarled.

It was more like stalking, which was something she was getting very good at these days. Before long, she'd have what she needed, Kate was sure of it. And then all of these troublemakers would go away and leave her family and her baby alone.

"Kate." Claire's brow lined as she watched her. "Did the left side of your face just twitch?"

"I just needed to get a few things at the grocery store, you see," Kate rattled off, her brain sputtering in panic. Claire had always been good at seeing through her subterfuge and lies. Working with her back here in the ravine everyday while trying to take care of these other problems was not going to cut it for Kate.

"You know Grady wants you to stay away from the grocery store."

"Too damned bad," she snapped, tossing aside the tote bag of food. "The sheriff does not get to run my life like … like … like he's my dad. I'm a free woman, allowed to do what I want when I want."

"You have a history of bad luck at the store." Claire's tone sounded wary.

"None of that stuff was my fault!"

Her sister's frown deepened. "If you really believe that, you're more delusional than I thought."

"You know what?" Kate fluttered her hands around, wishing she could fly away from everyone and their so-called warnings and concerns about her. "I'm tired of feeling like the birds and animals back here will be soon—always watched and monitored. Why don't you just tag me with some kind of locator beacon while you're at it and hook electrodes up to my head."

"Kate, you're leaning off-kilter. Bring it back to level."

"I'm perfectly lucid," she growled. "So stop giving me that evil eye."

"I'll stop giving you the evil eye when you stop flapping your hands around like you're showing off to the other birds. *And* you stop twitching." Claire stepped closer, reaching toward her face. "It almost looks as if you're getting shocked with bolts of electricity."

Kate knocked her hand away. "I'm fine." A breeze ruffled her hair, the air slightly warmer thanks to the rising sun. She took a deep breath. The skunk smell was gone, replaced by the soft, earthy scents of the desert.

"Okay then, you're fine and dandy." Claire returned to the shovel, eyeing the shallow hole she'd made where one of the stakes had been. "But tell me the truth, sister to sister, were you spying on Deputy Dipshit again?"

"No." At least not on purpose.

Kate's focus had been on Grady's ex last night. As Penny had mentioned, Elizabeth's family had some money. The fancy-schmancy Victorian-style house that sat up on the hillside overlooking Yuccaville's Main Street made that fact obvious.

"Good. But you'd better steer clear of Ernie from here on out. Grady can't keep springing you from jail without looking bad."

"I told you I was not following him." And that was the truth of the matter.

Kate walked over to the tote and took out the bag of cookies. It was time to change the subject. She stuffed a cookie in her mouth, almost drooling over the soft and sweet gingery-caramel goodness. After demolishing the cookie and pulling out a second, she asked, "Hey, is Grady's niece still screwing around with Jess's dad?"

"I don't know."

Steve Horner, aka the child support–skipping loser, had shown up suddenly last fall after ignoring his daughter for more than sixteen years. He'd claimed his sudden appearance in Jess's life had nothing to do with hearing that Ruby not only was getting married to Gramps, but also that she had come into some cash left over from her dead husband, Joe Martino. But everyone besides Jess knew better.

Speaking of Joe …

"What makes you think Joe might still be alive?" Kate asked, switching topics again while gobbling up a third cookie.

"Is this the subject we're going to stick with now, Dr. Jekyll, or is Ms. Hyde going to return to play some more spin-the-bottle in your head?" Claire pulled a pair of leather gloves from her backpack and handed them to Kate, taking the bag of cookies away from her.

"Bite me." She held up the gloves like they'd been dipped in anthrax. "Why do I need to wear *these*?" The leather was stained and hardened, probably from Claire's sweat.

"Just put the gloves on before I use them along with the shovel to perform a colonoscopy on you."

Nose wrinkled, Kate did as told. The fingers were scratchy inside, too. Nothing even close to the baby-soft, leather driving gloves Butch had given her for Christmas.

"As for Joe," Claire said after biting into one cookie and tossing the remainder back into the tote, "besides the cigar butts that were piled up in one spot over behind that cottonwood..." She pointed at a tree off to the side of the ravine. "There have been a few other things of Joe's that have been giving me heartburn. Things he left behind."

"Such as?"

"Well, for one, his childhood home."

"Ronnie told me about that iron lung you guys found in there, and some of the other creepy stuff." Kate flexed her fingers in the gloves. "But how does that tie into Joe being alive? Anyone could have left that stuff behind in the house."

"I don't know. It just seems like something Joe would do. I mean, consider all of the weird treasures he's hidden around this place." Claire walked over to the corner of the staked square. "On top of that, there's Humdigger Mine."

"What about it?"

Kate knew from Butch that Joe had owned Humdigger Mine, which was located on a small mountain in the middle of old Mr. Webber's land; and that Mac had needed Butch's help getting permission from the gun-toting geezer to go check it out.

"Someone has been hiding in there."

"I thought you said it might have been used in the past by mules." Kate meant the human kind that carried stolen or illegal goods from one place to another, not the long-eared, four-legged kind.

"Not mules, but coyotes."

"So, somebody moving people, not drugs or artifacts."

"Bingo, although it might have been used by some mules, too. Joe was connected with those two assholes who tried to drown me in a shaft."

"Yeah, yeah, yeah, don't cry me another river about having to swim with a dead body." Kate's pity-party violin strings were wearing out.

Claire's glare was ruined when a breeze blew her hair in front of her face. "Anyway," she said as she strode to her backpack and pulled out her red Mighty Mouse cap. "I wonder if Joe has been hiding in that mine for a while."

Kate scoffed. "The man's been dead and buried over in Yuccaville for a couple of years, Claire."

"He could have been coming and going during that time, using the mine to check up on his stuff now and then."

"This all sounds pretty flimsy. Next you're going to want my help gravedigging."

"And then there's Sophy." Claire returned to the stake in the corner of the square, her hat firmly in place.

"Joe's ex?"

"Yep." She stuck the shovel in the ground, hitting something hard judging from the clang of the shovel head. "Remember how she told Butch when he paid her a visit in prison that Joe was alive."

"Sophy is crazy."

"Maybe." Claire tossed the shovel aside. "But what if Sophy is right? And what if I'm right about the mine? What if Joe is alive?" She pointed at the ground near Kate. "Bring me that pickaxe, will you?"

Kate picked it up. "Would that make Gramps's and Ruby's marriage null and void?" She handed off the pickaxe.

"Really?" Claire looked at her as if she were suddenly sporting a unicorn horn. "That's the first concern you have about that selfish bastard still trolling around here?"

"What's wrong with that? I like Ruby a lot. She makes good cookies."

"That's your preggo brain speaking."

Scowling, Kate socked her sister in the shoulder. "If you'd let me finish, I was going to add that Ruby will be super pissed if Joe is still alive, especially after she almost lost the RV park to the bank because of the debts he left behind when he died—make that was supposed to have died. *And* she's going to be totally humiliated that he fooled her into believing he was six feet under, especially after she worked so hard at playing nursemaid to him."

"Okay, those things are true. But there is a much bigger problem if the bastard is still breathing." Claire nudged Kate aside and took a swing at the ground with the pickaxe.

A small divot was all that showed for Claire's effort.

"What's your version of the bigger problem?"

"I've been finding all his hidden treasures and giving them to the cops or Ruby." Claire took another swing, leaving a second small divot. "If he is still alive, he hid these treasures for a reason, probably planning to come back for them. Now, he's going to be super ticked if part of his stash is gone, and I'll be the one at fault in his eyes."

If Claire was right—somehow—then Kate's whole family was in trouble, not only Claire. Joe would want to take out Gramps, too, for stealing his wife. Kate's fists tightened. She was getting really tired of these cocksuckers taking aim at her loved ones.

Claire swung again. A slightly bigger divot was left behind. "Son of a moldy biscuit," she muttered, glaring down at the ground.

"So, what's the next step?" Kate asked, fully on board the Joe-is-alive train now and ready to kick some dead-man ass.

Claire glanced at her, a frown lining her face. "You mean digging out a place for the platform's piers? I think we're going to have to rent a gas-powered digging auger. We just hit caliche, which is basically Mother Nature's version of concrete."

"No, Bob the Builder, I'm talking about confirming that Joe is still alive and back in town to mess with us."

" 'Us'?" Claire's frown shifted north, giving her more of a worried look now. "I'm not sure. Maybe go back up to the mine. Or another trip to his childhood home. I didn't go up to the attic last time."

"We need to do that. Oh, and you could call Sophy," Kate suggested. "Maybe find out what she knows about him still kicking."

"No way. That woman tried to use me for target practice with her shotgun."

Kate pshawed. "You need to get over that already and move on. You're breathing just fine and she's locked away for a long time."

"Oh, really? How about I shoot you in the ass with some birdshot and we revisit this 'move on' advice of yours while they're patching you up in the ER?"

"I know!" Kate ignored Claire's silliness and reached down, grabbing the shovel. "I'll call Sophy, since you're such a chicken shit."

Claire's gaze tightened. "Stay out of this, Kate. This is not your problem."

"Uhhh, yes it is."

"No, it's not. Listen, you need to focus on taking care of that baby." Claire pointed at the ground. "And on helping me build this platform."

"No, *you* listen." Kate tapped her sister on the chest. "Nobody fucks with this family."

Claire cringed. "You're twitching again."

"Good. Now let's go get that gassy digger and grab some more cookies. We have some serious work to do."

Chapter Four

Death was the perfect hiding place for a thief.

Ronnie Morgan had little doubt that if Joe Martino was smart enough to figure out the trick of living through his own death, he would have. But Joe's legacy of crippling medical bills and pissed-off ex-partners spoke for itself. Not to mention that he thrived on sour cream and onion potato chips, cigarettes, and alcohol. His blood pressure and stress had raced neck-and-neck toward the grave, tag-teaming to take him out in one massive stroke.

A diet and lifestyle such as Joe's did not speak of a mastermind criminal capable of faking his own death; rather more like a two-bit fencer from the sticks who got his grubby mitts on a gold-plated coffin and waited one damned day too long to sell it for a higher price.

Here lies Joe Martino, a thieving son of a bitch.
He tried to fleece the Grim Reaper, but snagged only a single coin for
passage over the River Styx.

Claire must still be high on post-adrenaline fumes after evading that John Denver–loving serial killer, because there was no way in hell that Joe was alive.

With the jury's vote cast on the case of Joe Martino versus Death, Ronnie closed the bookkeeping files on Butch's laptop, collected the printouts of the last few months' expenses, and shut the door to the back office at The Shaft.

She pushed through the batwing doors, finding Mac behind the bar where he'd be working until the regular bartender, Gary, made it in later this afternoon. Dressed in jeans and a flannel shirt,

Mac seemed as much at home behind the beer taps as he would be hiking in the Rocky Mountains. He was also wearing his glasses today, sporting the brainy geologist look as well as brawny outdoorsman. Or was he a geophysicist? Or a geograph … ah, screw it. His previous job didn't matter now that he was going to be taking over The Shaft along with her sister.

"Claire's wrong." She dropped the printouts on the bar.

"About what in particular?" Mac asked, taking the expense sheets and spreading them out.

Ronnie could dance a jig about Mac and Claire wanting to keep her working on the bar's books after they took over the business. She needed all the money she could get right now, and while accounting hadn't been a career aspiration of hers, she'd taken several classes in college and was good with numbers. More important, though, keeping track of the finances at The Shaft over the last few months had given her a solid dose of much-needed self-confidence.

When she'd initially arrived in Arizona after weathering the first squall of her divorce shitstorm, her inner strength had been knocked to its knees, and her pride could barely even manage to crawl. Working at The Shaft had given her a solid dose of get-up-and-back-to-living gumption.

If only she could escape from her ex-husband's shadow and all of the ghouls who liked to hide there in the dark. There were too many hitmen taking aim at *her* now that Lyle was safely tucked away behind bars. Although the cheating jackass had been stuffed in one of the prison's industrial dryers recently and left to spin to death on high heat, so maybe his safety net had holes in it. Too bad he'd lived through the ordeal to continue causing Ronnie more headaches.

But she digressed, as she often did when her ex was involved. Back to that other no-good son of a bitch—Joe.

"Claire's wrong about Joe Martino." She flicked on the overhead lights, brightening up the rest of the place. "There's no way he's still alive. Ruby saw Joe dead and watched him be buried. How could he fake that?"

Criminy, what was next from her sister's overactive imagination?

"I asked Claire basically the same thing last night." Mac

glanced up at Ronnie, his brow furrowed over his glasses. "She said anything was possible with a con artist as skilled as Joe."

"Even coming back from the dead?" Ronnie turned on the neon open sign in the window next to the front door.

Mac grunted in reply.

A peek outside the door found a cloudless blue sky and an empty gravel parking lot, except for a dust devil spinning toward the highway. It carried pieces of a tumbleweed and a plastic bag with it. Across the street, a couple of cowboys were loading bulky, heavy-looking sacks onto a Chevy pickup in front of the hardware store. Kitty-corner from The Shaft, a dark SUV with shaded windows was filling up at Biddy's Gas and Carryout. The noon sun glinted off its windshield straight into Ronnie's eyes.

Ronnie shut the front door on the sunshine and fresh air, leaning back against it. The Shaft's signature scent of fried meat and beer, along with a hint of lemon-scented ammonia, was oddly comforting. This place had become her home away from no-home, being that the Winnebago she'd been borrowing had burned up, along with her clothes and the few remaining what-nots she'd managed to retain after losing pretty much everything in her divorce.

She returned to the bar, grabbing a clean server's apron from the shelf. Claire couldn't really be serious about Joe, could she?

"So maybe somebody hooked Joe's dead body up to a bunch of electrodes." Ronnie grinned at Mac as she tied the apron around her waist. "And then left him out in a lightning storm to be zapped in the keister a few times."

"I'd love to have zapped 'Sticky Fingers' Martino a few times myself for the hell he put my aunt through." Mac's focus returned to the papers in front of him.

A clanking sound came through the order window, followed by a hoot of laughter from Chester Thomas, Gramps's old Army pal. Back in the kitchen, Butch was showing Chester the lay of the land.

Ever since Gramps and Manny had both gotten hitched, Chester had nobody to hang out with while smoking cigars and talking about getting some tail. Not that it stopped him from trying, but Gramps and Manny were often busy being henpecked. At least those were Chester's words this morning when Ronnie had asked why he wanted to work at The Shaft when he was supposed to be enjoying retirement. He explained slinging burgers might help him keep out of trouble with the incoming "hot birds" at the RV park, or at least give him more cash to share with the dancing girls over at his favorite strip club, Dirty Gerties. Ronnie was more apt to believe the latter, knowing Chester's love for babes in mud-covered bikinis.

She tucked an order pad and a couple of pens in one of the apron pockets. "I'm worried Claire is following in Katie's footsteps."

Mac looked up. "You mean Kate's Dr. Jekyll and Mr. Hyde syndrome?"

"Well, let's not go that far. More like creating waves because still waters are boring."

One of his brown eyebrows lifted. "I thought still waters run deep."

"Shut up and just go along with me on this."

He chuckled. "Fine, but you know how Claire gets when she locks her teeth onto something, so good luck convincing her Joe is dead if she wants to believe otherwise."

"She's too stubborn for her own good." Penny had nailed that part of Claire's personality when listing those Aries traits. "She gets that from our mother."

Mac groaned. "Don't remind me of Deborah. I'm trying to enjoy what little time I have left before she returns to Jackrabbit Junction and starts hating me out loud again."

"What do we have? A week before she finishes the thirty-day program for alcoholics?"

"Your grandfather told Manny to keep her in Tucson an extra week. Something about having Deborah de-fanged and de-clawed before returning to the RV park to be safe."

Ronnie cringed. "Manny needs to get her a rabies shot, too." Truth be told, she wouldn't be thrilled to have her mother back. While drunk, Deborah and her verbal jabs were bad enough. But sober? Hell, a crocodile had a softer bite.

She rested her elbows on the bar. "So, tell me honestly, how serious is Claire about this Joe's-alive theory? Like to the point of carrying a spyglass around and searching the hills for him periodically? Or more like breaking and entering obsessed?"

She'd witnessed both of those behaviors in Claire over the past few months.

Mac frowned. "Serious enough to enlist Kate."

"Oh, shitballs."

What the hell? Did Claire need to live in a constant state of paranoia now—like some sort of adrenaline junkie?

Ronnie would prefer to live in a constant state of *chill* these days, but that wasn't in her cards thanks to Lyle, may he choke on a meatball in his cushy prison cell. According to the FBI, it was only a matter of time until another hitman came knocking, and now she had a Mexican cartel upping the ante.

Still frowning, Mac returned to his numbers.

Ronnie needed some music to take her mind off the messy world outside of the bar. Something light and happy. Something she could sing along to while she worked. Singing was supposed to fill the brain with dopamine, wasn't it? Or was it adrenaline? Either way, a good song might distract her from both her sisters' crazy notions.

And her mother's sharp teeth.

And Lyle's lies.

And Elizabeth's bullshit, too. Like Ronnie needed Grady's ex adding to her pile of craptastic problems.

Grabbing some quarters from the change bowl Butch kept behind the bar, she popped a handful into the jukebox and perused the list of songs.

The first one was a no-brainer: "Lovely Day." Bill Withers's voice alone was soothing.

Ronnie sang the chorus under her breath as she punched in the letter–number combination.

"Ronnie," Mac said. "I'm going to run back to the supply room to get some clean bar towels."

"Okay." Ronnie waved without looking his way.

Penny should be by soon to drop off her niece, whom Ronnie would be training today on the job. She really hoped this waitressing gig worked out for Mindy Lou. She also crossed her fingers that the troubled twenty-something girl didn't end up going home with a different guy every night and fall deeper into a pit of self-sabotage.

Another song snagged her eye. She punched in the combo for

"Jump" by The Pointer Sisters. Ronnie could use some jumping for love and happiness these days.

Poor Mindy Lou just needed the right people around to lift her up instead of beat her down. She could also use a break from loser guys, but that might take some time and confidence boosting to shake off the past and …

No way! Since when did the jukebox have "Upside Down" by Jack Johnson? Butch must have updated the song catalogue since the last time Ronnie scrolled through the list. She selected Jack's mellow song along with James Brown's hit about feeling good.

That left one more song.

She was punching in the combo for KT Tunstall's "Suddenly I See" when the front door opened. That must be Penny and her niece.

Turning with a big welcoming smile for Mindy Lou, Ronnie was surprised to see a face that was familiar—but not.

A tall woman wearing beige khakis and a desert-camouflage flak jacket over a brown thermal shirt didn't wait around to be greeted. She strode toward Ronnie, her gaze steadfast and narrowed below the bulky black beanie. There was something about her dark, almond-shaped eyes …

Where had Ronnie seen them before? It was somewhere recent. Was it at the RV park?

No, it was somewhere with food.

"Veronica Jefferson," the woman said, her voice deeper than usual for a female, yet smooth and commanding.

Who in hades was this long-legged stranger?

A more sphincter-tightening question was, how did she know Ronnie's married name? Everyone around these parts knew her as Ronnie Morgan.

If she knew Ronnie as a "Jefferson," did that mean …

Shit! A hired killer?

A dew of sweat coated her lower back. Her hands started to tremble. She needed to yank that beanie down over the stranger's eyes and make a run for it.

Although … a voice of reason spoke above the panic starting to riot in her head. The stranger could work for the FBI, who also still called Ronnie by her married name.

"Who's asking?" Ronnie glanced toward the bar, looking for

backup. Mac hadn't returned from the supply room yet, damn it.

"I'm not asking." The woman stopped a few feet away, out of reach. Her eyelashes were long and thick, and her skin looked like smooth, rich caramel. "I'm stating your name."

She was tall for a woman, topping out several inches above Ronnie. Upon closer inspection, there was something about the strong angle of her jaw that was familiar. And her nose, too, which was slightly aquiline.

Ronnie took a step back, bumping into the jukebox. She held out her hands in front of her, as if she could magically ward death off with them. "What's this about?"

"I need to give you something."

What? A bullet in the forehead? A knife between the ribs? Ronnie sucked in a breath.

Oh, God! Here she was. A killer sent to remove Ronnie's fingertips, which would be sent to Lyle one at a time until he gave up some stupid money-related secret.

She took another peek toward the bar. Where in the hell was Mac? How long did it take to grab a few bar towels, for fuck's sake?

"Give me what?" Ronnie whispered, having trouble getting the words out around her quivering heart, which had staked a new claim in her throat.

Her eyes darted to the front door. And where was Mississippi? The FBI agent was supposed to be making sure Ronnie saw the sun rise and set each day. This was not the time to be dilly-dallying on the job.

The woman reached inside her flak jacket ... For what? A 9mm handgun? A meat cleaver? A tiny truth-telling robotic bug to jam up Ronnie's nose so it could tap into her brain?

Jeez, she'd watched too many creepy movies with Claire over the years.

Ronnie tried to make sense of the words coming from the stranger's lips, but she couldn't hear them over the sound of a freight train rushing from one ear to the other. Shooting stars began spiraling through the air around the stranger's head. Pain blossomed in her chest as she struggled to breathe, unable to get enough air past the fear squeezing the life out of her windpipe.

Holy hell's bells! She had to get a hold of herself before she passed out or popped a blood vessel in her brain.

"Stop it!" she shouted in the nearly empty bar and slapped herself hard, making her eyes water.

The stranger stopped. Talking, at least.

So did the freight train and the shooting stars.

The tightness in her chest eased, making breathing possible yet again. "Whew!" She rubbed her stinging cheek. "That was a close one."

The stranger stared at her as if she'd sprouted a beanstalk from the top of her head. "Are you okay, Veronica?"

"That depends."

"On what?"

"If you're here to kill me."

The woman blinked, but that was it. "Of course I didn't come here to kill you." She laughed, but it sounded forced. "I came because you saved my mother's life yesterday in The Mule Train Diner in Yuccaville."

Her mother? Ohhhh. No wonder she looked familiar.

Well, didn't that make Ronnie look the fool? And here she'd been thinking Claire and Kate were losing their marbles. All it took was one stranger to walk into a bar and mention her married name and Ronnie ... Wait a second.

"How do you know my name?" There'd been no information exchanged at the diner yesterday.

"Hey, Ronnie," Mac called. He stood at the other end of the bar with a stack of white towels in his hands. "How about you introduce me to your friend." He dropped the towels on the bar and headed her way, his eyes full of questions. "On second thought, I'll introduce myself."

How long had Mac been standing there watching them? Long enough to see her slap herself? Dear Lord, she hoped not. She'd never live that down.

The woman's gaze flicked in Mac's direction as he joined them. "Mac Garner, soon-to-be owner of The Shaft." He held out his hand as he edged Ronnie aside, putting himself partly between her and their visitor.

The woman took his hand after a hesitation, transferring what looked like a wad of money into her other hand. "Sadie Jenkins."

"Nice to meet you, Sadie, and welcome to The Shaft." He pulled his hand free and thumbed toward the bar. "You want a beer?"

"No, thanks. I was just stopping by to give Ms. Jefferson a reward for her service yesterday."

Mac glanced down at the wad of bills now held out between them, before aiming a raised eyebrow at Ronnie. "Did you find her dog or something?"

"I used the Heimlich maneuver on her mom when she was choking on a grape."

"Oh, good." Mac visibly relaxed, until he looked into Ronnie's eyes and saw something there that made his brow line again. "So, is your mom doing okay, Ms. Jenkins?"

She nodded, stepping closer with the wad of cash held out in her open palm. "Please," she said to Ronnie. "Take this as a thank-you for saving her life."

Ronnie stared down at the bills. How much money was in that wad? The top one looked like a twenty-dollar bill, and there were a lot of bills there. If those were all twenties, that would be plenty to buy herself some new clothes and shoes to replace what was burned in the fire. Maybe even some extra cash left over to tuck away in the bank account she'd opened after Christmas to save up for her own car.

Ronnie started to raise her hand to take the money, but something tugged at her. Something to do with her morals.

She lowered her hand. "Keep your money. I helped your mom because she needed it. I'm just glad I was there when it happened."

Sadie shook her head. "Take the cash. *Please.*"

Ronnie and Mac exchanged wary glances at the rigid tone in her voice. It was more like an order than a request.

Ronnie pushed the woman's hand away. "I said I don't want your money, but thanks for the offer."

Sadie cursed under her breath, taking a step closer, and lowering her voice. "Listen, lady, I need you to take the money, so I can square my ledger."

That sure was a weird way of putting that. Ronnie's gaze dipped south from Sadie's pinched lips to the tendons showing in her neck. Who was this uptight, partially camouflaged lady in combat boots? An accountant for an elite group of highly trained Army Ranger CPAs?

Ronnie crossed her arms, meeting Sadie Jenkins's gaze head

on. "I'm sorry, but your ledger will have to remain un-squared, because I don't save lives for money. I do it because it's the right thing to do."

Their stare-off continued as Jack Johnson crooned on the jukebox about turning things upside down. Ronnie was feeling a little spun around herself at the moment.

Mac cleared his throat. "Maybe we should all share a drink and come up with some other form of reward."

"No." Sadie's nostrils flared. "Never mind. I'll make this right my own way." She crammed the money back into her pocket and headed for the front door without a single glance back in Ronnie's direction or anywhere else.

After the door closed behind her, Mac looked at Ronnie. "What in the hell was that about?"

She tried to laugh, but it sounded screechy around the edges. "I don't know. I just saved a life is all, same as anyone else would have done, given the circumstances."

He continued to search her face, pausing on her cheek. "Are you okay?"

Maybe. "Yeah, why?"

He grinned. "Because it's not every day that I see a person smack themselves as hard as you did."

A rush of heat spread up her neck. "I panicked, okay?"

He patted her shoulder. "Remind me not to freak out in front of you. That was one mean slap."

She held her fist up in front of his nose. "You will speak to no one of these events—family or lawman or foe—or I will rearrange your pretty nose, got it?"

She didn't need Claire or Katie finding out she was one stranger away from needing a straitjacket, nor Grady, for that matter. His brow was furrowed more than ever when it came to Ronnie and her sisters. Add to that pot of problems one ex-wife back in town, and it all added up to a big bowl of heartburn. Oh, and this being an election year for him only made it all even worse.

Mac touched his nose. "I've always thought of it as more of a regal nose, not so much *pretty*."

She moved her fist closer. "Mac, promise."

"Fine, Kate Jr." He knocked her fist aside. "But I reserve the right to laugh at the replay of you slapping yourself in the face whenever I need a pick-me-up."

She pointed toward the bar. "Just shut up and go do bartender stuff."

Laughing as he walked away, Mac did as told. No sooner had he rounded the bar, the front door opened again.

Ronnie watched as Special Agent Mississippi Brown slipped off his jacket and hung it by the door. He wore his usual uniform—black shirt, jeans, and boots, along with a matching cowboy hat. Not a lover of color, Mississippi aspired to be a shadow at The Shaft while he watched Ronnie's back. She didn't care if he dressed in pigtails and polka dots, so long as he shot first and asked questions later when the next hired gun came to town.

Mississippi tipped his hat at her, then sidled up to the bar and ordered his usual burger and side salad from Mac.

Ronnie harrumphed. Sure, *now* the FBI shows up.

Sadie Jenkins could have been a cold-blooded killer and shivved Ronnie thirteen times before anyone came running to see what all the screaming was about. That just confirmed what Ronnie had told Grady last night—she needed to play offense from now on instead of defense. Fluttering around waiting to be killed was for the birds.

And how exactly had that woman known Ronnie's married name? It was still on her driver's license, which Deputy Dipshit had probably seen. It was also probably listed in the multiple reports filed on her at the police station, including the ticket Grady had given her when she'd first come to Jackrabbit Junction.

Of course, the FBI had probably used her married name around Grady and his deputies, too. Hell, probably half of Yuccaville knew her other name by this time, which really sucked because she wanted to bury "Veronica Jefferson" in an unmarked grave. Both parts of that name reminded her what a fool she'd been for trying to live a life that fit her like boots that were two sizes too small. She still had calluses from the blisters of her past.

Today was a good lesson. Ronnie needed to start carrying some form of protection.

With James Brown singing on the jukebox about feeling good, Ronnie headed for the ladies' room to splash some cold water on her stinging cheek and check if she'd peed her pants in the thick of panic. It was a good thing she was wearing underwear today.

Chapter Five

*H*aving grown up with three older, much bigger brothers, Penelope Harrison had learned early on that whatever didn't kill her in this rough-and-tumble world had better start running—and fast. After all, she was a savage warrior princess. At least that's what her oldest brother had told her for as long as she could remember.

While her mother had regularly reminded her children that nothing good ever came from violence, revenge had served Penny well over the years. Whether it be handing out black eyes to schoolyard bullies or delivering sucker punches in dark parking lots when someone got too fresh, her retaliations were legendary in the small town of Yuccaville, according to the table talk during her family's holiday get-togethers.

But age and time had dulled her savagery. By her mid-twenties, the seemingly never-ending jokes from the local dipshits about her grade-school nickname, "Penny the Pounder," were tiresome at best. She started craving an escape from the day-to-day monotony of mining-town life, looking for big-city excitement far away from home. A place where nobody knew her history. After her application to the culinary school in San Francisco was accepted, she'd filled her SUV with all her belongings and hit the road.

That was the end of Yuccaville city limits for her, she'd thought, wiping her hands of the dusty old copper town.

Life was good in San Francisco, not to mention filled with great cuisine. While she was in culinary school, she'd landed a challenging job in a renowned upscale restaurant, moved into a small apartment in the Castro District, and met Vince Denson, who slowly but surely wormed his way into her guarded heart over the next year.

Ahh, Vince. Tall, dark, and FBI.

The fact that he would disappear for weeks at a time due to his job hadn't mattered, because when he returned home the sex was great and the meals were divine.

Although, thinking back, the sex wasn't really *that* good.

Penny did have a tendency to let passion overrule common sense, especially in bed. After her lackluster—and unsatisfying—deflowering in the cramped backseat of a rusted-out Trans Am up on Hanky-Panky Peak, she'd made a point of taking control of her own pleasure, running roughshod over her lovers. While some guys kicked back and enjoyed the ride, others complained about not getting to hold onto the reins.

Vince fell into the latter category.

Annoyingly so sometimes.

But Penny shrugged off his whining because lo and behold, it turned out that her warrior heart had an Achilles heel: lawmen.

That shouldn't have been a surprise, really, considering that her father had been a highway patrol officer who was killed on duty when she was four years old. Most of her memories of her dad were blurry, faded from time, but that uniform and badge he wore … those were still as clear as a bell. He would always be her knight in shining armor, and his bravery and dedication to protecting others set the bar high for any males wanting to court her.

Anyway, back to Vince and her warrior heart, which had been tamed by love, and probably blinded by the sparkles in her diamond engagement ring, if she were being honest.

Wedding plans were already on the horizon when Penny found out about the other woman. Actually, *women*. As in plural. As in four of them. All being juggled at the same time as Penny. An impressive feat, truly, for one whiny, cheating whorehound.

But not quite as impressive as how fast Vince had run when she scooped up the pieces of her broken heart and chased after him through their apartment with an electric cattle prod. His fetish for collecting oddball weapons while on the job sort of stung him in the ass. Or rather jabbed him in it. Repeatedly. One quick zap for each woman he was screwing behind her back. And a final long zap for herself.

Penny could still hear his squeals of pain.

The tomcat should have known better than to break the heart of a savage warrior princess known for her vicious retaliations.

Lessons were learned on that fateful day: Love hurt. Bad.

And not all lawmen were created equal.

Penny spent the next few weeks operating in zombie mode. At the restaurant, she kept dropping pans and dishes, confusing orders, and cutting her fingers. Multiple warning slips turned into a visit to the unemployment office.

Home in her apartment, she hid inside the four walls, beating herself up for how foolish she'd been to trust a liar. His betrayal sliced her pride to ribbons and made her question if she could ever trust someone with her heart again.

She was busy consoling herself with a lemon meringue pie late one night when her mother called to tell her she was needed back home. Penny bucked that notion. Going home equaled complete failure. She'd be returning to her starting point, only older now, and scarred. Soured on men.

No, home would be bad for her.

Then her mom spilled the beans about Grady's current location smack-dab in the center of hell. She told Penny how Elizabeth had lied about so many things. About loving Grady. About the true father of the child she'd carried in her womb for nine months. About her vow to stay with Penny's brother until death did them part.

Penny's stomach had burned at the news. That lying bitch and Vince needed to be tied up, dipped in honey, and left out for the fire ants.

Thinking back, her mom's sister, Aunt Millie, had pretty much predicted this at Grady's wedding when she'd whispered in Penny's ear that marrying Elizabeth was bad juju because, "that girl was rotten long before she was ripe."

It was no secret to those who knew Penny that she'd go to hell and back for someone she cared about, and she really loved her brothers. *And* her mother, who had recently fallen and hurt her hip and now needed some extra help at home while she mended.

So, home Penny went, returning to the dusty mining town she'd tried to leave behind for good, because her mother was right. Grady needed his family to rally around him. On a career path to become the county sheriff, he couldn't hide away in a big city like

Penny was. He had to stay put and face the sneers and whispers.

She'd be damned if she'd let Grady stand alone.

Back in Yuccaville, Penny kept her cool while out and about, mostly because her mom made her promise not to get into any fights. The last thing Grady's reputation needed was his sister locked behind bars for disturbing the peace.

Penny shrugged off the snide comments and spiteful rumors about her brother's inability to keep his wife satisfied, and shot back underhanded insults with a big smile and a pat on the back.

She slammed back beers with Grady when he needed to blow off steam. She commiserated alongside him about no-good lousy cheaters and cried on his shoulder about both of their shitty predicaments.

But Grady was losing too much weight and growing more distant from those who loved him most. And Penny felt herself slipping deeper into depression, her own life as messy on the inside as Grady's was on the outside.

One day, Aunt Millie stopped by the house and dragged Penny out of bed and into the sunshine. It was time to get back to the business of living, and Aunt Millie showed Penny a building in town that was for sale. After a few motivational kicks by her aunt, Penny dug into her savings, secured a loan, and opened The Mule Train Diner.

Those first couple of years weren't easy. Only able to afford a staff of two at first, Penny worked hard every day, managing and waiting on tables, cleaning counters and floors after hours. With time, though, she built a steady customer base, made enough money to make additional payments on her business loan, and stashed extra cash in her savings.

Things were looking up for her, but Grady was still bending under the weight of his troubles.

Then suddenly last fall, her brother started showing signs of life again. He laughed at Penny's lame jokes when he stopped by for lunch. He put Elizabeth's and his old place in town up for sale and began planning out his dream house in the country. He even shaved when he was off duty and started wearing cologne again.

After putting her head together with Aunt Millie, the two of them started snooping around town, searching for what had spurred this change. Penny's aunt soon figured out the answer—a woman. Better yet, a *non-local* female. Someone who hadn't been around to see Grady while he was in the gutter. Somebody who didn't care about his past.

The light was back in her brother's eyes, finally. After one look at Ronnie Morgan, Penny understood why Elizabeth's shadow no longer darkened Grady's days and nights.

So, for a minute—maybe two—both Penny and her brother were as happy as a puppy with two tails.

But then that blond Medusa and her hissing snakes slinked back to Yuccaville.

As if that weren't enough, the bitch wanted Grady back.

Why Elizabeth thought Grady still belonged to her in spite of her infidelity was beyond Penny. Not to mention the public humiliation he'd had to face day after day for months after she'd left him. And what about the kid the homewrecker had claimed was Grady's until the hospital bills were paid by his insurance? Where was that child? And the father—the real one? Had she left both behind in Nevada, thinking she could come home and pretend that whole shitshow never aired on all of the local channels?

And on top of that boot-scootin' bullshit, Elizabeth had the audacity to threaten Penny's livelihood if she didn't help convince Grady to return to the cheater's bed.

In fact, according to the text message that had come in this morning, she had until midnight to pick the "right team." If Penny chose unwisely, Elizabeth was going to destroy the reputation of The Mule Train Diner and drive Penny out of business.

Holy salami! That bitch's roof wasn't nailed on tight.

"Aunt Penny?" Mindy Lou snapped her fingers in front of Penny's face. "Are you in there?"

"What? Yeah. Of course." She shot a frown at her niece, who was riding shotgun in Penny's SUV. "I'm driving, remember?"

"I remember, but do you?" Mindy Lou pointed out the windshield toward the ditch. "You crossed the white line twice in the last minute, hitting the rumble strips both times."

"Says the woman who has been involved in not two, but three minor rear-end collisions."

Mindy Lou wrinkled her nose at Penny. "The last one didn't count. The old broad backed into me while we were at a stop light."

"That's not the story she told your uncle when he went to talk her out of pressing charges after you verbally insulted her intelligence."

"I didn't insult her intelligence. I told her that her motor skills were older than dirt." Mindy Lou shifted in her seat, chewing on her lower lip like she had when she was a kid in blond pigtails.

Those were much simpler days in the girl's life. Happier, too. Back before Mindy Lou's self-confidence was shredded by her ex-fiancé—a vain, heartless, dog turd of a man.

Getting royally screwed over by their lovers appeared to be a Harrison family curse. Lucky them.

"Aunt Penny, can't I just work for you in the diner instead of this waitressing gig way out here in the sticks?"

"Sticks?" Penny grinned at her niece. "What do you think Yuccaville is? A shiny metropolis?"

"You know what I mean. Until I get my license back, I can't even drive myself to work. At least I could walk to your diner."

"I don't need any extra help at the diner right now." She swerved over the white line again to dodge a chunk of a retread tire in the middle of the road, grimacing at the rumbling complaint from the tires. "Besides, you don't need to drive. Between your mom and dad, Uncle Grady, and me, we'll make sure you get to work. And in a few more months, you'll get your license back. By then, you'll have saved up enough cash for a car, since the insurance company totaled your old one after that 'broad' backed into you."

That was the goal anyway for Penny and the rest of her family, along with wanting to keep Mindy Lou from falling off the wagon and once again landing facedown in the gutter.

Mindy Lou had hit rock bottom a year ago when her fiancé told her she was too fat for him and dumped her for a skinnier woman. The poor girl had always struggled with her weight, and after that back-alley confidence beating, she gave up on herself.

She began smoking cigarettes soon after that to try to keep from eating. After losing a few pounds, she returned to dating, which Penny figured was probably to rebuild her self-esteem. Unfortunately, Mindy Lou's dating pool was filled with sharks, who offered her cheap compliments, along with booze and cigarettes, in exchange for even cheaper sex in skanky motels.

It had taken a family intervention to pull Mindy Lou out of her tailspin. She'd given up the dating scene for starters—along with the booze that came with it—and was able to see pretty quickly the true motivation behind those flattery-bloated pickup lines she'd fallen for in the past. She might be insecure with a bruised pride, but she wasn't dumb.

Giving up cigarettes was another story, though. That nicotine devil was a low-down, dirty fighter.

On the good-news front, a recent test at the doctor's office had come back clean of any type of sexually transmitted diseases. Thankfully, Mindy Lou had never been so drunk that she forgot to use a condom.

It was going to take Penny's niece some time to get back on her feet again. After some discussion, the family had figured a job outside of Yuccaville would be best, since so many of the locals still looked down their noses at a girl fresh from the gutter.

When Penny told Mindy Lou about this new job opportunity last week, she'd agreed to take it. But now that her first day at The Shaft had arrived, she kept fidgeting and worrying her poor lower lip.

Penny reached over and squeezed Mindy Lou's arm. "You're going to be fine, chickpea. Trust me. These people are not going to judge you. They're happy to have your help."

Mindy Lou let out a soft sigh. "Uncle Grady told me the same thing last night on the phone, but I really hate starting a new job and meeting new people."

In the midday sunlight, her niece looked ten years older than her twenty-three years. Mindy Lou's teal-streaked, bleached blond hair wasn't helping her on that front. Nor was her splotchy skin— a leftover from months of hard living and bad eating habits while looking at the world through cigarette smoke.

A couple of miles later, The Shaft loomed ahead on the right. Penny slowed and turned into the gravel lot, parking near the front door.

She turned to her niece. "You want me to stick around while you settle in?"

Mindy Lou stared out the windshield. "I'm not a kid anymore, Aunt Penny."

"Good. Then don't act like one today. Walk in there with confidence. Remember, you're a Harrison. We may take a beating now and then, but that won't keep us down for long."

Frowning, Mindy Lou asked, "What are they going to think of me? Especially after screwing around with Steve. I mean, he was almost old enough to be my dad."

That was true, and Steve Horner needed to be castrated for not only robbing the cradle, but for taking advantage of a girl down on her luck. But Penny would plot that revenge another day.

Like most small towns, one of the parties in a relationship tended to have a common denominator with several other locals. In Mindy Lou's case, Steve Horner happened to be the father of Jessica, as in Ruby Martino-Ford's sixteen-year-old daughter. Being that the Morgan sisters' grandfather married Ruby Martino last fall, Jessica was now their aunt by marriage. That meant that Mindy Lou had been sleeping with Ronnie's aunt's dad, which made the whole thing seem even more cringeworthy for Penny.

"Mindy Lou, look at me." Penny waited until she had her niece's full attention. "It doesn't matter what anyone else thinks of you. What really matters is what you have in here." She tapped Mindy Lou's forehead. "And in your heart."

"I know, but—"

"No buts. You are strong. You are beautiful. You are smart." Penny grinned. "And I know this for a fact because you take after me."

Mindy Lou leaned across the console and hugged her. "Thank you, Aunt Penny," she said in her ear. "You always know how to make me smile."

"Let's do this, chickpea." Penny hugged her back. "I'll order some lunch and stick around while you get your first day underway."

"Okay." Her niece pulled back. "Uncle Grady is picking me up tonight, right?"

"Yep." He'd stop by to play taxi for both Mindy Lou and Ronnie, who was supposedly going to be training their niece today.

Penny opened her door and hopped to the ground, glancing around. The lot was empty out in front of The Shaft. Near the back of the building, a handful of vehicles sat, reflecting the sun's rays. The closest was an old International Scout that was in dire need of a paint job—that must be Butch's newest project. Next to it was a dusty white Dodge truck, which Penny was pretty sure belonged to Mac Garner. The last one was a midnight blue pickup.

She grimaced. *Not him. Not today.*

Of all the gin joints in all the dusty pitstops in all the deserts …

Fiddle-dee-fuck.

Penny had hoped not to see the owner of that particular pickup again before the end of this decade. Or the next.

"What's wrong?" Mindy Lou hesitated at the front door.

"Uh, nothing." She shifted her gaze back to her niece.

"Then why do you look like you just sucked on a lemon?"

"I bit my tongue," she lied and joined Mindy Lou, steeling herself for what was waiting on the other side of the door. Or rather *who*. "You ready?"

"Nope." But Mindy Lou opened the door and led the way inside anyway.

Three pairs of eyes looked their way.

Penny had been right about the white pickup belonging to Mac. He waved at her from where he stood behind the bar, which had several papers spread over it. Penny hadn't seen him wearing glasses before. The female customers were going to enjoy being served beer by a brainy-looking hunk.

Butch was missing, but Ronnie was there, leaning on the bar across from Mac. She wore canvas tennis shoes, jeans, a serving apron, and a black button-up shirt with "The Shaft" embroidered above the breast pocket. Good, Mindy Lou would fit right in alongside of her—except for the teal-streaked hair. Ronnie's brown, shoulder-length hair hung straight today, the loose curls flattened, which made her look more sleek, less wild.

That left the long-legged guy sitting on the bar stool. Penny avoided looking his way, but she knew well enough that his eyes were a vivid green, like a rainforest; his hair was black, wavy, and silky to the touch; and his body was lean and tightly packed.

Pasting a smile on her face, Penny led the way over to the trio, deliberately not looking at FBI Special Agent Mississippi Brown.

"Sorry we're late," she said, glancing behind her to make sure Mindy Lou wasn't playing wallflower by the door.

Her niece had followed on her heels, but her smile was forced, same as Penny's. "Hi, I'm Mindy Lou," she said, her voice creaking at the end of her name. She tittered. "I'm nervous."

Ronnie came their way, her gaze warm and welcoming. "I'm Ronnie, and we've met before."

"We have?" Mindy Lou's eyes narrowed for a moment, and then widened in a flash. "Oh. God. No." Two dark pink spots warmed her cheeks. "Shit. Wow." Her gaze darted around, as if she were seeking a rock to crawl under, but then she seemed to give up and settled on staring at her sneakers. "I think I owe you some money."

"You don't owe me anything." Ronnie's voice was kind.

Penny frowned back and forth between the two women. When had this meeting taken place? Or maybe *where* was the better question, judging from her niece's pained expression.

Mindy Lou groaned loud enough to be heard over KT Tunstall singing on the jukebox. "Man, what are the chances. You must think I'm a real piece of work. "

"Nah. You hit a rough spot in the road." Ronnie shrugged. "Trust me, I've been over some rough road lately, too, so I understand."

"Maybe I should go." Mindy Lou glanced at the door.

"No. We need your help here." Ronnie rushed forward and pulled Mindy Lou into a hug, surprising both the girl and Penny. "You're the perfect person for the job."

"Why me?" Mindy Lou's voice was slightly muffled by Ronnie's shirt.

Ronnie stepped back and held Mindy Lou by the shoulders, smiling at her. "Because you're tough. Working here isn't for wimps."

"I am?"

"You are." She left Penny's niece standing with a bewildered expression and stepped behind the bar, hurrying back with a server apron. "I believe introductions are in order." She handed the apron to Mindy Lou. "This is Mac." She thumbed toward Garner. "He and my sister, Claire, are buying the bar from Butch, whom your uncle told me you already know."

Mindy Lou nodded.

"You'll meet Claire later this afternoon when she finishes up at the RV park, where she works as the resident handywoman."

"Handy*woman*?"

"Yep. Claire is really good with her hands."

"I'll say," Mac joked, grinning toward Mississippi, who raised his glass in return.

Ronnie made a show of rolling her eyes for Mindy Lou's entertainment, Penny could tell. "Mac thinks he's funny. Just pretend to laugh at his jokes, and he'll make sure you get your drink orders lickety-split."

"Okay," Mindy Lou said, giving Mac a shy smile.

"And this guy hangs out here more often than not," Ronnie said, poking Mr. FBI in the shoulder. "His name is Mississippi Brown."

"Seriously? Like the state?"

Penny tried not to grin at the disbelief in Mindy Lou's tone. She'd been doubtful, too, when she'd first heard his name. But then she'd found out about the FBI part and started cracking her knuckles in preparation to go round one with the government pawn. Unfortunately, she didn't heed Grady's warning to stop after the first match.

Giving Mindy Lou a two-fingered salute, Mississippi said, "You can call me Mr. Brown."

Mindy Lou glanced at Penny, who nodded while doing her best to not look in Mississippi's direction. "Okay," the girl said, her smile widening with more confidence.

"So, welcome to The Shaft." Ronnie pointed at the bar apron Mindy Lou was clutching against her stomach. "We have aprons here instead of club jackets."

Mindy Lou laughed. A natural laugh this time, which warmed Penny's heart. Maybe this would all work out after all. She crossed her fingers behind her back.

"Now, if you'll come with me to Butch's office," Ronnie said, waving for her trainee to follow as she headed toward the swinging doors. "There are a couple more forms you need to sign. After the paperwork is finished," she said, backing through the swinging doors, "we'll stop by the supply room to grab you a work shirt like mine."

Mindy Lou trailed after Ronnie, disappearing into the back.

That left Penny alone with Mississippi, the last guy on the planet she wanted to talk to after barking up the wrong tree last week.

Well, almost alone. Mac was still there, thank God.

The song on the jukebox ended, leaving the three of them in silence.

Awkward silence.

Nerve-racking silence.

Maybe she should leave.

No. She promised Mindy Lou she'd stay for lunch.

But that was before she knew *he* would be here.

Penny jammed her hands in her back pockets, glancing around the bar. She could play some pool to keep her hands busy. No. Mississippi liked to play pool. He might join her up there.

She puffed her cheeks and blew out a breath. Damn it, where was the usual lunch crowd? The Shaft was a popular eating joint in this area. It must be too early yet. What time was it, anyway?

Something clanked back in the kitchen. She peeked through the order window and a plate with a steaming burger and a salad slid into view. She caught a glance of Butch and someone older and rounder in the belly than the usual cook.

"You hanging out for a while, Penny?" Mac asked, watching her with a slightly raised brow as he set the food on the bar in front of Mr. FBI.

She would not look at Mississippi to see if he was showing any signs of interest in her answer. Nope. She would try to stay focused on Mac and Mac only.

While she was focused on him, Mac looked over at Mississippi. Like a lemming, Penny followed his lead.

Somehow, her gaze got stuck on Mississippi's hand. Actually, her focus was more on his long, tanned fingers, which were wrapped around his drink as he lifted it to his mouth and touched the glass to his ... *Oh, for the love of Pete!* She needed to get a grip. What was she? Sweet sixteen with a bubble-gum crush?

When she looked back at Mac, she realized her mistake in a blink. He'd zeroed in on her, catching her staring at Mississippi. Crap! She'd walked right into Mac's trap, and now she was breaking out in a sweat, damn it.

She tried to hide her flustered state of mind behind a broad grin. "Yep, I'm staying for lunch. I promised Mindy Lou I'd wait for her to settle into the job. You know how hard first days can be.

I was always a nervous mess my first day at any job, wishing I could sneak a shot of vodka to mellow out. Mindy Lou takes after me, the poor kid."

Great googly moogly, what was she saying?

Mac tipped his head slightly, one eyebrow raising.

"Not that Mindy Lou will drink on the job, of course. I was just ..." Penny paused to put her tongue in neutral for a couple of seconds while she took a deep breath. "I'm going to quit talking now."

Chuckling, Mac grabbed an order pad from behind the bar. "What would you like for lunch, Penny?"

The smell of Mississippi's fresh grilled burger tempted her, but she decided on a different course. "A club sandwich would be great."

"Got it."

"Along with a lemonade." She tried to laugh, but it sounded more warbly, like a jittery chicken. "I'm driving back to Yuccaville, so no alcohol for me today."

"Sounds good."

While Mac let the kitchen crew know about her order, she turned her back on the bar and opened her mouth wide, letting out a silent scream of mortification.

Stupid, stupid, stupid!

Criminy, who was running the show in her brain today? Goofy? Someone needed to cram a boot down her gullet.

She strolled over to the jukebox, needing to put some distance from the train wreck that had just happened in front of Mac. Maybe she should get her lunch to go so she could cram food in her big blabbing piehole in private.

"Penelope," Mississippi said, his voice low and close. Too close. Right behind her.

She slowly turned.

Sure enough, the green-eyed devil had snuck up on her.

She glanced toward the bar. Mac must have gone in back, leaving her holding this six-foot-tall, FBI skunk by the tail.

Chapter Six

*K*ate washed her hands in the sink of the campground restroom, cursing under her breath at her sister while she lathered with lavender-scented soap that was supposed to be calming, according to the description on the dispenser.

Claire was sooo wrong. This bathroom was not just "up the trail apiece." For a woman carting a baby in her womb, which kept bouncing on her very full bladder, it felt far enough from the bird watching platform that overnight mail would take a month to arrive.

A look at her face in the mirror after rinsing her hands made Kate pause. Her cheeks were pinker than usual today. That was probably due to having to work outside in the sunshine for the first time in … well, longer than she could remember. She needed the floppy-brimmed hat her mother preferred to wear about, like an old Hollywood starlet.

What couldn't be explained by the big bright sphere in the sky was the shape of her face of late. She turned her head one way and then the other. Her cheeks seemed fuller, softer, same as the rest of her pregnant body.

However, contrary to what Claire claimed earlier, Kate did not have the darting and whacky eyes of a psychopath. Nor was she foaming at the mouth. She leaned closer to the mirror. Well, maybe a little at the corners, but that was probably because of the dust they were kicking up back in the ravine.

She scowled at her reflection while flapping her hands to air-dry them. Somehow she needed to figure out a way to get out of helping Claire build this dang birder's perch. She was never going to get to the bottom of the origin of that knife or figure out if Joe was still kicking around at this rate. Especially not if she were stuck being her sister's lackey, like she'd been all morning, carting tools to and from the tool shed for seemingly no reason. If she didn't know better, she'd think Claire was trying to distract her with all of these inane tasks. But from what? Bird watching?

This lackey business was a job for a teenager who had nothing better to do than paint her nails and yak on and on about lip gloss and pop stars, and if Kate had to bribe Jess to take her place on the weekends, she would happily cough up the cash.

On Kate's way back out into the midday sunshine and fresh air, her phone started ringing. Hoping it was some low-level emergency call that would require her to tell Claire she needed to leave immediately, she pulled the phone from her back pocket.

The number on her screen made her stop short on the gravel drive. It was a phone number with a local area code, but not a number her phone recognized from her address book.

Desperate for any reason to get out of going back to work in the ravine, she accepted the call.

"Who's calling?" she asked right out of the gate.

"Who's answering?" a slightly wavery, female voice returned.

Kate tried to place the voice. It sounded familiar. Sort of. "You called my phone, so you should know who this is. Now, who are you?"

"*What* I am is more important if you are who I think you are, but if you aren't, then I'm of no importance to you. So we're back to you telling me who you are first."

Kate snarled up at the sky. "But you called *me,* and I don't trust *you* enough to give you my name."

"You're putting too much value in a simple name," the woman said. "It's not like I asked you to give me your social security number or your mother's maiden name."

Kate was still trying to mentally go through all of the females she knew or had met at some point who lived within this area code. Having worked at The Shaft for a while, though, made that list pretty long. "Maybe my name is top secret," she said to buy time.

"I doubt it."

Well, there was no need to be offensive about it. "I doubt yours is either."

The woman sniffed in Kate's ear. "Millie was right. You're a real pain in the keister."

Millie? A light blinked on in Kate's memory. "Is this Ruth?"

Ruth was a good friend of Penny's aunt, Millie. Claire had gotten into a scuffle with Ruth over computer time at the library last summer and had been banned from the place for six months because of it. Ruth had claimed she was attacked by Claire out of the blue, but the bruises left on Claire's arm and leg from Ruth's cane told a different story.

However, that was all water under the bridge now that Kate and her sisters had come to a truce with Millie and her gang of blue-haired library cronies.

"Maybe it's Ruth," the woman replied. "Is this Kate?"

Good gravy! Kate kicked at a patch of grass growing up in the midst of the gravel drive. "Yes! This is Kate!" she yelled.

Several grayish-blue scrub jays took flight from a nearby cottonwood tree, screeching back at her as they flew off.

"There's no need to get your dander up, girl. This is Ruth. We're on the same team, remember?"

"Did you call me simply to test my patience?"

"No. I have a message to relay to you."

"From whom?"

"Does it matter?"

Kate snorted. "Of course it matters who the sender of a message is."

"Not necessarily, especially if it's a warning."

Kate thought on that a moment. Ruth had a point. "Is this a warning message?" And if so, a warning about what? Something to do with Ronnie? Why else would …

"No," Ruth said, putting a stop to that slew of questions.

"So, it's just a plain old message then."

There was a short pause from the other end of the line before Ruth replied, "No, it's more like an intelligence briefing of an impending hostage situation."

"A hostage situation?" Oh, no! Kate's pulse raced from zero to sixty in a gasp's worth of time. This had to be about Ronnie! One of the hitmen must be here! Had they already taken Ronnie? No, Ruth had said it was *impending*. Shit! Did that mean there was still time to alert Grady?

"Wait," Ruth said, interrupting the shrieking in Kate's head. "Did I say *hostage?*"

"Yes!"

Ruth giggled. "My mistake. I meant *hostile*."

Kate blinked, feeling like she'd fallen off the back of a wagon and had the wind knocked out of her. "So, it's a hostile situation, and not anything to do with a hostage?"

"That's right."

She pulled her phone away and cursed in the other direction. When she returned to the call, she told Ruth, "You know, there's a *big* difference between those two situations."

"Not if the hostile situation ends with someone being taken hostage."

"Ruth," Kate said between gritted teeth. "What is the damned message you're supposed to give me?"

"Hold on a minute."

"Now what?"

"I can't remember why I called you."

Kate's shout of laughter spurred a bark-fest from two dogs at some nearby campsites. "You're kidding me."

"It's your fault," Ruth shot back.

"How is this my fault? You're the one who called me to deliver a message."

"And I would have delivered it already if you hadn't been such a bonehead about giving me your name."

Kate flipped off her phone. "You should've written it down first."

"And leave an evidence trail? Come on, child. Do you think I don't know big wood from kindling at my age?"

Kate wasn't sure how to answer that.

"Now shush up for a second and let me retrace my steps."

While waiting, Kate could hear something creaking rhythmically. Was that Ruth's cane? "Are you walking around right now?"

"Did I not just say that I needed to retrace my steps? I tend to forget my thoughts when I go from one room to the next, thereby changing the scenery."

After several more creaks, the sound of liquid trickling came through the phone next. What in the hell? "Are you getting a drink of water now?"

"No. I spent too long trying to give you my message and now

I have to tinkle."

"Oh my ... eww." Kate held the phone away from her ear and counted to ten while walking back to lean against the restroom building's sun-warmed wall. When she held the phone back to her ear, the tinkling was still playing through the line.

Come on! James Bond never had to deal with this type of buffoonery from his confidential informants.

"Are you almost done?" Kate asked.

"Just hold your horses." The tinkling was replaced by rustling, and then a definite toilet flushing. "Okay, now what were we talking about?"

Kate sighed, waiting to hear the sound of Ruth washing her hands. "The message from you."

"Oh, yeah." The creaking sound came again. "It's not from me. It's from the head honcho."

More creaking came through the phone instead of the splash of water running from a faucet.

"Ruth, are you going to wash your hands?"

"No. I don't need to. I'm at home."

"Yes, you do. That's how cholera is spread."

Ruth scoffed. "Cholera is spread by water contaminated with feces, Miss Know-It-All, not urine."

"Urine is close enough. You need to wash your hands."

The creaking stopped. "Urine is sterile."

"That's a myth. It has bacteria in it." Kate knew that because she had taught health during summer school one year, and a disease specialist had to come talk to the kids in order to earn community service hours for not paying his parking tickets on time.

"What's your source on that?" Ruth asked.

"Never mind my source. Just wash your hands."

"Do you want your freaking message or not?"

"Sure, after you wash your hands."

"For cryin' out loud." Ruth huffed through the phone. The sound of running water came and went. "There! Are you happy, Nurse Ratched?"

"Yes." Although she didn't think there'd been soap involved on Ruth's part, but whatever. "Now give me the damned message."

"I'm supposed to tell you that a certain someone is about to drop a can of pepper in Veronica's butter churn."

Kate opened and closed her mouth. Twice. But nothing came out.

"Did you hear me?" Ruth asked. "Hello? Hello?"

"Is pepper a bad thing to put in a butter churn?"

"Boy howdy, you must be the dull knife in the drawer."

Kate bristled. "I'll have you know that I have a very high IQ and have been a schoolteacher for years."

"Could've fooled me with the way you answered your dad-burned phone."

Kate took a deep calming breath, holding onto her stomach. Under her palm, she felt a small flutter. Then another. Was that the quickening feeling she'd read about in her pregnancy book? Or just a gas bubble?

She took another breath.

There it was again. Definite fluttering.

She gasped. "Ruth! I felt it move!"

"Nah. That's just ol' Copper Snake Mine blasting out a bigger hole in the ground."

"I mean my baby." She pushed her palm harder into the side of her belly. "I think it's kicking."

"Oh, yeah, you're the pregnant sister. How far along are you?"

"About twenty weeks."

"Well, that's just about right then. Do you know who put the bun in your oven?"

"Of course I know!"

"You don't need to get snippy about it, child. I wasn't calling you a soiled dove or anything of that sort. Just making sure. This town is often out of stock on both pregnancy and paternity tests."

Kate cradled her pregnancy bulge, awed by the reality of her situation. "Wow. There's a little human growing inside of my stomach."

"Actually, *Teacher*, the baby is in your uterus."

"You're ruining the moment, Ruth," Kate said dryly.

A chuckle came through the line. "Fine. But when you're done daydreaming about baby booties, what are you going to do about Grady's ex-wife unleashing a slander campaign against Veronica's reputation?"

All thoughts of the tiny life inside of her went up in smoke for the moment. "*That's* what your message is?"

"Yep."

"Where did you and Millie get this information?"

"We can't reveal our sources," Ruth said.

"And how much is this information going to cost me?"

"Millie will add it to your tab."

Kate held her hand over her forehead, feeling the frown lines under her palm. "Anything definite about what Elizabeth is going to do first?"

"Nothing is set in stone yet, but she was overheard talking on her phone about Veronica and someone named Lyle Jefferson."

Damn it! Elizabeth knew about Ronnie's ex-husband, which meant that if Elizabeth didn't already know about the federal investigation into Ronnie's life due to suspicion that she was involved with Lyle's illegal wheeling and dealing, she would soon.

If that became public news—or rather *when*, now that Elizabeth was causing trouble—how would the locals feel about their sheriff consorting under the covers with a possible felon? Or at least someone who had been married to a felon? Although, since Lyle had still been married to some other woman when he exchanged vows with Ronnie, they hadn't even been officially married all of that time.

"This could get really ugly," Kate said as much to herself as Ruth.

"Sure, like forty miles' worth of bad road ugly," Ruth said.

"You're not making me feel any better, Ruth."

"I'm just the messenger. Speaking of, I'm supposed to report back to Millie if you plan to run any sort of interference on this potential hostile situation."

There was no hesitation in Kate's mind. "Hell, yes!"

Her only dilemma was if she should rain hell down on Grady's ex on her own, or if she should tag-team with a partner on this one. As much as she preferred to stalk trouble alone these days, as she had done last evening, being pulled in too many directions at once might slow her down. A partner was probably for the best. It would be easier to delegate duties here and there, so she could keep her head low, especially when Butch or Grady were around.

Kate thanked Ruth for playing messenger, albeit a befuddled

one, and hung up. Next time, Millie should just tape a note to a blind tortoise for quicker delivery service.

Before returning to Claire and the ravine, Kate went back to the restroom. All of the excitement both outside and inside of her womb made her bladder antsy again. She pondered who to partner with on the Elizabeth front as she washed her hands, staring at the blonde in the mirror again.

Her first choice would have been Claire, but her sister was already spread too thin, not to mention she'd tattle to Mac about Kate hunting trouble, and Mac would then blab to Butch.

She couldn't tell Ronnie, since she was the one centered in the crosshairs. Besides, Kate might need to use her oldest sister as bait at some point, so it was best to keep Ronnie out of it for now.

She flapped her hands dry.

There was Millie and her gang of blue-haired bandidas, but Kate was already paying them to help her with that knife of Joe's. She didn't need to get in debt trouble with a rowdy bunch of extortionists equipped with canes and walkers. Although, it'd be fun to unleash the Geritol bruisers on Elizabeth's hide. Especially Aunt Millie.

In the mirror, Kate noticed a gleam in her eyes that hadn't been there before. She leaned closer to the glass. Her pupils looked wider, slightly dilated. Were these the eyes of a psychopath?

"Is that you, Ms. Hyde?" she whispered.

Her left cheek twitched, and then a cackle of laughter rang out from between her lips.

Shit. Maybe Claire was right.

Covering her mouth in case the foaming started next, she left the restroom and started back toward her sister.

As her shoes crunched on the gravel drive, she wondered how she was going to tell Ronnie about this news. What would she do upon hearing it? Would she go head-to-head with Elizabeth and risk Grady's future as a sheriff? Or would she slip away in the night, disappearing from their lives rather than tarring those she loved with the scandal coating her past?

Crippity-crap, Kate needed to get a jump on Elizabeth, but how? If not Millie and her pals, then who could …

She stopped in her tracks. "Well, duh."

There was one other posse member left to round up and ride

out with on this bitch-hunt. On second thought, maybe lassoing Aunt Millie to come along, too, might be worth the extra cost.

"Yes, that just might work," she muttered, back on track for the ravine. As she rounded the tool shed, another cackle escaped from her lips.

Chapter Seven

"One Mississippi," Penny counted aloud as she stared back at Mr. FBI. "Two Mississippi. Three Mississippi. Four Mississ—"

"What are you doing, Penelope?" he interrupted.

"Counting how many times you and I have locked horns in this very bar."

To be fair to him, she'd instigated three of the four bouts, taking her past mistakes out on him. Not that he had any trouble blocking her verbal jabs. He'd landed a few winners of his own in return.

Mississippi crossed his arms. "Could you be any more obvious about our situation in front of Garner?"

"What situation?"

"Don't be coy. Not after last week."

While he'd nailed it on her inability to act naturally around him a few moments ago, she refused to acknowledge her failure. At least to him. "As far as Mac knows, we're strangers."

"Wrong. Garner was here that night you first assaulted me back at the pool tables."

" 'Assaulted'?" she scoffed.

"That makes us something other than strangers in his eyes," he continued, cool and calm. His FBI training for handling tense situations rang through loud and clear. "And your inability to keep a poker face today was a telltale sign of something more, which you previously declared it wasn't."

"There is nothing more," she said, still determined to make that the case going forward. "And I didn't assault you."

"Dry-gulched me?"

"That night, I simply let you know I saw through your bullshit smoke screen, Special Agent Brown, and if you were going to pull the wool over anyone's eyes in this corner of the state, you needed to work on your disguise." But based on his choice of all-black clothing today, he hadn't listened.

His right eyebrow quirked. "In my world, threatening to rip off a man's family jewels and feed them to the local wildlife, and *then* stealing his drink borders on assault."

She made a "pfftt" sound, waving off his accusation. "If you can't handle the heat down in these parts, you should call in for a replacement."

In fact, him leaving the area for good would be perfect. She didn't need him sticking around long enough for anyone to connect the dots between them, especially her brother.

"So, if that wasn't assault, then I'm guessing you don't consider the shakedown you gave me at my pickup last week battery, either?"

"Shhhh." She pointed toward the order window. "Last week didn't happen, remember?"

"Oh, it surely did."

"We agreed it was nothing."

His focus slid south to her lips. "No, I specifically said it was *something.*"

"Really? Because I can barely remember it."

"Now who's blowing smoke?" His gaze returned north, his eyes slightly narrowed. "You were like a randy octopus."

Her face burned. "I'd had too much to drink."

"Not that much."

Damn him for noticing that fact. "More than usual. Besides, I thought we agreed that there'd be no further talk about it."

He rubbed his jaw, a small smile playing at the corners of his mouth. "If memory serves me right, you did say something about no talking right before you climbed onto my lap and stuck your tongue down my throat."

"Could you be quieter, please," she hissed, wishing she could sink down through the cracks in the plank flooring. "Listen, can we just pretend nothing happened and return to our regular old lives until you move on to your next assignment?"

"Hmmm." He pursed his lips, playing it up, she could tell. "Let me get this straight. You want me to act like you did not join me in the dark while I was enjoying a moment of stargazing, grab me by the collar, and slam me back against my truck."

"That's not quite a true account of my actions." She had actually gone looking for him outside after sneaking peeks at him back at the pool tables all evening; and when she'd found him, she'd plastered herself against his body. Him falling back against his pickup and banging his elbow on the mirror was an unfortunate side effect of a little too much vodka mixed with a lot of loneliness. Together, the combination had fueled her lust with extra oomph. "But close enough. So, you agree to pretend it didn't happen?"

He held up his finger. "I wasn't done, darlin'."

"There's no need to finish." Her humiliation was fully seared on both sides.

His chuckle sounded downright devilish. "That's not what you said the other night."

"*Ay, caramba.*" She squeezed the bridge of her nose. "I'm never drinking vodka again."

"You think it was the vodka that greased your wheels?"

"It's what I *know* greased my wheels. When I'm stone-cold sober, you're off-limits."

"Hmm." Mississippi took a step closer to her. "Off-limits, huh?"

Penny held her ground, lifting her chin.

"Here's my problem with pretending anything other than the truth, Penelope. As you so kindly pointed out before, I'm not the best thespian when it comes to fooling locals. I'm not so sure I can pull off this act you're expecting of me."

"Quit trying to sell snowshoes to a rattlesnake, Special Agent Brown," she snapped back. "I have first-hand experience dealing with your *kind*. I know all about the training they drill into you, teaching you how to tell lies without a single twitch."

His head cocked to the side. "Yeah, but I was sick the day they taught us how to handle a rogue female bent on molesting an innocent agent in and out of his own rig."

"Innocent?" she snorted. "If memory serves me right, you were more than willing."

"Ah, so you do remember some of the details. And here I thought you were too drunk on that vodka."

She closed her eyes, searching the insides of her eyelids for inner peace, but that well was dry more often than not of late. "Listen, let's just forget about the unfortunate slip of control on my part that night."

"But what about the love bite that's still showing on my ribs?"

Her eyes opened wide. "I did not bite you."

"I beg to differ." He started to unbutton his shirt. "Would you like me to show it to you right now?"

"Oh my—stop!" She tugged his hand down, holding tight when he tried to lift it again. "Fine, maybe I did leave a little bruise."

He grinned. "It's not little, Penelope. And actually, there's more than one."

Sweet-n-sour meatballs! What was wrong with her? Oh yeah, could it be that she hadn't had sex in over a year because she knew pretty much everyone in the whole damned county and couldn't risk doing the naked tango with anyone who might confuse lust for love? Dating a local guy meant running into him at the grocery store; or worse, him stopping by her diner and getting all pissed off when she gave him the "It's not you, it's me" speech. Not to mention that her brother was the sheriff, so any dalliances would undoubtedly get back to him in time.

Then along came this green-eyed demon, who surely wasn't long for these parts. Sadly, all it took was a splash of liquor after another lonely night of tossing and turning for Penny to forget about her aversion to guys like him.

"Here's the real problem with us pretending nothing happened," Mississippi said. "*You* can't."

She sputtered. "What the hell are you talking about? I can forget what we did."

"I didn't say *forget*. The word I used was *pretend*, as in you cannot pretend your lips weren't all over me. And your teeth." He reached out and ran his thumb along her jaw. "And your tongue."

Flashes of dark, steamy scenes full of warm skin and hot breath ricocheted through her mind. Memories the vodka couldn't blur, nor did she want it to, if she were honest with herself.

He leaned close to her ear. "You're thinking about it right now," he whispered, his breath making her shiver. "I can see it on your face."

"I am not," she lied, but there was no muscle behind her

denial.

"And," his whispering continued. "If I can see it, so can anyone else who's paying attention. Like Garner. And the sheriff."

She sighed, stepping away from Mississippi. Damn it, he was right. Grady would figure it out in a heartbeat if he caught them together. He'd been trained early on to read people, not just listen to them.

"My brother cannot find out that we had sex."

"I agree. The sheriff won't believe his sister started it."

Penny didn't bother denying her part in the act. Mississippi was right. She was the one who'd followed him outside and found him leaning against his pickup looking up at the stars.

She'd had a brief flash of clarity when she stopped in front of him, telling herself to scurry back inside and bury all the fantasies that had been playing in her head throughout the evening. But then he'd said her name with that slight drawl of his, warming her body from head to toe, and her reasons for leaving deserted her.

She'd slammed against him, sending them both reeling. But in her defense, he'd come back for her just as strong after catching his balance. Before she knew it, they were inside his dark pickup with the passenger seat tilted all the way back. Her pants came off first—well, one leg of them anyway. That was all they needed. Her hands were everywhere, feeling their way in the dark. His groans and whispers encouraged her to round the bases toward home.

Things had blurred a tad then, but she remembered enough to make her heart pound when she thought about him while alone at night in her bed. During that moment with him, the ache inside of her had eased. He'd made her feel wanted again. Exciting. Sexy. Not alone.

But now it was time to return to normal. She had a business to run. As the sister of a county sheriff whose world was rocked by a humiliating scandal in the past, screwing around in the front seat of a pickup in a bar's parking lot wasn't really smart.

"Okay," she said, leveling with him. "No matter which one of us instigated it, what happened cannot be undone."

"Agreed."

"And it cannot happen again."

He shrugged. "Probably."

"There's no probably about it. I'm the sheriff's sister."

"That is a fact."

"And you're only here temporarily," she said, but sort of asked at the same time.

"Most likely."

"So then, we agree to return to being aloof when our paths cross and to avoid each other as much as possible so these sorts of interactions rarely happen."

"Well, we can certainly give it the ol' college try."

"Great." She held out her hand to shake on the deal.

He took it and used it to tug her back into the hallway leading to the restrooms, pulling her with him into the small, secluded alcove between the video games lining the wall.

"What are you doing?" she said, trying to pull free of his grip. "We need to get back out there before Mac or Ronnie come back."

"Not until you answer two questions that have been weighing on my mind since you molested me."

She stilled. "I did not molest you. You kissed me back."

His smile was downright wicked. "I sure did."

Oh, boy. "What are your questions?"

"Why did you choose me that night?"

"You were convenient."

"Right." The glint in his eyes said he didn't believe that for a minute. "Convenient."

"That's what I said." She leaned back to check out front. Still empty. "What was the other question?"

"Are you always that feral of a kisser or did the vodka have you off your game?"

She gasped. "I wasn't feral."

He smirked. "If you say so, but I don't think I've ever had a woman's tongue doing what yours did in my mouth."

She huffed, trying to remember exactly how she'd been kissing him that night.

"What in the hell are you talking about, Mississippi?"

"At first I couldn't decide if you were trying to polish my back molars or tickle my uvula, and then it's like you got electrocuted mid-kiss."

Ignoring that first mortifying part of his recount, she focused on the last piece. "Electrocuted?"

"Yep. Your tongue started twisting and writhing. It was a bit distracting."

She glanced down at his belt buckle. "Not that distracting, apparently. You had no problem with the rest of the act." Neither had she, unfortunately.

"What can I say?" His grin teased. "You'd already taken off your shirt and bra." His gaze dipped to her chest. "You're built like a steep mountain road, Penelope, and I do appreciate a good challenge of curves."

"I am not a feral kisser." She reached out and tipped his chin up, making him focus on her face again. "I'll have you know that if I want to, I can turn your world inside out with my tongue alone."

He chuckled. "If you say so."

"If you think you're baiting me into kissing you again, it's not going to work."

"No baiting, I swear. Like you said, you're the sheriff's sister and I'm only here temporarily. It's best for both of us if you can manage to keep your hands to yourself whenever we're together."

She scowled. "Do you have calluses from patting yourself on the back so much?"

He laughed. His warm gaze stirred something to life in her in spite of her attempts to beat it down. "Penelope Harrison, I do believe I'm going to miss you after I'm gone."

"I know you will." She pointed her thumbs at herself. "Nobody does it like I do." That sounded far more confident than she felt, and before she could make a fool of herself in front of him yet again, she pulled free of his grip and returned to the bar.

"Order up!" Butch hollered shortly after she'd plopped onto the bar stool a few seats down from where Mississippi had been sitting before.

"Thanks, Butch," she called back.

He peered out through the window. "Oh, hey, Penny. I didn't know you were still here."

"I told Mindy Lou I'd wait for her to settle in."

Mac pushed out through the batwing doors, snagging the plate of food from the order window. He set it down in front of her, grabbing a napkin and silverware from behind the bar.

He glanced toward Mississippi's empty bar stool. "Where did he go?"

She nudged her head toward the back hallway. "The bathroom, I think."

By the time Mississippi returned to his stool, a group of four guys from a nearby ranch had settled in at one of the tables. She'd gone to school with two of them, and the others had run around with her oldest brother. She passed on their offer to join them.

It was all she could do to act naturally and not choke on her toasted club sandwich or freshly squeezed lemonade with Mississippi sitting so close. To keep from peeking at him, she focused on watching Ronnie show Mindy Lou the way to deliver their orders to the kitchen and how to pinch-hit for the bartender if he wasn't behind the bar.

When Mississippi finished his lunch he stayed put, chatting with Mac about the brewery addition he and Claire were planning to build on to The Shaft.

Penny listened to his smooth drawl, trying not to think about the rock-n-roll-hoochie-koo that had gone on in his pickup last week.

Or how good he'd smelled in the dark.

Or how she'd been on him like a duck on a june bug.

Or how she'd French-kissed him apparently like she was the local larynx inspector.

As much as she wanted to race home, shut the curtains, bar the door, and curl up on her couch with a pan of cinnamon rolls for sweet company, she slowly finished her sandwich and wiped the corners of her mouth.

At some point over the last few years she'd gone to seed. So be it. There was no shame in that. Her passion had been spent on something very worthwhile—her business, which kept her community flush with tasty baked goods.

Her phone pinged. She pulled it from her jacket pocket to see who'd texted her. A glance at the screen made her shoulders tighten. Her old sandbox buddy had texted for the second time today.

Scowling, she read what Elizabeth had written:

Don't pick the wrong team.

Below the words was a picture of a piece of pie on a plate. Cherry pie.

Yeah, so what, Penny thought.

Another picture popped up. It was the same pie and plate picture, only this time there was a big disgusting cockroach sticking out of the cherry goo. Below the plate was now one of her menus with the words *The Mule Train Diner* clearly visible. Her heart pounded in her throat.

Penny slammed her phone facedown on the bar. It appeared Elizabeth was going to come out of the corner swinging if Penny didn't sing praises to Grady about his ex. What a bitch! She was going to cram that cockroach down Liz's throat the next time she saw her.

"What's wrong, Penelope?" Mississippi asked.

She shook her head, glaring down at her phone. "Nothing."

"You sure? Because your face is telling a tale of first-degree murder."

"I reserve the right to remain silent."

And the right to hogtie Grady's ex-wife.

"Silent you may be, but you're clutching the bar like you're about to tear the top clean off."

She gave him a hard look. "This is not in your jurisdiction, Special Agent Brown."

Her phone pinged again before he could nose any deeper into her business.

She hesitated, not sure she wanted to see what else Elizabeth had in store for her. A picture of a dead rat baked into one of her cakes?

The phone pinged again.

Penny reached out and flipped the phone over, wincing in preparation for another sucker punch.

Kate Morgan's name was displayed on the screen along with two message notifications.

She leaned closer to check out the first: *I'm going to teach Grady's ex a lesson about messing with my sister.*

Well, it appeared Penny wasn't the only one daydreaming about retaliation this afternoon.

The second message read: *Your aunt is going to help.*

Aunt Millie? How in the hell had she gotten mixed up in this?

A third message pinged onto her phone. It read: *You want in on this posse run?*

So Kate Morgan was teaming up with Aunt Millie? Damn. That was like two twisty dust devils merging to form a major sandstorm. Did Penny want to risk riding along with those two? She'd worked hard to become a respectable member of the Chamber of Commerce. Kate, on the other hand, was unstable as old TNT these days; and Aunt Millie was bloodthirsty for revenge for her nephew, not to mention a borderline criminal on her good days.

Penny scrolled back to the doctored image of the pie. It was going to be like that, huh?

She sent Kate back a two-word reply: *I'm in!*

Chapter Eight

Wednesday, January 30th

Claire stood outside the RV park's tool shed listening to the birds cackle and tweet. All of this hubbub about a bird viewing platform had her paying extra attention to her winged neighbors.

Her comment to Gramps last night about this viewing platform intruding on the birds' personal space had earned her an eye roll along with the threat of him coming out to help her build the damned thing. She'd rather deal with her pregnant sister bitching about needing to pee all day than Gramps and his big ideas.

A cool breeze blew through the RV park, rattling the willows, cottonwoods, and mesquite. Claire shivered inside her flannel coat. She should have grabbed a scarf, but she didn't like working with anything wrapped around her neck while handling power tools. She blew out a breath of steam while fishing in her coat pocket for the park's set of master keys.

Winter mornings in southeastern Arizona could be downright chilly, especially before the sun crested the horizon and kicked on the heat. But this morning seemed especially chilly, and not because of the clouds to the east blocking the ball of fire from doing its job. It was colder because Mac had left for Bisbee before dawn and wouldn't be back until Saturday morning. And then he'd be home for only two days, leaving again on Monday morning to return to the jobsite for a full week.

As she unlocked the tool shed, she tried to imitate the warbly whistle of the cactus wren that sat nearby in a mesquite tree at the edge of the ravine. It was probably reporting to the other birds in the area that the annoying human was back and about to disrupt their peaceful world with that drilling auger again. Luckily for the birds, she was done poking holes in the ground for now. Today she'd be busy filling them back in with concrete.

She tucked the keys into her pocket, her thoughts back on Mac. Their last night together had been bumpy. They'd argued about the extra money needed for the brewery off and on throughout the evening while working at The Shaft. Claire had practically begged Mac to stay in Jackrabbit Junction and accept the extra financial help from Gramps. There was too much work to be done here for him to run off to Bisbee for five days a week. Too much of a load on Claire's shoulders for him to refuse Gramps's money merely because he didn't like borrowing from *her* family.

Mac held firm, though, no matter how many times they rammed horns over the subject. He was going to earn extra cash for the brewery his way. Period. End of story. No further discussion.

Grrrr.

After all the friction between them—and not the fun and sexy kind—the ground hadn't been the only thing frosty this morning while they ate the scrambled eggs and bacon Ruby had kindly woken up early to make for them.

Claire stepped inside the tool shed, breathing in the familiar, comforting scents of grease and dust. While it wasn't fresh-baked cookies or cinnamon and apples, it was what she knew well. Unlike the ins and outs of a relationship.

This was exactly why she'd avoided any kind of long-term commitment for years, especially after growing up around her parents' constant fighting. Compromise was no easy feat, and what was a relationship without compromise? Basically a dictatorship of sorts, and she chafed quickly when bridled.

Claire collected the tools she'd need for the day's work, tossing them into the wheelbarrow. Before she forgot, she grabbed an empty five-gallon bucket to set upside down next to the folding chair she'd brought along for Princess Pregosaurus, who was supposed to show up sometime after the sun crested the Tres Dedos Mountains. Although, as much as Kate whined yesterday, Claire would believe her sister was coming to help again when she saw her twitchy face in person.

Maybe she should text Kate and ask her to bring a cup of hot coffee out to the worksite. That might keep her sister from trying to weasel out of working.

Coffee …

When Claire had followed Mac out to his pickup after breakfast, carrying his travel mug of coffee for the drive south for him since his arms were full, she'd called a truce for the time being.

"I don't want to fight, Mac. Not with you leaving for a few days." She paused as he tossed his duffel bag and gear over onto the passenger seat of his pickup. "My grandma always told me that life is too short to waste being pissed off at the people you love."

That won her a smile. "I would've liked to have met your grandma." He held out his hand for the coffee.

"She also had a saying she'd picked up from somewhere that stuck in my head." She handed him the travel mug, which he placed in the cup holder in the console between the seats. "It was something about wanting to always be your favorite hello and your toughest good-bye. She'd say that to Gramps now and then when he was heading off to work for the day. I always thought that was nice, especially after so many years. And arguments."

Mac caught her wrist and pulled her in for a hug, whispering next to her ear. "You are my toughest good-bye, Slugger."

She buried her face in his chest, soaking up his usual scent—a fresh combination of sunshine, warm sage, and spicy mesquite. "Yeah, well, you're my favorite hello, so hurry up and get your sexy buns back here safe and sound."

He pulled away slightly and nailed her with a tough-guy glare. "Promise me you won't go up to Humdigger Mine while I'm gone."

As much as Claire wanted to know what stolen treasures Joe might have hidden in that mine, she wasn't dumb enough to go up there on her own. Besides, she'd had enough near-death experiences in the mines around here.

"As if I have time for anything other than work between the RV park and The Shaft," she told him.

He leaned down and kissed her on the forehead. "And promise that you won't sneak into Joe's old childhood home in the middle of the night."

"I'll be too tired in the middle of the night to do anything but snore," she assured him. And that was the truth.

Joe's old house would be way too creepy at night, anyway. If Claire were going to sneak in again, she'd find a way to do it while the sun was shining. Maybe through a basement window. The one she'd noticed the last time she'd driven past the house had looked big enough to squeeze her butt through, after she pried off the boards, of course.

Mac held her at arm's length, watching, probably waiting for any twitches or other tattletale signs of lying. "*And* promise that you'll stop with this 'Joe's alive' business until I'm back here to hear more about your theory on his zombified state."

Claire decided to consider that last bit as a request for her not to talk about Joe over the phone, which would be easy enough. "Got it. I'll fill your brain with news about pouring cement into round cylinders and screwing things."

He chuckled. "You can skip the cement details when I call and concentrate on the screwing part, only include me in the stories."

"With or without tools?"

"Surprise me, Slugger." This time he landed a kiss on her lips, but it felt short and bittersweet, tasting like good-bye.

After assuring her he'd call this evening after settling in at the jobsite, he'd hit the road. That left Claire with nothing better to do than make headway on the birding platform since the lumber for the brewery addition would be dropped off on Friday, according to the phone call Mac had received yesterday from the delivery company. The more she could get done back in the ravine this week, the better.

She rolled the wheelbarrow of tools out under the blue sky and then locked the shed behind her. Looking around, she tried to remember what else she'd need to get the piers poured later this morning after the sun had warmed the ravine up to the mid-fifties. She'd lugged most of the supplies out there yesterday afternoon, including a shitload of forty-pound bags of concrete mix that had her muscles still complaining, so she wouldn't have to mess with it all this morning, and then she'd covered her stash with a tarp and secured it with river rocks from the creek.

Oh. A second bucket for toting water for the concrete. That was the last thing. She grabbed the bucket, too.

As she rolled along the trail out to the building site, enjoying the view of the sun cresting the Tres Dedos Mountains in the east, she thought about Joe Martino and the stuff he'd hidden around the RV park and in Ruby's house. Cash, stocks, diamonds, mummified remains, silver bars, and more. Christ, this place was like a smuggler's cove with stolen bits of treasure tucked in here, there, and everywhere, including inside the mines Joe had owned in the surrounding hills. Hell, even back here in the ravine.

She shuddered about what else might be buried or hidden yet around Joe's old stomping grounds. Even more worrisome was who might be missing these "treasures" and would come looking with a gun, instead of a shovel, to find them.

Setting the wheelbarrow down next to her tarp-covered stash, she took a look around at the holes she'd made yesterday while Kate ate cookies and talked about the things she'd like to do to torture Grady's ex. Why Kate had become suddenly obsessed with Elizabeth partway through the day was beyond Claire, but it was better that woman be on the receiving end of Kate's ire than Deputy Dipshit, since a jail cell could be an end result with the latter.

Claire pulled the tarp off her supplies and then stretched her already-sore arms and neck before warming up her shoulder muscles. Mixing and pouring concrete was a younger woman's game. Too bad Mac wouldn't be around to massage her sore muscles later tonight, and then kiss her aches and pains better. She bent and touched the ground, stretching her hamstrings. A hot shower and a slathering of liniment would have to do the job in his stead.

With the sun's rays starting to warm the air down in the ravine, Claire got to work. She had the cylindrical form tubes leveled and ready for the concrete to be poured in them when the low growl of an engine rumbled along the ravine, interrupting the chattering and screeching from several western scrub-jays that had been keeping her company.

She rose from her knees and turned toward the RV park while brushing some of the dust off her pants. The Princess had arrived via motorized transport this morning, along with Chester, who was behind the wheel of Gramps's new UTV.

"Oh, good," Claire said to Kate when Chester shut off the

engine. "You brought me some free labor to help mix and pour concrete. It's my lucky day."

"I'm here for your visual pleasure only," Chester said, grinning between his whisker stubbles. His bristle-top hair was hidden under a red knit hat. "If you want me to put on a toolbelt and wiggle my hips, that'll cost you extra."

Kate pretended to gag. "Please, Chester. I just finished breakfast." She walked toward Claire while pulling on her work gloves. "I brought Chester along for one reason."

"To act as your chauffeur?"

"Okay, make that two reasons." Kate pulled out a small notepad from the tote bag she had hanging from her shoulder. The same bag as yesterday. And it was as bulky as it had been then, too.

Claire took the tote bag from her, checking inside. Sure enough, there were more protein bars, chips, and waters ... along with plenty of cookies. "You're going to grow out of your pregnancy pants if you keep eating cookies for breakfast."

"I can't help it. This kid likes sweets." Kate patted her belly. "I try to feed it salad or mixed vegetables, and I get heartburn."

Claire took out a bottle of water and twisted the cap off. After taking several deep swallows, she pointed her bottle toward the prep work she'd done so far. "Chester, how much would you charge me to help mix concrete and fill these forms this morning?"

He eyed the twelve forms in the ground, rubbing his fingers over his beard stubble. "I need to be at The Shaft by noon to help out in the kitchen today and spell Gary behind the bar when he needs a break."

Claire nodded, glancing at her phone to check the time. "That gives us three hours."

"I'll tell you what." Chester sniffed. "I'll do it for a week's worth of free lunches after you take over The Shaft."

"Deal."

Kate clapped her gloved hands. "Perfect. I also have a job for you today, Chester."

"Let me guess." Claire capped the water bottle. "He's supposed to drive you back and forth to the restroom six times an hour."

"That's not funny, Claire. In fact, that's on-the-job harassment. Pregnancy bladder is not a laughing matter."

"Shove it up your harassment, Princess."

Kate flipped her off. "I'll have you know, my job for Chester will interest you greatly." She lifted her chin. "In fact, you should probably pay for half of whatever he charges."

Claire rolled the wheelbarrow over to the stack of supplies. "Let's hear what this job of yours is before I agree to anything." She lifted a bag of concrete mix and dropped it into the wheelbarrow.

"You have an extra pair of gloves?" Chester asked, grabbing the hoe from the supply pile and chopping a hole in the bag of concrete mix.

"Sure." She grabbed the pair she'd brought along in case Kate conveniently forgot hers. "Along with a mask for the dust."

Kate stayed back as they dumped the bag of concrete. Once they'd finished, she came closer with the notepad and a pen.

"Are you going to interview us?" Claire asked, pointing at the pad.

"No, I'm going to show Chester the script I wrote for him."

"What script?" Claire asked.

"The one he'll read when we call Sophy later."

"Sophy?" Chester said. "You mean Sophy Wheeler?"

"The one and only." Kate leaned closer and whispered to the two of them as if the Secret Service might be trying to eavesdrop via remote listening devices. "Last night, I found Valentine's application and acceptance for phone privileges at the prison where Sophy is locked up."

Butch used to keep in touch with Sophy because he was taking care of her place when she was first sent to prison. Claire wondered where her sister had found the phone privileges info, and how she'd managed to keep Butch from knowing what she was up to. Because if he knew, Claire didn't think he'd approve of Kate going anywhere near Sophy—not even via a phone.

"I also found the phone number to call in order to reach an inmate, and the times when they're allowed to receive outside calls." She pointed her pen at Chester. "You can pretend to be Valentine and get some information for us."

"Do them there privileges also include conjugal visits with ol' hot-legs Wheeler?" Chester asked, eyeing Kate's notepad. "Or at least phone sex."

"Chester," Claire snapped, slightly indignant. "Sophy tried to kill me, remember?"

"Whose team are you on, anyway?" Kate chimed in.

"I'm on the team where I get some action for my efforts, and Sophy has some mighty fine curves that I only got to explore a little once, and then she practically broke my arm."

"There are no conjugal visits in this deal, buddy." Kate scowled at him. "But I will pay you with free food at The Shaft."

"I don't want your free food."

"But you wanted it from Claire, and it's made at the same place."

"That's her deal, not yours. I want something different from you."

"Like what?" Kate asked, distrust in her tone and eyes.

"Well, since you won't let me be a godfather to the bun in your oven, and I don't have any offspring of my own—"

"That you know of, anyway," Claire cut in.

"Right, that I know of." Chester pointed at Kate's belly. "I want you to include my name somewhere in the mix of your kid's."

Claire whistled. "That's a steep price to ask."

"Maybe, but so is asking me to call and consort with a known killer."

Kate scoffed. "Just a few minutes ago, you were talking about doing the horizontal version of the jailhouse rock with that same killer."

"I know, but then you shut the door on me getting to do the wild thing with Sophy, so the price went up."

Claire settled back on her heels, hands in her coat pockets, waiting to see how far Kate was willing to go when it came to finding out if Joe was still alive.

As if Kate were eavesdropping on her thoughts, she turned to Claire. "You're the one who wants to find out if Joe's alive or not. Why am I having to pay for this?"

"Because Mac made me promise this morning that I wouldn't pursue things having to do with Joe until he's back from Bisbee." Claire shrugged. "So, I back-burnered this Joe's-alive business."

She didn't want to spark any more arguments with Mac, especially when he was three hours away. Fighting over the phone with him always left her feeling like she'd been kicked in the gut.

"I could back-burner it, too," Kate said casually, trying to act as if it wouldn't be a big deal for her. But Claire could see the curiosity burning in her sister's eyes. Or maybe that was just Ms. Hyde peeking out at her.

"Okay," Claire said. "Let's forget about calling Sophy and get to work then."

Before Claire could move a muscle, Kate held up her hand. "Fine! Chester, I'll include your name somewhere in my baby's name."

"Don't you need to clear this with Butch?" Claire asked.

Kate waved her off. "He'll like what I pick out. He's easy that way."

Chester thumbed toward Kate's belly, winking at Claire. "Looks like he's easy in more ways than one when it comes to your sister."

"Is this the kind of lowbrow joking that I can expect from you while we work this morning?"

He nodded. "I guaran-damn-tee it."

"Fine. So long as we talk about Kate's sex life instead of mine." "Deal!"

A couple of hours later, Kate called a time-out.

Claire looked up from finishing filling a concrete form. "There are no time-outs in construction."

"Yes, there are," Kate said. "They're called breaks, and I'm blowing the break whistle." She held out her arm at a right angle. "Toot toot."

"It looks like you're trying to get a trucker to honk his horn at you," Chester said, taking off his gloves. He wiped his hands on his jeans and then took the cookie Kate was offering. He shoved the whole thing in his mouth, grunting in appreciation.

When he held his hand out for another, Kate held the cookie bag out of reach. "Not until you make the call to Sophy."

"That's blackmail," he said. "I suppose you'll withhold water, too, if I need it."

"No, the water is yours. It's against the law not to share it in Arizona."

Claire frowned, trying to remember if that was a fact, or if Kate was high on sugar and baby hormones.

"But," Kate continued, "I won't let you have any beer tonight after your shift at the bar if you don't make the call to Sophy now."

His forehead lined. "That's dirty pool."

"If you're going to play with the big girls, you'd better pull on your big girl panties."

Claire guffawed as she banged the concrete dust off of her Mighty Mouse cap. "Chester likes to wear big girl panties all of the time, Kate."

"Hey, no telling secrets here," Chester said, chortling.

Kate came over next to Chester. "Here's the script I want you to follow when you call." She held her notepad out for him to read.

His eyes moved back and forth and down the page. When he finished, he asked, "Don't you think she's going to know I'm not your baby's daddy when she hears my voice?"

"No, because you're going to tell her you have a cold." Kate poked him in the arm. "So make sure you cough a few times."

Claire moved closer. "Let me look at that script."

Pulling it away before Claire could see it, Kate shook her head. "I'm paying for this show. You just sit there and watch a master detective at work."

"Master detective, huh?" Claire smirked. "This should be fun."

Kate pulled out her cell phone and held it up in the air. "Reception is good." She glanced at Chester. "You ready?"

"Bring out the clowns, let's get this circus started. I'm getting hungry. The Shaft's grill is singing my siren song."

"Ten bucks says this goes sideways, Chester." Claire plopped down in Kate's lawn chair.

"Twenty." He raised the bet.

"Done." Claire grabbed another bottle of water and some cookies, kicking back with her work boots resting on the upside-down bucket.

"Don't be such a negative Nelly." Kate typed in the number and then handed the cell phone to Chester.

When he took it, the ringing stopped. He frowned down at it. "I think you hung it up when you handed it to me."

"No." Kate took it back, scowling at him. "You hung it up when your big chubby thumbs bumped the screen."

"My thumbs are not chubby. They're perfectly proportioned. Just ask the girls down at Dirty Gerties."

"Booooo!" Claire said.

Chuckling, he took the phone more gingerly this time when Kate handed it off to him.

Claire took a bite of cookie as she listened to the loud, clear ringing via the speakerphone. Today's cookie flavor was lemon with white chocolate chips. She drooled a little when she stuffed the rest of the heavenly morsel in her mouth. Ruby was on a roll lately. She must be stressing about Deborah coming home soon. Claire certainly was.

The ringing stopped midway through the third one. A robot-voice answered, announcing the prison's name and asking for an extension.

"Oh. Here. Let me." Kate leaned over and typed in some numbers.

A couple of more rings and a voice from Claire's recent past answered. "I thought you weren't going to talk to me anymore, Butch," Sophy Wheeler said.

Claire's jaw unhinged. How had Kate gotten through to Sophy so easily? She must have set the call up ahead of time, and Sophy had been waiting by the designated phone.

Kate held up the notepad in front of Chester, pointing at the page for him.

"Uh, yeah." Chester frowned down at the script, reading. "Well, I lied. I need some answers." He sounded stiff and new to the stage.

There was a long pause from the other end of the line. "Who is this?" Sophy asked finally.

"It's Butch."

"This is not Butch. I know his honeyed voice well enough, trust me."

Kate wrinkled her upper lip at the phone.

"It's Butch," Chester repeated. "And I was wondering if you'd be interested in selling your rest stop." He leaned closer to the notepad, squinting. "I mean restaurant."

"Who is this?" she asked again. "And why am I hearing birds? Are you on a payphone?"

"No, this is good ol' Butch and I'm just standing outside The Shaft talking to you."

"Why aren't you in your office, *Butch*?"

"Because it's so loud in there that a horned toad would go

deaf."

Kate glared at Chester, shaking the notepad in front of him, until he knocked her hand aside.

"Well, I'll be," Sophy said, her voice dipping down to that sexy drawl Claire had heard her use at The Shaft when ordering more beer at the bar. "Chester Thomas, you ol' sly dog. Why are you calling me pretending to be Butch Carter? You looking for a li'l conjugal visit via the phone? Want me to whisper sweet and nasty nothin's in your ear?"

Chester grinned, opening his mouth with what Claire was sure was a big affirmation, but before he could get a word out, Kate walloped him upside the shoulder with the notepad.

He scowled at Kate while saying, "You caught me, Sophy. And as much as I'd like to spend some time steaming up the phone with you, I actually do have a question that I need you to answer."

"Is this a question from Butch or that little hussy who used a baby-trap to hogtie him?"

Kate flipped off the phone.

"Actually, it's a question from the girl you tried to blow a hole clear through."

Claire sat up, lowering her feet to the ground, holding her hands out in a what-the-fuck gesture. Sophy wasn't going to give them any information if she knew Claire was behind this.

Chester waved off both her and Kate, who was busy stomping on the ground all around Chester as if she were stepping on ant hills.

"Let me get this straight, sugar," Sophy said, sounding not near as flirty as she'd been a moment before. "You want me to answer a question from the nosy bitch who landed me in this shithole?"

"Yep, that's the one. Although technically, you landed yourself in there by killing Joe's partner."

Claire frowned, reliving those terror-filled moments of staring down the double barrels of Sophy's shotgun.

"And why in hell should I help *her*?" Sophy asked.

Kate held up the notepad again, tapping her index finger on the script she'd prepared.

Chester took the pad from her and tossed it over his shoulder without even glancing at it.

Glaring up at him, Kate's left cheek twitched.

Uh oh.

"You're gonna help Claire," Chester continued, "because you want the same thing she does."

"And what's that?"

"Joe Martino's head on a platter."

Claire heard Sophy draw in a quick breath. Then she tried to hide her reaction with a laugh, but it sounded canned. "Joe? He's dead, remember?"

"Well, we thought he was, but then a few things here and there changed our minds about that."

"Like what?" Sophy took his bait.

Chester aimed a premature victory grin at Claire and then Kate. "I'm not going to go into that, unless you wanna play ball with us and quit pretending you believe that son of a bitch is sleeping under a green quilt with a tombstone headboard."

"Fine." Sophy gave in surprisingly fast. Too fast, in Claire's opinion. "What do ya need from me? And make it quick. The clock's tickin' on this call."

"Why did you tell Butch last fall that Joe is still alive?"

"Because he is."

"You have some proof to back up those words?"

"Maybe."

"Do I need to drive down there and seduce them out of you, hot legs?"

Sophy's laugh was husky—all tease and no substance. "You'd like that, wouldn't you, Chester the Molester?"

"You would, too, I'm guessing, after all these months of having no boytoys around to play back seat bingo with you. Or maybe you found a few girls willing to pet the kitty?"

Claire exchanged a grimace with Kate, who then wrinkled her nose at Chester.

He wiggled his eyebrows back at her.

"Okay, big boy," Sophy purred. "You want to know why I'm ninety-nine percent sure Joe is still breathin' topside?"

"I'm all ears."

So was Claire, who was sitting on the edge of her chair.

Kate, who had raced over and picked up her notepad, stood ready with pen and paper.

"I'll tell ya," Sophy said. "But I want a favor in return first."

Chester turned to Claire, his bushy eyebrows raised.

She licked her lips. Shit. Mac wouldn't be happy to hear she was making deals with this hellcat, but if Joe was really alive …

Besides, Mac had asked Claire not to go looking for Joe, and so far this phone call didn't qualify as an actual quest. She gave Chester a thumbs-up.

"What kind of favor?" he asked Sophy.

Claire stood and stepped closer, wanting to hear better over the bird tweets and screeches.

"One that requires help from a certain nosy bitch," Sophy answered.

Chapter Nine

The grocery store parking lot in Yuccaville looked like an old pickup truck rally was in progress. Sitting behind the steering wheel in Grady's truck, Ronnie blended in with all the others—well, almost. Grady's rig was relatively new in comparison, but it was dusty as hell, same as many of the dented, sun-faded rally participants.

She checked her cell phone for the time. Duty called. She had a half-hour to grab the items on the list Butch had texted to her. That would leave her enough of a window to swing by and pick up Mindy Lou, saving Penny a drive to Jackrabbit Junction.

Grady's niece was the main reason Ronnie was borrowing his pickup this morning. Normally, she shied away from driving his rig for multiple reasons—a couple were silly and had to do with where she felt they were (or were not) at this point in their relationship; others were more practical, such as a possible lack of insurance coverage and her qualms about operating a big vehicle.

Pocketing the keys, she pulled up Butch's list on her phone and headed inside the grocery store. The produce department seemed busier than usual this morning and filled with shoppers who had all of the time in the world to pick out the perfect apples or check every head of lettuce for the smallest sign of wilt.

She was almost through her grocery list with tomatoes being the final item when her cell phone pinged. Figuring Butch had something else to add, she pulled up the message. It wasn't from Butch. It was from a different area code, one she wasn't familiar with in these parts or from back home in South Dakota.

Leaning on the cart's handle, she checked the message: *I've been looking 4 U. Now U R mine.*

She froze and read the words again.

Who sent this? Glancing around, she looked to see if someone was watching her this very moment. But the other shoppers were still busy scrutinizing the fruits and veggies.

"Calm down," she whispered to the heavy-breathing neurotic woman in her head who wanted her to run back to Grady's pickup and hide inside with the doors locked.

She looked at the phone number again, pondering the area code: 323. Where was that from? She did a quick search for it on her phone ... Los Angeles. Okay, so who did she know from L.A.?

Uh, nobody, that was who.

But there were probably lots of cartel hitmen living there.

Her heart started beating in double time. Shit. She needed to get the hell out of here and back to The Shaft where Mississippi—and his gun—would be watching over her.

Glancing around again, she grabbed a plastic bag from the roll provided by the store and hurried over to the tomatoes. She just needed a dozen.

She tried to open the end of the bag, but her fingers were too sweaty and slid over the plastic. Scowling, she wiped her hands off on her pants and tried again, realizing she was trying to open the wrong end. Damn it, why didn't they print on the plastic which way was up? She flipped the bag around and tried to open it, but the bag slipped out of her hands and fluttered to the floor.

"Oh, screw you!" She bent down to grab it. When she came back up, someone was standing next to her.

She let out a yelp of surprise and took a wild, right-handed swing at the person before reason caught up with panic.

Sadie Jenkins leaned back, barely avoiding Ronnie's fist. "Whoa!"

"Sadie!" Ronnie clutched the plastic bag to her heart. "Jesus, I'm so sorry. You ... you scared the hell out of me."

The other woman's dark eyes roved over Ronnie's face. "Yeah, I can see that."

Her pulse still pounding in her ears, Ronnie glanced around the produce section. Several shoppers were watching her now, including an employee in a green apron, who was stocking the cucumbers. She focused back on Sadie, who looked like a tall ninja in her black seersucker-like shirt, pants, and combat boots. All she was missing was a hood to replace the black stocking hat she was wearing. And a samurai sword.

Sadie took the plastic bag from Ronnie and opened it, grabbing a tomato and slipping it inside. "You're a pretty uptight babe, aren't you?"

Ronnie grasped the edge of the tomato display to hide her shaking hands, smiling as she tried to pretend her heart hadn't nearly exploded a moment ago. "You surprised me, that's all."

The frown Sadie gave her made it clear she wasn't buying Ronnie's line of hogwash, but she shrugged and handed her the bagged tomato. "How many more do you need?"

"A dozen total," she said.

Together they picked out the tomatoes in silence.

"So, what's your deal today?" Sadie asked as Ronnie tied the plastic bag shut.

"I'm getting a few groceries for The Shaft," Ronnie answered, ignoring the deeper question.

"Right." Again, it was obvious Sadie saw through Ronnie's smoke, but she didn't push for more.

"What are you doing here?" Ronnie asked, realizing that Sadie had no cart or basket of her own.

"Taking care of a few things." She reached into her back pocket. "Which reminds me, I wanted to give this to you."

Ronnie frowned down at what looked like a credit card. "What's that?"

"It's a thank-you for helping me." When Ronnie just looked at Sadie, she added, "And my mom."

Ronnie shook her head. "I told you I didn't want anything for that."

"I know, but where I come from, you reward people for saving lives." She held the card out toward Ronnie. "Please, take it."

Ronnie didn't. "Where is that?"

"Where is what?"

"Where you're from."

"Around here," Sadie said and took a step back.

"You mean Yuccaville?"

"I mean in this general area."

"Of the county," Ronnie pressed.

"Yep."

Something didn't add up with Sadie and her mom. "How did

you find out my name?" Ronnie asked the question she'd wondered since Sadie had come into The Shaft yesterday.

"I asked one of the other customers who was in the diner."

Ronnie thought back to that moment, trying to remember who else had been there. She didn't remember seeing anyone she knew outside of her sisters and Penny. Especially anyone who might know her as "Veronica Jefferson" rather than Ronnie Morgan.

"What did this customer look like?"

Sadie waved her off. "That's not important." She held out the card again, practically shoving it into Ronnie's hand. "Please, take this gift card as thanks. It would mean a lot to me if you'd just let me even the score."

"I really don't think—" Ronnie started.

Sadie leaned closer and whispered, "It's a thousand-dollar gift card."

Ronnie frowned down at the card Sadie held between them. A thousand dollars, huh? She could buy a good amount of clothes with that in Tucson, including a few nice pairs of shoes. Maybe even something sexy to keep Grady's focus on her and not his damned ex with all of her curves and cute blond hairdo.

She started to reach toward the card, but then paused. Then again, good deeds were done from the heart, not for money. If she were going to try to clean up her act for the sake of Grady's future as the county sheriff, she needed to act like he would in this situation. He would never take money for saving a life. No, that was his job every day—helping citizens stay safe.

Shaking her head, she pushed Sadie's hand away. "I told you before, I don't want a reward for saving your mom. I'm just glad I was there to help."

Sadie growled, rolling her eyes. "You're a real pain in my ass, Veronica." She pocketed the card. "There must be an amount that would change your mind."

"No."

"Two thousand?"

That would buy her even more much-needed clothes. "No money."

"Five thousand?"

Now Sadie had to be messing with her. Ronnie laughed. "You're funny."

"I'm serious."

"Yeah, right." Ronnie patted Sadie on the shoulder. "I gotta go." Mindy Lou would be waiting for her by now. She pushed her cart toward the cashiers.

"Veronica," Sadie called after her.

She looked back as she rolled along. "Call me Ronnie. And tell your mom I hope she's doing well."

Sadie scowled after her.

While the cashier rang up her goods, she took another glance at her phone and breathed a sigh of relief at a lack of any more messages.

Outside in the parking lot, Ronnie rushed to Grady's pickup, breathing easier after she'd closed and locked herself inside. The cab smelled like him—a hint of bay rum with spicy undertones. His scent calmed her nerves, but her hands still trembled when she grabbed the steering wheel and turned out of the parking lot.

I've been looking 4 U. Now U R mine.

Criminy, who in the hell had texted her that message? Should she try calling the phone number back and see who answered? She glanced in the rearview mirror a few times as she turned right and then left on her way to pick up Mindy Lou, checking to see if anyone was following her. The street was mostly empty behind her, none of the vehicles taking the same route as she was.

She checked the phone when she paused at a stop sign, reading the cryptic message again. Was it really meant for her? It could be a message for whoever had this phone number before her. She'd only had it for a little over a month. Or maybe the sender had texted the wrong number by mistake.

Should she show it to Grady? God, he had so many things on his plate already. She hated to add to his load if this was simply a wrong-number text. She could show Mississippi. Right, and then send the FBI after some poor person who didn't mean to text her number. Their life would become a nightmare. She knew that from her own experience with the FBI and some of their initial false accusations.

Maybe she should start with Claire and Katie and see what they thought. They might know how to find out more about where that text came from without making a big deal out of something that could be nothing.

Mindy Lou was waiting under a patio awning next to Penny's front door when she pulled into the drive at the address Grady had written down for her this morning before he'd headed in to work. The girl stood up from a wicker chair with orange cushions, grabbing a travel drink cup from the ledge of the stucco wall surrounding part of the patio.

Ronnie had never been to Penny's place before. It was a cute adobe mission-style house with a yard that looked like a desert garden. Ocotillo, cholla, and prickly pear cacti were mixed with a couple of mesquite trees and boulders placed here and there. The windows had deep red shutters on both sides with yellow sunflowers painted on them. The patio's roof and columns looked like they were of the same wood as the beams sticking out of the stucco walls.

Mindy Lou pulled open the pickup door, smiling at Ronnie as she climbed inside and clicked into her seatbelt. "Thanks for taking me to work."

Ronnie spared one last look at Penny's house, wondering if it was as stylish on the inside as the curb appeal hinted. She backed onto the street, checking again for any suspicious vehicles, seeing nothing but the usual sort—older pickups and dusty cars.

"Happy to give you a lift. I usually need one myself."

"You don't have a car?"

Ronnie shook her head. "I'm saving up for one, though. Most days I hitch a ride with one of my sisters or your uncle."

Mindy Lou took a drink from her cup. "I lost my license for six months for driving without insurance after an incident with an old broad. Then the bank came and towed my car away because I hadn't made any payments in a while. So, I'm starting back at square one."

"What a coincidence, I just recently made it up to square one from deep in a hole. We can move forward together."

"Deal." Mindy Lou reached forward and turned the radio dial from Willie Nelson's song about a train called The City of New Orleans to Bad Company going on about … Well, being bad company. Ronnie could relate these days.

"You really like Uncle Grady, don't you?" Mindy said, out of nowhere.

Ronnie's cheeks warmed. She hadn't expected to talk about

Grady this morning, certainly not with his niece. "Sure. He's a great guy."

"Yeah, but a little bossy."

Ronnie chuckled. "More than a little sometimes."

"I think that comes with the badge." Mindy Lou took a sip from her cup, staring out the windshield. "Do you love him?"

Wow. So, they weren't going to dawdle with weather talk this morning.

Ronnie weighed her answer, not sure how much Grady had told his family about her or their relationship. Sure, they were sleeping together, but it wasn't like she'd moved in with him or they'd discussed future co-habiting arrangements. Although he had offered to let her stay at his place on a more permanent basis after Gramps's Winnebago had burned up, Ronnie had resisted committing to anything on that level. Once she moved in, there wasn't an easy way to back out if she needed to make a run for the hills emotionally.

She supposed if she'd gone to his mom's birthday party earlier this month when he'd asked instead of chickening out, she would be more comfortable with telling his niece the truth this morning.

"Well, we haven't really … " Ronnie paused, not wanting to say something that could get back to Grady and cause her even more problems. "I mean, we've really only been together for … " She shifted in her seat. "I don't know if he would like … " She corralled her bumbling tongue and took a breath. "Fuck it. "Yeah, I love him."

Mindy Lou grinned at her. "Good. He deserves someone better than that rich bitch."

"You mean Elizabeth."

"Yeah. What she did to him was so wrong."

"I agree. My ex royally screwed me over, too, so I get how that feels."

"My great-aunt, Millie, thinks you're pretty badass."

"She does?" That was quite a compliment from Millie, who was the ringleader of her own band of ass-kickers.

"She said you have a posse."

Shazbot. Millie needed to keep that under wraps. Grady got squinty-eyed whenever anyone brought up the posse.

"Well, my sisters and I and a couple of others formed one

when we were kids, but it was just for fun. Sort of like a club, you know."

"That's not the way Aunt Millie described it."

Ronnie gripped the steering wheel tighter, imagining how lined Grady's forehead would be if he were listening in on this conversation. "She's exaggerating. Your aunt Millie is a real cutup."

"That's true." Mindy Lou leaned back as they headed out of Yuccaville and hit the open desert. "You're gonna need more help, you know."

"What do you mean? At the bar?"

"No, with taking on that cheating bitch. Elizabeth's family practically owns half of the town. They've been here for generations and multiplied like jackrabbits."

Ronnie growled under her breath. Jesus, she didn't need to deal with this right now. Not when she was getting creepy texts and watching in the rearview mirror all of the time for someone hunting her down.

"You have any advice for keeping Elizabeth at bay?" she asked Mindy Lou, forcing a smile. She would keep her shit together, dammit, come hell or hired hitmen or rich bitches.

"I sure do." Mindy smiled back, only hers had a sharp edge of malice. "You need to let me join your posse crew. After spending a few months down and out with other gutter dwellers, I know some people who might be able to help you take Ms. High-and-Mighty Elizabeth down a few notches."

Chapter Ten

The lunch rush at The Mule Train Diner came and went, leaving Penny free to return to her office and finish the bookkeeping paperwork for last year's taxes so she could ship it all off to her accountant. Another profitable year was in her rearview mirror now. If things kept going at this rate, she'd have her loan for the building paid off years early.

But thanks to Elizabeth, that was turning into a big IF.

Penny's blood boiled as she reread the copy of a new one-star review of the diner, which had been forwarded to her email inbox an hour ago by an anonymous sender going by the username of GoldieDare75. Her focus got stuck on several of the words in all caps throughout the review, as the author had obviously intended: REVOLTING, MOLDY, STALE, DISGUSTING.

The game was definitely on. Elizabeth had followed through on her threat, starting the attack on Penny's livelihood with a terrible review posted on multiple well-known food sites that had been so kindly included in the email body.

That no-good, malicious, vicious, two-timing troll!

Penny picked up the stress-relieving ball sitting next to her coffee cup and squeezed the hell out of it. What she needed now was a voodoo doll with a few strands of the bitch's hair sewn to it. And several stick pins. Maybe a lighter to heat things up, too.

At the sound of footfalls coming through the kitchen, she closed her laptop. She didn't want her assistant manager, who'd been prepping the diner for tomorrow's morning shift, to know about Elizabeth's review. Not yet. Not until Penny had a handle on her rage, and she was able to think beyond the urge to hunt down her brother's ex-wife and cram Elizabeth's review in her big, fat mouth.

She didn't look up at the knock on the partially closed office door. "Come in," she said, covering her face with her hands, afraid her anger was all-too visible to those who knew her well.

Son of a fucker! How was she going to stop this bullshit? Kate Morgan had told her that they'd meet to make an attack plan soon, but how much damage could Elizabeth do to The Mule Train Diner's reputation before then?

The door creaked open.

"Thanks for prepping for tomorrow," Penny said, still shielding her face behind her hands. "If you'll flip the closed sign and lock the front door behind you, I'll see you in the morning."

"She already locked the door," said a voice much, much deeper than her assistant manager's. "But she's sticking around until I leave to make sure I wasn't lying about being a friend of yours."

Penny lowered her hands and stared up at the last person she'd expected to see this afternoon—or wanted to see after yesterday's face-burning bumble-fest. "We're not friends."

Mississippi sat down in the chair across from her, stretching out his long legs and crossing them at the ankles. He looked well-rested and unruffled by whatever life was currently throwing at him. And yet rugged around the edges. Dangerously rugged, unfortunately.

"Aren't we?" He tipped his head slightly. "Maybe 'amorous adversaries' is a better description for this thing we have going on between us."

Sitting back in her chair, she stared at Mr. FBI. He'd mixed it up today, wearing blue jeans instead of black. His cowboy hat was cream colored, making his hair look even darker. What was up with that? Was this his version of being in disguise?

She wished she'd taken the time to wash the flour and kitchen grease off her face before he'd shown up, or at least let her hair down and run a brush through it. Thankfully, with her job, a day's work often left her smelling like pies instead of sweat and grime.

"What are you doing here, Mississippi?" she asked, not in the mood for his twisted version of flirting this afternoon. Not after that damned review.

He took off his hat and sat it on her desk. "This is nice." He glanced around her office, taking in the plush couch and the framed photos of cacti and Sonoran Desert views on the walls, showcased by the recessed lighting. "Who's the photographer?"

She was, but she didn't want to chit-chat about her hobbies at the moment. "I repeat, what are you doing here?"

He held her stare, his game face in place. "We need to talk, Penelope."

"I'm pretty sure we said all that was needed to be said yesterday."

His descriptions of her kisses would haunt her until she was well wrinkled, and she wanted to hide under her desk about his "randy octopus" comment. Sheezus! Talk about sucker punching a girl's ego and leaving it gasping for breath on the floor.

"You certainly said plenty," he said with a slight smirk, finger-combing his hair, which erased the hat lines. "But I didn't necessarily agree with it all."

She really didn't need to deal with him today on top of everything else, especially after being up since five this morning to make the ten pies she'd donated to the Humane Society's fundraiser event.

"Fine, what do we need to talk about this afternoon, Special Agent Brown?"

If grins could swagger, his would do that and wiggle its eyebrows, too. "You know, it's kind of sexy when you say my work name in that molar-grinding tone. Next time you join me in my pickup and crawl on my lap—"

"Shhh." She hopped up and rushed to the door, closing it and then leaning against it for good measure. "There will not be a next time when it comes to me and your pickup." And especially not his lap.

"Are you sure? Because I think you could use some more practice at throwing a leg over the saddle, what with the way your boot heel got wedged between the seats last time."

Must he continue to remind her of how she'd lacked finesse that night? She crossed her arms, hitting him with a laser glare. "I'm one hundred and ten percent positive."

"That seems overly confident."

"*If* I need more practice," she continued, "I will find someone who will be less critical of me while my pants are down. Now, what is it you came here to talk to me about?"

"Our future."

"Our?"

He nodded once. "As in us."

"There is no *us* in the future. As you told me last week, according to your superiors, you wouldn't be hanging around town much longer."

"Well, about that." His grin flatlined. "I received word this morning to the contrary."

Hell's bells and blueberry pie! "What do you mean?"

"Things changed. I'm going to be here for longer than originally planned."

Of course he was, because Mars was transitioning per her Scorpio horoscope and Uranus was ruling at the moment, shaking up her life regarding matters that had been resistant to change. And stagnant. Including her love life.

"How much longer?"

He laced his fingers together over his stomach. "Well, that's not been made crystal clear, but let's just say that I'm gonna need to switch vehicles again and move to some new digs that charge by the month instead of the week."

So at least a month then. Crap. Penny couldn't tell if her chest was full of butterflies or boa constrictors about this news. Rather than focus on her own turmoil about having Mississippi around to continue to tempt her, she added one and one together. "Ronnie is in big trouble, isn't she?"

He nodded, his expression grim, matching how she felt. She could only imagine how her brother was handling this. Grady probably wanted to fly Ronnie to the dark side of the moon and hide her away deep in a crater until it all blew over.

"Are they sending more of your kind to help?" she asked.

"My kind?" He rubbed the back of his neck. "And what *kind* would that be, Penelope?"

"You know, heartless Bureau-brainwashed robots in suits," she jested. Kind of. Kind of not. Her ex had fooled her into believing he had a heart. Silly her for her naivete.

He chuckled. "I'm not heartless. There's a beating organ in here." He tapped on his chest. "It's small and thorny with a crusty layer or two around it, but it's definitely in there."

"It's cute that you believe that." She stepped away from the door and moved to the front of her desk, sitting halfway on it as she looked down at him. "So, are you getting extra suits to keep an eye out for hired hitmen?"

"Don't forget the hitwomen, too," he said, his gaze focusing on her lips. "You ladies can be even more deadly given the right motivation."

"Answer the question." She nudged his boots. "More help or not?"

His focus returned north. "Not."

"What a bunch of assholes. Why in the hell not?"

"Maybe they think I can handle this on my own."

"You along with my brother, you mean."

"Right, the sheriff, too."

"And Kate and Claire and Aunt Millie and Mac and—"

"Point taken, Penelope," he said, rising out of the chair. "I'll do my best, but I'm only one man, after all."

He'd taken that wrong, but she didn't correct his thinking. It was better for him to believe the worst when it came to her so that what happened last week in his pickup wouldn't happen again. A few walls between them would be a good thing. Maybe even a fence or two, as well.

"So," she said, clasping her hands. "What's your reason for coming here, exactly? Just to let me know you'll be around to avoid for longer?" He could have just sent word through Grady or Ronnie rather than deliver that news in person.

"Something like that." He reached down and grabbed his hat from where it sat on the desk next to her hip. "And to see if you'd be willing to rent me your upstairs apartment." He pointed at the ceiling.

She blinked. "You want to rent my apartment?"

He nodded.

No. Nope. No way. That was too close to home. "It's a mess up there," she lied.

"That's not what your brother said this morning when I asked him for some rental suggestions."

Doh! Of course Grady would offer up her apartment, because he'd be thinking the extra cash would help her. Grady also probably liked the idea of having Mississippi close to his place here in town, which was less than five minutes away. That would help keep his blood pressure down, since Ronnie stayed over there somewhat often and Grady was periodically called away in the middle of the night on sheriff's business.

"Grady's version of clean is different than mine."

"He seems to run a pretty tight ship over at the sheriff's office."

She frowned. "I don't think the apartment is up to your standards."

"What do you know of my standards?"

"Well, for one thing, there aren't any black leather furnishings, spiky sculptures, or gun racks up there."

He raised one eyebrow. "You think I'm into dark torture lairs?"

Maybe she did, which was kind of sexy, truth be told. "I only have your choice of clothing to go off of."

"And what exactly is spiky in my attire?"

"Your personality."

He laughed. "Says the bristly cholla cactus in the room."

"I thought you said I was curvy like a mountain road."

He sobered, his gaze slowly traveling over her. "On the outside, sure." His lips tightened. "But on the inside, you like to poke, stick, and stab me at every opportunity."

That assessment was spot-on from the moment she'd found out he was an FBI agent. She'd needed a punching bag after her ex betrayed her, and Mississippi had looked tough enough to take a hit that first night. She'd been handing out the verbal version of knuckle sandwiches ever since.

Logically, what happened with her ex had nothing to do with Mississippi. But when had logic ever run the show when it came to emotions? Especially when lust came on scene.

"Listen, Mississippi, I'm not sure you renting my upstairs is a good idea."

"Because you don't like getting paid well from the government?" he asked, straight-faced.

How well? The extra money would be nice. Really nice. But … "No, because of what happened." When he continued to stare at her, she added, "Last week." Still, he didn't react. "With us. In your pickup."

"Oh, I see." He nodded, holding his hat by the brim. "You're afraid that if I'm upstairs here, you won't be able to keep from assaulting me again, only this time in my bed instead of my pickup."

Her whole body heated from the humiliation erupting from her pores, but she lifted her chin. "We already covered this and it was not assault. You enjoyed it as much as I did."

"You're right, Penelope." He took a step closer, his gaze suddenly intense. "Every single moment."

"Even when I went all 'octopus' on you?" she whispered, her mouth suddenly dry.

"Even when," he said. "You were wild and weird and sparking with a lot of 'wow' through the very end."

She wasn't sure how to take that, especially the "weird" part. But she did know that renting to him would make it hard for her to focus on work. This place was where she came to destress, spending hours in the kitchen trying out new recipes for pies and sweet rolls and more. If he was right above her, it would mess with her mind.

She cleared her throat. "I don't think it's a good idea to have you upstairs."

"I do."

"I come in here sometimes during off hours and make a lot of noise."

"I promise not to come down and interrupt."

"The smells from the kitchen might tempt you."

His smile was downright devilish. "I can assure you that it's not the smells that will be tempting me."

She pointed at him. "See, that right there is a problem."

"No, this is only me flirting with you, Penelope. But you do tend to make a guy stop what he's doing and take notice."

"Flattery won't get you the apartment, Special Agent Brown."

"Okay, but maybe this will." He reached into his back pocket and pulled out a wad of folded hundred-dollar bills. Without looking at her, he started counting them aloud.

"Seriously, stop."

He kept counting.

"Mississippi, you don't want to live up there."

He continued counting while nodding.

She put her hand over his, forcing him to stop. "There's no

bed," she lied.

He paused, staring up at her through his dark eyelashes. "The sheriff seemed to think otherwise."

"Fine, there is a bed, but it's very hard. Like sleeping on the ground."

"Penelope, I've slept many a night in my pickup. A bed, even a hard one, is a luxury."

Actually, it was a very nice bed that she'd bought from a previous employee who'd been renting the apartment for a year. The woman had resigned to go chase her dream of acting in a sitcom, ending her lease. Penny hadn't heard of that dream being fulfilled yet, but she'd been happy to support her ex-employee's dream by paying a good amount for her queen-size bed.

"I start work really early," she told him, and that was no lie. "And I bang pots and pans around when I work."

"I've been waking up extra early since I stopped smoking and started going for early morning runs."

She was running, too—out of reasons not to rent to him, at least. "The hot water heater is small."

"I take quick showers."

She tried to think of another excuse, but came up blank. Except for one last thing that might be a deal breaker. "There's no sex allowed up there."

He leaned back, his smirk returning. "None at all?"

"Nope." It was her apartment and she got to make the rules, including one that applied only to him. "If that's a problem for you, Special Agent Brown, then you should probably look into other accommodations."

He shrugged. "Fine, no sex will be had in the apartment." He held out his hand. "Deal?"

She hesitated.

"I'll pay double your normal rent."

Holy big buckaroos! Dollar signs popped up behind her eyes. But then her principles spoke up. "Fine, but that price includes both room and board."

His eyebrows shot upward. "When you say *board*, you mean—"

"I'll give you a key to the diner's kitchen."

"Wow. That's generous, Penelope."

She shrugged. "So is your rent payment."

"Will that include a piece of pie now and then?"

"Sure. Or cake or sweet rolls. Whichever you prefer."

"Great." He smiled, looking relieved. "When can I move in?"

"I don't care. Tonight, if you want."

He tossed the stack of money onto her desk next to her laptop. "Tonight it is."

She went around behind her desk and pulled the key for the upstairs apartment from her drawer. The level-headed half of her brain remained unsure that this was a good idea, but the money would come in handy, especially with Elizabeth trying to decrease her clientele via bad reviews.

Grabbing a business card with her cell phone number listed, she held it and the key out to him. "If you need anything else from me, you know how to reach me."

He took both from her, his smile heating her up like a sunny day in August, making her swelter on the inside. "Oh, one last thing, Penelope."

"What's that?"

He reached toward her, his palm warm when he tipped her chin up and ran his thumb down her cheek.

What was he doing? Was he going to kiss her? She needed to stop him. Right now. Immediately. She opened her mouth to object, but then hesitated, waiting for him to lean closer.

His green eyes held hers for a few heart-palpitating seconds. "You had flour on your face," he said, lowering his hand.

Of course. It mixed smoothly with the egg left there from last week. She was well on her way to making humble cake frosted with a rich, creamy layer of mortification at this rate.

"Was that all of it?" she asked, wiping off where he'd touched.

He stepped back. "No." He pointed at her forehead. "There's some there, too."

She ran her shirt sleeve over her face, scowling. "Go away, Mississippi."

He backed toward the door, settling his cowboy hat back on his head. "I was just trying to be helpful, ma'am."

"You can shove your help up your ass."

"We're going to have fun being neighbors, Penelope, I can tell already. Lots of fun."

"Get out now, before I decide to sneak upstairs tonight and kill you in your sleep." When he hesitated in the doorway, she glared hard at him. "I'm not joking. Ask the last FBI asshole in my life what I did to him that sent him to the ER in tears."

Mississippi raised his hands in surrender and backed out, closing the door behind him and his laughter.

Penry sagged against her desk, scowling down at the pile of cash. "Shoot or sugar! What have I done?"

Chapter Eleven

K ate, order up!" Gary, the bartender, called out across the room.

Dodging Mindy Lou, who was carefully weaving between tables while balancing a tray with baskets of sandwiches and fries on her shoulder, Kate started toward the end of the bar where Gary was waiting for her. The overhead bar lights reflected in his thick glasses, making it hard to tell if he saw her wave in acknowledgment or not. Midway there, Kate had to change course, road-blocked by a group of twenty-somethings congregating around their pal's cell phone to watch whatever was on the screen.

The Shaft sure was busy tonight, Kate thought, especially after a relatively quiet few weeks. But with three waitresses, plus a trainee, Gary behind the bar, and Butch back in the kitchen teaching Chester the ins and outs, the place was easily manageable. And while the Dancing Winnebagos RV Park just down the road was filling up on the reservation front, Claire had told Kate earlier that most of the birders weren't rolling in for another month, so it was a good time to train new staff and change out the management. Come spring, this place would be a madhouse. She hoped Claire and Mac knew what they were getting into here.

Tonight was also a good time to plot the demise of a certain blond-haired, pain-in-the-caboose ex-wife who thought she was going to hop back on the gravy train—or rather the "Grady" train—and chugga-chugga back to the way things used to be in the past with her hunka-hunka law dog love.

"You doing okay?" she asked Gary when she reached the bar, grabbing the two mugs of beer he slid her way that went with her order. "You need a break?"

He shook his head. "Oh, Kate," he said as she started to lift the tray. "Butch wanted me to tell you, after you drop those off, he needs you in the kitchen."

Right now? She glanced toward the order window and ran into Butch's steady stare.

"Why?" she asked loud enough for Mr. Carter to hear through the window. Was Butch going to chew on her again about carrying too much on her tray? She wasn't *that* pregnant yet, damn it.

"He didn't say," Gary answered, not realizing the question wasn't for him. "Maybe he needs a break."

Meanwhile, the blue-eyed devil in the kitchen wiggled his index finger at her, giving her the come-hither sign.

Grumbling under her breath, she turned away and carted the order to the two cowboys tapping their toes over by the jukebox to The Guess Who's "No Sugar Tonight," which was going to be a true story for Mr. Valentine Carter if he didn't stop eagle-eyeing her.

Contrary to what Gary thought, Kate doubted Butch's summoning had anything to do with taking a break. In fact, she'd caught him watching her through the order window several times over the course of the evening, and he wasn't admiring her figure. Oh, no. She'd lay money on him playing watchtower guard, thinking he had his little woman under his thumb and well within his control. But Kate was on a mission tonight, and she'd be damned if he was going to stop her from doing what needed to be done.

"Here we are," she said, lowering the tray to the table.

A commotion over by the door, followed by a shout out from one of the guys holding down a bar stool, caught her attention.

A look toward the door found Penny, fresh in from the cool night, wearing a black puffy vest, jeans, and boots. Laughing, she waved at the dude at the bar and then glanced back toward the pool tables, doing a double take. Her eyes narrowed, along with her lips.

Kate followed Penny's line of sight, curious what had caused her smile to flatten out so quickly. Both pool tables were busy, the closest one in use by a couple of older guys wearing leather chaps and jackets with various patches on them partially hidden under their long gray beards.

At the other table, Mississippi was racking up the pool balls.

Across from him stood a woman holding a pool cue. Her hair was long and straight and dark blond. Her skin tanned. Extra tanned actually, like she'd spent a month working road construction without the proper sun protection. If Kate had to guess, she'd place her somewhere between her mid-thirties and … wait. Upon closer inspection, Kate recognized her from the RV park. Earlier today, the woman had been walking her miniature poodle toward the laundry. The dog's yellow leash had matched the smiley faces on the blonde's harem pants.

Another shout from the dude at the bar pulled Kate's gaze to the door again.

Son of a prickly pear! The sheriff was in town.

As she watched, Grady shucked his black sheriff's coat as he scanned the room.

A layer of sweat coated Kate's skin. The urge to shield herself behind her empty tray was strong. Great. Just freaking great. Penny was supposed to come alone. Kate should've made that more clear in the text message she'd sent, because the last thing she needed tonight was the sheriff here keeping his eye on her, too.

* * *

Ronnie knew the moment Grady entered The Shaft.

It wasn't because of some passionate undercurrent linking them together. Nor was it due to a soul mate sort of awareness that made her heart palpitate or her skin tingle, like she'd read about in one of Manny's romance books while working the register in the General Store for hours on end.

The reason Ronnie knew Grady had stepped into the bar was because she happened to be looking at Katie at that very moment, and she saw the whole left side of her sister's face twitch, as if she had bitten down on a live wire.

Ronnie would have laughed at Katie's reaction if she hadn't been so tightly wound herself today. That creepy text she'd received this morning while she was at the store about having been "found" had kept her on guard throughout the day. And then learning Mississippi's news about him having to stick around longer due to the FBI expecting to catch even more hitmen in their butterfly net thanks to Lyle's big mouth had raised her stress level a few more notches.

From where she stood in the middle of the bar, Ronnie could see the tiredness lining Grady's face. She wondered if it was simply that his day had been hell. Or had the forewarning from the FBI spurred reactions similar to hers—frustration and fatigue?

Ronnie could add the urge to take flight as a third reaction for her. Unfortunately, heading south of the border was no longer an option for hiding out, not with a Mexican cartel or two pissed at her ex for blowing their chances at collecting more illegal firearms.

Maybe she could hop a freighter ship to the Far East. Wait, was hopping a freighter even still a thing? Was it like stealing away in a train boxcar with a backpack full of clothes and cigarettes? Anyway, if she could somehow sneak on board a boat, she might be able to slide into obscurity under some tropical forest's canopy on the other side of the world.

Then again, humidity always made her cranky and left her chapped in the most uncomfortable places. Ronnie sighed. Until she could come up with a less sweaty—and less buggy—place as an escape, she was stuck standing her ground here in Jackrabbit Junction. She just prayed that when hell tiptoed into town, the devil left her family and friends alone.

Ronnie swung by to check in with Mindy Lou, who was taking orders at a table of mixed-age book club buddies who met at The Shaft weekly to drink beer. Every now and then they brought a book along, but not tonight. They were in their usual spot, which was back near the pool tables where Mississippi was racking up a game of pool next to some busty blonde wearing too much eyeliner and swoopy, fake eyelashes.

She paused for a moment, watching Mississippi and his pool buddy. Ronnie preferred it when he played pool alone while on duty. Then his focus was on making sure she didn't end up dead before the night was over.

From what she could tell, this blonde seemed to be doing her best to distract him by laughing too loud and tossing her hair back and forth like a prancing pony. Ronnie couldn't quite tell if Mississippi was enjoying the attention or playing along to hide the fact that he was the recess monitor in this beer-filled version of a school yard.

As she continued to assess the situation, Mississippi sank the red-striped eleven ball in a corner pocket. He paused then to scan the room while taking a drink of iced tea. When he noticed Ronnie looking his way, he nodded ever so slightly at her before continuing his perusal of the land. His gaze paused on where Grady and Penny were sitting, his focus seeming to get stuck there until the blonde came over and shoulder bumped him, pointing at the table.

That was curious. Ronnie made her way toward the bar, pondering what she'd just witnessed. Was that extra-long stare directed at Grady's back or Penny's? Or was Mississippi just lost in his FBI thoughts about hitmen and the Bureau's bullshit, like Ronnie had been repeatedly this afternoon?

"You waiting for me?" Gary stepped into her view, dragging her back to the here and now.

"Yeah. Will you let Mindy Lou know I need her to take this order to table six when it's ready, please?" She handed it off. "I have to talk to the sheriff about a problem that's cropped up."

"Sure." Gary set the order on the counter, frowning across the bar at her. "Is this about my cousin's newest game?"

"By cousin, you mean—"

"Elizabeth," he confirmed.

Ah, the complexities of small town life where everyone was related to each other, and the neighborhood dogs got married and had puppies.

"What new game are you referring to?" Ronnie asked, trying to act as if her neck wasn't bristling at merely the sound of Elizabeth's name.

"The one where Liz goes around town telling everyone that she and Grady are back together and planning to renew their vows."

"You're fucking kidding me." Ronnie's mouth gaped. Wow, that bitch was entering the ring swinging.

"I wish I was, but I stopped by the bank on the way in today, and one of the tellers who went to school with Liz asked if there would be another wedding ceremony to make it all official." Gary shook his head. "I don't know what Liz is thinking. This is not how you win a guy back after you shit all over his pride." He winced. "Excuse my French."

Before he could elaborate further, Gary was called away by a customer further down the bar, leaving Ronnie huffing and puffing, wanting to blow Elizabeth clear into orbit. It took a few deep breaths and a short, curse-filled rant to let off enough steam so that Ronnie didn't pop her top right there and then. Kaboom!

That rotten, cheating skank was not going to get Grady back, no matter how delusional she was.

Ronnie and he had talked about his ex-wife last night after they'd crawled into bed. Grady had assured her that any flames he'd felt for Elizabeth were well doused. The remaining ashes had been swept up long ago and the fireplace boarded over. After several more avowals regarding the shift in his feelings between then and now, he'd pulled Ronnie close and shown her how hot and bothered she made him—even when she wore flannel pajamas to bed.

Several chanted "ohms" later, Ronnie headed for where Penny and her brother were sitting. As she came up behind Grady, he took a sip of his drink—something cloudy in a tall, skinny glass. Lemonade with a kick of vodka? Probably just lemons squeezed in sparkling water with a squirt of desert honey—one of his favorite virgin drinks. Tension-filled or not, Grady drank alcohol only when he was wearing civilian clothes, and tonight he was still in uniform.

It was because of that uniform and them being in public that Ronnie kept her greeting casual. "Hey, Sheriff Hardass," she said, resting her palm on his shoulder as if they were just pals who didn't take showers together with extra-steamy and satisfying endings. "You have a minute?"

She wanted to touch base with him privately about the FBI crap and maybe see what he thought about that text message she'd received.

His shirt was warm, same as the flesh underneath the fabric, which she'd run her nails all over this morning before he'd headed off to work. He looked up, his amber eyes searching hers for who knew what, but she knew that look of his. It appeared the sheriff was still on duty.

"I have a whole bunch of minutes for you, Ms. Morgan, clear through until morning."

"I thought you were on call tonight, Grady," Penny said.

"I switched with Gonzales. He needs to head to Tucson

tomorrow for some sort of family deal."

"Good," Ronnie said for Grady's ears only. "Then come with me for a few minutes."

As he rose from the bar stool, Penny aimed a smile at Ronnie. "Thanks for taking such good care of Mindy Lou yesterday. She came home talking my ears off about how much fun she had working with you."

"I'm glad her first day here went smoothly. Is she living at your place now?" Ronnie wasn't sure where Mindy Lou had landed after her unfortunate go-around with Jess's dad last month.

"At the moment." Penny shot her brother a slight glare. "I was going to let her rent the apartment above the diner, but now it's occupied."

He nudged Penny's shoulder as he passed behind her. "You're welcome."

His sister scowled back. "I might regret renting it to him, you know."

"You need to let go of old ghosts," Grady told her. "Like I have." He smiled down at Ronnie. "Lead the way, Ms. Morgan. It's always more fun to follow you, especially when you're wearing tight jeans."

"These aren't that tight." Especially since she was struggling to keep weight on due to all her stress and anxiety. As Ronnie pushed through the batwing doors, she asked over her shoulder, "Who's Penny renting to?"

"Your FBI shadow."

She frowned as she passed the kitchen and opened Butch's office door at the end of the hall, holding it wide for Grady. "Mississippi is going to be staying above your sister's diner?"

He nodded as she closed the door behind him. "It's a nice apartment. He told me he'd pay her double the normal rent, so it's a win-win."

Ronnie leaned back against the door. "You sure about that?" When he raised one dark eyebrow, she explained, "Her history with one other FBI agent in particular would lead me to think she might still be pissed at anyone associated with those three letters."

Ronnie had heard about Penny's ex-fiancé and his love of philandering, which explained her allergy to black suits and FBI badges. Ronnie had suffered from a similar, raised-hackles reaction upon first meeting Mississippi. And while her own history with the Fricking Bunch of Invasive assholes also included sex, Penny's was actually performed voluntarily *with* one of them. Whereas Ronnie's sex acts only starred her ... and then were widely viewed by the pompous, FBI sons-a-bitches thanks to the hidden cameras Lyle had planted and aimed at their bed and the master shower.

Either way, though, both Penny and Ronnie had been fucked by the FBI.

Grady shrugged off Ronnie's concern. "Penny told me a few weeks ago that she'd pretty much forgotten about her ex-fiancé and moved on."

Moved on? Really? After being betrayed like that? Had Grady forgotten that his sister was a Scorpio? Even Ronnie, who was minimally versed in astrology, knew never to piss off a Scorpio— especially the females. Let alone betray one. There'd be no forgetting or forgiving, only castrating and burying in a shallow grave in the middle of the desert.

If Grady believed his sister had truly moved on, then his brain was telling itself tall tales, but Ronnie let it go for now. She needed to talk to him about her own issues that had the FBI still crawling all over her.

"What about you?" she asked.

He took a step closer, tipping up her chin. "What about me, Veronica?"

She could smell his work rig on him, a mix of seat leather cleaner and dust, with a hint of his bay rum aftershave underneath. Reaching up, she finger-combed life into his dark locks, trying to erase the crease from his sheriff's hat. "Are you pissed about the FBI sticking around longer?"

His gaze stayed fixed on hers as her fingers trailed down the side of his face. "I'd rather see his taillights driving away for good, since that would mean your troubles are over."

"Not all of them. You'd still be here," she teased, wrapping her arms around his neck.

"Yeah, but admit it, you think I hung the moon." He leaned down and kissed her, taking his time about it.

At first she could taste the lemon on his tongue, but no underlying liquor, which answered her earlier question. But then she could only taste him, and for a moment she let go of everything but Grady. She pressed against him, wanting to feel his strength, to absorb some of his resilience, to steal a pinch of his grit.

"I missed you, babe," he whispered when he came up for air, his hands busy showing her which parts of her anatomy he missed the most.

She needed to tell him about that text yet, but as usual, his touch started spreading small fires under her skin, making her burn for more. "You just saw me this morning."

"But not enough of your skin." His lips trailed along her jaw, while his fingers began to unbutton her shirt. "There were covers in the way. Not to mention those damned flannel pajamas."

She smiled up at the ceiling, giving his lips more access to her neck. "That's because you insist on keeping your house so freaking cold."

"So, if I turn up the thermostat a couple degrees, you'll sleep naked?"

"A couple degrees will get you silk pajamas instead of flannel." When he growled in complaint, she nuzzled his cheek. "But come summer, you might get your wish."

"I don't want to wait until summer." He finished with her shirt, his warm hands sliding inside along her ribs.

"Grady, hold on a min—" She paused, sidetracked by the magic he was working with his thumbs, but then her mind refocused. "We can't screw around in Butch's office."

"This isn't screwing around." His words came out slightly muffled as he kissed the spot below her ear that made the lower half of her body tingle and quiver.

She moaned. "What is it then?"

"I'm just searching you for dangerous weapons." He pulled back enough to look down at her bra. "A front clasp. Damn. It must be my lucky day."

With a flick of his fingers, the clasp was undone. Before she could protest, he'd backed her against the door and kissed her again.

His lips demanded submission while his hands frisked her like a pro, tugging her shirt free of her jeans and peeling it partway off her shoulders. She pressed against him, from top to bottom, all her worries and fears temporarily buried.

She pulled free of his kiss, shifting her mouth to his cheek.

The beard stubble tickled her swollen lips. "Grady," she breathed more than said before nibbling on his ear lobe.

He groaned in response, stepping back enough to make room for his hands to do more investigating.

"You are forgetting to search inside my pants."

As his hands slid toward her waistline, the office door shoved open, sending Ronnie bumping into Grady.

"What the …?" A voice came from the other side of the door, and then, "Hold on, Mac."

Grady was able to step aside before a second, more forceful shove sent Ronnie pinballing into Butch's desk while trying to pull her shirt together.

"Oh, my— Come on!" Claire shouted from where she stood in the open doorway. "What is wrong with you two?"

Ronnie kept her back to the door while trying to refasten her bra. "There is nothing *wrong* with us," she said over her shoulder. "We just got carried away."

"Same song, different verse," Claire scoffed. "I'm surprised you didn't steal my keys to use the Jeep again as your lovemobile."

"I told you we didn't have sex in there," Ronnie snapped.

"Not for want of trying," Claire shot back.

Grady cursed, grabbing a pillow from the office couch to shield his own reaction to their screwing-around. "About that night, Claire," he started.

The sound of footfalls rushing up the hall drew a second, louder round of cursing from Grady. He stepped between Ronnie and the rest of the world, blocking her from view. "If you'll just give your sister a moment to—"

"What's going on?" Butch interrupted him, looking over Claire's shoulder.

"Jeez and crackers!" Ronnie muttered, finally fastening the stupid bra and moving on to the buttons of her work shirt. "Nothing is happening here, dammit."

Never mind that something might have happened if they hadn't been interrupted. Thank the Maker that her pants hadn't been around her ankles when Claire shoved into the room. She might have landed bare-ass up on the couch.

"Christ, Harrison!" Butch said much louder than he needed to in Ronnie's opinion. She peeked around Grady's shoulder, scowling at Butch. "Not again. What's with you two and this place? You'd think I was running a brothel here with the good ol' sheriff being my top customer."

Grady tossed the pillow aside and crossed his arms. "Real funny, Carter. But if memory serves me right, someone got pregnant in this very room thanks to you."

"What's going on?" Chester asked, nudging Claire farther into the room so he could see better. His gaze met Ronnie's, and then a grin covered his face from ear to ear before he turned on Grady, pointing the spatula he was carrying at him. "Well, well, well. If it ain't the age-old tale of the local sheriff giving the buxom serving wench a private li'l pat down in the back room."

"Cram it, Chester," Ronnie said, finishing with her buttons and tucking her shirt back into her jeans.

"What was that, Mac?" Claire spoke into her phone, turning aside. "No, it's Ronnie and Grady right here in Butch's office." She snorted. "No, not on the desk. Some vertical slap and tickle against the door."

"We were not slapping," Ronnie defended.

"But they were getting mighty tickly," Chester hollered so that Mac could hear him.

Grady scrubbed his hand down his face, covering his mouth and shaking his head.

Chuckling along with Chester, Claire listened on her phone for a moment. Then she laughed again. "Mac says that you should know better, Ronnie. Screwing around is allowed only in Butch's supply room."

"Ha ha," Butch said, pointing at Claire. "It's going to be you guys' supply room soon enough, then it's my turn to have sex all over the place in there."

Claire wrinkled her nose at him. "Mac, we'll have to keep it stocked up with condoms," she said into the phone. "Hey, I have a money-making idea. We could rent the room by the quarter hour and charge extra for local law dogs."

Butch shook his head at Grady. "Why can't you be more like Mac and Claire and screw around outside behind the building where management won't walk in on you?"

"It's too cold outside right now," Chester said in Grady's defense. "Take it from a member of the North Woods Frozen Blue

Balls Sex-capades Club, Minnesota Local Chapter 24. The sheriff will freeze his twig and berries clear off." He held up his index finger. "Although I have heard some wild tales from the girls down at Dirty Gerties about fun adventures with popsicles."

"Enough!" Ronnie said, turning to Grady. "Why aren't you saying anything to defend your honor in front of these three stooges, *Sheriff?*"

"Four," Claire said, pointing at her phone.

Grady sighed. "I reserve the right to remain silent rather than fan the flames."

Katie shoved Chester aside, moving up next to Claire. "What's going on back here? We're waiting on you guys to cook some orders. The locals are getting restless out there."

"Claire interrupted your sister and Harrison getting busy in here," Butch told her.

"On the couch?" she asked, frowning at Ronnie and then Grady. "Come on, have some respect." She rubbed her round belly. "That's where Valentine and I conceived our child."

"We should call it the love couch," Chester declared, pointing the spatula at the piece of furniture as if he were knighting it. "You could charge extra to rent it out. It's a guaranteed baby maker."

Ronnie looked at the couch, grimacing. "I'm not sure that's a good selling point in a brothel environment, Chester."

"That's it." Claire thumbed toward the door. "Everyone out. I need to talk to Mac in private about something."

"You're going to have phone sex in here, aren't you?" Chester said, and then howled with high-pitched laughter as Claire tried to kick him in the backside, sending him racing out of the room.

"After you, Sir Sheriff of Naughty-hand." Butch grinned, holding the door wide.

"Keep it up, Carter," Grady said as he paused in front of Butch. "And I'll arrest you."

"For what?" Butch asked.

"I don't know, but I'll come up with something requiring an anal cavity search by that ham-handed doctor down at the local clinic."

Butch let out a shout of laughter at Grady's back as the sheriff headed down the hall.

Katie rushed over to Ronnie and whispered, "You don't need

to worry about Grady's ex anymore. I have your back."

Before Ronnie could ask what Katie meant by that cryptic message, her little sister scuttled over to Claire and said something to her, too.

Claire rolled her eyes and pushed Katie toward the door. "Get out of here, Ms. Hyde." She pointed her cell phone at Ronnie. "And take your sleazy-easy sister with you."

Chapter Twelve

*C*laire ushered everyone out, closing and locking the office door behind them. She leaned against it for good measure. Then she remembered that Ronnie and Grady had been about to have sex—or something close to it—against the door and moved to Butch's desk.

She'd escaped to the office to talk to Mac because the bar was way too loud, not expecting to walk in on a makeout session. Especially not one including her older, wiser sister.

The Ronnie that Claire had grown up with never would have sneaked into the back room at a busy bar to screw around. That was more Claire's style. And their cousin Natalie's. Not toe-the-line Veronica Morgan.

Who was this new woman, and how in the world did dating a county sheriff turn Ronnie into a wild, wanton badass when being married to a true-blue criminal for years had kept her a boring Stepford wife? Oh, the irony.

But back to her phone conversation with Mac ... which had nothing to do with Sophy Wheeler. Claire knew better than to open that can of worms with Mac, especially over the phone. And she certainly didn't need Kate whispering in her ear not to tell him about the call to Sophy or her deal offer, as if Claire's brain were the one with the surplus of mad monkey hormones these days.

"Okay, Mac," Claire said now that she was finally alone with him in the quiet office. She put the phone on speaker so she didn't have to hold it to her ear anymore. "It's just you and me now."

"Is the door closed?"

"Closed and locked."

"Good. You know, maybe we should have sex in that office as soon as the papers are signed."

"Why? Is this some sort of marking your territory thing?"

"No. More like exorcising everyone else's sex demons."

She smiled. "Fine, but this time it's your naked ass on the cold desktop, not mine." She moved around the desk, dropping into Butch's cushy leather chair. "Now, what were you saying about the jobsite?"

"It's a mess." He sighed, sounding as tired as her aching muscles felt after another day of double duty between building that damned platform and slinging drinks. "I'm going to be up late each night this week going through the paperwork and double-checking that the supplies will be here in time to keep the crew moving."

Claire leaned back in the chair and kicked her feet up on the desk, listening as Mac continued sharing his frustrations with her. She closed her eyes, wishing once again that he hadn't opted for the consulting job. That he'd stayed put here with her, so she could look into his hazel eyes before drifting off to dreamland after an exhausting day. These long-distance phone calls were supposed to be a thing of the past.

She stifled a yawn. Sitting still for so long was dangerous. It would be easy to take a cat nap now that all of the commotion out front had been dulled to a low rumb ...

"Claire?" Mac asked, hauling her back from the edge of dreamland.

"What?" She opened her eyes, glancing at the clock on the wall. She needed to keep awake for another hour to help wrap things up out front.

"I miss you."

"I miss you, too."

A silent yawn came and went. Crap, she was so tired. Maybe she should move around a little, do some jumping jacks. Yeah, that would do the trick.

"How's the old town of Bisbee doing these days?" she asked, rising from the chair. She walked around the desk and headed for the couch, and then did an about-face, returning to the desk before bending and touching her toes.

"I don't know." Something creaked on his end of the line, sounding like a chair maybe. Or the bed. "I've been too busy making phone calls and trying to line up the holes in the Swiss cheese slices here to even look outside."

For a moment, she contemplated telling Mac about Kate's crazy plan to follow through on Sophy's request in exchange for information on Joe just to take his mind off his work woes, but there was no way anything to do with Sophy would go over well with him. Mac would tell her she was nuts to even open a dialogue with that deranged woman, and then after they'd ended the call, he'd stay up for part of the night worrying about Claire.

She stretched her sore neck muscles side to side. No, mentioning Sophy's name alone would be bad. Mac needed to focus on this job this week. The sooner he got things done, the quicker he could come home. Then maybe she could convince him to take more of her grandfather's money for the brewery. She'd do whatever it took—begging, bribing, seducing. She wanted him back here for good.

Someone knocked on the door. Five quick raps. Pause. And then five more raps.

"Hang on, Mac. Someone's at the door." Claire unlocked it, pulling the door open.

Kate stood on the other side, a frown puckering her brow.

"What do you want now?"

"Are you still on the phone with Mac?" Kate asked.

Claire nodded, holding her index finger up to her lips to shush her sister before she opened her big mouth and landed Claire in hot water with him.

"Did you tell him about you-know-who?" she whispered.

Jumping Jehoshaphat! Claire rolled her eyes at Kate's monomaniacal obsession with that woman.

"If you roll your eyes at me one more time tonight, Claire Alice Morgan," Kate said loud enough for Mac to hear, "I'm going to fill your underwear drawer with fleas."

Laughter came from Claire's cell phone. "I'd pay to see you wiggle and dance, Slugger."

"Careful, Garner," Claire warned jokingly, walking over and picking up her phone in case she needed to mute it quick due to Kate's loose lips. "Or I'll send my sister down to work at the jobsite with you, and let me tell you, those baby hormones have her more than a little cranky in the morning."

"Real funny," Kate said, flipping her off.

"Why, thank you. Now what do you need? Mac doesn't have

long until he needs to crash, so make this quick."

"I need your help."

"Right now?"

"Yes."

"You'll have to wait until we're done having phone sex," she said, pretending to kiss the phone.

Kate snatched it out of Claire's hands. "Mac, Claire will call you back shortly," she said and ended the call.

"Hey! What the hell?" Claire took her phone back. "We were having a conversation."

"I don't have time for you and your conversating crapola. I have something to tell you and it has to be now. But you can't tell anyone else about this."

"Shittlesticks, Kate. You're just a twisted mess of secrets these days all wound up in a tight mysterious ball. Maybe I don't want to know whatever it is that has you acting like you've been possessed by an electric eel tonight."

"Yes, you do, Claire."

"What makes you so sure?"

Kate walked by her and approached the three-shelf bookcase next to Butch's filing cabinet.

"Couldn't this have waited until I finished with Mac?"

"No. Butch is keeping close tabs on me tonight, barely letting me out of his sight. But right this moment, he's too busy cleaning up a mess in the men's bathroom to shadow me, so this has to happen now."

"What mess?" Claire asked.

"Someone dropped a glass of beer on the floor."

"Who would take their beer to the …" A light flickered on in Claire's head. "Really, Kate? That's a pain in the ass to clean up."

Her sister's cheeks turned bright pink. "You don't understand. I just needed five minutes to take care of this, but his eagle eyes were unblinking." When Claire continued to glare at her on Butch's behalf, Kate huffed. "Fine, I'll make it up to him the next time we have sex."

"Gah! Stop!" Claire held up her hand to ward off any further visuals.

"You're such a prima donna," Kate said, pulling a book off the shelf.

"Says the woman who used to never leave the house without her shoes and purse displaying the proper brand names."

Kate lifted another book from the shelf, handing it and the other one to Claire. "That was a different life starring men who were mere shadows of Valentine."

"Whatever. Just tell me what is so important that you had to run interference with Butch when he's supposed to be training Chester on the line?"

Kate handed Claire a couple more books, and then reached behind the remaining ones on the shelf, extracting a hidden book with a black cover. "There's something I need to show you." She held the book against her chest.

Claire eyed it. "Is that another first edition of Joe's that you found down in his basement office?"

"No." She lifted her chin. "But before I show you this, I want you to promise me two things. One, that you won't be mad; and two, that you'll help me figure out a mystery."

No. Claire didn't have the time for another mystery, nor the brainpower. She was maxed out between the physical labor on her plate and this whole Joe's-alive distraction. Hell, just tying her shoes each day was puzzling enough right now.

"I don't have time to read that book and decipher any clues. I barely have time to eat right now, and that's a bigger crime than anything possibly hiding on those pages."

"This is not about the book." Kate flipped open the cover. "It's about this."

Inside the book was a hollowed-out compartment. Crammed within that compartment was a wad of tissue paper with decorations of different-colored versions of potted cacti.

"About what? Some fancy tissue paper?" Claire asked with a healthy dose of sarcasm.

"No, smart ass." Kate lifted out the tissue paper, carefully unwrapping a knife hidden within it.

Not just any knife either. It was the one their mom had pulled from her purse during her post-wedding bridal shower at Dirty Gerties before Christmas. At least Claire was pretty sure it was the same one. Although that memory was fuzzy thanks to the cognac their mother had been insisting Claire and Ronnie guzzle along with her.

God, that night had been such a disaster. If Claire never drank cognac again, it would be too soon.

"So there *was* a knife." Claire scowled at her sister, who'd later played dumb about it. "I knew it!"

"You were pretty drunk by the time Mom started waving this around." Kate held it up, careful to only touch it along the edge of the handle.

"Not that drunk." Claire cautiously took the knife from Kate, using some of the tissue paper to protect it from her skin oils.

The artifact was even more interesting now that she wasn't seeing double or triple thanks to the cognac. She stared down at the jade handle, studying the carvings on it. It certainly looked like some ancient Maya handiwork, but shouldn't the carvings on the handle be more worn? The leather binding appeared sturdy and tight yet for having lasted through a lot of centuries. Maybe the knife actually started out as a collector's piece for some Mayan king, or priest, or some other member of nobility. That would explain the lack of wear.

"I figured Mom had hidden it somewhere later that night while she was drunk and we'd probably never find it again." Claire blew out a breath. "Shit. Another damned treasure."

"Joe had some really sticky fingers."

"Yeah, and now we're stuck dealing with the pissed-off people missing their fenced goods."

"Millie and I suspect it might have been stolen from the private collection of an antiquities dealer."

"Millie?" Claire frowned at her sister. "You don't mean the sheriff's aunt Millie, do you?"

Kate nodded. "My donations to her and her gang of blue-haired bullies are keeping them in bingo cards these days."

"Son of a mother-humper." Claire groaned. "Not this again."

Someone pounded on the door, making both of them jump and Claire almost dropped the knife.

"Kate!" Butch hollered from the other side of the door. "Are you in there?"

"See what I mean," she said to Claire and took the knife, gingerly wrapping it in the tissue paper before sliding it down inside her sock. After lowering her pantleg, she returned the fake book to its hiding place.

"Kate," Butch said again, pounding harder. "I heard your voice. Open up."

Claire helped Kate shove the books back onto the shelf, and then her sister hustled over to unlock the door.

"Hello, Valentine," she said when she opened it, greeting him with a flirty smile. "I was just consoling Claire for a moment about Mac being gone. Did you get that little mess cleaned up in the bathroom?"

Butch stalked into the room, squinting at Kate and then Claire, his blue eyes narrowed in suspicion. "Your sister looks just fine to me."

"Of course she does." Kate moved around him so that Butch was the monkey in the middle. "Claire is tough. She's never been one to wear her feelings on her sleeve, but I can see how sad she is that Mac is gone again." Kate gave Claire a pointed look from behind Butch.

Claire took the hint, giving Butch a sad puppy-dog face. "Yes, I'm very upset on the inside. Mac is my sunshine. Without him the world seems dark and full of despair."

Behind Butch, Kate mimed smacking her forehead and looked to the heavens. Then she grabbed Butch's hand, tugging his focus back in her direction. "Now, what is it you wanted to talk to me about, hot stuff?"

She batted her lashes at him so hard that Claire practically felt her hair blow back.

Butch's gaze narrowed even more as Kate walked her fingers up his chest. He caught her hand, holding it still. "Kate, you're a real minx, you know that?"

"I'm sure I don't know what you're talking about. Like I said, Claire needed me." Kate glanced over at Claire and winked.

Or maybe that was a twitch.

Criminy, Claire needed her, all right. She needed Kate about as much as she needed a tarantula hawk wasp jammed up her nose.

"Butch, if you don't mind me borrowing your office for a little longer," Claire said, needing a break from crazy Kate, "I'm going to call Mac back quick. I forgot to tell him one last thing."

Kate shook her head violently.

"About the brewery addition," Claire added for her cuckoo sister's peace of mind. "I'll be out front in a few."

Butch backed out into the hall, tugging Kate along with him. "No problem. It's slowing down out there. Your sister will make sure your tables are taken care of, won't you?"

"Of course."

Another wink came from Kate.

Claire stood staring at the closed door for a few seconds after they left, scowling in Kate's choppy wake.

First the call with Sophy and now this Maya knife. Each of these on their own was a lot to hide from Mac, and Claire and he were supposed to have an "open and honest" rule now in their relationship. Although Mac had sort of kept his plans to do consulting work to himself until the last minute.

Wait, to be fair to Mac, he had mentioned the possibility to her. He'd just kept from her the fact that he'd left the door wide open.

Claire blew out a breath. To tell or not to tell.

Really, there wasn't much to say at this point. The call had been made to Sophy, but Claire had only heard the high-level version of the offer—to exchange one favor for another. She didn't know the exact favor yet, so keeping quiet about that wasn't really withholding that much. And as she surmised before, with Mac so far away from Jackrabbit Junction, Claire merely mentioning the name "Sophy" to him would only make him lose sleep. Right now, he needed to be alert on the job, finish up quickly, and then hurry home. Period. End of story.

Home.

She smiled at the warm, heady feeling that came with that word in relation to Mac.

Okay, so that was the plan. Hold onto this crap until Mac came home on Saturday, then she'd spill and see what he thought about both of her problems—Sophy and the knife, plus get his take on the new ideas she'd come up with for the brewery addition while working on Gramps's platform the last couple of days.

She pulled up Mac's number. Before she could send the call through, someone knocked on the door again.

"You've got to be kidding me." Cursing about the lack of privacy around this gin joint, Claire yanked open the door.

She was expecting to see Kate, figuring she'd somehow fooled Butch and escaped again.

But it wasn't Kate.

Or Butch, Chester, or Ronnie.

Claire stepped back in surprise, her hand covering her chest. "What in the hell are *you* doing here?"

Chapter Thirteen

enny frowned down at the note Kate had slipped her almost ten minutes ago as she passed by Penny's bar stool. She struggled to reread the words in the thick shadows.

Meet me on the back patio in ten minutes. ALONE!

It'd been fifteen minutes since she got the note. No, make that sixteen.

Shivering in the cold breeze blowing in off the desert, she leaned against the side of the building. She should have grabbed her vest before leaving the bar to come out here, but with the way Kate's gaze had been darting around when she handed off the note, like her eyeballs were rolling loose in her head, Penny hadn't wanted to draw attention to her soon-to-be whereabouts before slinking outside.

Especially not from her brother, who'd been sitting next to her since returning from his meeting with Ronnie in Butch's office. He hadn't mentioned what Ronnie had needed to talk to him about, so Penny hadn't pressed, but the pained expression that kept flitting across his face when he thought nobody was watching sure had her itching to ask.

Kate had also given Penny the shush sign when handing off the note, making it obvious that this was something to keep under the radar. Especially when it came to Butch, who seemed to be overly preoccupied with Kate's whereabouts tonight. Penny had to wonder if Kate had been overdoing it lately, worrying Butch about her and the baby's health. The soon-to-be momma certainly seemed to buzz around the bar like a worker bee running late for the tulip train in spite of her pregnant belly.

Seventeen minutes.

Penny had waited the initially required ten minutes per Kate's note, sipping on her glass of ginger ale and prickly pear syrup as she kept a sneaky eye on the clock, before excusing herself to go to the restroom. On her way across the bar, she'd cast a glance toward the pool table where Mississippi was lining up a shot, playing yet another game of eight-ball with the big-boobed, glossy-lipped, Charlie's Angel wannabe who kept staring at his ass when he was taking his shots.

Wasn't he supposed to be on duty watching Ronnie's back instead of flirting with that blond tart? Penny gritted her teeth, reminding the jealous oaf in her head that who Mississippi flirted with was not her business. A single night—no, make that a single half-hour—of making out, followed by sex, did not give her the right to expect anything else from the vexing rogue. This was true even more so since Penny was the one who'd insisted that one game of half-naked bronco busting was all that was allowed.

But that fine-looking devil had better not bring that hussy back to her diner, damn it. Penny had laid down the law about sex, and she'd meant it. Even though it really wasn't her business—and probably not even legal—and she'd never given a rat's ass before about sex happening or not upstairs.

Eighteen minutes.

She shivered again, sliding her hands under her thin sweater to keep them warm against her stomach. "Come on, Kate," she said, her teeth chattering as she stared up at the stars glistening in the dark sky. Sprinkles of sugar, her grandfather used to call them, she remembered with a sad pang in her heart for happy days gone by.

The stars were pretty much the only thing about this place she'd missed while living in San Francisco. Well, the stars and her family. She hadn't missed the small-town gossip mill, though, nor the politics. And she especially hadn't missed her mother trying to set her up with every Tom, Dick, and Billy Bob driving around with jacked-up pickups and overinflated egos.

Just yesterday, her mom had stopped by the diner to let her know that one of Penny's old high school boyfriends was single again. His third divorce was final now, it seemed, and he was back on the market sporting three kids and only a few hundred a month in alimony. Penny could hardly contain her joy at the package deal her mom had been trying to sell her.

She checked her phone. Nineteen minutes.

Another shiver racked her as the patio door opened.

"Penny?" Kate whispered, sticking her head out. The steady boom-boom-boom of Queen's "We Will Rock You" seeped out, drowning out the sound of the wind making the nearby creosote bush branches clatter.

Finally!

"Over here," Penny called.

Kate stepped outside and closed the door behind her, joining her in the shadows. "Thanks for meeting me out here."

"No problem. What's up with the top-secret meeting outside in the freezing cold?"

Sighing with an extra dose of drama, Kate glanced back toward the door. "Valentine thinks I'm up to something. He keeps following me around, making it hard to take care of business."

Poor Butch. Penny was pretty sure he had his hands full and then some with the youngest Morgan sister. Just wait until that baby was born.

A strong gust whipped through the patio, making one of the hanging planters thump against the wall. Kate jumped at the sound, her gaze darting toward the door yet again.

"Since we are standing here in the shadows," Penny said, "and you keep checking over your shoulder, I'm assuming you are up to something worrisome for Butch or one of your sisters. Is this clandestine meeting about Elizabeth?"

She sure hoped so, because that stupid review about her diner still had her gnashing her teeth.

"Partly. But first I need you to hide something for me." Kate leaned down. When she came back up, she had what looked like a tissue paper–wrapped hot dog in her hand. "Can you keep this somewhere tucked away for a while?"

"Tucked away where?" Penny looked at the wrapped object Kate held out, not sure she wanted to touch it and get herself mired in whatever Kate was up to tonight. "What is that? Are those cacti on the tissue paper? How cute."

"This is a secret." Kate took Penny's hand and placed the thing in it. It felt hard under the tissue paper. "A big one."

"Your secret feels heavy already. I'm not sure I want you to share it with me."

"Don't be a whiner-forty-niner, Penny. It's an old knife."

Penny unwrapped part of it, holding it up in the light coming through the patio door. The black blade reflected the light. "How old? Is this obsidian?"

"Like ancient Maya times old." Kate pointed at the black blade. "Your aunt has been helping me look into it. I'm pretty sure it's something that Joe Martino skimmed when he still lived here and tucked away for later."

Penny frowned at Kate. "The same Joe Martino who was married to your new step-grandma?"

"The one and only." Kate opened her mouth, like she was going to tell Penny something else about Joe or her new grandma, but then didn't.

Lowering her frown to the tissue-wrapped knife, Penny asked, "And why am I the one holding it right now?"

"My mom found it down in Joe's old office and brought it to the strip club for her bridal shower. When everyone else was wasted, I took the knife and hid it away to protect it from being seen by anyone else in the club. You never know who might be slinking around Yuccaville these days, and the last thing Ronnie and Claire need is more trouble hunting them down."

Penny nodded, but still frowned at the knife. "That doesn't explain why I'm here holding it right now, though. Or why you want *me* to hide it away."

"You know," Kate said, crossing her arms. "You're a bit like your brother."

"Which one?"

"The sheriff one."

"I have a feeling you don't mean that in the good, upstanding citizen sort of way."

Kate chuckled and touched her nose. "You get your teeth locked onto something and you won't let loose." She paused as a cutting breeze whipped past them, pelting them with some dust and tumbleweed twigs. "Listen, I need some time to figure out the full story behind that knife, but Butch has been watching me 24/7 lately, which I think is partly your brother's doing and maybe both of my sisters' faults. Everyone thinks I'm on the verge of a breakdown or something, so they monitor me day and night." Kate tapped on the tissue-wrapped knife. "I'm afraid Butch will find this and turn it over to your brother."

"And that would be bad because?"

"Because your brother is the sheriff," Kate said it as if Penny had feathers for brains.

"I know that, but would Grady holding onto this artifact really be so bad?"

"Hell, yes! He'd tuck it away in evidence and then Deputy Dipshit would get his hands on it. Who knows what would happen to it then? Maybe Ernie would just keep it for himself when it should be in a museum somewhere. Or maybe he'd try to sell it on the black market, which would draw attention to it being here in Jackrabbit Junction where my family lives. Or maybe he'd use it to say Claire or Ronnie or I stole it and get us thrown into the big house. Or maybe—"

"Okay, okay. I get it. You don't want Ernie to have it."

Kate's upper lip curled in a growly scowl. "That guy is as crooked as a bent nail. If he finds out that we've been finding treasures at the RV park, he'll go out of his way to get the feds involved and have Ruby's place shut down."

"I'm sure Grady wouldn't let that happen."

Kate guffawed. "Grady wouldn't have a choice in the matter if the feds got involved." She reached out and re-wrapped the knife in tissue paper, and then closed Penny's palm around it. "You need to hide this for me where nobody will find it. Not your brother, not Deputy Dipshit, and especially not Mississippi with his FBI badge."

Kate might be right. They already had enough FBI in town with the green-eyed scoundrel inside playing pool with that blond charmer.

"Okay, I'll find a hiding spot for it for now, but if shit hits the fan, you have to promise me you won't tell Grady about my involvement. He already rides me enough for the stupid speeding ticket I got last year."

"Deal."

Penny held up the wrapped knife. "You really need some sort of protective case for this."

"I carved out a spot for it in a book and had it hidden away on a shelf in Butch's office for the last couple of days, wanting to give it to your aunt or you for safer keeping." Kate pushed Penny's hand lower, glancing at the door again. "But I couldn't fit the book down my pants or in my boot when he almost caught me showing it to Claire, and then he was right on my heels again as soon as I left his office."

Penny only made sense of half of that, but she held onto the knife anyway. Now, where to tuck it away until she escaped back to Yuccaville?

"Oh, by the way," Penny said. "Elizabeth posted her first shitty review today for my diner." She growled. "That bitch started out with a solid jab right to my eye."

"Oooo! She's such a shrew. What was your brother thinking when he married her?"

"I've asked him that too many times to count over the last few years. He mainly claims she misrepresented her attributes, playing up the good girl act while lying behind his back."

" 'Good girl,' huh?" Kate wrinkled her nose at that moniker. "That sounds boring."

"Yeah," said the Scorpio in Penny, who preferred her life and her men on the wild side. Although her actions of the last year or two told a much more boring, mundane story.

"Is that what your brother wants? The perfect little sheriff's woman without any tarnish in the corners? Someone who dresses like a 1950s Hollywood wife and toes the line to the point of losing touch with her true self?"

Penny picked up on the sharp teeth in Kate's questions, feeling a bit defensive of Grady suddenly. "Well, we've never really discussed that aspect of a wife for him, but I think his issue with Elizabeth centers more on her deception. Not on the actual persona of some sort of textbook wife."

Kate harrumphed. "Ronnie used to be all about using the correct fork at dinner and keeping the linen napkins pressed and the silver polished. But those days burned up along with her pride when Lyle got busted by the feds."

"Exes are assholes. I think we're both fully on board that train of thought," Penny said, entertaining the dark fantasy of stringing up her ex by his testicles and batting him around like a piñata. *Whack! Whack! Whack!*

"Toot toot," Kate said, pulling Penny back to the moment.

She returned to her current, more pressing problem. "Now, about this damn review made against my diner. You mentioned in your text yesterday something about taking Elizabeth down. Do you have any plans yet?"

Kate nodded. "So far, I have one idea, but I haven't run it by the rest of the posse yet."

The posse could wait. She was now front and center in Elizabeth's sights. "What is it?"

"I'm going to—"

The patio door opened. "Kate? Are you out here?"

"You've got to be fucking kidding me," Kate whispered, silently shaking her fists at the sky. "Yes, Valentine. I'm out here talking to Penny."

He stepped out onto the patio. "Why out here? It's freezing."

Penny shivered in agreement.

"Because it's too loud in there and I was hot." She fanned herself. "We're just enjoying a little girl talk. Hint, hint."

He sighed. "I get it, but Claire sent me to find you."

"Why?"

"Because there's someone here to see you."

"Me?" A squeak came from Kate, and then the left side of her body twitched enough for Penny to see it in the shadows. "It's not one of Grady's law dogs, is it?"

Butch took several steps closer, his gaze narrowed. "Why would the police be after you again, Kate?"

"No reason, I swear."

Penny saw Kate cross her fingers behind her back. Shit. What had Kate gotten herself into now?

"Kate," Butch started.

"I was joking, Valentine." She laughed a little too fast to be normal, and then let out a strangled screech. "Oh no! Please tell me my mom isn't back in town already."

"No." He cringed visibly. "If it were your mother, we would've been forewarned by a plague of grasshoppers. Followed by all of the beer in the joint turning to blood."

"I've heard Grady talk about Kate's mom," Penny said. "His face gets all scrunched up at the mention of her name."

"Yeah, Mom isn't a fan of your brother. I don't think it's personal, really. More to do with the badge he wears and how many times he's tossed Claire and me in the hoosegow. Especially since we've been innocent a couple of the times."

"Cut the man some slack," Butch said. "He's just doing his job. Besides, breaking and entering is a legitimate crime. And let's not forget that he let you off with only a hard glare about locking his deputy in a jail cell."

"You did that?" Penny asked.

Kate's chin jutted. "Ernie had it coming. Trust me."

"Oh, I don't doubt it about Ernie." Penny smirked. "He's not a fan of women, unless they are taking their clothes off over at Dirty Gerties. I was actually referring to the breaking and entering Butch mentioned." Grady hadn't told her about that.

Kate waved off the B&E as if it were yesterday's boring news. "One of these days, I'm going to teach Deputy Dipshit a lesson."

"No, you're not, sweetheart." Butch wrapped his arm around Kate's shoulders, kissing her temple. "Now come inside and introduce me to this guy that showed up at the bar and has your sisters fawning over him like he's a rock star."

"Really?" Kate looked up at him. "Did you happen to catch his name?"

Butch pulled open the patio door, holding it for Kate. "Luke Beals."

Kate gasped. "Luke!" She let out a cheer and raced inside.

"You coming?" Butch turned to Penny.

"In a minute." She needed to plant the Maya knife in a better hiding place before returning to her brother's side.

"Okay, but if you don't come inside soon, I'll have to turn in a missing person's report with your brother." After a small salute, he closed the door behind him.

Shivering as another cold blast rattled past her, Penny made sure the knife's obsidian blade was safely wrapped in the cacti tissue paper and then untucked her shirt. She slid the knife inside her pants, partway inside her underwear elastic, adjusting it so that it wouldn't stab her when she sat on the bar stool. She straightened her shirt, making sure it hid all evidence when it draped down to mid-zipper. That should do if she didn't lift her arms at all.

Happy to return to the land of heat, Penny hurried inside.

Mississippi stood by the *Big Buck Hunter* video game, arms crossed, blocking her path. "Star gazing?"

She shrugged, then remembered she needed to keep her arms down. "Just getting a little fresh air."

"You should be careful. It could be dangerous out there alone in the dark."

"I'm not afraid of being alone." She looked him up and down, noticing the blue pool cue chalk, thigh-level, on his black jeans as well as his shoulder. She liked the way his dark shirt made his green eyes more piercing, dang it. "I'm more worried about why you're standing here, obviously waiting for me. Am I on a list of possible suspects now?"

His face softened with a grin. "Sure. I got a call from headquarters and they want me to start shadowing you now, too. It seems you have a reputation for harassing poor, nice FBI agents who are just trying to do their jobs."

"You're not nearly as likable as you think you are."

"I beg to differ." His focus dipped to her lips. "I think that somewhere underneath your layers of barbed wire and Kevlar skin, you really like me."

Maybe she did.

And maybe she needed to have her head examined.

" 'Like' is a strong word." She hooked her thumbs in her front pockets to keep from reaching out and brushing the blue chalk off his shoulder as an excuse to touch him. "Why are you waiting here for me?"

He shrugged. "Could be I was missing your scowling face."

"I'm not sure where you'd find the time to miss it, what with your blond girlfriend glued to your side."

One dark eyebrow climbed upward. "Jealous?"

Of course, dang it. Mississippi was hers alone to hate–lust after. "Merely concerned for her welfare."

He knew better. His cocky grin said so.

"I was at the bar when Butch came from this direction. He asked me to do him a favor and make sure you made it inside okay."

Kate must be sidetracked with her visitor, allowing Butch a spare moment to watch out for someone else. "Well, thanks for checking up on me, but I'm good. You can get back to your pool game."

"That's over." The way he said that made it clear he meant

"over" in every sense of the word.

"That's too bad." Penny had little doubt the blonde would've been happy to continue playing out in his pickup.

"Why is that?" He leaned back against the video machine.

"Because she was easy on the eyes."

"You like long-legged blondes, do ya?"

"No, but I know an attractive woman when I see one."

His gaze held steady on her. "So do I."

Was he flirting with her or just stating a fact? "Good. We're on the same page then."

"And what page would that be, Penelope?"

"That you were playing pool with a pretty woman."

He shook his head slowly. "You're wrong."

"About playing pool or the pretty woman?"

"About us being on the same page."

What page, dammit?

He stood upright. "I need to get back to work. You want to join me for a drink, landlady?"

And continue with this back-and-forth mental fuckery? "No, thanks. I think it's time for me to head home."

Unfortunately, Penny would have to give up on a posse planning meeting tonight. With the way Butch was shadowing Kate, the chances of getting her alone again were slim. Elizabeth's bullshit would have to wait another day.

Not to mention that Penny had an ancient Maya knife stuck down her pants that was sliding slowly south. Hopefully her underwear would hold it in place long enough for her to say her good-byes without having to make adjustments. She doubted Grady, or anyone else, would believe she was rearranging her "junk" when she suddenly grabbed her crotch mid-conversation.

Mississippi checked his watch. "What time do you typically start banging pots and pans around in the diner?"

"Five. I suggest you buy some earplugs."

"So that means fresh coffee and cinnamon rolls will be there by the time I wake up?"

Be where exactly? Their deal was for room and board, not room and maid service. "If you think I'm going to serve you breakfast in bed, you can just lie there and keep dreaming."

"I didn't say 'in bed,' Penelope. However, if you want to

explore that idea—"

"No!" She held up her hand, trying to stop him, and then remembered the damned knife and lowered her hand just as quickly. "I was thinking about you being in bed and ... I mean, I wasn't thinking about you *in* bed, per se, only that ... well, if you were in bed, I wasn't going to ..."

Dear Lords of the Universe! How hard would it be to literally swallow her own tongue right now?

One look at him and her cheeks burned even hotter. The son of a bitch was obviously trying not to laugh, and only barely succeeding.

"I'm not adverse to the idea, Penelope," he said, his attention drifting south over her shirt, getting snagged along the route here and there.

She held very still, praying the knife didn't suddenly slip faster and end up as a noticeable bulge behind her zipper.

"Especially," Mississippi continued in a velvety voice, "if you delivered the goods wearing a French maid outfit."

His gaze returned to hers. There was no mistaking what sort of breakfast he'd want from her when she showed up in that costume.

She gulped.

"Actually," he said as he stepped closer, speaking for her ears only. "Scratch the apron and feather duster. With your gorgeous hair and amazing curves, I'm thinking more along the lines of a red and gold bustier, a short blue skirt with white stars, and a shiny tiara."

Penny pursed her lips. "Don't forget my golden lasso of truth and red boots."

"Red and white boots," he corrected. "And make sure you're wearing those bracelets of submission." He seemed to be struggling to keep his grin in check. "We should probably establish a safe word before we get started with that lasso. I have a feeling you might enjoy dominating me a little too much."

Yep. She definitely would. She sniffed, trying to play the cool cucumber when she felt like she'd just swallowed a handful of ghost peppers.

"As I said before, Special Agent Brown, you can just lie there in bed and keep dreaming."

He sucked air through his teeth. "I think my dreams tonight will be extra relaxing thanks to you, Penelope."

Her face warmed at the image of him in the sheets thinking about her ... or about Wonder Woman. Either way, he was naked in the sheets, and her brain needed to do an about-face and close the door on that peepshow right now.

She cleared her throat. "I should've clarified earlier that flirting with your landlady isn't allowed."

"No sex *or* flirting? Is this an apartment or a monastery I'm renting?"

"A bit of both." The Maya knife shifted in her pants, sliding down her belly another half an inch or so. *Yikes!* Time to go. "There are fresh sheets and blankets in the closet next to the bathroom. Sleep tight."

Head down, she glided as smoothly as possible toward the front door, pretending she was balancing a teacup and saucer on her head. She paused long enough to make sure Grady would be taking Mindy Lou home after her shift and then grabbed her vest on the way out.

Before she climbed inside her SUV, she glanced around to make sure she didn't have an audience and extracted the stupid knife, tucking it in the pocket in her driver's side door.

Inside her vehicle, she rested her head on the steering wheel. If this was a sign of what was to come with Kate Morgan, Penny was going to need to start buying tighter underwear.

The drive home in the dark was uneventful, leaving her mind plenty of opportunities to replay her ridiculous conversation with Mississippi.

Great globs of goulash, the man must think she was the biggest fool north of the Mexican border. First, she threw herself at him out of the blue last week and had randy octopus sex with him in his pickup. Then tonight, she brought up serving him breakfast in bed, and proceeded to stumble through the following *tête-à-tête* as if her tongue kept slipping on banana peels.

What happened to her old, sexy, confident self? Since when had flirting become so damned awkward? Maybe *old* was the key word there. Had her libido been broken along with her heart back in San Francisco?

Penny parked in front of her garage, which was currently filled with boxes of Mindy Lou's stuff. She grabbed her purse and the Maya knife. It really was pretty tissue paper. Butch must use it to ship cacti from his nursery.

Her solar walkway lights lined the path to her front patio. Shivering once again in the cold night breeze, she pulled out her keys to unlock the front door only to pause at the sight of an envelope duct-taped to it.

She stared at her name written on the letter, not recognizing the writing. Her gut tightened.

Stepping back from the door, she peered up and down her street. The neighbor's wind chimes dinged and clanged. Several houses down, a tumbleweed meandered across the road. A couple of coyotes howled and laughed up on the hillside behind her house, their calls sounding more lonely than eerie.

No sign of human life to be seen.

Penny returned to her door and pulled the envelope and tape free, scowling at the sticky spot left on the wood.

She unlocked the door and stepped inside, securing the deadbolt as soon as she'd closed out the world. She turned on the overhead hall light and tore open the envelope. At the sight of the familiar writing on the paper inside of it, she sighed with relief. Aunt Millie must have had one of her friends deliver the note.

Come to the library tomorrow at 2:30 pm. We have something you're going to want to see.

Penny took the paper along with the tissue-wrapped knife into her bedroom, hiding both in a shoebox in the back corner of her closet. Tomorrow, she'd take the knife to the diner and hide it there. She had the perfect little cubby hole for it.

After a quick hot shower to help her relax, she climbed into bed, double-checking that her alarm clock was set.

Okay. She would not think of Mississippi Brown tonight. Not about his eyes or his ass or his lips. Nope. She would meditate her way to sleep by trying to conjure each variety of cacti she'd captured in her camera lens over the last few years, one at a time.

When she went to put her phone on silent mode, she noticed a text from a number she didn't recognize.

She pulled the message up on the screen:

Grady and Elizabeth sitting in a tree, K-I-S-S-I-N-G.
First comes love, second comes marriage, third comes a visit to Penny by the
local health inspector.
Good luck with your white-gloved colonoscopy!

She slammed her phone down on the bed and flopped back onto her pillows.

"Son of a fucking bitch!" she yelled at the ceiling.

Chapter Fourteen

Thursday, January 31st

It had been a while since Ronnie slept with anyone other than Grady. So, when she awoke with the early morning sunshine blasting her through a strange window, it took her several blinks to remember where she was and how she'd landed in Claire's bed.

The previous evening's highlights replayed in her head—getting caught screwing around with Grady in Butch's office; nearly falling over at the sight of her cousin walking unannounced into The Shaft; staying up late with Claire and Luke in the General Store while reminiscing about old times and catching up on their current lives.

It had been ages since Ronnie had seen Luke, who traveled all over the place, working on government-based construction projects for long periods of time. He'd pulled into the RV park yesterday with his fifth wheel, and Gramps had given him a space back near the new restrooms. How long he'd be here depended on how long he wanted to take a break between jobs, according to him.

A few years younger than his sister, Natalie, Luke had set his sights on traveling the world early on, whereas Nat had been happy to stay put in the Black Hills. He shared his sister's brown hair color, strong cheekbones, and full lips, along with a stout work ethic and a wicked sense of humor—the latter blending well with Claire's and Katie's.

Chester was going to be giddy to have a new testosterone-filled male to pal around with after being stuck with Ronnie and her sisters as his main companions for the last few weeks.

And Claire was thrilled to have extra help with building the bird viewing platform. She'd told Luke about the brewery last night, too, obviously fishing to see if he was interested in working on that project—which he was. So, Claire had gone to sleep with a smile on her face. Ronnie only hoped that Mac would feel the same about more of Claire's family getting involved with their bar baby. Having lived with Mac and Claire in Tucson for a couple of months, she'd learned that he liked to be part of the planning as well as the doing.

But that was Claire's problem, not hers.

After a nice slow stretch, Ronnie sat up. She frowned at her sister's clothes strewn here and there and everywhere, and then chuckled. Some things never changed. Poor Mac. A life with Claire meant messy days and crazy adventures. He'd spend half of his life cleaning up the disasters left in her wake. The guy must really be nuts about her sister to want to tie himself to her with a bar and a house and maybe someday marriage, if Claire ever fully got over being allergic to matrimony.

Ronnie looked into the mirror above the dresser, staring back at the wild-haired woman sitting up in the bed. Then again, she wasn't much different from Claire nowadays, clear down to the Foghorn Leghorn T-shirt she'd borrowed from her sister to use as pajamas. Chaos ruled Ronnie's days and anxiety whispered sweet terrors in her ears most nights. The fact that Grady wanted her in spite of the nightmare her life had become still floored her.

And if that bitch ex-wife of his thought she could flounce back in, remove the knife she'd buried in his back, and return to his warm bed again, she had another think coming.

A glance at the clock had Ronnie scrambling off the bed and fishing through Claire's clothes for something to wear for the day. She really needed to go shopping and stop bumming off her sister. Stupid fire. Gramps's Winnebago was yet another victim of her mother's post-divorce spiral. Ronnie hoped like hell that her mom didn't rush back here before she'd figured out how to work through the issues that had made living near her over the last few months absolutely hellish.

She headed to the bathroom to shower and get ready for another day of work at The Shaft. The toiletry bag she kept at Ruby's place was basically a clone of what she kept under Grady's sink, just in case she needed to come back "home" for a night or two. As much as she loved playing house with him night after night, the idea of jumping fully into his life still filled her stomach with killer bees.

Okay, today's to-do list started with a trip to Yuccaville to pick up a few cleaning supplies for The Shaft. She liked it better when Katie had taken care of the runs to the grocery store, but there were only so many times Grady could let her sister out of jail after getting into altercations in the parking lot without slapping Katie with a misdemeanor.

Ronnie's problem with picking up groceries was that she often felt like someone was following her. Even more so after that text she'd received at the store yesterday. She'd shared that creepy text and the phone number from which it came with Grady last night before he took Mindy Lou home, asking him to look into who was behind it without involving the FBI. He'd left her with a worried frown on his face, promising to check it out first thing this morning. A quick check on her phone as she toweled dry showed nothing from him on that front yet.

By the time Ronnie made it out to the kitchen, Claire and Luke were long gone, as was the breakfast Ruby had made to spoil her visiting step-grandson. Ronnie grabbed a mug from the cupboard and poured herself a cup of coffee.

"Where's Gramps?" she asked as she joined Ruby at the table.

Her step-grandma was enjoying a glass of tomato juice and a piece of toast while looking through a printout filled with columns of names and phone numbers.

She looked up at Ronnie, a smile warming her freckled cheeks. "He went out to check on the supplies in the restrooms with the dog," Ruby said in her soft southern drawl, leaning back in her chair. Her red hair was pulled back in a ponytail this morning, but some of the curls had escaped already. "Said when he finished restocking them, he was fixin' on heading back to the ravine to check on Claire, Luke, and Kate. Although I'm not certain Kate has shown up yet because her car isn't out front, but maybe Butch dropped her off when I wasn't payin' attention."

Oh, dear. Claire was not going to love having a supervisor on site. Gramps might be very generous to his family and rock-solid as a leaning post when dust devils tore through any of their lives, but when it came to supervising construction projects he was a royal pain in the ass. And so was his dog, Henry, although Katie had always adored the nosy beagle. Barking orders and nitpicking details was his specialty—Gramps, not the dog—especially after a lifelong career of being a general contractor.

Claire was the only one in the family who stood up to him when he snarled at the end of his chain. She would growl right back. Actually, Ruby did, too, now. Ronnie tended to scuttle away when Gramps's neck bristled, not wanting to get bit; whereas Katie cranked up the honey production, trying to sweeten his saltiness, which made Ronnie and Claire roll their eyes. This was why in Gramps's opinion, Katie could do no wrong.

Ruby pointed toward the stove. "There's leftover ham in that pan, if you're looking for some protein with your yogurt this morning."

"Thanks." Ronnie scooped up one of the two pieces and stuck it partway in her mouth as she grabbed some pineapple yogurt out of the fridge. She joined her step-grandmother at the table, settling in for a quick meal before hitting the road.

"Did Claire mention anything about leaving her keys for me?" While collapsing on the bed last night next to her sister, Ronnie had asked if she could borrow Claire's Jeep to get to Yuccaville this morning, since she didn't have any wheels herself and Claire would be busy most of the day working on the platform out back.

Ruby nodded. "She said to tell ya they're hangin' on the key rack and not to get a scratch on her Jeep, or she'll burn the few clothes you've bought since the fire."

Ronnie smiled. "I'd expect nothing less from Claire."

"So, how's it happen ya spent the night here last night, darlin'?" Ruby asked. "You didn't get into a tussle with the sheriff, did ya?"

"No tussle. Mindy Lou needed a ride home last night when her shift was over. Grady was pretty wiped by then, so I told him to take his niece home and then grab some shut-eye. I got a ride back here with Claire so I could catch up with Luke and find out what he's been doing since we saw him last."

"Well, I sure am glad to hear that all is still good with Grady and you. Especially after what I overheard the other day when I was gettin' my hair done in Yuccaville about that ex-wife of his."

After talking to Gary last night about Elizabeth's lies, Ronnie had an idea about what Ruby had heard. "Grady and I are fine. Better than fine, actually."

If only Ronnie didn't have such a black cloud following her around thanks to Lyle, making her afraid of the shadows and shrouding her future possibilities with Grady. The last thing she wanted to do was smudge his shiny badge with her muddy past.

Her uncertain future was one of the reasons she tiptoed around Grady whenever he mentioned something about her moving in with him after his new house was built. She loved him, but the guy deserved a woman who would be free and clear to put down roots, especially if he continued on as the sheriff of Cholla County after this year's election.

Ruby's eyes narrowed. "I'd hate for that ex-wife of his to ruin the good thing Grady and you seem to have goin'."

Me too. Ronnie dipped her spoon into the yogurt, scooping out a minuscule bite of pineapple that was sweet on her tongue. "What are you looking at there?" She pointed her spoon at the papers in front of Ruby.

"Next month's reservations. Thanks to Jessica's website, we're almost clear filled up." Ruby leaned both elbows on the table. "Ronnie, I'd like to hire you to help me with my tax bookkeeping for last year. I need to hand it off to the CPA your grandfather hired in the next month. The work is partly done, but with the increased spending done to build the restroom and the back deck, plus some influx of capital thanks to your grandfather, there's a good amount left to do." She held up the papers with the reservations. "And I'm too busy trying to run the place with all of these extra folks millin' around now."

"I'm happy to help you out in exchange for the spare room you provide whenever I need it." Ronnie glanced at the time and then got serious about finishing her yogurt. "And food," she said between spoonfuls.

Of course, her helping Ruby was based on her making it through the next month without being snuffed out by one of her ex-husband's enemies. With the way Lyle's troubles kept rolling downhill and burying her up to her hips in alligators and electric eels, she wondered how much longer it would be until Mississippi came to her with the news that a permanent change of name and zip code was needed to keep her safe.

Where did they hide people away in the Witness Protection Program, anyway? She'd always figured a small town in the desert would do, but she'd already tried on this dusty identity and was well on her way to wearing holes in the knees and elbows.

"I appreciate your help, darlin'," Ruby said. "If you don't mind, I'll gather the paperwork and get you set up in the basement office next to the laptop computer Mac brought from Tucson. Then you can stop by whenever it works with your schedule at the bar."

"Sounds great." Ronnie set her spoon and the empty yogurt carton down. "I might bunk with Claire a few times a week while Mac's down south, so that I can get up early and dig into your bookwork."

Ruby reached across the table and squeezed Ronnie's arm. "Honey, you know you're welcome to stay anytime. I was just telling Harley this morning that it might be good to build a couple of one-room cabins in those camping spots between here and the laundry. That would give us some room to house more family, like you if Grady is out of town, or Luke or Natalie when they come to visit." She wrinkled her freckled forehead. "Maybe even your mother, if Manny gets tired of her bitchin'."

Ronnie grimaced, reaching for her coffee. "Let's not get ahead of ourselves here. I prefer Mom being in a house on wheels. That way, Manny can roll her out of here now and then to give us all a break."

Ruby chuckled. "I like the way you think, Ronnie."

After gulping down her coffee and checking in with Butch via text to confirm what all he needed from the grocery store before she picked up Mindy Lou for work, Ronnie said good-bye to Ruby. She hit the road in Claire's Jeep.

Yuccaville was busy this morning with more traffic than usual clogging up Main Street.

"What the heck?" Ronnie turned down a side street. Had there been a parade this morning? Was it some holiday she couldn't remember? That would explain why Grady was taking so long to get back with her on her anonymous texter.

The same was true in the grocery store parking lot. People were hurrying in and out of the store, leaving carts in the way and driving like assholes. Ronnie was forced to park clear at the back of the lot, so that Claire's Jeep didn't get any door dings from the big pickups spilling over the lines in the few remaining close-up spots.

Inside the store, Ronnie grabbed a basket instead of a cart since her grocery list was short today. Dodging busybodies who came rushing out the end of an aisle without worrying who might be walking past, she grabbed the two jugs of ammonia Butch needed, a package of sponges, and a can of vanilla, double-shot espresso coffee for herself. Her late night was going to catch up to her at some point today.

The self-service cashier line took twice as long as usual due to the extra shoppers. She pocketed the can of coffee and sponges, leaving both of her hands open to carry the jugs of ammonia. When she headed outside into the cool morning sunshine, a loud rumble of exhaust greeted her.

She waited outside the store's doors as a pack of motorcycles rolled along in front of her, backing up the lot's exit. Inching along behind them was a mud-rimmed, jacked-up old Ford, followed by a sparkling clean, blue pickup. As the line of traffic crawled forward, Ronnie glimpsed between the vehicles and saw a familiar face dressed in a desert camouflage coat.

"Sadie," she called out with a smile, happy to see a familiar face in the crowd, but the growl of exhaust drowned out her voice.

She set one of the jugs at her feet and waved, but Sadie seemed to be focused on the driver of the blue pickup. Like super focused. So much so that Sadie didn't notice the dually truck that was backing out right behind her.

With a black water tank filling the truck's bed, Ronnie doubted the driver could see Sadie out the rear window. The stack of two-by-six boards jutting out the back of the bed should have made him extra cautious. Hell, the red flags dangling off the end of the boards certainly caught Ronnie's eye. Unfortunately, Sadie was standing right in his blind spot, seconds from either getting jousted by the boards or hit by the back bumper.

"Sadie!" Ronnie yelled, taking several steps out into the street, but the blue pickup rolled forward and blocked her, coming to a complete stop right in front of her.

Scowling at the meathead in a black beanie behind the wheel, who was staring out at her like he knew her, she motioned for him to back up. "Get out of the way!"

Instead, he rolled down his window and leaned forward.

Behind his head, through his passenger window, Ronnie could see Sadie reaching into her jacket for something, clueless that she was seconds away from getting creamed.

"Shit!" Dropping the other jug of ammonia, Ronnie raced around the back of the blue truck.

"Watch out!" she yelled as she sprinted toward Sadie. She came at her from the side, grabbing Sadie by the coat and yanking her out of the way with only a second or two to spare.

Sadie grunted in surprise, stumbling along with Ronnie between a van and a compact car.

"Damn, girl," Ronnie said as they righted themselves. "You came this close to getting clocked."

"What?" Sadie adjusted her coat, zipping it up to her neck. She frowned at the white dually pickup.

The driver was apparently still oblivious that he'd almost hit a pedestrian, because he was already easing into traffic without even glancing their way.

Turning back to Ronnie with a furrowed brow, Sadie ordered, "Stay right here, Veronica."

Ronnie watched her rush out into the path of traffic. Where was she going now? Did she have some kind of death wish this morning?

Sadie jogged after the blue truck driven by the meathead with the black beanie, which was now turning out of the lot. But if she were trying to catch it, she was too slow. She paused off to the side of the line of traffic, staring after the rig until it disappeared around a corner the next block up. When Sadie returned, a scowl was firmly in place, sending even more deep vertical lines up the middle of her forehead.

"Do you know that guy in the blue truck?" Ronnie asked.

"No," Sadie said quickly. "Why? Do you?"

"Not at all, but you were so focused on him that you didn't even realize that other bozo was backing into you."

"I was just distracted by something," Sadie said. She rubbed her hand down her face, her dark eyes narrowed as she looked at Ronnie. "Oh, hell! You saved me, didn't you?" She sounded pissed about it, too.

"Not on purpose," Ronnie said, feeling defensive.

"You even went out of your way this time." Sadie growled and shook her fists at the sky, clearly annoyed.

"I didn't really risk my life. I mean, the traffic was creeping along." Unlike now. It appeared with the bottleneck of bikers gone, things were moving smoothly again in the parking lot.

"What is it with you and this guardian angel shit?"

"Golly gee." Ronnie crossed her arms. "I'm sorry I didn't want to watch you get your head bashed in, but blood and brains weren't on my grocery list for today."

"Damn it." Sadie scowled toward the store. "Now I owe you double."

"You don't owe me anything!" Ronnie didn't get it. Why was Sadie's anger aimed at her instead of the jerk who had almost rammed her? "I was just here at the right time."

"Once again, Veronica races to the rescue," Sadie complained.

Someone needed to file a police report this morning, because Sadie had been robbed of all her common sense.

"Christ," Ronnie said under her breath. "Listen, Sadie, let's just chalk this up to a bout of bad luck and call it good. I need to get to work now."

Ronnie hurried back to where she'd left the jugs of ammonia, which were still sitting next to the curb. Unfortunately, the jug she'd dropped had cracked upon impact with the cement, but it was a small fracture and had leaked only a small trickle onto the ground.

Crud. She hesitated on taking it with her to The Shaft, not wanting it to leak in Claire's rig. But she didn't want to go back inside the busy store and buy another one either, so she picked up the jug and tipped it so that the crack was facing upward. Maybe there was a way to get it to The Shaft without further spillage. She grabbed the other jug by the handle and strode toward Claire's Jeep at the back of the lot.

Sadie joined Ronnie along the way, matching her stride for stride in her combat boots and black pants. "You have to let me pay you back for saving my life, Veronica."

"I told you before, I don't want your money." She paused next to Claire's Jeep and set the uncracked jug on the ground, carefully balancing the other one while she fished for the keys.

Sadie took the cracked jug from Ronnie, freeing up her hands. "You don't understand. I can't have my ledger unbalanced like this."

"What is with you and this 'ledger' of yours?" Ronnie gave her a sideways scowl. "Are you an accountant?"

"Sort of."

"Well, you're just going to have to figure out how to get by with an uneven balance sheet, because I don't want your stupid money."

She unlocked the Jeep and set the undamaged jug on the floor behind the driver's seat. Then she took the cracked jug from Sadie. "You think this will spill if I wedge it in here somehow with the crack facing up?"

"Yes, I do, and I also think you're making my situation way harder than it's supposed to be."

"Because I kept you from getting clocked in the head today?" Ronnie scoffed. "That doesn't make any sense."

She walked around to the back of the Jeep, opening the tailgate. Maybe Claire had something that could keep a dripping jug from leaking.

Sadie followed Ronnie. "It makes total sense if you knew me."

"Well, I don't know you. And frankly, I'm starting to regret saving your mother from choking on that dang grape. No offense to your mom, of course."

Ronnie frowned at the black crate in the back of the Jeep. It held several of Claire's tools and a blanket, but nothing that would help with the leaky jug.

"And then you had to go and pull me out of the line of fire today," Sadie added to Ronnie's list of life-saving faults.

"Yeah. What in the hell was I thinking?" Ronnie shook her head in exasperation. "Silly me. I should have just let you get clocked and maybe run over by those double back tires."

"They would have flattened me into a human pancake covered in blood syrup."

Ronnie cringed. "Gross."

"Yeah, I've seen how that ends before."

"Right." Wait, was she serious?

Sadie unzipped her camouflage coat and pulled out a roll of duct tape from somewhere. Then she fished into another side pocket and came out with a black jackknife. In a flash, she had the crack in the plastic bandaged with the tape. Then she stuck the ammonia in the crate taped side up and secured it with the blanket so it wouldn't move.

"There." Sadie tucked her knife and duct tape back into her coat. "You should be good until you get to The Shaft."

Ronnie stared down at Sadie's bulky coat. What else did she carry in her pockets? "Do you always come to the grocery store with duct tape and a big knife hidden in your coat?"

"Sure," Sadie said. "You never know who might need sliced or taped."

"You mean *what*."

"Is that a question?"

"No, you said 'who might need sliced.' I was correcting you so that it was 'what might need sliced.' "

Sadie smirked. "Your constructive criticism has been noted, Veronica, and fuck you very much for it."

"You're beginning to sound like my sisters." Ronnie closed the back of the Jeep, returning to the driver's side. "Thanks for your help with the jug. Now we're even."

Sadie huffed. "Please. I taped a jug. You saved my life. Twice now."

"No, I saved two different lives—yours and your mom's."

Sadie's eyes widened slightly. "Yeah, that's what I meant. By saving my mom, you saved me, because I'd have died from a broken heart."

"Okay, then my non-heartbroken pal, I'll see you around." She smiled at Sadie, because the woman still looked miserable about not getting creamed by that pickup. "Cheer up, frowny Fran. Next time I'll let you *almost* die."

Sadie stepped back as Ronnie closed the door and started up the Jeep. In the rearview mirror, she watched Sadie's scowl as she drove away.

"That was kind of weird," she muttered to herself, focusing back on the road in front of her.

What were the odds of her running into Sadie at the store again, anyway? Maybe she should mention something to Grady about the woman now. But it was the only grocery store in Yuccaville, and Grady had enough on his plate, including that anonymous text message, about which he still hadn't gotten back to her.

Also, Sadie obviously wasn't out to hurt Ronnie. On the contrary, she seemed more clumsy than dangerous.

Maybe Elizabeth had hired Sadie to follow Ronnie around solely to mess with her. But if that were true, Sadie wasn't very good at her job, and she kept bumbling her stalking routine.

Ronnie turned onto Penny's street. Up ahead, Mindy Lou stood out by the mailbox, waiting for her with a smile. When she pulled up, Grady's niece hopped inside.

"Nice wheels," she said to Ronnie.

"It's Claire's Jeep."

"I like your sister's style. She's pretty funny, too."

"Yeah, she's always been the comedian in the family." Ronnie had often wished she had Claire's sense of humor, especially when it came to some of the mishaps with her own love life. "And Katie was the spoiled one."

"What does that make you?"

"The oldest and wisest sister," she said, grinning at Mindy Lou. "Actually, I was the most boring."

"You don't seem so boring to me, or to my uncle, judging by the way he keeps eyeing you while you work." The girl set her purse on the console between them and then buckled in. "You actually remind me of Aunt Penny—strong and reliable."

Reliable was still boring. However, Ronnie would prefer to be unexciting right now. Especially to someone who might be looking to cut off her fingers, wrap them in a bow, and mail them to Lyle.

"Guess what I heard through the grape vine?" Mindy Lou asked as Ronnie pulled away from the curb.

"What?" She paused for a stop sign.

"That Uncle Grady has proposed to Elizabeth again."

Ronnie stomped on the brakes, sending Mindy Lou reaching for the dash. "He what?"

"Yeah, that's what I said. And according to the person telling me this juicy rumor, Elizabeth happily said 'Yes!' So, stay tuned for more details on their upcoming nuptials."

Ronnie's blood bubbled and boiled. "That bitch is messing with the wrong *other* woman."

Chapter Fifteen

I think we need to call Sophy Wheeler," Kate announced to Claire from her high and mighty perch on the lawn chair. Give her a feathered cap, and Kate would fit right in with the pair of Gambel's quail meandering between the birding platform and Jackrabbit Creek, clucking and crowing with their jaunty black topknots curving forward off the top of their heads. "And we need to do it right now."

The queen has spoken!

The Mad Red Queen was more like it, Claire thought, shaking her head.

For the last ten minutes, Kate had wasted a lot of hot air about how the sheriff's ex-wife needed to be taken down a notch and then run out of town. Her reasoning included a long list of Elizabeth's crimes not only against Ronnie and Penny, but against humanity in general. Claire figured her banana-brained sister was only a few baby hormone flare-ups from shrieking, "Off with her head!"

She looked up from tightening a lag bolt into one of the three beams that Luke and Chester had helped her haul out to the platform earlier. "I think we should finish securing these beams to the posts first." Claire pointed at the box on the ground near Kate's upside-down bucket footstool. "Grab a few of those bolts and bring them over here, Pregzilla."

"You didn't say *please*."

Claire made a face at Kate. "Kiss my grits, chicken lips, and bring me the damned bolts."

Kate walked over with a handful of bolts from the box. "Quit putting this phone call off, you big wuss." She blocked the warm late-morning sun, casting Claire in her shadow. "Let's make the call to Sophy before Chester and Luke get back with the rest of the beams."

"They're bringing joists, not more beams."

"Nobody likes a know-it-all, Claire."

"Then how in the world do you live with yourself, Miss My-IQ-Is-The-Highest?"

Kate jammed her hands on her hips, which made the baby bump under her red sweatshirt stick out even more. "You're stalling."

Maybe, but for good reason.

"We need to wait for Chester. You were perfectly fine with him being here the last time we talked to her." Claire moved to the next concrete footer, holding her gloved hand out for Kate to give her one of the bolts.

Truthfully, she wanted Chester to make the phone call. He'd made a good buffer between Claire and the shotgun-happy harpy last time.

"Yeah, but Luke is here today." Giving Claire one of the bolts, Kate frowned toward the RV park. "I don't think we should involve him in any of our adventures."

Claire had felt the same last month when a diamond killer was hunting her and Ronnie, and Luke's sister had shown up. But in the end, Natalie was family, so she'd been dragged into the posse and had ended up helping take down the killer. Without Natalie, Claire might still have a target on her ass.

Hell, if Joe was truly back from the not-so-dead, she could still be wearing a bull's-eye yet.

She squinted up at Kate. "Why not include Luke? I thought you were big on family bonding."

Truthfully, Claire had her own reasons for *not* wanting to drag Luke into several of the dust devils swirling down in these parts, especially considering the level of troublemakers they'd encountered over the last year. However, she could definitely use his help building the platform, and maybe the brewery, too, if he stuck around long enough. With Mac bouncing back and forth between Bisbee and Jackrabbit Junction, Luke showing up right now was a godsend.

Make that a *Natalie*-send, since Luke had told Claire last night that his sister had phoned him a couple of weeks ago. Natalie had put a bug in his ear about coming south to help his cousins the next time he was in between contracting jobs, such as now.

Kate squatted next to Claire, casting another glance toward the trail back to the RV park. "Family is important, but we don't need another person nosing into our business. Right now only Chester, me, and you know about Sophy. I think we need to keep it that way." She focused on Claire, a mob boss glare in place. "You didn't tattle to Mac, did you?"

Chuckling, Claire tightened the lag bolt. "No, Ms. Hyde. We haven't had a chance to talk since last night when you hung up on him. Before I could call him back, Luke showed up, so I texted Mac that my cousin was in town and I'd catch up with him tonight when he was back in his hotel room."

"Good. Mac will screw everything up."

What? Since when had Mac become Kate's enemy?

"How will Mac mess up your diabolical plans? The poor guy is three hours away working his sweet buns off."

"Mac is wily."

Claire's guffaw echoed through the ravine. "Mac is not wily. He's the least crafty person I know. He tells it as it is, straight and clear, whether you want to hear it or not."

And sometimes Claire didn't, but Mac's honesty and rock-solidness were some of his finest qualities. Boulders were less sturdy than him in a storm, and Claire had been through enough tempestuous situations since meeting the guy to know this for a fact.

"He's not a saint, Claire."

"He's surely not," she told Kate with a grin. "A saint wouldn't do the wicked things Mac does to me during sex."

Kate cringed. "Come on! I'm going to be working with that man on a daily basis soon. I don't want to think about you and him doing anything more than playing patty-cake."

"Is it naked patty-cake?" Claire teased, laughing at her sister's visible squirminess.

"Stop before I throw up the eggs and toast Ruby made me for breakfast."

"Fine, wimp. But quit making Mac out to be a villain."

"Tell him to quit watching me through his X-ray vision goggles."

"He's not 'watching' you, Kate. He's 'watching out for you' because he cares about you. That's what Mac does. He's a protector."

"I'm a protector, too," Kate said, thumbing at her own chest. "That's all I'm trying to do around here, make sure nobody hurts my family, but you guys keep calling me 'crazy' and trying to keep me tied up and locked away." She stood and kicked at a tuft of weeds. "I'm not even allowed to go to the damned grocery store anymore."

"Because you keep getting into altercations there."

"None of those were my fault."

"None?" Claire stopped tightening the bolt and stared up at Kate.

"Well." Kate crossed her arms. "It might be possible that one or two of them could maybe have been caused by a slight lack of patience on my part, but each time I was merely trying to stand up to bullies, and you know that, Claire."

"Jeez, Kate. Could you fit any more qualifiers into that half-assed acknowledgment of guilt?"

"Probably."

Claire shook her head and returned to the bolt. "I'm not sure we should call Sophy without Chester because she might not want to talk to you. And I seriously doubt she'll be willing to speak to me."

"Why not you? She's the one who tried to shoot *you*, remember? Not the other way around."

"Of course I remember that, spudnut. But I'm the one who sneaked not only into her shed, but her house, too. She doesn't take kindly to trespassers." Sophy had made that clear while her double-barreled shotgun was aimed at Claire.

Kate blew a raspberry. "That's in the past. Now that she's spent a few months in prison, I'm sure she's moved on to a new woman to hate. Someone who is even more annoying than you. Although after putting up with your bossy butt for three decades, I find it hard to believe such a person might exist."

Claire flipped off Kate's wide grin. "Bite my bossy butt."

"I'll leave that to your great protector when he gets back from Bisbee." Kate pulled out her cell phone. "Fine. If you don't want to do the talking, I will. I've been around enough outraged parents to be able to handle talking to a vindictive ballbreaker like Sophy."

"Kate." Claire stood, frowning as her sister scrolled on her phone's screen. "This is a bad idea. Besides, don't we need to let Sophy know ahead of time that we're calling so that she's waiting by the prisoners' phone?"

In Claire's imagination, there was a line of payphones on a wall where the prisoners were allowed to make and take calls. She'd seen that in a movie once or twice. Or maybe there was only one payphone with all sorts of graffiti written on the concrete block wall next to it.

"What happened to you, Claire?" Kate tapped on the phone's screen. "You used to run headlong into trouble without worrying if it was a good idea or bad."

"You're right, I did. And then I got shot, drowned, clocked upside the head with a shotgun, and forced to tread water at the bottom of a shaft next to a dead body. Excuse me for entertaining caution these days when it comes to staring death in the face yet again."

Kate rolled her eyes. "Leave the drama to Ronnie. That's her specialty." She tapped on the phone screen again, and then lifted the phone to her ear. "I'd like to speak to ADC inmate number 550279."

Claire leaned back on her heels, frowning at her sister, who had rattled off that number from memory. And what had happened to the robot-voice answering machine? Had Sophy given Kate some other number to call at some point?

Did Butch have any idea how much Kate was burrowing around under the surface these days? Because Claire was beginning to wonder what exactly her little sister was up to when she wasn't here in the ravine with her, bitching about having to help build a birding platform … if one called sitting on her butt in a lawn chair while watching Claire work "helping."

"Yes," Kate said into the phone. "Sophy Wheeler is awaiting our call."

Claire's heart began to pound harder and faster. Shit. Were they really doing this right now? She looked toward the RV park, wishing Chester was rumbling this way in the UTV so he could do the talking. But the path was empty.

"It's ringing," Kate whispered and put the phone on speaker.

Her eyes were bright with excitement when she looked up at Claire. Then the left side of her face twitched several times, like it'd been struck by a series of lightning bolts. Maybe it wasn't excitement she saw in Kate's eyes, rather a glimpse of the mad monkey who was running the controls at the moment.

"Here." Kate caught Claire's wrist and shoved the phone into her hand. "You do the talking."

"I don't want to talk to her!" Claire shoved the phone back at her sister, but Kate dodged and darted out of reach.

"You're late," Sophy's voice came from the phone before Claire could chase down her bratty sister.

Claire stared down at the phone in her hand as if it had a pair of antennae, bulging eyes, and sharp pinchers.

"Hey!" Sophy said. "Either start talking or the deal is off, and you can try to find out about that thieving, backstabbing bastard on your own."

"What do you want me to say?" Claire asked her old nemesis while glaring daggers at her sister.

Silence came through the line for a couple of seconds.

"Welllll, I'll be." Sophy was long on the drawl and short on the honey, her tone downright scathing. "If it isn't the nosy, trespassing two-bit sneak."

"Hello, Sophy. Life's been good with you gone."

A crusty laugh came through the speaker, sounding like two packs of cigarettes a day for thirty years or so. "I bet it has. Especially with you stumblin' onto Joe's hidden treasures left and right. You do know that he's gonna skin yer hide when he realizes you've done gone and fucked up his retirement plans, don't ya?"

"*If* Joe is still alive," Claire said, "that dickhead is going to be living out his golden years behind bars. Same as you."

"Oh, sugar, I'm sorry to piss in your punchbowl, but one of us ain't gonna dance to that jailhouse rock tune."

"What's that supposed to mean?" Claire asked.

"For one thing, Joe ain't gonna be found that easily." Sophy sniffed. "And frankly, I'm not so sure you have the backbone to hunt him down and trap him. And I know you don't have the smarts."

"You underestimate me," Claire said.

"Me, too," Kate chimed in.

"Who is that?" Sophy asked.

"Kate Morgan."

"Ahh. The one who's been sending me the emails."

Claire gave Kate a dirty look. How deep was her sister in this Joe business already? Hip? Neck? Over her head?

"So, you two bumpkins think you can handle Joe Martino?"

"Maybe," Claire said, unwilling to admit otherwise in the face of Sophy's doubt.

But probably not. Hell, there were mornings when Claire wasn't sure she could handle fastening her bra right, let alone hunting down and capturing a longtime, conniving thief who'd managed to fake his death so well that even his wife didn't suspect any different.

"You two greenhorns do realize that he's killed before—and more than once—for lesser crimes than someone stealin' one of his sparkly picks?"

"Quit trying to scare us, Sophy," Kate said, sounding tougher than Claire felt at the moment.

Criminy, how many people had Joe killed? And how exactly? Was it via a sniper rifle while he laid low back in a ravine like the one they were standing in right now?

Claire scanned the trees and scrub brush farther back in the ravine, a fresh bead of sweat on her upper lip. And had the creep been smoking cigars while he waited for his target to line up in his crosshairs? Because she had a fresh stash of cigar butts from nearby this very spot that were now sealed in a baggie back at Ruby's house.

"As Claire told you," Kate continued, "we're ready to deal. Tell us what you want in exchange for proof that the bastard is alive."

"It's your funeral."

Claire hoped like hell it wouldn't come to that.

"I need you to sneak into my house." Sophy's voice had lowered to a whisper. "Butch should still have the keys."

Do you know where the keys are? Claire mouthed to Kate.

Kate shook her head.

Damn. Step one, figure out where Sophy's keys were.

Kate turned suddenly toward the RV park. "Oh, crap," she whispered.

Claire heard it then. A low rumble.

She looked over her shoulder. Chester and Luke were on their way back in the UTV with a small trailer loaded down with joists bouncing along behind them.

Wait, that wasn't Chester. It was … Oh, double crap!

Her stomach tightened at the sight of Gramps sitting next to Luke. If he found out they were talking to Sophy, he'd chew them ten ways from Sunday.

"What happens after we get inside your house, Sophy?" Claire pressed, exchanging a worried grimace with Kate.

"Go to my bedroom. You remember where that is, don't you, trespasser?"

"Of course."

Sophy huffed. "Under the dresser, you'll find what I need. As soon as I have it in my hands, I'll give you what you need."

Claire turned so her back was toward Gramps and Luke, not wanting them to see she was on the phone. "How are we supposed to get whatever we find to you while you're in prison?"

"That will be the easy part. Drop it in the mail."

"What's the tough part?" Claire glanced toward Kate and did a double-take. Her sister had a goofy smile on her face, hamming it up for Gramps and Luke as they pulled to a stop several yards away.

"Stayin' alive, sugar. Joe is gonna want to string you up and gut ya when he finds out you gave the diamonds he'd hidden in his El Camino to the law. And when he figures out what other treasures you've stolen from his retirement stash, he'll cut out your tongue and choke you to death with it."

The line went dead as the UTV's engine cut out.

Bloody blazes! Must Sophy be so graphic about how Joe would be killing her?

Claire pocketed Kate's phone and then turned to greet her grandfather and Luke, pretending she hadn't just learned the Grim Reaper would be swinging for her soon … again.

Chapter Sixteen

I, Kate Morgan, current commander-in-chief of the Prickly Pear Posse, officially call to order today's meeting."

Kate smiled at Penny, who'd shown up at the library meeting five minutes late still wearing a ketchup-stained apron with her diner's logo on it. At least she'd made it, saving Kate from being the sole worm repeatedly henpecked by the three attending members of the Geritol Gangsters.

"Did she say 'commander-in-cheese'?" Aunt Millie asked her second-in-command, Ruth. "My hearing aids aren't working so well today."

Penny leaned forward, looking closely at her aunt's ears. "That's because you don't have them in, Aunt Millie," she said loud enough for her aunt to hear.

"Shhhh," said the librarian at the front counter, frowning at Penny.

"Sorry, Ginger," Penny called back.

Ruth pointed her knitting needles at Kate. "What did the fertilized chubby bunny call us?"

Kate couldn't tell where the bulky, black hand-knitted sweater Ruth was wearing ended and where whatever black knitted creation the woman was working on now started. The old lady was one big bundle of yarn with pointy needles sticking out.

"I'm not a chubby bunny," Kate told her. "I'm pregnant."

"I know," Ruth said. "That's why I said you'd been fertilized."

"I think she called us some kind of prick," Greta said, lifting the reading glasses chained around her neck onto her nose.

Greta was the third member of Millie's gang of silver-haired bullies who'd shown up for the meeting. Built like a ripe, bottom-heavy pear, Greta was outfitted in a pink, blue, mustard yellow, and beige splotched sweater, with rhinestone sequins edging her pants, jacket, and glasses. According to Ronnie, the bling-covered woman could speak and read German, loved Humphrey Bogart, and thought mariachi players were really "sexy." Kate had to wonder if she was color-blind, too. Who wore that color combo these days? It was like somebody had eaten a shoulder-padded jacket from the late 1980s and then puked it back up onto Greta's chest.

The other two missing gangsters, whom Kate had only met one time, were stepsisters. Millie had informed her upon arrival that they couldn't make it this afternoon because they were on a double date with a guy. Penny had explained to her aunt that officially a double date meant two and two. Then, in turn, Millie had informed Penny that at their age, finding one guy who could still get the job done was like discovering a diamond in the rough. The chance of finding two roosters was slim, especially in a hard-working town like Yuccaville, where men started working at the mine at a young age and were lucky to make it past their sixtieth birthday party.

"A prick, huh?" Ruth snorted at Kate. "Sweetie, we're not men."

"I know you're not men." Kate crossed her arms. "I said 'prickly,' not prick."

"Who's being prickly now?" Millie snapped back.

Penny's aunt looked like she'd wandered in off the street fresh from a Day of the Dead parade. Behind the splattering of colorful candy skulls on her loose-fitting top and stretch pants, there were yellow, green, blue, and red flowers mottled on a black background. The whole ensemble dazzled all rational thoughts in Kate's head every time she stared at Millie too long. Knowing Millie's *modus operandi*, Kate figured she probably dressed this way on purpose to distract innocent passersby right before crushing their toes with her dingle ball–decorated walker.

Greta peered at Kate over the top of her reading glasses. "I think you're still mad at Millie for the tussle you started with her last summer."

"And lost," Millie added.

"I did not start that tussle, and I'm not mad at Millie anymore." Although given the opportunity to put a tack on the battleaxe's chair, Kate might be very tempted.

"What's a prickly bare pozzie?" Millie asked, her gaze drifting down to the front of Kate's pants. "Is that what you young girls call it when you give your hoo-ha a mohawk?"

Kate and Penny exchanged appalled looks.

Ruth cackled. "Kids these days think they invented microphone checks. They forget we were catching the crazy turkey long before they were born."

"What's a microphone check?" Penny whispered.

"Does 'catching the crazy turkey' mean chasing down wild turkeys?" Kate asked. She'd done that last Thanksgiving with her sisters. Were wild turkey roundups a common practice in southeastern Arizona?

All three of the older dames snickered at Penny's and Kate's ignorance.

"She's not much of a commander-in-cheese," Millie said to her pals, thumbing toward Kate.

"She said 'commander-in-chief,' " Penny told her aunt, adding extra enunciation to her words.

The librarian shushed Penny again, louder and longer this time.

"Sorry, Ginger." Penny added a wave as an addition to her apology.

Someone nudged Kate's shoulder. She looked around at the freckled face and long auburn eyelashes of Ruby's daughter, who was also Kate's sixteen-year-old step-aunt now that Gramps and

Ruby were husband and wife.

"How long are we going to be here?" Jessica whispered, smelling like the strawberry bubble gum Kate had seen the girl stick in her mouth earlier. "Hailey's foster mom just texted her. She wants some deets."

Early this morning, Butch had dropped Kate off at the RV park so he could change the oil in her Volvo and try to figure out why it was making an odd pinging sound when it idled. Having no car meant that Kate had needed to borrow Ruby's pickup in order to make it to Yuccaville in time for this secret meeting that she'd set up with the Geritol Gangsters and Penny. Unfortunately, borrowing Ruby's truck meant having to pick up Jess after school, along with a ninth-grade girl named Hailey, whom Jess was tutoring.

So now, Kate had Jessica and Hailey here in the library, along with Millie and her crew plus Penny, and none of them were letting her get a word in edgewise about the stupid old knife, which was why she'd called this meeting to order in the first damned place.

"What are deets?" Greta asked, glancing over her reading glasses as she pulled a ball of pink yarn from her knitting basket.

"I think they're one of those electronic cigarettes," Ruth answered.

"Deets is short for 'details,' you twits," Millie told them.

Kate checked her phone for the time. She had a little longer until Butch would probably call to check on her and see how her fake baby doctor's appointment went this afternoon. As much as she loved Butch, this constant supervision was getting out of hand. Next, he'd have the sheriff slap an electronic ankle shackle on her so she could be monitored at all times. Sheez o'mighty. It wasn't like she was going to do anything to wind up in jail again. It was simply a trip to the local library with two kids in tow.

"Tell Hailey's foster mom that you're going to be here at the library tutoring her for another half-hour," Kate said, and nudged Jess away. "Now go back in the study room and close the door."

She wanted the girl out of earshot for this business about the knife. Ruby didn't know anything about the ancient artifact that Deborah had found in her basement office, and Kate wanted to keep it that way for as long as possible.

"Fire, chill out. Claire's right. You're all pissy with lots of preggertude lately." Jess stomped off.

Whatever, Claire!

Turning back to Penny and the gangsters, Kate tried again. "I called this meeting to order to discuss a particular artifact that was found at a location I'd rather not say at this moment."

Ruth leaned over to Greta and whispered loud enough for all of them to hear, "Millie said she found it at the RV park down in that basement office."

"Why on Earth would some old-fashioned knife be down there?" Greta asked.

"It's not just old," Kate clarified. "It's ancient."

"So is Greta," Ruth said, smirking at her friend. "Hell, she used to babysit Hitler when he was just a baby."

"That's not funny, you ol' cow." Greta leaned over and poked Ruth in the shoulder with a knitting needle, earning a small shriek in return.

Millie fiddled with one of the twisted dingle balls on her walker. "Was this basement office the same place where that thieving donkey-dick, Joe, kept the antique watch Veronica was researching last fall?"

"Yes." Kate rubbed her hands together. "Now, before we go any further, do you ladies understand the full meaning of the word 'secret'?"

Ruth scowled. "We've been keeping secrets long before you first sucked eggs, chubby bunny."

Kate scowled back, not liking her new nickname. "I'll have you know that I have never sucked eggs in my life."

"Your loss, *fräulein*," Greta said. "Sucking eggs is a real treat."

Penny grinned at Kate. "Is this what you were hoping to achieve when you called this meeting to order?"

"Who did she call?" Millie asked, leaning closer to Penny while cupping her ear. "Is she ordering pizza, because I'm feeling a bit peckish."

"I said 'called this meeting to order,' " Penny clarified. "You really need to start carrying your hearing aids in your purse, Aunt Millie."

"Shhhh!" The librarian stood up this time to give Penny a hard glare.

Whoa, Kate thought. That was a lot of aggression steaming

out of one skinny librarian's blow hole. If Penny didn't watch it, she'd be banned from the library for six months, like Claire had been since last August.

Penny winced. "Sorry again, Ginger." She leaned forward and whispered to the group, "Why am I the only one getting shushed here when you guys are talking louder than me?"

"Because Ginger doesn't like you," Greta said.

Penny's mouth gaped. "Since when? What did I do to tick off Ginger?"

"Nothing, most likely," Ruth said, clacking away with her knitting needles. "But according to what the girl was telling me earlier, her cousin heard from someone else that you were badmouthing her behind her back a few days ago."

Wow, that was a lot of "hers" for Kate to sort through.

Penny's brow lined. "I was badmouthing Ginger?"

"No, Ginger's cousin." Millie huffed. "Maybe *you* need to get some hearing aids, Penelope Sue."

"Why would I badmouth her cousin?"

"Because her cousin runs the deli at the grocery store where you buy the meat and cheese for some of your lunch sandwiches."

Penny's frown deepened. "I didn't say anything about Ginger's cousin. Everything has been same as always in my dealings with the deli."

"Are you sure?" Kate asked, wondering if Deputy Dipshit was out stirring up trouble by spreading rumors. This time he was taking aim at Grady's sister instead of the Morgan girls. Maybe he'd heard that Penny was now a member of the Prickly Pear Posse. That stinky weasel needed to be taught a lesson once and for all.

"I'm positive," Penny said.

"Hey, Ginger," Millie called out loud enough to potentially earn a mouthful of shushing.

But Ginger looked their way with a smile for Millie. "Yes?"

"Who told your cousin that news about Penny backstabbing her?"

"I heard it from a very reliable source." Ginger glared a pair of holes at the supposed guilty party. "Penny, you of all people should know to be careful about running your big mouth in a small town."

"Who's your source?" Millie pressed.

Ginger lifted her chin. "Your soon-to-be niece once again—

Elizabeth."

Penny growled, muttering loud enough for Kate to hear, "That lowdown, dirty rotten skank."

"Congratulations on Grady's impending nuptials," the librarian said to Millie. "Elizabeth is such a nice girl. And so pretty, too."

Something fired in Kate's chest, singeing her esophagus.

No way. Nope. Nuh-uh. That wasn't happening. There was no way in hell that lying, uppity bitch was stealing Grady from Ronnie. Not while Kate was on duty.

For the moment, she curtailed all thoughts about the knife and centered her full attention on the librarian, whose head was apparently jammed so far up Elizabeth's ass that she could perform a thorough exam for polyps.

Kate cleared her throat. "Excuse me, Ginger. I'm new around this town, so maybe I'm confused about something."

"What's that?" Ginger asked, her composed, how-can-I-help librarian smile in place.

"Is this 'Elizabeth' you're talking about the very same philandering strumpet who just a few years ago was not only knocked up with another man's baby *while* married to our wonderful sheriff, but who also lied to him and all of the other shit-for-brains yokels—such as your pissy-faced self—in this fantastically turdy, one-donkey town?" Kate grinned extra wide at the librarian's pinched expression. "Or am I thinking of the wrong, no-count, sleazy, cheating fuck-tart?"

* * *

"And that's how Kate got banned from the library for six months." Penny ended her tale and blew out a breath, shaking the tension from her sore, slightly chapped hands.

She'd busted her buns all morning, giving the diner a good cleaning in preparation for a visit from the health inspector— damned Elizabeth, the delusional punk-ass hussy. Scouring, scrubbing, and polishing had almost made Penny late for the library meeting. Then Ginger, the librarian, had delivered that sucker punch, leaving her winded. How was she going to patch up the mess with the cheesed-off cousin situation at the deli?

"I appreciate the update, Penny," Grady said from the other side of his desk in the Cholla County sheriff's office. "But my question had nothing to do with what happened at the library. I'm more interested in hearing about how you ended up *here* this afternoon." He tapped his index finger on the desktop. "And why Kate Morgan has parked herself in one of my jail cells again."

"I can't speak for Kate. I'm not her attorney."

His amber-colored eyes narrowed, reminding her of their father. "Of all people," he said quietly, "you, the sheriff's sister, should know better than to get into an altercation with a deputy."

"Don't lecture me on how my actions affect your job, Grady." She crossed her arms. "Trust me, I learned years ago that so long as I live in the same town as you, I have to cruise at a certain speed and not cross the center line."

Especially when it came to her vices.

And her sex life.

His success came with sacrifices. Same as hers, actually. But she was too frustrated with him at the moment to give him any leeway.

"Answer the question, Penny," he said, sounding more weary than angry.

"It's Elizabeth's fault."

"Was she at the library with Kate and you?"

"Not in the flesh."

His brow wrinkled.

"Quit giving me that look, Grady. This is not Kate's fault. Your ex-wife is responsible for stoking several fires around town with her lies and slander, including this current blaze that was sparked by what Ginger told us at the library."

"That you were talking bad about Ginger's cousin?"

"Well, yes. That was the part that pissed me off because it's a lie that Elizabeth told in order to screw with my livelihood."

"And that lie is what set Kate off?"

"No, weren't you listening earlier?"

"The sheriff never listens when it comes to me," Kate hollered out from the jail cell down the hall.

Grady had tried to coax Kate out of her cell after he'd first arrived at the office and sent his deputy, Ernie, home. But Kate had refused to come out until the sheriff would acknowledge that she was totally innocent.

"Kate," Grady called back. "If you're going to insist on being part of this conversation, then join us at my desk. Otherwise, butt out."

"You butt out," Kate shot back. "You big galoot."

With a scowl adding even more lines to his face, Grady returned to Penny. "What lit the jailbird's fuse this time?"

"Your ex is also spreading word around town that you have asked her to marry you again." Penny smirked. "Congratulations, Grady. Elizabeth has accepted. Maybe the next kid will actually be yours."

Grady's jaw tightened. "Christ." He sat back in his chair and shook his head.

"So, you see, it's not Kate's fault."

"Really? You'd state that in a court of law?"

Uhhhh. Well. "It's not solely Kate's fault," Penny amended. "She was standing up for her sister, as any good sibling would do." Same as Penny had for Grady when it came to Elizabeth's attempts to blackmail her into switching teams. "When you look at the big picture, the match was lit by your ex."

His jaw tightened visibly.

Leaning over the desk, she added, "It's time for you to do something about her forked tongue, Grady, and these tall tales she keeps spreading around town."

He appeared to think on that for a moment, then sighed and shifted in his seat. "Connect the dots for me here. How does this tale of yours go from Ginger sharing the latest rumor about Elizabeth saying we're getting married again, to Kate knocking down my deputy and sitting on him in broad daylight right outside the library, to my deputy being accused of assault and attempted battery and Kate almost being charged with disturbing the peace?"

"It's your deputy's fault!" Kate called out from the cell at the other end of the hall.

"You're a broken record, Kate," Grady returned. "Well?" he pressed Penny.

She leaned back and looked down the hall. "Hey, Kate, you want to tell him the full story?"

There was a moment's pause, and then, "No. He'll believe his sister before me."

Penny turned to Grady. "Kate was in the process of doing as asked—exiting the premises—when she backed into your deputy."

"Backed into him?" At her nod, he pressed, "Explain."

"Kate was walking backward out through the library's doors, delivering a final message to Ginger, so her attention was directed inside the building."

"Let me guess, this so-called final message included a lewd gesture along with instructions of where the librarian could shove it."

"I was defending *your* girlfriend," Kate hollered from the other end of the hall. "Something that you might want to try if you know what's good for you, because if you hurt my sister, I'm going to hurt you."

Grady stood and walked over to the door at their end of the hallway leading to the cells. "Are you threatening an officer of the law, Kate?"

Silence.

As Grady turned back to Penny, Kate answered in a quieter, but firm voice. "You bet your ass I am, Sheriff. Ronnie's been screwed over enough this decade."

He paused and looked up at the ceiling. Then, without a word, he closed the door leading to the holding cells and returned to his desk, both eyebrows raised as he stared at Penny. "Continue with your story."

"As I said, Kate was backing out of the library while giving a somewhat dramatic exit performance. She wasn't looking where she was going and ran smack-dab into Ernie, who appeared out of nowhere."

"You mean my deputy just happened to be walking by at that very moment?"

"I know, it seems oddly coincidental." The scene replayed in Penny's head, including the rush of panic when Kate's arms flailed wildly as she started to fall. "But I was following her out, so I saw it all firsthand. One minute the path behind Kate was clear, the next, your deputy was there. And he wasn't merely passing by either. He was right in the way, so their feet got tangled and they both fell. Thankfully, Kate landed on top of him, which was a good thing because he broke her fall. Otherwise, she might have hurt herself, or worse, the baby."

"So Kate didn't intentionally sit on my deputy's back for any length of time, holding him down?"

"No. She did sit there for a moment, probably to figure out what had happened and to catch her breath."

Grady nodded slowly. "And the claim that Kate purposely tried to knee Ernie in the groin?"

"When Kate was struggling to push to her feet, she accidentally kneed Ernie in the upper thigh near his dick. Although, according to Aunt Millie, who used to chitchat with Ernie's ex-girlfriend—the one who worked in the kitchen over at the senior center—your deputy has a very crooked penis that veers sharply to the right, like almost ninety degrees, which makes you wonder what—"

"Penny," he interrupted. "Why does that even matter?"

"Well, it's kind of a memorable piece of information, you have to admit. But my point was that Kate's knee would have missed your deputy's penis by a few inches, which, coincidentally, the ex-girlfriend also told Aunt Millie was the size of Ernie's—"

"Penny!" Grady made a pained face. He blew out a breath and then asked, "How sure are you that it was an accident? Kate and Ernie have a bit of a history."

"Trust me, Grady. If Kate wanted to knee Ernie in the dick or balls, she would have done so well enough to make the mayor's son sing soprano for the rest of his spoiled rotten days."

She'd never understood why Grady had hired Ernie. While her brother denied it had anything to do with the chump's dad being the mayor, Penny wasn't sure that her brother hadn't somehow been blackmailed into it.

"Truthfully," Penny said, pausing to glance toward the empty desk where Ernie had been sitting a short time ago until Grady had shown up and sent him home. "I sort of think Kate might be right about your deputy being up to something fishy."

He growled under his breath. "Please tell me you're not going to jump on Kate's bandwagon about Ernie having some personal vendetta when it comes to her."

"Well, he was johnny-on-the-spot as she came out of the library. Like I said, it's an odd coincidence. Almost as if he'd been spying on her and waiting for the exact moment to throw himself in front of her."

"You mean behind her."

Penny ignored the skepticism in Grady's tone. "And why was Ernie still in uniform? You said his shift was over an hour earlier. Shouldn't he have been able to shower and change and be long gone by then?"

"I think you're trying too hard to pin the tail on that donkey."

"Well, Ernie always was an ass, even when he was in grade school. Remember when he got busted for chasing and kicking Miss Grover's favorite rooster and claimed he was simply defending himself when it attacked him. She made sure an article was written up in the paper with the truth—that Ernie was the bully, not … what was that rooster's name?"

"I think you're running off the rails here, Penny."

"Maybe I am, but you need to remember that Ernie set precedence with that rooster and has a history of covering up the truth." She leaned closer to Grady and lowered her voice. "Now, what are you going to do about Elizabeth telling everyone you two are getting married again?"

He squeezed his forehead. "Other than continuing to refute her claims, there isn't much I can do."

"Have you talked to her about putting a cork in her cakehole before someone crams a fist down it?" At his raised brow, she shrugged. "Just speaking in general, of course."

"I've been trying to avoid Liz since she returned to town and stay focused on the job at hand. Lord knows there's enough going on around the county to keep me busy, let alone the crazy shit Kate keeps doing."

"And how is this avoidance game working out for you?" Because Penny would love to do the same, but Grady's ex insisted on stirring up shit.

He shrugged. "Liz has shown up at the house a couple of times and brought me dinner at work like she used to when we were married, but I've managed to put a stop to both."

Or had his actions merely encouraged Elizabeth to double-down elsewhere? "What about Ronnie?"

"What about her?"

"What does she have to say about Elizabeth showing up at your place?"

"She was at work both times."

Penny tilted her head. "Did you tell her about these visits?"

"There's no need. I sent Liz on her way. Nothing happened."

"That's a mistake. Ronnie is going to find out, and if the news isn't coming from your lips, she'll be hurt—at the least. More likely, though, she'll be pissed as hell. And then her sister sitting back in your jail cell will form a hanging committee that will hunt you down and string you up." Penny snickered. "Knowing how fond Aunt Millie and her cronies are of Ronnie, they'll probably provide the yarn."

He shifted in his chair again. "I really don't want to talk about Liz to Veronica."

"Why not?"

"Because Veronica has enough headaches dealing with her ex-husband. If I can just figure out a way to make Liz see that there's no future with me, I think she'll return to her own whacky world, and life can go on as it was before."

"So, you'll live here in the same small town as Elizabeth and simply wave whenever you see each other at the store?"

"Ideally, she'd leave town, but either would work." When Penny gave him an incredulous look, he shrugged. "I'm selling the house and moving to my new place closer to Jackrabbit Junction in a few months. I figure two mature adults should be able to co-exist in the same county."

"With a past as drama-filled as yours?"

"That was years ago. People have moved on."

Penny snorted. "Did someone knock you upside the head with the stupid stick this afternoon, Grady, or are you so mired in your work that you have no clue how much the people in this county have not moved on? Not even an inch. And now with Elizabeth running around town and talking up your impending nuptials, you're front-page news again."

He shook his head. "I think you're exaggerating things a little. You've been hanging around Ernie and Kate too much."

"And I think you need to get your head out of your ass and accept that Elizabeth is not going to just fly away. For some silly reason, she has set her sights on you again, and she is hell-bent to win you back, even if it takes every single lowdown, cheating, conniving method to pull it off."

Grady laced his fingers together on his desktop, his mouth set in a grim line. "Well, if you're right, Liz is doomed to fail. I'm nuts about Veronica."

That was good to hear, because if he returned to lapping at Elizabeth's heels, Penny would join Kate and Aunt Millie in stringing her brother up.

"How nuts?"

"I asked her to move in with me."

"And?"

"She said no."

"Why *no*? Did she give you a reason?"

He nodded. "Because I'm the sheriff, and I live in a town where everyone knows my business."

So, Ronnie was worried about the townspeople thinking badly of her? She didn't seem like the type to really care that much about what other people thought.

"She says my role is supposed to be a position of respect. Apparently, in Veronica's mind, being sheriff comes with a chastity belt along with a badge and gun."

Ah, Ronnie was worried about *his* reputation. That was a fresh change from Elizabeth and her me-me-me attitude. But still … "Most of us who know you are aware that you and Ronnie are more than just pals. You haven't been hiding her under a rock or pretending otherwise. What's the difference between openly sleeping together and actually living in the same house as you?"

Especially considering that Ronnie's temporary residence had gone up in smoke. Penny would think that an opportunity to live in a house would be nice, and Grady's place was very comfortable. For a guy who worked long hours and wasn't home much, he kept a clean pad.

Maybe Ronnie didn't like how far Grady's place was from her family in Jackrabbit Junction. Or maybe she just wasn't ready to take their relationship to the next level yet.

He shrugged. "It makes a difference to Veronica, so I need to give her some more time. I'm hoping that moving to the new house in a few months will solve this issue and she'll join me there. It's far enough out of town that people won't be able to nose into our business so easily."

"How far along are they on the house now?

"The framework is done. I figure at the rate they're going, we could be there in a little over two to three months. It wouldn't be quite finished, but close enough to move in."

"Have you thought about eloping to Vegas and putting Elizabeth's rumors to rest?"

"You're assuming I want to get married again."

She was. Back when she'd first returned from San Francisco, they'd both agreed marriage was for the birds. But Grady had changed over the last few months, his rough edges smoothing out. Penny saw the way he looked at Ronnie. Her brother was smitten. She'd assumed he'd changed his mind about wedding rings now.

Grady picked up a pencil from his desk, tapping it on his palm. "One of Veronica's main concerns is how her blemished history, including her ex-husband's illegal dealings, might tarnish my reputation as sheriff. She thinks any sort of public commitment will only make things worse for me."

Crap. That left room for Elizabeth to pound a fat wedge between them and really muck things up all around.

"Could Ronnie's past cost you the election?"

Grady scratched at something on the desk. "Possibly."

"Especially if Elizabeth blows things out of proportion and puts together a nasty smear campaign," Penny surmised.

"Yeah."

"Are you nuts enough about Ronnie to risk losing the election?"

He looked at her with a frown burrowed deeply into his forehead. "Well, that's—"

Bzzzzz.

The sensor for the front doors interrupted them.

Claire rushed into the sheriff's office. Both her face and red Mighty Mouse cap were dusted with dirt.

"I've come to pick up your prisoner so I can transport her to Jackrabbit Junction where the father of her child is waiting with a ball and chain." Claire glanced around the room, her gaze settling on the closed door leading to the cells.

"It's unlocked," Grady said.

"That door?" Claire pointed at it.

"Yes, as well as the cell door. Your sister has shut herself inside the jail cell and refuses to come out."

"Not again." Claire walked over to the door and pulled it open a crack. "Kate, get your ass out here." She joined Penny and Grady at his desk. "So, what did she do now? Gramps told me to come pick her up. He didn't explain how it came to this."

"She got into another altercation with my deputy."

"Oh, hell," Claire said. "Not Deputy D—"

The door leading back to the cells crashed open and Kate strode out. "Sheriff, I'd like to make a citizen's arrest."

Grady leaned back in his chair, crossing his arms. "And who would you be arresting?"

"For starters, your deputy."

"You can't make a citizen's arrest of another officer of the law, Kate. That's out of your jurisdiction."

"I figured you might say that." Kate's gaze narrowed. "Then I'm going to fire up a case for internal affairs. Your deputy is participating in illegal activities."

"Sweet Jesus," Grady muttered.

"On top of that, I believe he is conspiring with your ex-wife to slander my sister and yours."

"Do you have any proof of this, or am I supposed to just take you at your angry word?"

"I have proof." Kate pulled out her cell phone and tapped the screen. She carried it over to Grady and held the phone in front of him. "See."

"What's this?" he asked, frowning down at the phone.

"It's your ex-wife." Kate pointed at the screen. "And that's her sharing a drink with him at that sleazy bar down by Roadrunner Auto Parts."

Claire came closer and peered over Grady's shoulder at whatever was on her sister's phone.

"This doesn't prove anything, Kate," Grady said. "Liz and Ernie have known each other since they were kids, same as the rest of us who grew up here. This could be simply two old friends sharing a conversation over beers."

Kate sighed, as if Grady were an A-1 dimwit. "Don't you think it's suspicious that your ex-wife returns to this corner of Arizona and instantly wages a campaign against my sister? Is it too much for your follow-the-rules, law dog brain to imagine that she and your deputy, who has made it no secret that he is out to get me, might conspire to drive us Morgans out of the county and will use whatever means to succeed—legal or not?"

Grady shook his head. "That's a stretch for sure, Kate."

Claire took the phone from her sister and looked at it closely. She flicked her finger back and forth over the screen.

Penny was tempted to move next to Claire so she could see the picture, too.

"Not that much of a stretch, Sheriff." Kate turned to Penny. "You know how sharp her claws can be when she doesn't get what she wants."

Penny did. She also knew that Ernie was a half-assed lawman who had a job in part because his daddy was the mayor and Grady couldn't fire him unless he had solid evidence of Ernie screwing things up beyond fixing.

"Trust me, I understand that Liz is making it known that she's not happy about Veronica and me being together," Grady said. "But I think that you're looping my deputy into this because you don't like him."

Kate huffed. "It's not as simple as me disliking your deputy, Sheriff. Ernie is now stalking me because he's obsessed with throwing me in the clink, like he did today."

"Kate, Ernie didn't actually throw you in jail," Penny reminded her. She wasn't trying to undermine Kate, but Penny had gone on record with her account of today's events. They needed to keep to the facts. "You came in here of your own free will with Grady's deputy following you and demanding that you 'halt and desist' while he radioed the whole thing in."

Penny would have laughed at the time if she hadn't still been so concerned about any lasting effects from Kate's fall, and if Ernie hadn't been making such a commotion in public while trying to get Kate to stop from illegally jaywalking across the street to the sheriff's office.

"You walked into the jail cell on your own and then demanded Grady be called," Penny added.

"An act that I did for my own protection. I knew that if Ernie thought he could get away with it, he would go as far as to hide the pens on his desk so he could try to add larceny to my list of crimes."

Grady grumbled a string of curses. "I need a vacation."

"You need a new deputy," Kate said. "What kind of training

would I need to go through to get hired on here?"

"No." Grady stood and walked over to the front door, yanking it open. "Claire, take your sister home. And take mine with you while you're at it."

"I can walk, thank you," Penny said as she passed in front of him with her chin held high.

Kate followed, with Claire bringing up the rear while still looking down at Kate's phone.

She frowned back at Grady as he locked the doors behind them and then turned away. "He can't lock the doors, can he?" Kate asked. "It's not even five o'clock yet."

"They don't usually lock the doors at all unless they are all out on a call," Penny told her. "He's making a point."

"What's this?" Claire asked after they walked several steps away from the front of the sheriff's office, holding Kate's phone out.

"What's what?" Kate took the phone from her, but held it out for Penny, too.

"You see that right there in your picture? Next to the booth right behind Elizabeth and Deputy Dipshit?"

"What is that?" Kate enlarged the picture. "A chair leg with a wheel?"

Why would a chair have a wheel? Penny tried to block out the sunshine so they could see the screen better.

"It's the front of a walker," Claire told them.

"Oh!" Kate pulled the phone away. "That's nothing."

"And," Claire continued, "if you enlarge the picture enough, you can see a few of the red dingle balls hanging off the front corner of it."

Red dingle balls ... Aunt Millie!

"How long ago did you take this picture?" Claire asked.

"Umm, somewhat recently," Kate said, looking away while grimacing.

"How recently?"

"Maybe Monday-ish."

Claire's gaze narrowed at she stared at her sister. "That explains your absence Monday night."

Absence from where, Penny wondered.

"Listen, I just happened to see Elizabeth enter that bar when

I was running some errands and parked nearby to watch."

"To spy, you mean," Claire accused.

Kate shrugged. "It was a lucky coincidence that I caught her meeting with Ernie."

"This picture has stalker and stakeout written all over it, Kate." Claire snorted. "You're one to talk about citizens' arrests for performing illegal activities when you're doing almost the same crap to the sheriff's deputy."

"I'm protecting myself here. He's the one who started all of this." She pointed at the picture. "And now Elizabeth is joining up with him."

"You think it's a coincidence Aunt Millie was in the booth right behind Elizabeth and Ernie?" Penny asked.

Claire gave her sister a smirk. "What do you think, Kate?"

After a glance back at the sheriff's office, Kate moved in closer to Penny and whispered, "I may have asked your aunt to check into Elizabeth's day-to-day activities after she threatened you and Ronnie at the diner."

"Well, that explains why my aunt isn't trying to clobber Elizabeth in that picture."

Penny glanced back at the sheriff's office. It was a good thing Grady hadn't taken a closer look at the photo or he might have seen their aunt's walker.

"Now what?" Kate asked.

Claire pointed at her sister's phone. "Now you delete that picture."

"This is evidence."

Penny agreed with Claire. "You should probably save it somewhere other than your phone for safekeeping, because Grady might ask to take a second look. Trust me, you don't want him to do that."

"Okay, that I will do."

Penny's phone rang. She pulled it out and frowned at the phone number belonging to her assistant manager. "Hello?"

"Penny, we have a visitor."

"The diner should be closed."

"I know," came a whispered reply. "But it's the health inspector and she wants to talk to you."

"Ahh, balls!"

Chapter Seventeen

Friday, Feb 1st

Ronnie stood at Grady's kitchen sink, staring blankly out the window into his backyard.

She wasn't really seeing the large old barrel cactus that had been here since he and Elizabeth had bought the house, or the tall ocotillo reaching for the sky behind it, or the needle-covered cholla and prickly pear sharing the same small cacti garden. The flagstone walkway and thorny shrubs lining parts of it were a blur, too, same as the leafless desert willow back near the detached garage with last year's dried bean pods still shivering in the morning breeze. The carved stone bench under the green limbs of the paloverde tree and the spinning kinetic metal wind wheels weren't reeling her in either.

Nope.

Since she'd woken up this morning alone in Grady's bed, her mind was locked onto one thing and one thing only—Lyle's latest fuck-job of her life.

Because of her rotten choice when it came to picking a husband years and years ago, she was now a wanted woman.

Oh, the irony. For so long, back when Lyle would disappear for days on end, sometimes weeks, she longed for someone to want her. Really want her. Not for her ability to host a party for well-to-dos. Not for her knowledge of how to perfectly set a table. Not for her fake blond hair or her fake eyelashes. To want her, the real her.

Now she was wanted in all senses of the word. Ruby wanted her to help with bookkeeping. Butch wanted her to take on Kate's old duties. Claire and Mac wanted her to continue working at The

Shaft after they bought it. Grady wanted her in his bed every night. And all sorts of strangers wanted her dead—or at least close to it. Or whatever it would take to hurt Lyle for screwing them over. A toe. A pinky finger. An ear. Maybe even her whole head before it was all said and done.

The thought of what was waiting outside of these walls every day had her wanting to burrow under Grady's bed, but she couldn't keep living like this. Scurrying through her days and nights like a lizard running from one hiding spot to the next was no good in the long run. She was turning thirty-six in a few days. She needed to get her shit together, put her past behind her, and figure out what she wanted for the rest of her life. Or at least for the next few years.

Blinking away her worries and wonders, she finished her cup of coffee and rinsed the mug in the sink. On a high note, it turned out that the anonymous text she'd received while in the grocery store was from some poor sucker who was given a wrong number at a bar by a girl he thought he'd impressed on the dance floor. Grady told Ronnie last night that the guy had nearly swallowed his tongue when a sheriff from Arizona called back to ask what in the hell he meant with that text.

Her phone pinged on the way out of Grady's front door. Speaking of texts ...

She pulled it from her purse as she made her way down the sidewalk to his truck, which she was borrowing yet again.

She made a mental note:

Get-Shit-Together List—
Figure out how to buy own vehicle in spite of bad credit.

In the meantime, Penny was supposed to bring Grady by The Shaft later this evening so he could use his own rig to drive Mindy Lou home after her shift was over. Ronnie planned to spend the night at Ruby's place, wanting to get some bookkeeping done in the morning before heading back into work.

As she tapped the text message to open it, she heard a diesel engine idling nearby. She looked to the south. Across the street a couple of blocks down was a gray pickup. A big and bulky-looking shadowy figure sat behind the wheel, but Ronnie couldn't see any details due to the glare of the morning sunshine on the windshield. The truck looked clean as a whistle, though. At least from this distance.

Something about the whole scene made her think of when those first two FBI guys had come to town before Mississippi took over. They'd been so obviously not-locals.

The text was on the screen when she looked back down at her phone. It was from Butch. Today's grocery list included a few more vegetables and a big pack of napkins.

It was funny how they'd run low on different items in between stock deliveries. Sometimes napkins, sometimes cleaning fluids, sometimes hamburger buns. Once she'd even had to pick up four boxes of condoms of varying sizes to fill the vending machine in the guys' bathroom. Boy, had that purchase earned her a set of raised eyebrows from the checkout guy at the drugstore.

She called Butch back but got his voicemail, so she left a quick message saying she was running a little late this morning but was on the way to the store now and would be at work soon to help open. Pocketing her phone, she fished the keys for Grady's pickup from her coat pocket and unlocked the door.

"Morning, Veronica!" a voice called from behind her.

She screeched in surprise, dropping her purse when she whirled around.

"Sadie," Ronnie said, holding her palm over her thumping heart. "What are you doing here?"

The question was silly, sort of, because Sadie was jogging in place in front of her, breathing somewhat quickly. She was obviously out for a run. Her black spandex pants and zipped-up utility jacket matched her stocking cap and ... combat boots. Who jogged in combat boots? She had to be ex-military. Didn't they run in boots during basic training? And that utility jacket—that wasn't normal running gear either. Ronnie preferred something body-fitting and lighter weight when she jogged or walked.

"I like to run around town in the morning." Sadie stopped jogging in place and scooped up Ronnie's purse for her. "Is this where you live?"

Something about Sadie being here right now made Ronnie hesitate before answering that question. This was the third day in a row that she'd run into the woman. Or rather the woman had run into her.

"It's where I sometimes spend the night." Ronnie didn't

elaborate about it being Grady's place.

"Ahhh, I get it," Sadie said with a grin and a wink, handing Ronnie back her purse. "Hey, do you mind driving me to the store?"

Ronnie clutched her purse to her stomach. "I thought you were out jogging." Couldn't Sadie jog to the store? It was only about six blocks away from Grady's place. Why would she need a ride when she was this close?

"I was, but my knee is starting to tighten. It's an old injury that flares up now and then. If I take it easy for an hour or two, everything will loosen again and be fine."

"How do you know I'm going to the store?"

"Because I overheard you on the phone as I was coming this way. I didn't mean to eavesdrop, I've just always had really good hearing."

Ronnie glanced up the street and then back toward the south, wondering from which direction Sadie had come.

The gray pickup was no longer idling. The form behind the wheel was not there either. Ronnie tucked a loose strand of hair behind her ear as she eyed the pickup and the area surrounding it. When had the driver gotten out? Her heart pounded in her ears.

Ronnie hadn't heard the engine cut out or a door slam or anything. She should've been watching, paying attention instead of looking at her stupid phone.

She tried to take a breath and suddenly couldn't. She coughed, her lungs felt like they were full of sludge.

Where was he? Had Sadie been behind the wheel? No, the driver had been bigger and bulkier than Sadie, with shoulders twice as wide. Then who was it and where had …

Take back control, damn it!

Control started with breathing right. She took a deep breath. Then another. And another.

"Are you okay?" Sadie asked.

Ronnie was now, mostly. "Listen, I can take you to the store, but I'm running late and still have to pick up one of my coworkers, so I can't drop you off back at your place afterward."

Not that she knew where Sadie's house was. Ronnie just wanted the woman to know that there were people expecting her to show up at certain places today. In other words, she would be missed if she didn't arrive on time. This was a self-defense tactic she'd learned years ago and decided to use in case Sadie wasn't as harmless as she had seemed so far.

"Works for me," Sadie said with a smile.

They climbed into Grady's rig. Ronnie scooted the seat forward so she could reach the gas and brakes while Sadie buckled up.

"So," Ronnie started as she shifted into drive. "Are you done being mad at me for saving you yesterday?"

"I'm a little less mad now." A small smirk settled on Sadie's face as she stared out the windshield.

They drew closer to the gray pickup. Ronnie slowed down, trying to see through the shaded side window.

"Look out!" Sadie yelled, jerking Ronnie's attention forward again.

"What?" Ronnie didn't see anything in the road, but her pulse was now rocketing between her head and toes.

"Sorry, it was a lizard. I didn't want you to hit it. Those little guys are so cute."

"Holy hairy moly, Sadie. That's the second heart attack you've almost given me this morning. Are you trying to kill me? And after I saved your bacon, too. Have you no respect for your guardian angel?"

Sadie settled back into the seat with an audible huff. "Just drive me to the damned store, woman."

As they bumped along the streets, Ronnie shot a couple of glances at her passenger. "What do you do for a living?"

"I'm an independent contractor."

That sounded important, but vague.

"In what?"

"The health industry."

Did that mean she was a nurse? Or a doctor? Or a pharmaceutical sales rep? Whatever she was, Sadie was being tight-lipped about it, so Ronnie switched to a different subject. "How's your mom doing?"

"Great. My turn now. How's it happen you *sometimes* spend the night in town?"

Ronnie shrugged. "Sometimes I don't feel like going home to the rest of my family." Again, she made sure to let Sadie know she wasn't alone very often, just to be extra safe.

"I get that." Sadie nodded. "But you don't stay here in Yuccaville at your *sometimes* place every night?"

"I like the option to choose."

That was sort of true. After what had felt like living in a fortress mostly alone for years while Lyle traveled constantly, not having an official home had its merits. Although it would be nice to have a small place to accumulate some new clothes. She'd been wearing her sisters' stuff for long enough.

"You going to be there tonight again?" Sadie asked.

"Why do you want to know?"

"Just wondering if you want to go for a run with me in the morning. Running is more fun when you're not alone."

Ronnie glanced Sadie's way. "That sounds suspiciously like an offer of friendship."

"Well, I'm not going to ask you to wear my ring or high school letter jacket."

Ronnie chuckled. "I'm not going to be at my *sometimes* home tonight. I have another job in the morning that I need to go to."

"Cool."

"But if you want to exchange phone numbers," she said as she pulled into the store parking lot, "I can text you the next time I'm in town and available for a morning run. Although I'm not very fast and probably can't run as far as you."

"If you're interested, I can show you some breathing techniques that will help with your stamina."

That sounded for sure like something taught in the military, didn't it? Or in the health profession?

After Ronnie parked, they exchanged numbers.

As she shut and locked the door, she asked Sadie, "You heading inside?"

"No, I'm gonna go next door for some coffee." She pointed toward the small café the next block over. "Rest my knee for a while before walking home. Maybe ice it."

"I'll see you around, Sadie." Ronnie tossed a quick salute her way. "Try not to get yourself killed in the meantime."

Sadie shook her head, muttering under her breath as she walked away with a slight limp.

* * *

Claire was washing her hands in the campground bathroom when Kate rushed inside and closed the door behind her, leaning against it as if she were holding back a horde of zombies.

Huh. Another day, another cuckoo version of Kate.

"You're late, jailbird." Claire grabbed a paper towel from the dispenser. "I'd dock you an hour's pay, but sitting on your bumpkin with your feet up on a five-gallon bucket while you watch me toil away isn't really working."

Kate waved her off. She reached into her pants pocket and pulled out a keychain with three keys hanging from it, holding it out toward Claire. "*Voilà!* Sophy's house keys have been found. Now, when are you gonna go?"

"When am I gonna go?" Claire tossed the paper towel in the trash. "Don't you mean when are *we* going to go?"

"No, I mean you." Kate scowled. "After the crapshow in Yuccaville yesterday, Valentine is keeping me on a short leash because the sheriff is breathing down his neck. Damned nosy Grady. If he'd just do something about his stupid deputy."

After Kate's most recent stunt at the sheriff's office, Claire wasn't surprised by Butch's increased monitoring. She'd overheard Grady talking to him last night about trying harder to keep Kate away from Yuccaville and his deputies.

"Is he tracking your phone yet?"

"You mean Deputy Dipshit? The chum-head better not be or I'll—"

"I meant Butch."

"Oh." Kate's eyes narrowed to tight, menacing squints. "Valentine better not be tracking me. Not if he wants to keep Big Jim and the twins healthy and happy. I'll rip them clean off, I swear."

"Big Jim and ..." Claire cringed, realizing which parts of Butch's anatomy were at the risk from Kate's potential wrath. "Kate, please refrain from telling me your nicknames for Butch's nether regions in the future. I have to work with him every night. Now every time the name 'Jim' comes up, I'm not going to be able to look the guy in the face."

"I'm sorry. Does that hurt your delicate sensibilities? Try

having a stranger do a rubber-glove inspection of your hoochie-coochie every few weeks."

Claire rolled her eyes. "Kate, your cannon is loose. Lash that sucker back down. And that's not a stranger examining you, it's your OB-GYN."

"You can stack a bunch of letters after your name on a piece of paper and nail it to the wall, but in the end—in *my* end, anyway—you're still an uninvited guest at my private party who is sticking your fingers where they don't belong."

Claire sighed, staring at her reflection in the mirror over the sink. "How did it come to this? I just needed to pee and then grab something from the tool shed. Where did I go wrong?"

"You asked if Butch was tracking me."

"Oh, right. And did you give me an answer in the midst of that churning dust devil of a reply?"

"I checked the location settings on my phone and I should be off-grid. However, Valentine told me he'll be texting me throughout the day, and if I don't answer within a few minutes, he's going to come looking for me." Kate harrumphed. "That man is making me barking mad."

More like howling mad. Like a monkey. Ever since the baby hormones started coursing through her body months ago, Kate's brain had been hanging from the chandelier and throwing bananas and poo at anyone passing too close.

"Listen, Mad-dog Morgan," Claire said, moving toward the door. She wanted to get back to the platform where Luke and Chester were enjoying some quiet sanity well away from Kate while making progress on the build. "I understand how frustrating it must feel to be under a microscope, but you have to admit that if you hadn't holed up in Grady's jail cell yesterday, Butch wouldn't have you on lockdown today."

"That wasn't my fault." Kate walked over to the three bathroom stalls, pushing the door open on each.

Claire crossed her arms.

"It wasn't, Claire, so don't be giving me *that* look."

They'd already had this discussion on the way home from jail. "You entered the holding cell of your own free will. How can that not be your fault?"

"I had to do it for my own protection."

Kate moved to where Claire had been standing and started checking her reflection in the mirror above the sink. Claire watched as her sister adjusted her sunhat and then batted her lashes at the knucklehead staring back at her.

"I think you need to go to Sophy's today when you're done out back," Kate said, glancing at Claire before returning to her self-inspection. "You need to get whatever is under the dresser in her bedroom and then bring it to The Shaft later and show me when nobody else is around."

"I can't go there today," Claire told the preening peacock.

"Why not?"

"Because the lumber for the brewery is supposed to arrive sometime this afternoon. I'm waiting for a call from the delivery driver, so I can meet him there."

"That won't take all day. You can sneak over to Sophy's afterward."

"No, I can't. You of all people know how busy The Shaft is on Fridays. Butch will need all hands on deck, so as soon as Luke and I finish screwing on the composite decking, I'll be donning an apron and helping serve the masses."

Kate scowled. "Claire, we need to get whatever Sophy has squirreled away to her as soon as possible. If Joe is still out there creeping around, waiting to strike, we need to beat him to the punch and attack first."

"If Joe is still out there, Kate, we probably need to tell Grady and let him and his deputies do the attacking."

"Grady is never going to believe Joe is still alive unless we deliver him on a silver platter with an apple crammed in his mouth."

"I disagree. With the right proof, I think Grady will listen to us. After all, he has a vested interest in this family now."

"Not according to his ex-wife." Kate finished dolling up and turned her back on the mirror. "Did you know Elizabeth is telling people that he asked her to marry him again and that she said yes? That mad dreamer needs to be taught a lesson about lying."

Elizabeth was totally unscrewed and rattling as she rolled, there was no doubt about that, but this particular problem was out of Kate's jurisdiction. "Does Ronnie know Elizabeth is saying that stuff?"

Kate shrugged. "If she does, she's not letting on about it. And don't you go telling her, either. Ronnie has enough trouble with the potential killers coming for her. She doesn't need to deal with an out-of-whack ex-wife who can't seem to decipher fiction from fact."

"It's not like I was going to run out of here and find Ronnie. I am a little busy at the moment working on a bird viewing platform, remember?"

"What's Luke's story?" Kate said, switching gears.

It took Claire a blink and a head shake to catch up. "What do you mean? He's here to help out and meet his new step-grandmother."

Luke hadn't been able to make it to visit Gramps and Ruby when they'd traveled to South Dakota last fall, so this was his first time getting filled full of sweets and treats by Ruby, and she was doubling down. If Claire didn't stop sharing in the candied fruits and sugary cookies of Ruby's labor, she'd have to switch from jeans to sweatpants soon.

"I don't think that's the only reason he's down here," Kate said.

"Well, Natalie did contact him and let him know we could use his help when he had some free time."

"I don't think that's the real reason, either."

"Okay, Detective Bigbrain, why is Luke here?"

"I think it has something to do with woman troubles."

"Kate, why do you have to go fishing for drama? We have all sorts of nets full of it without you trolling for more."

"Mark my words, there's a woman haunting Luke."

"How about I mark your forehead with a good old-fashioned knuckle-rub instead?"

"You wouldn't hurt a pregnant woman."

"True, but I might give you a wedgie." Claire pointed at the door. "Now, can I get back to work?"

Kate rushed over and blocked it. "Not until you promise me you'll take the keys to Sophy's place and go get whatever is hidden under her dresser today." She held up the keys again. "Come on, I spent half the night searching for this, tiptoeing around the house while Valentine slept."

"I told you I have the lumber coming today."

"Fine, then go tonight."

"I'm working, remember?"

"You'll be off by midnight."

Claire scoffed. "You want me to go to Sophy's place at midnight and sneak inside her dark house to find some sort of proof that the man who we thought has been dead for over a year is still alive?"

"You don't need to sneak. She gave permission. And turn on the lights while you're there."

"Kate, why would she leave the power on? That's a bill to pay and she's behind bars for a long time yet."

"So take a bunch of flashlights."

"No way. I'm not going up there alone in the dark."

"Why? Are you too chicken?"

"Yes." And Claire wasn't ashamed to admit it. "I'm very chicken. That's the place where I was shot."

"You didn't actually get shot. You fell and hit your head."

"Sophy shot at me, I just happened to knock the shotgun barrel aside first."

Kate snorted. "That's not the same as being shot."

"Tell you what, I'll aim a double-barreled shotgun at you and pretend to pull the trigger and see if you can tell the difference between attempted murder and straight-up murder."

"Sheesh. Talk about being a drama queen, Claire. I'm not asking you to face off with the devil in the dark, only to go to an empty house and find whatever clue is under the dresser. Then come home. Easy-peasy."

"I'm not going up there alone. Period. End of story. I'm walking away from this." She nudged her sister and the keys aside and pulled open the restroom door.

Kate followed her out into the late morning sunshine, which warmed the top of Claire's head in spite of the cool breeze that kept ruffling her collar today.

"You know I'd go with you if I could, but there's no way Butch will let me escape while he's on watchtower duty."

"Then Sophy's secret will have to wait until you can get away."

"That could be weeks, Claire."

"Then we wait weeks. I'm a little busy building a few things right now, in case you haven't noticed."

Kate grabbed her elbow, tugging her to a stop. "You're stalling."

"I'm not going up there tonight, Kate."

"Fine, but at least take these damned keys. If Valentine realizes they're gone, he'll frisk me from head to toe, so I need them out of our house."

Claire took the keys and pocketed them. "There. Happy? Now let me get back to work. I'm hoping Luke and I will have the decking secured before I get the call about the lumber being here."

"You're not going to tell Mac about the Sophy deal when he gets here tomorrow, are you?"

Claire wasn't sure. She didn't like hiding things from Mac, but if he didn't ask about Sophy, which he shouldn't since he had no idea they'd called the prison beauty queen, it wasn't really "hiding," was it?

"I'm not planning to go out of my way to let him know about any of this, if that's what you mean."

Kate's lips pursed. "I don't think that's the same thing as what I'm asking."

"It's the best you'll get from me at the moment."

They walked along in silence for a few steps.

"Oh," Kate said. "Have you had a chance to think about that ancient knife?"

"Shhhh." Claire looked around, worried about eavesdroppers. "That's not something you just announce out loud like that."

"I wasn't announcing anything," Kate snapped. "I was inquiring."

"Well, inquire more quietly next time. You never know when someone might be listening in around here."

"Fine," Kate whispered. "How's this? Quiet enough?"

"No. I'd prefer you were totally muted and mimed your thoughts and ideas from here on out."

Kate held up her middle finger in front of Claire's face. "Like this?" She held up her other, too. "And this?"

Claire knocked both of her hands away. "Grow up already. Your sister is turning thirty-six in a few days, which means we're getting older, too."

"What are we doing for Ronnie's birthday party?"

"I don't know. You're the party planner, not me." Claire

veered toward the tool shed. "Maybe she doesn't want a party. Have you checked with her?"

"Ronnie needs a party. She's had a shitty year and we need to help her put the past behind her and start fresh for the last half of her thirties."

"I still think we should check with her before throwing any parties," Claire said. "If she wants a quiet night with Grady instead, we need to be considerate."

"Fine, I'll sleuth around to find out what she wants. In the meantime, I need you to help me figure out the origin of that kni—" She stopped. "That special *thing* I mentioned a few minutes ago."

"I already know the origin."

"You do? Did you do some research on it?"

"I didn't need to." Claire lowered her voice. "The origin is the Maya people."

"Oh, you!" Kate backhanded her shoulder. "You know what I mean. We have to find out where it came from before someone comes looking for it here."

Claire already had put some thought into that knife and its origins—the post-Maya ones. Something didn't feel right about it. Having worked on some of Joe's other mysteries, Claire realized that the puzzle of the knife was too easy. Sure, it could belong to some rich collector of ancient artifacts, but if she'd learned anything about Joe, it was that he had more eccentric tastes when it came to his fenced goods. That didn't mean he liked to collect rare gold-plated trinkets, more that he liked to use elaborate brainteasers to conceal where he stowed the stuff that he stole.

The knife was too simple all around. An obsidian blade. A jade handle. Tucked away behind some books—a simple hiding place.

Claire wondered if the trick to that particular fenced good had something to do with the carving on the jade handle. She would have liked to see exactly where their mom had found the knife and how it had been placed. If it were pointed in a particular direction, or at some book, or at another item on the shelf in particular. Or maybe at a certain wall in the office.

The way Joe's puzzles worked was rarely as simple as taking the artifact at face value. Especially an item that wasn't locked away in his wall safe behind the bookshelf or hidden down a mine shaft.

"I'm going to need to see it again," Claire told Kate.

"I can arrange a meeting for that."

"What are you, some kind of arms dealer now?"

"I told you before, I'm an ace detective."

"More like an ace criminal, according to Deputy Dipshit."

Kate snarled. "Mark my words. I'm going to find out what Elizabeth and Ernie are up to and remove both of those bungholes from the equation."

Claire frowned. "Careful there, Kate. If the sheriff hears you say stuff like that, he'll lock you in his cell simply to protect the general public."

"Did you know that Elizabeth is messing with Penny now, too?"

Maybe, but Claire played dumb. "Like how?"

"She's posted bad reviews about The Mule Train Diner on multiple online sites and is spreading rumors that Penny is talking bad behind her business associates' back."

Yeah, Claire knew all about that. "She sounds like a real sweetheart of an ex-wife. Grady and Ronnie know how to pick winners, don't they?"

"Don't tell anyone else this, especially Mom, but I think they're good for each other." Kate sniffed. "I sure wish he wasn't a lawman, though. If Ronnie marries him someday, we're going to have to either toe the line for the rest of our lives, or commit crimes behind our sister's back."

"You really think Ronnie wants to get married again? Last time she talked to me about her future, another husband wasn't on the list of wants she mentioned."

"When was that? Back when she was living with you and Mac in Tucson?"

"No. It was last month."

"Really? I wonder if Grady knows that. He seems really keen on her."

"Keen?" Claire chuckled and unlocked the door to the tool shed. "Who are you? Beaver Cleaver's mom?"

"There's nothing wrong with the word *keen*. For example, I'm very keen on you getting your ass up to Sophy's place today. The sooner we get her what she wants, the sooner we can figure out how to find Joe." Kate shuddered. "I really don't like the idea of him waiting out there somewhere, watching us. He's probably planning on taking out Gramps for marrying Ruby."

"If it's not Joe watching us, it's one of the people he's skimmed from looking for their goods, or it's one of Ronnie's hitmen." Claire searched the hills around the RV park. "Do you remember what it was like when we lived in South Dakota and didn't have someone trying to hurt us?"

"Yep." Kate pulled out her phone. "It was a real snooze-ville."

Yeah, it sort of was, but … "Sometimes a dull life doesn't sound too bad, especially these days."

While Kate played with her phone, Claire stepped inside the tool shed and grabbed a charged impact drill battery to take back to the worksite. She looked around the small, crowded shed to make sure there wasn't anything else they needed.

When she stepped outside, Kate was talking to a young girl with light pink hair. Something about the girl's Cleveland Browns paint-streaked sweatshirt reminded Claire of Jess. It could be that she was young and bouncy and chewing bubble gum. Or, now that Claire looked closer, maybe it was that the sweatshirt was Jess's.

Claire approached Kate, glancing around to see if there was a parent or some other responsible adult lurking nearby.

The girl gave Claire the stinkeye. "Who are you?"

"An adult who lives here. Who are you?"

"I'm Jess's best friend."

"Since when?"

Claire knew all about Jess's life, whether she wanted to or not. From the first time they'd met back by this very tool shed, Jess had made a point of oversharing her life story and had continued ever since to fill Claire's ears with jibber-jabber about lip gloss, nail color, and which girl was French-kissing what boy in the halls each day during school.

The girl's cheeks darkened. "Since last week when she started tutoring me."

"Ohhh." Claire nodded. "You're Hailey."

The girl gasped. "How do you know my name? Have you been stalking me?"

"Sure, kid. That's what I do in all my spare time. I go around stalking gum-chewing nimrods who like to skip class so often that they're failing math and English even though they are supposedly really smart."

That pretty much summed up what Claire had been told about Hailey, Jess's newest "project." Oh, and that she was a foster kid who needed a good friend.

Hailey pouted. "I only skipped class three times."

"That's three too many," said Kate, the ex-teacher. "School is your job at this point in life. Take it seriously and respect your teachers."

Hailey raised her hands in surrender. "Sheesh, Kate. Take it easy on a poor kid who came out to bring you a message."

"Why couldn't Jess play messenger?" Kate asked.

"She's working the register at the store."

Claire stuffed the drill battery in her toolbelt. "She could have texted one of us. Why aren't you two in school?"

"Teacher workday," Hailey explained, adding, "Jess can't find her phone and her mom said she's not allowed to leave the register except to go to the bathroom." She shook her head. "Adults can be so bossy. It's like they think we have no lives outside of serving them."

"What's the message?" Claire needed to get back to the worksite. They were on track to get the decking finished today if they kept at the pace they'd been working so far. Kate had delayed her enough as it was.

Hailey looked back toward the General Store, a frown lining her brow "Well, it was ..." She chewed on her lower lip and squinted. "Umm. Jess said that ... shoot, what was it?" She jammed her hands into the front center pocket on the sweatshirt. "We were talking about irrational numbers and the phone rang and ..." She bounced up and down a couple of times, as if that would jumpstart her brain, and then she frowned at Kate and Claire. "Dang it. I can't remember."

"Then it must not have been very important," Kate said.

Hailey tipped her head sideways, eyeing Kate. "Are you really banned from the library for six months?"

"Yes."

"You did cuss a lot at the librarian."

Kate glowered at the kid. "I know. I was there."

"Jess said you went to jail, too."

"Jess is technically wrong."

"I saw the whole thing."

Kate's forehead turned a shade of pink that almost matched Hailey's hair. "It wasn't one of my finer moments. You probably shouldn't repeat some of the words I said."

"I don't think the librarian has heard some of those words before."

Claire probably had. Kate had the biggest potty mouth of all three of them. It was probably due to that big IQ she liked to blab about to everyone and their brother.

"When I said I saw the whole thing," Hailey said, pausing to blow a bubble and then pop it herself. "I was talking about the part afterward when that sheriff's deputy got out of his pickup and rushed over right as you scurried out the door."

"I didn't scurry." Kate bristled. "I walked out backward while stating the final arguments for my case."

Hailey chewed her gum, nodding. "That deputy was a jerk. He's the one who got in your way."

"Right! That's what I told Grady," Kate said to Claire.

"And I'm sure he made a note of that," Claire returned. After all, the sheriff knew Kate and Deputy Dipshit had a turbulent history.

"I think the deputy was just pissed because he dropped his knockers."

"He's always pissed when it comes to me," Kate muttered.

Claire frowned at her sister and then Hailey. "You should watch your language some," she told both of them. They didn't need Hailey's foster parents calling Ruby to bitch about …

"Wait." Claire turned to Hailey. "What did you just say?"

"Deputy Dipshit was pissed," Hailey said.

Claire held up her hand to stop the kid. "Where did you hear that nickname for him?"

Hailey pointed at Kate. "She called him that when they were having their yelling match outside the library."

When Claire glared at her sister, Kate grimaced and looked down at her shoe, kicking a stone away.

"Listen, kid," Claire said. "Please don't use that name for the deputy again. It could get you in big trouble." She shot Kate another glare for her lack of control when it came to flapping her gums. "Kate and Ernie have known each other for a while and don't get along well. They both tend to call each other not-so-nice names."

Although, to be fair to her sister, Claire had started calling Ernie that after the first time he'd shown up during a potential crime situation and acted like a total dipshit while talking down to her.

"That's enough, Mother Teresa," Kate said to Claire. She frowned at Hailey. "I screwed up. Don't be like me."

"You mean pregnant and nutty as squirrel poop?"

Kate's gaze hardened in a flash. And then her left eye twitched. Twice. "I'm starting not to like you, Hailey."

Hailey took a step toward Claire. "She's scaring me," she whispered out of the side of her mouth, smelling like bubble gum.

"She's been scaring me for most of my life," Claire told the girl. "You said something about the deputy dropping some 'knockers'? Do you mean like a pair of brass knuckles?"

"I don't know what brass knuckles are." Hailey was still watching Kate with a wary look. "I said 'knockers,' which is what a little kid I used to live with called binoculars."

"So, the deputy had a pair of binoculars with him when he crossed to where Kate was?"

"He had them in his monster truck. When he hopped to the ground, they fell out. I think they broke, because I saw glass fly."

"Maybe he keeps them in his door," Kate said. "I'm pretty sure he's a hunter judging from that sticker on his back window of a deer with a target over it."

Hailey nodded. "If so, he was hunting you yesterday."

"Why do you say that?" Claire asked.

"Because I saw him staring through them at the library for a while before your sister started screaming at that Ginger woman."

"I wasn't screaming." Kate huffed. "I was making a point."

"How long was he spying on Kate?"

Hailey shrugged. "I wasn't watching the clock, but I'd say he must have been sitting across the street playing peekaboo pretty much since Kate and Jess and I got there."

Claire turned to Kate. "Why do you think he was eyeballing you?"

Had Kate done something before showing up at the library that would have gotten his attention? Something like trying to lock him in his own cell again?

"Because he's stalking me. I keep telling people that, but nobody believes me, especially not Grady. He thinks that I'm—"

"Oh! Oh!" Hailey held up her hand, waving it in the air as if she were sitting behind a school desk.

"What?" Kate asked, exasperated.

"Jeez. You'd make a mean teacher."

Claire laughed. "She has you pegged."

Kate jabbed Claire in the shoulder with her index finger. "Keep it up and I'll peg you to the wall of your tool shed."

Ignoring her sister, Claire looked at the pink-haired gum chewer. "Did you have a question, Hailey?"

"No, but I remembered what I was supposed to come out here to tell you guys."

"What?" Claire and Kate said at the same time.

"Jinx!" Hailey giggled.

"Hailey!" Kate snapped.

"Fine. Sorry for breathing wrong, meanie." She sniffed. "Jess talked to someone on the phone, and when she hung up she told me to come warn you. She said you should hide."

"Hide?" Kate repeated as if Hailey were speaking a foreign language.

"Why?" Claire asked.

Hailey shrugged. "Something about Jess's stepsister being on her way home."

Kate looked at Claire with wide eyes. "Mother!"

"Son of a b—" Claire remembered Hailey at the last minute. "Big-butted baboon!"

Chapter Eighteen

Mac was back and he was tired as hell.

When he'd turned in his resignation earlier this month, he'd figured that his days of driving for hours in the dark to get to Claire were over. But here he was again, bleary-eyed and exhausted as he rolled into the gravel parking lot in front of The Shaft.

He didn't even bother going to the RV park first, the lovesick fool that he was. It was Claire first, sleep later.

He parked his rig and breathed a sigh of relief. He'd made it home in one piece after several ten-plus hour days on the job and too many long nights on an uncomfortable bed in a hotel with walls made of paper.

Pausing for a moment to stretch under the stars, he listened to the sound of the wind whispering over the valley, rattling the nearby creosote bushes and mesquite trees. It smelled different here than it did in Bisbee. Fresher maybe, since there was very little humanity in and around Jackrabbit Junction. Or maybe it was psychological, and what he was smelling was home sweet home.

Any signs of life at The Shaft were hidden behind closed windows and doors. But outside in the parking lot, vehicles were parked this way and that since there were no designated spots. The metal and glass glistened under the orange parking lot lights.

He spotted Claire's Jeep near the back of the building where she usually parked. Mississippi's pickup was next to it, along with Grady's and Butch's rigs. Good, the gang was all here. It wouldn't be long before the place would be his and Claire's, and then he could stay in one place for weeks on end. Just a few more consulting jobs to go.

As he stepped inside the bar, heat and humidity thick with the scent of cologne, perfume, and grilled meat greeted him. The din of conversation held steady at a low rumble, interrupted with a squeal of laughter from over by the jukebox where Supertramp was singing about taking the long way home. What a coincidence. That was Mac's theme song tonight. He took off his coat, searching for Claire somewhere in the sea of bodies.

He spotted Gary behind the bar first, and then noticed Grady sitting at the far end of the bar, his back partially turned toward Mac as he frowned out over the crowd. Stepping farther into the room, he saw Ronnie and Kate weaving through the tables, delivering trays of food and drink. Then he found Mindy Lou, who was taking drink orders back at the pool tables from Mississippi and a couple of cowboys. Her hair looked darker tonight, almost brown.

"Order up!" Mac heard Chester call out above the hubbub. He caught a peek of Butch through the kitchen window behind the bar.

Where was Claire? The bathroom?

Mac peeked over the batwing doors, checking to see if a light was on in Butch's office.

Somebody stuck something pointy into his lower back.

"Hands in the air, desperado," Claire said, her breath warm on his neck.

Mac smiled and lifted his hands.

She prodded him forward. "Butch's office. Now."

He led the way, glancing toward the kitchen as they passed. The place was on fire tonight. Literally. But it was only a small fire on the grill, where Chester stood over a flaming burger while slapping out the flames with a spatula. Butch stood next to him, laughing, a small fire extinguisher on the counter next to him.

Mac didn't realize he'd stopped in his tracks until Claire bumped him along. "They've got that under control," she said and pinched him through his jeans. "Move those sweet buns."

As soon as they were inside Butch's office, Claire closed the door and leaned against it, her chest heaving slightly. While he was admiring her heaving parts, he noticed that she'd spilled something on her black workshirt. It looked like a dollop of mustard. It must have been a busy evening for her not to take the time to clean it off.

His gaze shifted upward. Her hair was hanging loose around her shoulders, looking silky and shiny, making him want to touch it. Higher yet, her eyes sparkled as she smiled at him, welcoming him home.

One of these days, Mac was going to convince this woman to marry him. For now, he'd take a good, long kiss instead.

"You're home early," she said, holding out her hand for him to take. "Was it that you couldn't stay away from Jackrabbit Junction, The Shaft, or me?"

"Yes." He caught her by the hand and pulled her in for a welcome-home kiss and maybe something more while they were at it. "But mainly you, Slugger."

She pressed against him, all warm, soft, and delicious. "I missed you." She wrapped her arms around his neck.

"Good." He nibbled on her jaw, making his way toward her ear.

"You didn't tell me you were coming back tonight."

"I wanted to surprise you."

The sound of her soft sigh eased his road-weary soul. "I like surprises."

"What else do you like?" He nuzzled her ear.

"Kittens and puppies."

Her skin smelled sweet with a hint of the pear-scented soap he'd given her for Christmas. "Everyone likes kittens and puppies, Claire."

"I also like you."

"Oh, yeah?"

"Yep. A lot."

"Show me." His hands spanned her hips, squeezing.

"Mac." She tipped her chin up, giving him easier access as his mouth slid lower toward her collarbone.

"What?"

"There's something I should probably tell you."

He pulled her shirt free of her jeans, reaching under it, wanting to feel the warm, supple skin he knew waited there. "You can tell me later."

"But I think—"

"No thinking." His fingers skimmed her ribcage, inching around to her back and southward. "Just skin and touching." He pulled back enough to stare into her dark eyes. "Kiss me, you saucy serving wench."

She chuckled, framing his face. "As you command, my lord."

"That's better." He leaned down to make it easier for her, waiting for her lips to brush over his.

Claire had a way of kissing with her whole body that left him winded at the same time as charged up and ready to barrel into battle. It was some sensual combination she did with her lips, her fingers, and her hips. No, it was more than that. Her tongue was involved, along with sultry sighs and moans that overheated his brain and everything else below it.

Many nights when he was alone in their bed in Tucson and she was here in Jackrabbit Junction, he'd tried to figure out her secret behind turning him inside out. But thinking about it had only made the ache to be near her sharper.

Claire trailed her fingers along his neck, sending a rush of shivers down his back. She kissed the corner of his mouth. Then his cheek. Then back to his lips, full on this time. Her tongue got involved, toying with his, teasing him into following her lead, giving him a taste of something sweet and fruity, leaving him wanting more.

She pulled back enough to breathe his name and take his hand in hers, lacing her fingers through his as she stared up at him. "Mac."

Claire.

Her lips moved as she said something to him, but he wasn't listening. He was too busy thinking about how much he wanted this right here every day—Claire, a life together, family and friends all around, maybe even a kid or two, and a dog or a cat or both. He'd even adopt a tortoise if it would help keep her at his side for the rest of his days. Those guys lived a long time.

He'd spent what little free time he'd had in Bisbee scouring real estate offerings in this area. In between figuring out options for where they could live, he'd researched the costs of building a new house on a chunk of land, including how much it would run to dig a well and set up a rainwater collection system, to hook up to solar and go off-grid, and to install a power station for charging a vehicle. He planned to keep his pickup, but he also wanted an economy vehicle to drive to and from The Shaft and around

Yuccaville. Or maybe a plug-in hybrid. Change everything up. What the hell.

Claire waved her hand in front of his face. "Did you hear me?"

He nodded, but then changed course. "Not really. Sorry, it was a long drive home."

"But you're listening now?"

"Sure, but I can't guarantee for how long."

"Because you're tired?"

"Because I'm touching you." He trailed his fingers along the smooth, warm skin of her lower back. "Your body has a way of fogging up my brain even when I'm wide awake."

She smiled. "Defog for a moment and focus on what I'm saying. I have to tell you about—"

A staccato of knocking sounded on the door.

"Claire, are you in there?" It was Kate.

"What do you need, Kate?" Claire called back.

"I'm sending out a Mac alert."

Mac raised one eyebrow. Claire shrugged in reply, and then twirled her index finger next to her temple.

So, Kate was still crazy. Nothing new on that front.

"I think I saw him over by the door a few minutes ago," Kate continued. "And I'm pretty sure his pickup is in the parking lot."

"Got it," Claire said. "I'll be out in a minute."

"Hurry up, it's busy out here," Kate said, her voice louder now. "And remember, keep your big mouth shut about working with our chain-gang pen pal. What's good for our goose is not good for your eagle-eyed boyfriend."

Jesus, what were Kate and Claire up to now?

Claire cringed. "Go away, Kate."

"Fine, you party-pooping sourpuss! This is me leaving while I'm giving you the bird."

Mac stepped back from Claire. He needed some space to think straight. He watched her, waiting to see if she would finish what Kate had started.

"I was going to tell you," she said. "It's what I've been trying to say since we came in here."

"I'm listening now."

Claire took a deep breath. "Okay, here goes."

He braced himself for something about the bar acquisition

paperwork or maybe the lumber delivery. But what had Kate meant by that "chain-gang pen pal" part?

"You and I are going to sneak into Sophy's house tonight around midnight to look for something under her dresser."

His brain tumbled backward onto its ass. "What?"

"Actually, it's not really sneaking, I guess, because Sophy told us we could go inside her place and Kate found the spare set of keys Butch was holding for her." She jammed her hands into her back pockets. "Those keys save us from landing in jail with a B&E charge on the docket, and with Kate staying put here at the bar where she'll be under constant watch by Grady and Butch, nobody will think twice about you and me leaving a little early to go home and catch some sleep. Wink-wink."

"What?" Mac said again, still trying to wrap his mind around the first part.

"Oh, that reminds me, we need to let Ronnie know you're home or she'll try to sleep in our bed. She's staying the night at the RV park so she can get to work on Ruby's bookkeeping early tomorrow before running to Yuccaville for supplies. She could have slept in Manny's Airstream, but he brought Mom home this evening, so we're all trying to avoid *that* nightmare."

"Christ." Mac scrubbed both hands down his face.

"Oh! And I need to introduce you to Luke. He's been so much help with Gramps's birding platform. We finished with the deck today. Tomorrow, we'll get started on the railing and the steps up to it. Gramps is now flapping his gums about us installing a more permanent pathway out to the platform rather than just a boardwalk, but that's a lot of cement or pavers or whatever he wants to use, so Luke and I are trying to change his mind."

"Holy fuck, Claire. How long was I gone?" He crossed to the couch so he could sit for a minute to let it all sink in.

"Too long." She came over and sat next to him. "You missed Kate and Penny going to jail. I had to go spring them. Well, officially Penny wasn't in jail and Kate shut herself in the cell and wouldn't come out until she knew Grady was there to make sure Deputy Dipshit didn't try to pin some trumped-up charges on her. Turns out he was spying on Kate and then got in her way and knocked her down."

"Kate fell?" Mac looked sharply at Claire, who didn't seem too concerned about that. "I take it the baby is okay."

"Yeah, she fell on top of Ernie and flattened him on the sidewalk like a squished rat. Unfortunately, she didn't break his spleen or give him any career-ending injuries, but he was pretty butt-hurt and embarrassed, from the sounds of it. As soon as Grady arrived at the sheriff's office, though, he dropped all talk of charges. It probably helped that Penny was at the library and witnessed the whole thing after their posse meeting with Aunt Millie and her fellow bruisers. Ernie knows better than to mess with the sheriff's sister. Not to mention that Penny is a Scorpio."

Mac frowned. "What's that have to do with Kate and Ernie?"

"Don't piss off Penny. She'll plot ten different ways to kill you in your sleep before you have a chance to say you're sorry."

"What about you?"

"Me? I'm an Aries. I'll straight up kill you and then get back to work."

"That's comforting."

"Speaking of work." Claire stood and held out her hand for him. "It's busy out there and I don't want Kate overdoing it tonight. She needs to be sharp in order to cover for us while we're up at Sophy's house."

Standing, he took her hand. "You're assuming I'm going with you."

She smiled at him as she led him toward the door. "Have I told you that I love you?"

"Declarations of love aren't going to cut it."

"What if I offer to kiss things better when we get back home in bed?"

"Which things in particular?"

She opened the door, letting in the clamor from the kitchen crew and the crowd out front.

"Use your imagination, big boy." She wiggled her eyebrows at him in Groucho Marx style.

"That's not sexy," he called after her, watching her walk away as he closed the door behind them.

"Yes, it is."

No, it wasn't. And why in the hell were they going to Sophy's house in the first place, damn it?

"Claire, wait!" He strode after her.

Chapter Nineteen

Saturday, Feb 2nd (just after midnight)

Every surface in The Mule Train Diner sparkled under the bright kitchen lights. The stainless steel countertops, the grill, the double oven, and the sink all positively gleamed. The floor was clean enough to eat off after Penny scrubbed tile by tile with a brush and ammonia water. The marble-topped baking table looked brand-new. Every single one of her temperature logs had been updated to the new format, fully filled out per the specifications, and clearly displayed.

Penny searched the room for something to clean or organize. Short of slapping a fresh coat of paint on the walls and ceiling, she was done. Hell, even the lights themselves had been de-greased and polished until they gleamed.

Yawning, she tugged off her elbow-length rubber gloves. What Penny wouldn't do to figure out a way to have Elizabeth receive as thorough of a colon inspection as the health inspector had given the diner today. The no-good worm-tongued, scumweasel of a dumpster twat's day of reckoning was coming.

Penny had spent the last six hours taking care of the boxes checked on the health inspector's worksheet, figuring the Draconian woman and her dour personality would probably return tomorrow or the next day for a follow-up inspection. While the violations were on the non-critical list, aka the "blue items" on the inspection sheet, Penny fully expected a return visit thanks to Elizabeth's apparent pull with somebody high up in the health department.

Grady needed to do something about his lying sack of shit ex before Penny did it for him and took Kate's place behind bars.

She sniffed her shirt and cringed—grease, dirt, and sweat. Her pants weren't much better, especially at the knees and butt. Even her hair felt stringy and grimy. Gross. There was no way she was sitting on the cloth seats of her SUV covered with this muck, not after having the interior detailed last week.

A glance at the clock set her in motion. Mississippi would be at The Shaft another hour yet, so she had enough time to clean up and skip out of here before he returned. She didn't want to take a chance of running into him and giving him the idea that she'd stuck around to see him.

Tugging off her shirt, she slipped out of her bra and stepped out of her jeans and undies, wadding everything up in a ball and stuffing them in a garbage bag. At the sink, she turned the water on warm and grabbed a clean rag from the stack, lathering it with the citrus-scented soap made with aloe and vitamin E that she used to keep her hands from drying and cracking.

She hurried through her equivalent of a sponge bath, including a quick hair wash. Then she grabbed the spare sweatpants and T-shirt she kept in her office for times like these. She dressed in a flash, pausing long enough to apply some lotion to her knees and elbows and hands, which all had taken a beating during her hours-long cleaning marathon.

The couch in her office tempted her. She needed to be back at work in only a few shakes, but there was that dang Mississippi factor to consider.

"This randy octopus has her pride," she told the couch.

After sliding on her quilted vest, she grabbed her purse, keys, and bag of dirty clothes and then closed her office door behind her. She paused for one last admiring look at her clean kitchen, breathing in the fresh, clean scent of lemon and ammonia.

"Fuck you, Elizabeth."

Without further ado, she shut off the radio and exited stage left. When she opened the back door, someone was standing in the dark, waiting for her, blocking her path.

She gasped and swung her purse, walloping the prowler upside the head.

Whump!

* * *

Same time, different place …

Claire leaned against the backside of Sophy's house in the deep shadows. Waiting. Listening. Shivering.

Nearby, a loose piece of the shed's corrugated tin roofing rattled and creaked with each puff of cold breeze swirling past. A pack of coyotes yipped and barked farther up the canyon, sounding like a rowdy bunch of hellions leaving a bar after closing time and heading out to look for trouble. Somewhere closer, javelina were milling about. She could smell their pungent musk whenever the wind paused to take a breath.

She tucked her hands in her armpits, doing her best to hold in the trembling that was trying to travel south to her knees. God, this place still gave her the creeps, even after all these months. Apparently, nearly being blasted in half by a shotgun at close range had long-term effects on her psyche. Go figure.

"If we have the house key," Mac said, joining her after finishing his perimeter check, "and we were given Sophy's permission to be here, then why are we tiptoeing around this place like a pair of cat burglars and sneaking in the back door?"

"Because I don't like the way things feel out here in the dark." She stared toward the shed, trying to see into the darkness beyond. "And going in the front feels too exposed."

He pulled her close, resting his chin on the crown of her head. "I don't like the way things feel here in the daylight, either, but someone was determined to drag me to Sophy's place tonight in spite of my request to table that idea until less paranoid thinking prevailed."

"Kate wouldn't stop badgering me all night."

"She's certainly relentless when she sets her sights on a notion."

"And rabid. She sinks her teeth in and won't let go."

"Reminds me of someone else I know." He squeezed her in a warm hug. "The teeth part, not foaming at the mouth."

"Hey!" Claire poked him in the ribs. "You're supposed to be comforting me, not taking potshots when my defenses are down."

"Your defenses are never fully down, Slugger." He leaned back, staring at her. "Your fortitude and grit are admirable traits.

But they do lead to heartburn when I'm a phone call away from you rather than only in another room."

She patted his chest. "I'm glad you're here now."

"I'm not so sure I am." He kissed her on the forehead. "Come on, let's go inside, find whatever it is Sophy wants, and then get the hell out of here. Preferably in one piece without any bullet holes."

She followed him, holding the screen open and handing off the set of keys that Kate had given her.

Without the man in the moon showing his face tonight, Sophy's place had been dark when they'd pulled up, hair-raisingly so. Mac had left the Jeep's headlights on, which helped brighten up the place some, but it also created spooky shadows at the fringes of Claire's vision that seemed to shift and sway.

As Mac unlocked the deadbolt, she huddled close to his side, glancing behind them. At any moment, she half-expected to see a dark, sinister form walking toward them.

Gadzooks! She was losing it.

Trying to distract her overactive imagination, she looked up at the swath of stars overhead. The Milky Way was really putting on a show tonight. So many stars. Where was the Big Dipper? There were too many stars to see it easily.

"Got it," Mac whispered.

Thank Jupiter!

"Let's go." He opened the door.

She followed tight on his heels, closing the door behind her and locking it. They didn't need anyone else joining them unannounced and scaring the piss out of her.

Mac hesitated for a moment in Sophy's laundry room, clicking his fancy flashlight a few times, apparently trying to decide if he wanted a bright narrow beam or a wide less-intense spread.

Claire shined her plain old flashlight around the room, spotlighting a jug of bleach, several bottles of degreaser and stain remover, and an empty laundry basket that sat on the counter next to the washer and dryer. It was almost as if Sophy were here yet, coming and going in between running Wheeler's Diner during the day and sneaking into Joe's mines at night, looking for more of his hidden treasures.

The place still smelled of stale cigarette smoke and dust, with a hint of something a little sweeter, similar to the last time Claire was in here. She sniffed. Was that Sophy's favorite perfume, Tabu? She knew that fragrance all too well thanks to Sophy and Henry, Gramps's ornery dog. Claire sniffed again. No, this was more subtle than the mix of jasmine, amber, and other floral notes. Less feminine, too.

"What are you doing?" Mac asked, shining his light in her direction.

"Sniffing the air."

"Why? Did you turn part hound dog while I was away this week?"

"For your information, Mr. Smartass, things smell different in here than I expected."

"Different how?"

"I don't know, just different than before."

He sniffed. "It stinks like stale cigarette smoke, dry rot, and old linoleum." He thumbed toward the kitchen. "You ready to go find your bargaining chip, or did you want to stand here all night in an old house full of mold and decaying who-knows-what and play the 'Guess that smell' game some more?"

* * *

Same time, previous place ...

"Ouch!" Mississippi said, holding the side of his face. "Jesus, Penelope. You could at least warn a guy before you clock him with a twenty-pound bag of flour."

With her heart still pounding out a panicky beat, Penny stepped back, leaving him room to join her inside. "It's not twenty pounds, you big baby." When he squinted at her in disbelief, she shrugged. "It's a wallet full of change and a paperback book."

He continued to glare at her.

"What? I like to read when I have a spare moment or two. How was I to know you were going to play boogeyman at my back door in the middle of the night?"

"I wasn't playing boogeyman." He closed the door behind him. "I was simply acting the part of a paying renter."

"Yeah, well I was just leaving." She pointed at the door, and then felt like a cold shrew for her attempted hit-and-run. "Listen, I'm sorry I whacked you. I wasn't expecting you back this early. It's not even closing time at The Shaft yet."

"The place died down early, which was surprising since it's Friday night. Anyway, Ronnie took off. She's staying at the RV park tonight so she can work there in the morning on some bookkeeping, which left me free to harass some other innocent woman." He moved his jaw around, tapping his cheek where her purse had left a red mark. "Those were Ronnie's words, not mine."

"So, you chose to harass me?" Should she feel flattered about that? Actually, she was a little, dang it.

"I chose nobody," he said. "I had two thoughts in mind as I drove back here. One was all about food and the other centered on that cushy bed upstairs."

Of course it had nothing to do with her. For crying out loud! It would be amazingly wonderful if she could manage to converse with this man and not make an ass of herself. Just once! Was that too much to ask?

"Okay," she said, anxious to leave before she crammed her other foot in her mouth, too. "I'll leave you to it then."

When she tried to move around him, he caught her by the arm. "Wait. Now that we're both here, what about staying a little longer and sharing my late-night snack." He held up a bag that smelled like old grease. "I'm buying."

"I can't. I've been here since this afternoon, and I have to be back in about five hours to start baking pies. Saturdays are crazy busy. I need some sleep."

He reached out and captured a tendril of her hair between his fingers, leaning closer. "You smell nice, clean. Did you shower upstairs?"

"No! Of course not!"

He grinned, letting go of her hair, but still holding on to her arm. "Whoa there, spitfire. I wasn't accusing you of a crime. No need to contact your attorney."

"I know, it's just that ..." She closed her eyes, wishing she'd have gone home as soon as she'd finished cleaning and avoided this whole cheek-burning scene. "I would never impose on your space like that, or enter your place without invitation, unless I was concerned for your safety." She pointed toward the sink. "I did a quick wash-up."

"Stay and eat with me. Please. I get tired of eating alone." He let go of her and started taking off his coat. "You have a couch in your office. You could crash there for a few hours when we're done, then you don't have to drive home."

"I like a bed better." As soon as the words left her stupid pie-hole, she cringed.

"Me too." His gaze traveled south of her chin.

Thank God she'd zipped her vest up, covering her T-shirt. Her lack of bra would be obvious otherwise.

"I should go." Before she made an even bigger mess of things here in her clean, sex-free kitchen.

"Come on, Penelope. Stay a little longer." He hung his coat on one of the wall hooks next to the door. "Keep a lonely guy company."

All sorts of reasons why she should go home played through her head, but his forlorn tone made her hesitate. She understood loneliness too well. She ate, drank, and slept loneliness on many days.

"It's the least you could do after trying to knock me out." He pushed up the sleeves of his waffle-knit shirt as he returned to where she stood. "I might have a concussion. You should stay and make sure I don't pass out."

She rolled her eyes. "Now you're reaching."

He held up the greasy bag again. "I got a spare burger."

"No." She took the bag from him and walked back into the kitchen, tossing his bribe where it belonged—in the trash.

"Hey!" He came up behind her, reaching for the bag of greasy grossness.

She batted his hands away, shoving him toward one of the stools at her baking table. "Sit down and let me make you a proper sandwich."

"Those burgers were made of meat and buns," he grumbled, taking a seat. "How is that not proper?"

She ignored his grousing and opened the door to one of her industrial-size refrigerators. "Do you like roast beef and red peppers?"

"Sure, but I don't want you to mess up your kitchen." He glanced around the room. "Is it just me, or is this place really shiny tonight?"

"Thanks for noticing. I spent the last six hours cleaning it from top to bottom."

"Is that normal? Like a once a week or month task?"

"No. I try to keep a clean kitchen, but this extra-polishing was an inspired job."

Inspired by a cold-hearted, crafty bitch. Penny had fantasized about the many ways she could murder Elizabeth in her sleep before deciding that a quick death was too kind for Grady's ex. A bit of torture and some maiming would be more satisfying, and then sending Elizabeth running out of town with her tail between her legs would make a nice finale.

She pulled out one of the roasts she'd prepared earlier for Saturday's lunch crowd. "This beef is some of the best I've found," she told Mississippi, looking for something neutral to fill the silence. Maybe if she talked food, she'd keep from saying something else that sounded half-baked. "It's from a butcher outside of Tucson who keeps his own herd. He feeds them a mix of fresh grass and corn."

It wasn't from the local grocery deli in town where Elizabeth had told some tall tales and screwed Penny over, but that deli did have some of the best cheese and cold cuts when she needed to resupply on short notice. If she didn't fix that situation, she would run into trouble during desperate times.

Next she grabbed the grilled peppers that she'd marinated in herbs, lemon juice, olive oil, and honey, along with some butter lettuce and her homemade mayonnaise with curry that she knew would bring out the flavors in the meat and peppers instead of smothering them.

"I didn't mean to make you have to work on my account."

She glanced at Mississippi. He was resting his forearms on the table as he watched her work. Under the bright lights, he looked worn around the edges, bordering on haggard. Unfortunately, that didn't make him less handsome. It just made her want to lead him into her office, lay him down on the couch with his head in her lap, and trace the lines on his face until he relaxed and fell asleep.

"This is easy stuff," she told him. And she needed to do it. She wanted to make him something good. Something that would impress him. Maybe even make him forget for a minute what a nincompoop she was in his presence more often than not.

"One sandwich or two?" she asked.

"Two—one for me and one for you."

She was about to tell him she didn't want anything, but after all that cleaning, she was hungry, too.

"How was The Shaft tonight?" She grabbed one of the hefty loaves of sourdough bread she'd made yesterday morning, cutting it in half and slicing some pieces from the center where the dough was soft but the crust was nice and crunchy.

"Busy initially, but boring mostly." He yawned, covering his mouth with the back of his hand.

"Anyone there worth an extra look?"

Like a certain long-haired blonde with a pool cue and mad crush on him? Or a new woman who didn't kiss like she was being electrocuted at the same time. Or someone even more worrisome who might want to hurt Ronnie?

"I saw Mac Garner come in a little after ten." He rubbed his eyes. "He'd told me he wouldn't be back until Saturday, so I was surprised to see him." He stretched his neck from side to side. "He took off with Claire the same time I left."

"Did Grady show up?" Like he was supposed to?

"Yep. He took your niece home. Ronnie was acting off tonight, though. Not just with your brother. I mean in general. Actually, she's been that way for a few days now."

"Off how?" She layered the meat, peppers, and lettuce on the mayonnaise-slathered pieces of bread.

"More skittish than usual."

She sliced the sandwiches in half, making the pieces easier to bite into when in the company of a guy who made her stomach gallop in spite of her attempts to corral her attraction to him.

Glancing his way, she asked, "You think there is something behind her change in behavior?"

Could this odd behavior be spurred by one of Elizabeth's attempts to dislodge Ronnie from Grady's side? Penny had been so busy lately defending herself from the conniving troublemaker that she hadn't thought about what might be going on in Ronnie's world.

"Hard to tell. Ronnie seems to go through waves of high anxiety depending on the updates we receive about her ex-husband's bullshit." He shook his head. "Can't say I blame her. Being a moving target 24/7 has to be nerve-wracking."

"And exhausting." She filled two glasses of water and delivered them to the table.

Just a week of taking potshots from Elizabeth had Penny wanting to bite off customers' heads and yell at the pushy old ladies feeling up the tomatoes in the grocery store.

She plated the sandwiches, adding some curled slices of navel oranges from a shipment of fresh citrus and produce that a friend had picked up for her southeast of Phoenix. As she set the plates down on the table in front of him, he hopped up and grabbed the spare stool she kept next to the sink, setting it down beside his.

"Thanks," she said, sighing as she dropped onto the stool. Her feet were tired buckaroos, wanting to be propped up for a few hours along with the rest of her body.

"This looks so good," he said, sitting and scooping up the sandwich. He smiled at her, adding more lines fanning out from his eyes. "I hope it's better than those two amazing burgers I had in the bag you tossed."

She laughed and lifted her own sandwich. "I'll let you be the judge."

The sandwiches went down easily, with only a few words shared in between bites, along with several words and groans of appreciation from Mississippi. When they finished, he insisted on washing their plates in the sink while she sat and watched.

He pushed the sleeves of his shirt higher, up over his elbows, bending over slightly as he scrubbed and rinsed. Penny stared her fill, admiring his long legs, broad shoulders, and everything in between when she should have been grabbing her things and zipping out the door. But she wanted to enjoy this quiet moment with him for a little longer. Usually, they were battling on some level in each other's company. Tonight, they'd called a ceasefire.

When he grabbed the clean towel she had hanging next to the sink, she told him, "You can just let the dishes air-dry in the rack."

He dried his hands before hanging the towel back the way she'd had it.

"Do you want some dessert?" There were a few pieces of pie left over from lunch yet in the fridge.

"Yes," he said, returning to where she sat.

"Let's see." She closed her eyes, trying to remember exactly what she had. "I have some leftover white chocolate cheesecake and some pumpkin cream caramel pie. A couple pieces of pecan pie that's based on my mom's favorite recipe. Oh, and there's some lemon meringue left, along with a single piece of s'more pie." She opened her eyes. "What sounds …" She trailed off at the intensity in his gaze. He was hungry, all right, but clearly not for pie. "Good?" she finished in a whisper.

"You know what I want," he said, staring at her mouth.

"No," she lied.

Mississippi reached down and cupped her chin, rubbing his thumb along her lower lip. "And you want it, too."

"No, I don't," she lied again, her voice sounding hoarse.

He smirked. "Penelope Harrison, you are a lousy liar."

Chapter Twenty

Same time, previous different place …

Let's go get that damned bargaining chip, smartass," Claire told Mac. She shined her light around Sophy's laundry room again, pausing on a corner closet filled with brooms and mops and a few old coats. "Before I chicken out and hightail it back to the RV park without you."

"I have the key to your Jeep," Mac reminded her. "So you're not going anywhere without me, Slugger."

He'd made a point of taking it from her before they'd left the safety of her vehicle, as if he didn't trust her. Wise man.

"Okay," she said. "You lead, I'll follow."

He headed into the kitchen. In the beam of his flashlight, dust particles swooped and swerved. The silence in the house felt thick, like she was hidden under a cloak. Besides her ears ringing, she could hear her heart pounding. The lily-livered organ needed to slow down and quit panicking. That same order went for her lungs and their panting breaths.

She stopped in front of the kitchen sink. The Wayne Newton salt-and-pepper shakers were still on the windowsill where she'd seen them before. The Las Vegas pictures and postcards remained taped on the refrigerator and cupboard doors, too. Same as Claire had felt in the laundry room, it was as if Sophy were still coming and going. And still obsessed with having that glittery Las Vegas life.

Claire stared out the window into the darkness. Without the moon, she could hardly make out anything.

"Do you see something?" Mac asked from where he waited in the archway that led into the dining room.

"No. It's too dark."

"Then stop staring out there. You're freaking me out."

She shined her light in his direction. "You're supposed to be a big, brave manly man who stands tall in the face of danger," she teased. "Otherwise, why do you think I brought you along?"

Actually, Mac was pretty damned gutsy. How many times had he gone into one of his aunt's dark, creepy mines all by himself for hours on end, mapping out the different drifts, stopes, and shafts? Then there was the cave-in. Oh, and that time with the dead guy. And of course he'd had his own heart-palpitating run-in with Sophy and her gun.

"I know exactly why you dragged me here."

"I didn't actually drag you." When his gaze narrowed, she changed her story. "Well, you weren't kicking and screaming or anything like that. Just complaining."

"You basically blackmailed me, woman."

"What? Blackmail?" She feigned innocence. "I did no such thing."

"What do you call threatening to come up here on your own tonight if I refused to ride along?"

She called it a well-played case of hoodwinking. Of course, she was guilty as charged. Same as her crazy sister, Claire wanted to know if Joe was out there watching and waiting. Her ass was on the line, along with Gramps's, if Ruby's dead husband was still sharing oxygen with the living. Claire had known there was no way Mac would let her come here without him. The protector in him wouldn't stand for that, and she loved him that much more because of it.

So, she'd pretended she had the balls to come up to Sophy's alone. The poor, tired guy had followed her across The Shaft's parking lot to her Jeep, listing the reasons coming up to Sophy's was a bad idea the whole time, even after climbing into the passenger seat and buckling up. Underneath her false bravado, she agreed with him. Coming up here could be dangerous. But Claire's spare time was in short supply and Kate was right, damn it—there was no better time to pull off this covert mission than in the middle of the night when Butch and Grady and Gramps (and anyone else who might object) were otherwise preoccupied.

"I wouldn't call it blackmail, per se." She held the flashlight beam under her chin, widening her eyes and giving him her best creepy smile as she added in a Dracula voice, "I just vanted your company, Renfield, and in exchange I vill grant you a little immortality."

He held up his hand and started ticking off his fingers. "First, I'm not your deranged and devoted servant, Count Dracula—well, I'm not deranged usually, only when you're around. Second, I don't eat flies or spiders. Third, Renfield dies at the hands of Dracula, which seems fitting with you luring me up here tonight."

"Nice! You know your classic horror literature."

"Please. It's *Dracula*."

"You still have two points left to make with that hand, wise guy."

He frowned at his fingers, as if he'd forgotten he was holding them up. "Fine. Fourth, you wanted me to come along tonight because you find me swoonfully sexy. And fifth, your life has no meaning when I'm not by your side."

She giggle-snorted. "Have I told you how swoonfully sexy you are when you show off your big brain?"

He returned to her side, took her by the elbow, and led her toward the dining room. "Move your beautiful ass, Claire. I want to go home and sleep. Preferably next to you naked. Or mostly naked. Or even fully clothed. Hell, I don't care as long as you're there and my eyes are closed."

The round table in the dining room had a loose stack of mail precariously piled on one end.

Claire picked up a letter from AARP that had almost slid off the edge and tossed it back on the top of the stack. "I wonder when Dory was last here."

Initially, Sophy had been paying Butch to watch the place after she'd landed behind bars, a task that he'd done out of his own moral debt for her help with setting up his business when he'd first arrived in the area years back. But then she'd pushed her luck and pissed Butch off, so he'd told her she needed a new caretaker. However, according to Kate, he'd agreed to keep Sophy's spare keys for the time being in case her new caretaker—which turned out to be that jackass, Dory, who worked for Tucson Power and Electric—lost his keys.

"Judging by Sophy's mostly empty mailbox," Mac told Claire, which she'd checked while he'd unlocked the padlock on the driveway gate, "I'd say Dory was here sometime in the last week or two."

"You think she gets much mail these days?"

"Probably just the typical sales sort of stuff." He pointed at the AARP envelope. "Like life and car insurance offers."

They moved to the living room next. The shades were drawn in this room, and the air smelled like the 1970s had been holing up in here with a carton of unfiltered cigarettes and a six-pack of cheap beer.

Mac pointed his flashlight beam at the large, ancient console television. "This sucker must weigh a ton."

"That there is a classic piece of art." Claire joined him in front of it. "Maybe we can buy it from Sophy and use it for a conversation piece at The Shaft. Set it over by the pool tables. Hell, for a few extra bucks, we can probably get this light-up version of the old Vegas Strip, too." She tapped her flashlight on the framed picture above the TV. "Retro art can be a real crowd draw."

"You're cute when you're talking shit, you know that?"

She patted him on the butt. "I'm always cute. Remember that the next time we're arguing about the business."

Mac shined his flashlight around the room, only to bring the beam back to the brown couch. "That looks used."

"If it's as old as the other stuff in here, it's well-used."

"No, I mean it looks *recently* used."

She followed him over to the couch, knocking her shin on the glass coffee table. "Damn it. I do that every time."

"You've only been in here once before."

"Yeah, well, I did it then, too." She stared down at the rumpled couch with well-worn armrests. "What makes you think this was recently used?"

"The blankets are still spread out on it." He looked back toward the dining room, frowning. "When you dragged me in here last time—which I'll remind you was against my will then, too ..."

"This is me playing your sad song on a teeny violin," she said, pretending to hold a small version of the instrument, using her flashlight as the bow.

He stole her flashlight. "Anyway, the last time I was here, the blankets were folded precisely and stacked on the floor next to the couch. I remember that detail because they looked so straight and perfect compared to how messy the rest of this place was. Then I learned that Sophy's dad had been in the Army, and I figured maybe he'd taught her some old military way of folding."

"Maybe Dory likes to take naps here."

Claire looked around for any other signs of someone hanging out in the room. The ashtray was empty. Not clean exactly, but no butts were left in it. There were no glasses half-full of water or beer or whatever else Dory might like to drink sitting on the coffee table. No food wrappers wadded up and tossed into the corners.

"Maybe we should hurry up and get out of here," Mac whispered.

Now who was acting out *Dracula*?

"Maybe we should." Claire took her flashlight back from him and stepped into the hall leading toward the bedrooms and single bathroom. There were four doors, all closed, same as they'd been the first time she was there.

"Why are you stopping here?" Mac asked when she paused partway down the hall. "Sophy's room is at the end."

"I know. But I'm curious."

She opened the door and stepped into the narrow room where Sophy had stored a bunch of Joe's fenced antique pieces that she'd taken from the thieving bastard's hiding places. Claire wasn't sure whether Sophy had stolen the pieces from her ex-husband before or after his death, but she had a good idea of the value of most of the pieces, and there had been close to a hundred thousand dollars' worth of goods stacked in here.

But they were gone now.

"I wonder what she did with it all," she said, shining her light around the empty room.

"Whatever the law didn't take she probably sold for money to buy cigarettes in the big house." He put his arm around her and turned her back toward the hallway. "Come on, Slugger. My pillow is waiting."

They moved to Sophy's bedroom next. Like the last room, this place looked barren. A lumpy bed remained with an old-style embroidery duvet covering it, as well as the dresser that had been there before, but the bottles of perfume and other trinkets that had covered the top of the dresser were gone. Next to the bed, Sophy's reading glasses were gone, too, but the Vegas ashtray was there. The room still smelled like her: a bit smoky, a bit sweet, a bit alarming.

"Where exactly is Sophy's all-important commodity supposed to be?" Mac asked.

"Under the dresser."

Claire dropped to her knees and peered underneath the chest of drawers. A solid layer of dust bunnies stood guard, blocking her view. She blew at them, realizing how asinine that notion was a moment too late.

"Don't say a word," she said in between sneezing and coughing. She scrubbed her face with the arm of her coat.

Mac kneeled next to her, clearly trying not to laugh. "When I think of all the dead skin cells …" he started.

Oh, ick! She shined the light in his face. "Stop it, or I swear I'll collect a few of the dust bunnies from under there and stuff them in your mouth after you go to sleep."

"You Morgan women are a vindictive lot."

"And don't you forget it." She ruined her threat with a pair of sneezes.

"So, did you see anything while you were whispering sweet nothings to the wads of dust and hair and skin flakes under there?" He made a wry face. "You know, there might even be some cockroach wings mixed in with that stuff."

She scowled. "What is wrong with you?"

He shrugged. "I'm feeling some residual frustration from your blackmail attempt."

"It was not an 'attempt' since you're here with me."

"So you admit you're guilty."

"I admit to nothing. You'll have to torture me to find the truth."

"The rack it is. Don't worry, I'll be gentle when I strap you down."

"You better be or I'll tell my mom on you."

Claire had yet to see her mother in person since her return from Tucson, due in part to Claire's busy schedule, but mainly because of some tactical maneuvering on her part. However, Deborah and Manny were indeed back at the RV park according to Ruby, who'd been making dark chocolate brownies with peanut butter cup centers when Claire had headed to The Shaft to meet the lumber delivery guy.

"Your mother's forked tongue doesn't scare me."

"You say that now, but wait until she's standing over our bed in the morning with her red glowing eyes and pointy horns."

"You think she'll be any nicer now that she's sober?"

Claire laughed in reply and then leaned down to take another peek under the dresser. She shined her light along the wooden underbelly, finally seeing an envelope duct-taped to it toward the back corner.

"Can you lift one side of this thing, tough guy?"

"You just want to see my brute force in action."

"You caught me. I'm only in this relationship for your grand displays of strength, Mr. McMuscles."

Mac stood and opened the top drawer for a better grip. He raised the side of the dresser enough for Claire to reach under and pull the envelope free while trying not to roll around in the dust bunnies.

"What is it?" he asked as he set the dresser down.

"An envelope." She held it under the light, noticing a slightly brownish-yellow stain on one corner. "It looks like coffee was spilled on it."

"Or a rodent peed on it." When she wrinkled her nose up at

him, he shrugged. "What? We don't know what's been in this house since Sophy's been gone. Or even before she was gone. She wasn't the best housekeeper, if you'll remember."

"How would a rodent pee on something taped to the bottom of a dresser?"

"Maybe it peed on it before she taped it there."

"Why would she keep an envelope that's been peed on?"

"Because she's unhinged from breathing in too much hair spray, diner grease, and cigarette smoke over the years."

Mac had a point. "I think Joe pushed her off the deep end. Sophy wanted what he wouldn't give her for too long. All of that frustration and anger and hatred cracked her brain in half."

"Don't forget the jealousy when it came to how much Joe liked my aunt." Mac pointed at the envelope. "Are you going to open that or am I?"

"Kate's going to be bummed she wasn't here for this."

"Kate shouldn't have put her own ass in jail again."

Holding the envelope by one of the clean corners, Claire let it rest partially on the dresser while she tore it open. Inside were several sheets of paper. She pulled them out and smoothed them flat.

Mac shined his light on them.

"They look like sheets from an address book," she said. The lines on the paper did, anyway. "But the words are all scrambled and include symbols and numbers."

"It's some sort of code. Is that Sophy's handwriting?"

Claire leaned closer. "Actually, the shape of some of the letters reminds me more of Joe's sloppy scrawls, but I'd have to compare it to one of the documents in Ruby's basement to be sure."

After a few more seconds of looking at the scribbled gibberish, Claire folded the papers and stuffed them in the inside pocket of her coat.

"What about the envelope?" Mac asked.

"After what you said about the piss? No, thanks." She carefully flipped the envelope over once more. "Besides, there's nothing written on it, so we might as well trash it."

Claire carried it down the hall to the bathroom where cans of hairspray still lined the back of the vanity. Sophy's hair must be flat as a pancake in prison. That alone probably made her fantasize about filleting Claire every morning for her part in putting Sophy behind bars.

After she dropped the envelope into the trashcan next to the open-lid toilet, she cursed. "You can't leave it here," she told her reflection in the mirror. Dory might see it and realize someone had been in the house, alerting the authorities—aka Grady. And then shit would really hit the fan for Kate.

Maybe she should bury it under the mountain of envelopes on the table. Shining her light toward the trashcan, Claire reached down to grab the envelope. Something glinted in the corner next to the sink as her light skimmed over it.

Was that a candy wrapper? She bent closer. Actually, it looked like a ... "Oh, shit."

What were the chances of finding one of those here?

"Mac," she called out.

"I'm right here," he said quietly from the doorway.

"Come look at this?"

He hesitated. "At what?"

She pointed downward.

"Is it a dead rat in the toilet?" he asked, still holding back.

"No."

"A mouse then?"

"No."

"A pocket gopher?"

"Criminy, what is it with you and rodents?" She nailed him in the face with her flashlight beam. "Would you get your sweet cheeks over here and take a look."

Cringing in anticipation, he stepped closer. "It's a cigar butt."

"What?" She was spotlighting the wrapper in the corner, clear as day.

"What do you mean *what?*" He pointed at the toilet bowl. "There's a cigar butt partway hidden in the trap."

"I wasn't looking in the toilet."

"There's this, too," he said, nudging the Vegas ashtray on the vanity. It was mostly empty but for the ashes lining the corners.

"Someone was smoking while on the pot," she stated the obvious.

He chuckled. "Your detective skills are incredible, Slugger. You should see if Grady will hire you as a contracted sleuth. We could use the extra cash for the brewery addition."

"Too late. Kate's applying for that job, and maybe signing up to be a deputy, too."

"Lord help us all then."

Claire bent down and reached to the floor next to the trashcan, snagging the gold-foil cigar wrapper while being careful not to touch the toilet.

"You're going to shower before joining me in bed tonight, right?" Mac joked as she set the wrapper on the vanity and leaned over it.

"I thought you liked it when I'm dirty." Was that a black panther on the cigar wrapper? Or a jaguar? Either way, the cigar was from Cuba, according to the writing under the animal.

"I like it when you *talk* dirty." He moved back to the doorway. "Have you ever seen Dory smoke a cigar?"

"No." She looked up from the wrapper. "I think these are very expensive cigars. The illegal kind."

She took out the sheets of address paper with gibberish scrawled on them and used them to scoop up the wrapper, carefully folding the sheets around it and pocketing it all.

"Since when did you become a cigar guru?" Mac asked as she stepped out into the hallway with him.

"Since I found that stash of cigar butts back in the ravine last week." And she'd later found a gold-foil wrapper caught in the spines of a nearby cholla cactus when she'd searched the area.

Mac followed her as she made her way back through the house and outside into the darkness. As she waited for him to lock the place up tight, she thought about Joe and what she knew of his sordid history—theft, betrayal, selfishness, greed. There'd been lies. So many lies. Not to mention murders, too, according to Sophy.

After they'd climbed into the Jeep and Claire had locked them inside, Mac handed her back the Jeep key.

"Maybe Sophy skimmed a stash of Joe's fenced cigars at some point," Mac said. "Dory could have found them while taking care of her place."

"And then what? Dory sat on the toilet and smoked one while nosing through Sophy's mail?" Claire shook her head. "I don't think so."

She started the engine and did a U-turn, kicking up some gravel in her haste to get out of there.

"Okay, Sherlock, spit it out. What's your theory?"

"I suspect Joe's been using Sophy's house to hide out while he spies on Ruby and the RV park." She slowed as they approached the gate at the bottom of the drive, frowning his way. "I know you don't believe me, Mac, but I'm telling you, that man isn't dead."

Chapter Twenty-One

Mississippi was right. Penny was a bad liar.

He was also right about her knowing exactly what he wanted, and her wanting that very same thing herself. Damn him for tempting her.

Actually, this was her own fault. She was the one who'd followed him out to his truck and ambushed him. If she'd only kept her hands to herself.

She should leave the diner.

She should grab her purse and dirty clothes, tell Mississippi good night, climb into her SUV, go home and go to bed. Alone. The End.

But she didn't move. Instead, she held stone-still on the kitchen stool while he continued to stand over her, holding her chin, staring at her with an intensity that left no doubt of his own longing.

She waited for him to bend down. To lean in. To kiss her. To start what she really wanted to enjoy finishing.

Come on, she silently willed him. Sex in her work kitchen would be a first for her. Wait. On second thought, she'd spent six hours cleaning this place from top to bottom, so maybe they should move to her office before any clothes hit the floor.

Mississippi made his first move—back to the other stool, putting breathing room between them. "Lemon meringue," he said, as if she were standing in front of him with an order pad and a pencil.

Lemon *what?* She stared at him, her sex-hungry brain busy grinding gears, having trouble shifting into reverse.

He shrugged. "I'm a simple guy who likes a simple pie."

Oh, jeez on toast! He was talking about dessert. As in eating it. Right now.

Truly, Penny needed to finish feeding this man and then get the hell out of Dodge before she made a big bumbling fool of herself for the umpteenth time.

She practically vaulted off her stool. "Of course. Lemon meringue. One slice coming up."

At the refrigerator, she tried to soak some of the cool air into her sweaty, embarrassed pores, taking her time dishing up his dessert. When she returned to the table with a fork in hand, she had her body under control again.

Mostly, anyway.

"Where's yours?" he asked after she sat the plate down in front of him and then plopped down on the stool without any for herself.

"I had some earlier."

"Which is your favorite?"

She shrugged, happy to focus on work, which didn't leave her hot, horny, and humiliated more often than not. "It changes based on the day and the time of year. I've done a lot of experimenting, so I've had a lot of pie in my time. It's hard to pick one or two … or even five."

He forked off the tip of the triangular piece, getting a good amount of meringue along with the lemon. She watched him slide the bite into his mouth, holding her breath a little, while she waited to see if he liked it. She'd squeezed those lemons herself early this morning.

Actually, that was yesterday morning. Which reminded her yet again that it was time to skedaddle and get some rest or she'd be asleep on her feet midway through the list of pies she needed to make later this morning.

"Damn, Penelope." He swallowed, pointing the fork at the pie. "This is incredible."

"It was better when it was fresh."

"I can't imagine how it could be better." He forked off another piece and stuck it in his mouth, groaning as he chewed and swallowed.

"You don't have to try to make me feel good about the pie."

Making pies was one thing she knew she could do well.

"I'm not." He paused to take a drink of water. "I'm just enjoying the best lemon meringue pie of my life." He smiled at her. "If you could give me a minute, pretty lady. I'd like to be alone with this pie."

She laughed and stood. "Actually, that's a good idea. It's really late, so—"

"Penelope," he said, rising as well.

"Yeah?"

"Will you do me a small favor?"

"Sure."

He took a forkful of pie filling, minus the crust, and held it up. "Take one bite.'

She shook her head. "It's all yours."

"Please." He moved the fork closer to her.

After a moment, she shrugged. "Okay, fine."

She opened her mouth, and he carefully fed her the bite of pie. The lemon still had a good kick, which was offset wonderfully by the meringue. Although it wasn't quite as stiff as it had been this morning.

She swallowed and licked her lips. "Those Meyer lemons add a lovely natural sweetness and depth. Next time, I think I might try—"

"Penelope."

"What?"

"I want to kiss you now."

"You do?"

He nodded slowly. "I want to taste the lemon and sugar on your tongue."

She gulped. "I'm not sure that's a good idea."

"Oh, I think it's a great idea, but I'm not going to kiss you against your will."

Silence filled the room. Over by the sink, the clock ticked away the seconds.

"Well?" His gaze held steady on hers.

He really meant it. He'd taken the first step by telling her what he wanted. Now it was up to her to take the next.

It was time to go home now.

Yep.

Definitely.

She took the fork from him and loaded it up with more sweet pie filling, sticking the bite in her mouth. Then, without letting her brain overthink things, she swallowed the lemon creaminess and reached up, pulling his mouth close to hers.

"All right, Mississippi. Try me."

He came in smooth and sweet, like the pie. His lips coaxed hers apart, making room for a sweep of his tongue. A groan followed from low in his chest. His fingers threaded her hair, tipping her mouth up for another taste. The second kiss went deeper and longer, his tongue exploring and teasing.

"Christ," he rasped when he pulled back slightly. "We need to try this over and over with different pie fillings."

Her laugh came out husky and thick in her throat. "Pie with Penelope. I could charge patrons per kiss," she joked.

"No way." Mississippi sat down on the stool again. "This was my idea. I get to decide who tastes the pies, and it's me and me alone." He scooped up another bite of filling, this time feeding it to himself. After a moment of savoring the taste, he swallowed, set the fork down, and caught both of her hands, pulling her to her feet. "It's your turn. Kiss me."

"What are the magic words?" she teased, moving closer, squeezing between his thighs, looking at him eye to eye.

Mississippi lifted her hands to his mouth. His gaze never left hers as he kissed the sensitive center of one of her palms and then the other. His lips tickled her skin, sending shockwaves deep down to where her body throbbed for more of him.

"I'd like more Penelope, please," he said, releasing her hands.

"That'll do." She took his face between her hands and kissed him like she'd been wanting to do since he'd walked into her kitchen.

She didn't bother with starting slow. Nope. She went in full speed ahead, pushing against him hard so that he had to grab her and hold on tight.

And he did just that, gripping her hips and drawing her even closer, flattening her curves against his rigid muscles.

But this wasn't close enough. She wanted to feel skin. Everywhere.

She reached down, grabbing his shirt hem, yanking it up. "Get rid of this thing."

"Are you always like this?" he asked, pulling off his shirt.

"Like what?"

She ran her lips down his neck and along the hot skin covering the ridge of his collarbone. When she came to the swell of muscles rounding his shoulder, she bit lightly, making the muscles there tighten.

"Vigorous."

"You mean like a randy octopus?" she kidded, trying to make light of their first round of rumpy-pumpy in his truck.

"More like a dominant succubus." His hands rounded her hips and slipped inside the waistline of her pants, his fingers sliding south over her bare skin. "Oh, sweet Jesus," He let out a shaky breath. "You're not wearing any panties."

She ran her tongue along the curve of his ear. "Do you want to touch me?"

A strangled-sounding laugh was his reply.

"Tell me where," she whispered.

"Not in your kitchen."

Not in my what? She pulled back, frowning down at his closed eyes. Had she heard that right, or was her overheated brain short-circuiting? Did that mean … Oh, shit. Had she mistaken his comments about her assertiveness as a good thing? A lot of guys didn't like women who were forceful in bed, such as her ex. Maybe it was an FBI thing—the whole need to retain control of a situation at all times. Ah, hell. Would she ever manage *not* to come across as a huge horny toad to Mississippi?

She reached down and removed his hands from her pants and then took a step back from him and the situation. "I'm sorry. I overstepped your boundaries again." She reached for the plate of half-eaten pie. "I'll just clean this up and let you get some rest."

He caught her arm in a steel grip as she lifted the plate. "Put it down, Penelope."

As she set the plate back onto the table, he stood. "You can take it upstairs if you'd like."

Why would she? "I don't want to take the pie upstairs."

"Okay. But I'm taking you." He pointed at the ceiling. "There's a nice, soft bed that's waiting for us." He grabbed his shirt and slung it over his shoulder while keeping hold of her arm. "And while my landlady says I'm not allowed to have sex up there, I'm hoping she'll give me some leeway tonight."

Should she? Have sex, yes. But what about going upstairs? They'd be setting a precedent.

"Come on, Penelope. We're two single adults." He tugged her along behind him as he threaded through the kitchen toward the stairs leading to the upstairs apartment.

Penny pulled him to a stop at the first stair step. "This is a bad idea, isn't it?"

The first time they'd screwed around, it had been an impulsive parking lot romp with liquor involved. In the light of day, that was easy to write off as a one-time fling. Lesson learned about mixing liquor and a good-looking, undercover agent. If they were to go up these stairs, take off each other's clothes, and spend the rest of the night touching and kissing—and licking and tasting—this would no longer be a simple matter of drunken horseplay. This was a fully sober decision to go to bed with him. And then what?

"Don't put too much thought into it," he said, lightly tugging on her. "Just let this happen."

He was right. She was being silly. Why would she want to stop it? Mississippi was offering what would probably be at least one orgasm, free of charge. Free of entanglements, too. So what if he'd be hanging around a little longer than she'd originally thought? It wasn't like he was putting down any roots. In time, he'd leave the area for good and nobody would know any different. Except her. But she'd be okay. Her heart wasn't in this. It knew better than to take any risks after the last betrayal.

"Of course." She followed him up a couple of steps. "We'll just marinate the loin and then I'll head home."

He stopped and turned back to frown down at her. The shadows in the stairway adding a touch of *Phantom of the Opera* drama to his expression. "Did you say 'marinate the loin'?"

"Yeah. You know, make some bacon."

His frown deepened. He let go of her arm.

"Sink the sausage?" she threw out, surprised he hadn't heard the previous two nicknames for getting busy.

"Penelope," he started and then shook his head. "Did they teach you this food-related sex slang in culinary school?"

She tipped her head, staring up at him. She hadn't really talked to him about that part of her past. Maybe he was just taking a wild guess based on her pie-making abilities. "How do you know I went to culinary school?" Had he checked up on her?

"Kate filled me in about San Francisco."

If Kate had told him about that, then she must have also talked about Penny's ex-fiancé. Oh, God, another rush of embarrassment heated her face. "You must think I'm some kind of FBI rodeo buckle bunny."

He lifted one dark eyebrow. "I've never put the FBI and rodeo riders in the same category before."

She shrugged. "You both last about eight seconds before packing up your saddle and heading to the next town."

"Wow." He reached out and tapped her shoulder. "That's some chip you have there."

Yeah, it was, but she hadn't been the one who chiseled it deep into the bone. She raised her chin. "Tell me I'm wrong. Tell me that you haven't enjoyed a woman in different ports of call and then packed up and moved on to the next assignment without looking back."

He crossed his arms. "I thought you said you weren't looking for anything long term."

"I'm not."

"Then what's going on here?"

How had this gone south so quickly? Her body still wanted him. Throbbed and ached for more of what they'd started with the sweet pie kisses. But her pride now stood in the way.

She sighed. "I don't know. It's late. I'm tired. Let's just call it a night." She turned to start down the steps.

"Penelope, wait."

She looked back at him. "What?"

"Sit down next to me." He dropped onto one of the wooden stair steps and patted the spot next to him. When she hesitated, he held his hands out, palms up. "Please. Just for a minute."

She sank down next to him, keeping a small space between them, and laced her fingers together over her knees. "Okay, I'm sitting."

He glanced her way. "Tell me what happened."

"The bastard screwed around on me." She kept it simple.

"Not with your ex. I meant tell me what happened between us

here, just a few moments ago."

Oh, jeez. Penny covered her hot face. "Damn it. Why can't I just be normal around you?"

"You're not being normal?"

She scoffed. "Not even remotely. For some reason, I turn into a flustered, feather-brained goofball who goes back and forth between throwing herself at you in some ridiculously mortifying way or saying stupid, awkward shit that makes me sound like I'm brand-new to flirting and ..." she almost said *making love*, but stopped, unsure if that sounded too emotional for what they'd done in his pickup. "And other copulating techniques," she finished, and then cringed.

What in the hell were *copulating techniques?*

Mississippi chuckled. "I find you refreshing, Penelope, in a quirky yet very sexy way."

" 'Quirky'? A few days ago, you told me that when I was kissing you in your pickup, it was as if I were being electrocuted. That's not quirky, Mississippi. It's plain weird. And maybe borderline creepy, too."

He laughed, capturing one of her hands and holding onto it when she tried to pull away. "You are not weird or creepy or a goofball. Maybe I'm doing something that is throwing you off your game." He sobered. "Or maybe it's the fact that I remind you too much of the last guy who screwed things up by being a selfish, philandering prick."

So, Kate had told him about Penny's ex. "You're different than him," she admitted, staring down at their linked hands. "I didn't think so at first, but now that I know you a little better ..." She shrugged.

"Not all of us FBI robots are the same."

"Yeah."

"Some of us know a good thing when we see it."

She wasn't sure where he was going with this, so she just kept her pie-hole shut and waited.

"Some of us know better than to get involved with anyone connected with a job," he continued, "yet I can't stop thinking about the county sheriff's sister, who knocked me for a loop last week out of the clear blue."

She smirked. "You're just trying to cheer me up."

"That's not entirely true."

"Then what is the entire truth?"

"I'm trying to get into your pants again, especially now that I know you're not wearing anything under them."

She smiled, bumping shoulders with him. "You're a lot funnier than he was."

"And I'm better in the sack, too."

"Well, you are certainly willing to be tested on that."

He looked down the stairwell, his forehead lined.

She bit her lip and looked down the stairwell, too, wondering if she'd said the wrong thing again.

"Penelope," he said, his voice barely above a whisper.

She glanced his way, getting snared in his gaze. "Yeah?"

"Come here."

She knew from the look in his eyes what he really meant by those two words. She leaned toward him.

He met her halfway, holding her still while they shared a slow kiss that started out soft and tender, growing steadily with heat and depth and the need for more.

Without overthinking things, she turned and straddled his lap, her knees bracketing his hips on the hard stair step.

"Penelope—" he started, but she cut him off with her mouth.

She didn't want to ruin another kiss with any more talk or tussles. She didn't want to think about her past or either of their futures. All that mattered was feeling wanted, maybe even needed, for just this moment in a shadow-filled stairwell far away from the rest of the world and the problems and frustrations that came with it.

Fortunately, he obliged. His hands kneaded her thighs and hips as she pressed against him. His tongue kept pace with hers.

He groaned. But it didn't sound wanting or hungry, more like something was hurting him. Maybe it was her weight. And then he grunted, shifting under her.

She pulled back. "Are you okay?"

"No."

"You want me to get off you?" She started to push away, but he held her in place, shifting again.

"Okay, that's better."

"You sure?" She stayed up on her knees, holding her weight

off him.

"Yes. The step was digging into my back." He pulled her back down onto his lap. "Take off your vest."

She blinked. "Take off my … ?"

"You heard me. Vest. Off. Now." He glanced down. "My shirt's off. It's your turn to even the score."

"I don't have a bra on," she said, as if that might be a problem for him. Idiot! "I mean, that's not really a showstopper, I just …" God, she was doing it again. What was it about Mississippi that turned her into a fumbling dolt?

"I've known that since I walked in the place, Penelope."

"It's a thick vest."

"Not that thick. And you aren't exactly flat-chested." He started to unzip her vest. "Come on. I want to see you. Last time it was too dark." He paused to kiss the underside of her chin.

She unzipped the vest and shrugged it off.

He leaned back, resting his elbows on an upper step as he stared. "That's a good start. Now take the T-shirt off."

She pulled her T-shirt over her head, managing to elbow the wall in the process, before tossing it behind him on the stair step.

He stared at her chest for several seconds.

Penny rubbed her throbbing elbow, afraid to say anything and screw up the moment.

"Damn," he said in a delicious, husky voice. "Mind blown. Appetite whetted. Pulse electrified. Body ready to be enslaved, abused, ridden hard, you name it. I'll attend your every need, woman, or let you attend mine, I don't care. Just let me know when I can start."

She chuckled. "Do you always approach sex like you're working a crime scene, listing off your thoughts on the matter?"

"Usually I keep it all in my head, but I made a special case for you."

"You don't have to flirt with me to make it to first base, Special Agent Brown. If my shirt's off, I'm waving you into home."

"I'm not flirting. I just really like *everything* about you."

Then why wasn't he touching her yet? "Except that I'm the sheriff's sister."

"I don't have a problem with that, but your brother might want to fill my ass with lead for the lewd acts I'm about to do to his sister."

What kind of lewd acts? She shivered in anticipation. Maybe he should list those off, too.

"Then stop talking about it and finish what you started with the pie-tasting experiment." She could think of several more places she'd like to lick pie off of him.

"I like your aggressive confidence when it comes to sex, Penelope." He leaned forward, angling his head, his mouth almost touching hers. "I like it a lot."

She licked her lips. "I'm a Scorpio. Domination comes naturally, same as breathing." She leaned back slightly, lifting one eyebrow. "Are you sure you don't have any hangups when it comes to sex with a woman who doesn't let inhibitions get in her way?"

"Are you for real?"

"You tell me." Lifting his hand to her mouth, she bit down on the end of his index finger, then blew on it and licked it better.

He sucked air through his teeth. "I think you just fried all my circuits."

"Take off your pants, Mississippi. It's my turn to check out the goods, and by the way, I like to touch before I buy."

He reached down, unbuttoning and unzipping in a flash. As he lifted his hips to slide out of his pants, the sound of glass crashing somewhere below made them both freeze.

What was … *Fuck!* Penny lunged to her feet, grabbing her T-shirt and vest. She tiptoed down the steps, pulling on her vest as she went. Mississippi caught her before she reached the bottom, his pants back in place.

He pulled her behind him and shushed her with his index finger over his lips. Then he peeked out into the kitchen, his hand raised to keep her in a holding pattern.

Penny listened for the sound of footfalls or additional signs of an intruder as she slowly, silently zipped up the vest and stuffed her T-shirt in one of the pockets.

He stepped out into the kitchen, waving for her to join him. When she got close, he whispered in her ear, "I think it came from out front."

She thought so, too.

Penny grabbed a butcher knife from the knife block next to the prep table. If someone was in her diner, she wasn't going to hide away and wait for anything to get stolen. She started toward the dining room area.

Mississippi didn't let her get very far. He held her in place, taking the knife from her. "Wait here."

She shook her head and mouthed, "I'm coming."

He scowled but then turned and led the way.

Out in the dining room, nothing moved. Penny pointed out the light switch to Mississippi. He nodded and tucked her behind him before turning on the overhead lights.

They looked around, but the place was empty except for an audience of tables and chairs.

And a brick sitting on the floor, along with broken glass.

"How original," Penny muttered.

"Stay put, Penelope." Mississippi pulled on his shirt and hurried out the front door.

While he was gone, Penny slipped behind the lunch counter and picked up the phone. She punched in Grady's phone number.

She had little doubt who was behind breaking her plate-glass window. Elizabeth was going to pay for this out of her own pocket, or Penny was going to rip out all of the cheating dirtbag's hair and sell it for cash.

When Mississippi returned, she was frowning down at a piece of paper she'd found taped to the bottom of the brick.

"I didn't see anyone," he said, breathing fast. He must have run the block and then some. "They probably threw it at the glass and then took off. It might've been some teenagers out messing around. Or maybe someone hoping to raid your cash register but chickened out."

"It wasn't a teen." She held out the paper to him. "Grady is on his way."

He took the note, frowning down at it, and read aloud: "This tastes better than anything you make." He looked up at her. "What the hell?"

"What the hell indeed," Penny huffed. "Mark my words, Elizabeth is going to get her ass kicked, beaten, and run through a meat grinder before I cram it down her throat."

Chapter Twenty-Two

Ronnie's day was off to a shitty start.

To begin with, she'd slept like hell. Mac had arrived home last night, which meant instead of sharing Claire's comfy queen-size bed at Gramps's and Ruby's place, Ronnie had to choose between the couch in the rec room or the trundle bed in Jessica's room. Both were lumpy. Neither offered her much peace and quiet.

In the end, Ronnie rejected the couch, because Henry was already asleep on it when she got there, and the spoiled beagle was snoring loud enough to wake the dead.

She tiptoed upstairs into Jessica's room, only to find the girl still awake and reading. Unfortunately, Jessica put the book down after Ronnie set up the trundle bed and then the non-stop talking began. On and on in the dark, filling Ronnie's ears with poppycock about high school crap, cute boys, college dreams, favorite new songs, and blah, blah, blah; until Ronnie buried her head under the pillow with the hopes of either suffocating to death or falling asleep.

Sleep had come first, but only in short spurts in between tossing and turning. By morning, Ronnie realized two things upon waking. One, she'd overslept, screwing up her pre-dawn plans to make solid headway on the bookkeeping, damn it. Two, Henry had relocated to her trundle bed at some point, and the bad dream she'd had about being trapped in a dumpster surrounded by rotting food had been spurred by the dog's stinky breath.

"Gross, Henry." She sat up, scrubbing her face with her T-shirt. A glance at Jessica's bed found the pillow empty and covers thrown back.

Ronnie and her achy bones creaked and popped down the

stairs and into the kitchen where coffee usually awaited, along with Ruby, and sometimes Gramps or Chester.

But not today. The kitchen was a ghost town.

What the hell? Where was everyone? More important, what lowdown, lousy bastard took the last cup of coffee without making more? Whoever had done it needed to be shot and left to hang for the buzzards to pick clean.

Ronnie prepped a new pot and hit the brew button. The lack of fresh coffee was probably her mother's fault. Claire and Kate had warned her that Deborah was back from rehab. It would be typical for the sober version of her mother to want to torture her daughters for her own warped entertainment, starting with removing all caffeine from the premises.

While waiting for the coffee to brew, she headed down to Ruby's basement only to find the door locked. So, she went in search of another human, finding Jessica minding the store.

The tired and grumpy teenager didn't know where her mother was, only that she'd left with Gramps earlier and would be back late. Jessica also claimed to be clueless about a spare key, bemoaning the fact that *everyone* treated her like she was a kid and *never* told her anything. Jessica did know, however, that Claire was already out working at the birding platform with Luke. So, apparently, *somebody* had told her *something* at some point—a fact that Jessica didn't like pointed out. The bag of pretzels that hit Ronnie in the chest shortly thereafter made the teen's feelings clear.

After throwing the bag of pretzels back at Jessica, who dodged and giggled, Ronnie went out onto the front porch to call her sister or cousin. When neither bonehead bothered answering their phones, she jogged all the way out to the frickin' platform. Once there, she learned that Ruby and Gramps had gone to Tucson for the day, and that a spare key to the basement office was hidden in a beer stein behind the bar in the rec room.

Back at the house, Ronnie found the spare key, smelling burning coffee coming from the kitchen. Figuring the pot had overflowed, she hurried into the kitchen and then screeched to a stop. A lake of coffee covered the counter. Below it, brown liquid cascaded down the cabinet into a growing pond on the floor. She reached over the mess and picked up the nearly empty pot. Upon closer inspection, she found several cracks across the bottom of the glass.

During cleanup, Jessica waltzed in the kitchen. At the sight of Ronnie mopping up the mess, the girl suddenly remembered a message for Ronnie from Ruby—something about not making coffee in the pot because Gramps had set the glass carafe down on the counter too hard this morning and cracked it.

No shit, Goofus McDoofus.

Rather than bite Jessica's head off, Ronnie finished cleaning up, dried her hands, and headed to the basement to get to work on Ruby's books. Unfortunately, running the register at the General Store was slow and "totally boring," which meant Jessica kept dropping by to pick up where she'd left off last night—more chatter about school and boys, with some brain-curdling bits about nail polish and lip gloss thrown in for extra torture.

Just when Jessica finally seemed to be running out of things to talk about, Deborah came down the basement stairs. Dressed in a flowing white pantsuit like some kind of blond angel, she shooed Jessica back to work, planted herself in the chair across from the desk where Ronnie had bookwork spread out, and announced that her therapist suggested she have heart-to-heart talks with each of her daughters about their relationships over the years.

"Clear the slate," Deborah told Ronnie. "So we can all start again fresh."

Like hell they could!

The slate would need to be broken into pieces, ground to dust, and then shipped to the moon. After all that, maybe they could find a way to start up once more with less hostility about the past. But things would never be "fresh."

At that point, Ronnie gave up on getting any bookkeeping done. While Deborah continued to paint rosy pictures about rehab and therapy, Ronnie crammed the paperwork back into the file drawer.

With a quick, "Gotta go, Mother," she made her escape, pocketing the spare keys to Claire's Jeep on her way out. She stopped in the General Store long enough to pay for a can of mocha-flavored coffee and to tell Jessica where she was going and in what vehicle, then she hit the road.

As she passed the Yuccaville city limits sign, she glanced at the time. She was running early—a little over an hour. A text from Butch had come in right after she'd left the RV park with his grocery list for the day. The list was short, thankfully, so she had time to swing by Grady's for a cup of coffee—or something more invigorating, if he were up for it.

Last night, he'd mentioned heading out to his new place in the afternoon to see how the house building was going. He'd invited Ronnie to join him, if she had time. She'd been tempted then and still was, but she was wary of the hope-filled daydreams this might inspire about a future for her that still seemed very cloudy.

She turned onto Grady's street, keeping her eye out for idling pickup trucks or other strange vehicles filled with shadowy forms. The sight of a sporty red Lexus pulling into Grady's driveway made Ronnie tap the brakes.

Who was ... The driver's side door opened and a blonde climbed out.

Elizabeth!

Ronnie veered to the curb about a block away on the opposite side of the street, slinking low into her seat. From her sneaky viewpoint over the dash, she could see Grady clearly when he opened the door. He was dressed in the blue and black plaid flannel shirt Ronnie had given him for Christmas, along with a pair of jeans.

Elizabeth, meanwhile, was wearing a professional snake charming outfit—oxblood leather coat and matching boots, with skintight pink pants in between.

How would Grady react to his ex-wife standing on his front porch in her hoochie-mama outfit? Ronnie crossed her fingers he'd slam the door in her face.

But he didn't. Instead, he held the door wide and waved the man-eater inside.

After the door closed behind them, Ronnie sat higher behind the wheel. Was this really happening? Was Grady inside his house with his ex-wife this very moment doing who knew what?

She pinched her forearm. Yep, this was no nightmare.

Jumping Jezebel! Now what?

Ronnie drummed her fingers on the steering wheel, reviewing the facts as she knew them.

Fact 1: Last night at The Shaft, Grady hadn't mentioned

anything about a breakfast meeting with his ex-wife.

Maybe this meeting was about more than breakfast, and you're going to sit out here like a pathetic fool while she bonks your soon-to-be ex-boyfriend.

No. Stop. Ronnie wasn't going to cruise down Jealous Avenue this morning. She wanted to give Grady the benefit of the doubt, which led to …

Fact 2: Grady loved her. He'd said as much several times. He'd shown her how much he cared about her in more ways than she could count. Something might be going on in that house, but knowing Grady's reputation for being fair and just, it was probably nothing more than what Deborah had wanted earlier with Ronnie—to talk about their relationship woes and clear the slate so they could continue to go on about their daily lives in the same county.

Ronnie hoped this was the case. She truly did, but …

Fact 3: Elizabeth was a cold-hearted, calculating bitch who'd pretended to be pregnant with Grady's baby only to screw him over royally after the birth. And now the femme fatale wanted him back.

However, the man behind the badge, whom Ronnie had come to know intimately, wasn't going to forgive or forget about his ex-wife's mistreatment merely because she claimed to have had a change of heart.

Fact 4: Ronnie was running early this morning. She had time to let the situation play out and determine how to proceed when Grady's ex left.

Which had better be real goddamned soon!

Fact 5: There were more chickens in the world than humans, and Ronnie's unwillingness to go up to Grady's door and find out what the hell was going on inside added one more mark on the chickens' side of the table.

Twenty loooong minutes later, Elizabeth strode out onto the porch. She turned back to Grady, her hands flailing as she pointed wildly here and there, stabbing at gnats for all Ronnie could tell. Meanwhile, Grady stood in the doorway in his wide-legged "I'm-the-sheriff" stance, his arms firmly crossed.

Neither party looked like their Saturday morning was off to a happy start.

"Excellent," Ronnie said, taking a sip from her can of coffee as she watched the performance play out on Grady's porch.

If only she could clearly see their facial expressions to know if …

Oh! Pause the scene! Claire had some binoculars somewhere in the Jeep, Ronnie remembered. They were actually Chester's, but Claire had confiscated them after she'd caught the old buzzard scrambling halfway up a tree trying to peep on a pretty redhead who was sunbathing topless on the roof of her camper.

Ronnie reached under the driver's seat without luck. They weren't under the passenger's seat either. She opened the console between the seats.

Bingo. She extracted them from their case.

Binoculars in hand, she settled back in her seat to continue watching the show. Her toes were crossed that the climax was up next and despair would ruin the day for Elizabeth, bludgeoning to death all hope of reconciliation for the abominable cheating skank.

Ronnie focused on Grady's face. His jaw was scruffy, so he must not have shaved yet. He looked tired, too. Like he'd had a rough night. Huh. Had he been called into work for some reason?

He wasn't supposed to be on call officially, but that didn't mean much. When Grady was needed, he went no matter if it were day or night. His dedication to the job and the people in his county was one of many things Ronnie admired about him. That dedication was also one of the main reasons she hesitated to move in with him.

Did she want a life with someone who worked 24/7 at a very dangerous job? Would she wonder every time he left in the middle of the night if he might not come home again? Did she want to have children with a man whose livelihood put not only him in danger, but also his family? She more than anyone had learned the hard way that criminals didn't stop at killing just one person—family was fair play, too.

Hell, did she even want to have children? She was about to turn thirty-six. If she were going to have a kid, time was running out.

And maybe Grady didn't want kids. Maybe Elizabeth had killed whatever interest he'd had in fatherhood when she'd jumped up and down on Grady's heart—and pride—before leaving town with the kid and its biological dad.

Up on the porch-stage, Elizabeth stepped close to Grady, touching his chest.

Ronnie bristled behind the binoculars. "Keep your hands to yourself, two-bit tempter."

She cheered when Grady removed Elizabeth's hand as if it were covered with oozing pustules.

Elizabeth pouted up at him. She pointed at his face and then toward the house.

What were they arguing about? Him selling the house? Did she want a portion of the proceeds after it sold? Maybe it wasn't about the house at all. For all Ronnie could hear from her vantage point, they might be arguing about if the moon were made of rock or cheese.

She cracked the Jeep's window and put her ear to it, but she was too far away to hear anything besides a pair of loud-mouthed birds in a nearby paloverde tree and the rumble of a diesel pickup a couple of blocks over.

A jogger ran past on the other side of the street.

Ronnie did a double-take. Was it Sadie? No, it was a guy in sweatpants and a nylon jacket. He glanced up at Grady's place as he started to pass in front of the house and then stopped, jogging in place while calling out something.

Elizabeth turned. In a blink, her pinched expression was replaced by a fake, sugary-sweet smile. She waved and laughed at whatever the jogger said, clearly overacting in Ronnie's opinion.

Or was Elizabeth slipping back into the role of a lawman's wife? Ronnie would need to work on perfecting that smiling-through-the-shitstorm look if she were going to shack up with the sheriff for the long term.

Grady's ex tried to link arms with him, a possessive move. But Grady wasn't having it. He untangled Elizabeth's arm from his and took a step away.

Ronnie cheered, fist-pumping the air. "Ten points and a gold star for Sheriff Hardass."

She lowered the binoculars slightly, reaching for her can of coffee. As she lifted the dew-dampened can, her focus still on Grady's porch, the coffee slipped from her grip. She reached with her other hand to help stop the can from falling while still holding the binoculars, but she was too slow.

The can fell straight down. Lucky for her, it landed in the drink holder spot with only a few splashes of coffee escaping onto the console.

Whew! That was close. Claire would kill her if she spilled her drink on the Jeep's carpet. Claire still blamed Ronnie partly for the pie catastrophe that happened over Thanksgiving.

Ronnie leaned across and forward to get one of the napkins Claire kept in the glovebox, bumping the horn with the binoculars.

Honk!

In the still morning air, she might as well have sounded a ship's horn.

Fuck nuggets!

She slid down into the seat, her heart pounding. Maybe that had been louder inside the Jeep than it was out.

A peek over the dash made her groan.

Now *she* was the star of the show.

* * *

"Hey, Kate?"

Butch's voice interrupted Kate's erotic dream starring him without many clothes on, lots of heavy breathing, and a bag of dill pickle–flavored pork rinds.

She opened her eyes to find him standing in the bedroom doorway, dressed in blue jeans and a long-sleeve Route 66 T-shirt. He looked downright hunky in the early morning light. Or maybe it was just pregnancy revving her hormone-fueled sex drive to life yet again. Lately, she couldn't seem to keep her hands off Butch. Or off pork rinds, no matter the flavor. Hungry and randy. Shamalama ding-dong! She really needed a break from this second-trimester rollercoaster. But in the meantime …

"Howdy-ho, cowboy," she flirted in a twangy voice while kicking off the covers. "You here for more bedroom rodeo fun? All I'm asking for is a solid, hard-riding eight seconds this time."

He scowled, leaning against the doorjamb. "Woman, you're tough on a guy's ego. You know I kept things going for more than eight seconds last night, in spite of your burlesque striptease act."

"Not the second time."

"You barely gave me a chance." He pointed at her. "Your

tongue should be classified as an illegal weapon."

Patting the bed next to her, she stared at him with wide, googly eyes. "Come play with us, Valentine," she teased, mimicking the creepy dead twins in Stephen King's *The Shining*.

"No." He shook his head. "That's not sexy, Kate. And neither is the lady in the bathtub scene, so don't be reenacting that the next time we screw around in there."

She pushed up onto her elbows and hit him with her best come-hither slow blink. "*Mein Herr* Carter," she said, switching to a German accent, "please, von't you bring me Herman von Longschlongenstein now? I vant to pet him."

He snort-laughed. "That's a new one."

"You like? *Ja*?"

"No. You sounded like a German-dubbed Sean Connery for a second there, and he doesn't light my fire. Although he made a good James Bond."

She cleared her throat, this time aiming for the queen of England giving a Christmas speech. "How about Prince Everhard of the Nether Regions? I think that has a nice royal ring to it, don't you?"

"Do you lay awake at night coming up with nicknames?"

"Maybe, baby." She winked. "You don't happen to have any *chicharrones* hidden in your pants, do you?"

"Pork rinds in my pants? Is that a pickup line?"

She slowly licked her lips, turning up the sex-kitten act. "Give me some pork rinds, *Señor* Stud. Your kid is hungry."

"Pork rinds for breakfast?"

She nodded again, continuing in her breathy voice, "I do love me some fried pork skin."

"Jesus, Kate." He scrubbed his hand down his face. "You have me running hot and cold at the same time here."

Welcome to her pregnant life. Kate tugged the comforter over her now-chilled feet. "So, I'm turning you on in spite of weirding you out? That's interesting."

"Not really. I'm turned on whenever you're around. You drive me nuts."

She patted her belly. "You made me nuts with your nuts, so we're even." She glanced at the clock. "Oh, bollocks. I'm late. Claire is going to bust my balls."

"That reminds me why I came in here," Butch said. "I got a call from Sophy Wheeler when I was in the shower."

Kate froze. "You did?" Why was she calling Butch? "How strange."

"I know. She left a message."

Oh no! Sophy wasn't supposed to tell Butch about Kate's emails. Kate had made that clear from the get-go. "I thought you weren't talking to her much anymore."

"We haven't really communicated since last fall."

"What was the message?"

"She is considering selling her place and wondered what I thought she should ask for it." He scratched his jaw, his face lined in thought.

"Are you going to call her back?"

He shrugged. "Maybe I'll look into it. Right now, I need to get going. Have you seen the keys? They're not where I thought I left them."

The keys? Kate's breath caught. She sat up in bed, something that was getting harder to do the bigger her belly grew. Did he mean Sophy's house keys? The ones Claire still had? Dang it, why did Sophy have to pull this shit about selling her place right now?

"I don't know anything about any keys!" she declared more vehemently than she'd meant to, judging by his wince. "Why are you blaming me?"

"I wasn't."

Panic shot through her, heating her from head to toe, making her heart race and her body warm again. "All I've done day after day is go to work with Claire and then come straight over to The Shaft, like you and Grady and Mac insist."

Well, except for that side trip to the library … and then jail. Dang Deputy Dipshit. Butch would have been none the wiser about her library visit if that idiot hadn't tripped her up during her grand exit.

"Mac?" Butch frowned. "He hasn't even been around to—"

"I'm like some prisoner now, practically shackled to your side." She shoved her bed-tangled hair out of her eyes. The anger and frustration that had been churning inside of her for weeks boiled to the surface. "You're probably monitoring my comings and goings with some fancy tracking device."

She could feel her emotions racing out of control. Her hold on the reins was slipping again. Oh, boy! Why was it so hot in here? She needed to get away from Butch before she did something crazy.

"Kate." Butch held his hand out. "Calm down."

Calm down? Now, there was a novel idea. Why hadn't she thought of that? It was so simple. Never mind the hormones raging throughout her body, making her want to cry one moment and beat someone with a rubber chicken the next. Or the fact that none of her clothes fit anymore. Or that she'd found her first stretch mark yesterday morning. Or that her legs were often waking her up in the night with never-ending cramps while Butch snoozed away, skipping through dreamland with Mr. Sandman.

"Calm down, you say?" she snapped.

She rose onto her knees, pulling up her pajama shirt so he could see her burgeoning belly in the clear light of morning. The elastic waistline of her satin panties had slipped down again, unable to stay in place around her growing baby.

"I would love to calm down," she told him. "But my damned underwear don't fit anymore and they keep getting into a big, mad twist."

"Kate, listen," he said. The mollifying tone in his voice made her want to hit him with a pillow.

"What?" She tugged her sad underwear up over her stomach for the umpteenth time and let her shirt drop.

"What's going on?"

"Nothing."

Why did he have to be so damned good to her? Her anger deflated, her frustrations cooled. Oh crud, now tears were threatening. She knee-walked to the end of the bed, needing to escape before the pendulum finished swinging the other way and she turned into a silly snotty bawl baby. Stupid hormones!

"Everything's fine, Valentine." She avoided his gaze, swiping at her eyes. "It's all peachy-keen and swell. Just out of this world wonderful."

He met her at the foot of their bed, taking her by the shoulders and staring down at her.

"I'm not crying, dammit."

He brushed away a wayward tear. "Of course you're not. But

your left eye is twitching."

"I don't want to talk about it."

"I read that shifting hormone levels in the second trimester can cause rapid mood swings."

Him and that freaking pregnancy book! She leaned her forehead against his sternum. "This is all your fault."

"I know, sweetheart."

"If you didn't have such overachieving, insanity-inducing sperm."

He chuckled. "You bring out the best in my boys."

"Why do you always have to smell so good?" She breathed in his clean scent, kissing his neck. "How am I supposed to resist you?"

"All the extra blood flowing through the lower half of your body now can really up your sexual appetite."

She pulled back, scowling up at him. "I sort of want to bite you right now."

"Which explains last night," he continued. "And the night before that. And the other morning when you jumped my bones in my office at The Shaft." He gave her a wicked smile. "And last weekend when you joined me in the shower and got me all steamy and lathered up. That book is right. Your breasts have easily grown a cup size. I wonder—"

She held her fist up in front of his face. "If you don't stop reciting shit from that baby book, I'm going to shove the damned thing up your ass sideways. And it's a hardback, so you're going to walk bowlegged for a while after I'm done."

"Sounds kinky." He grinned, his blue eyes raking over her. "You're really sexy with your wild hair and pink cheeks. Maybe we should continue this conversation in the shower."

Maybe they should.

No. Wait. Gah! She batted his hands away and shoved him back a step. "Stay away from me, baby maker. I don't need you sexing me up this morning. I'm already late for work."

He chuckled, taking her elbow to help her off the bed. "I'm sure your sister will let your tardiness slide. She has your cousin there to help now, too."

"Claire's a bossy bully on the jobsite. She takes after Gramps. Why didn't you wake me when you got up?"

She pulled free of his grip and stepped gingerly across the carpet. Her feet were swelling up more often than not lately, especially after a busy shift like last night. Pregnancy was not for wimps, and she was only halfway there. Not to mention the grand finale when the watermelon had to push out through the tiny keyhole.

"Because you were up late giving me a hands-on demonstration of how wonderful it is that there is extra blood flowing south of your belly button."

She scowled his way as she searched through her underwear drawer for some panties that actually fit, frowning as she cast aside all the sexy and lacey ones that she used to wear. "You don't take me seriously anymore, Valentine."

He came closer, picking up underwear from the floor along the way. "I take you whatever way I can get you, with or without underwear."

"Hardy har har." She took the underwear back and set them on the dresser to box up with her other clothes that no longer fit. "You read that book and think you have me all figured out, but there is more going on underneath my skin than what you read on those pages. I'm more than just an incubator for our child."

That was something everyone kept seeming to forget.

When she tried to turn away from him, he stopped her. "Kate, wait."

"What? I need to get dressed and head to the RV park."

Claire and Mac had been going up to Sophy's last night with those keys Butch wanted. She needed to know what they found and send it off to Sophy so she'd tell Kate how she knew Joe was still alive. And then Kate needed to sneak home at some point and put the keys back where she'd found them. Or at least close by so that Butch might think he'd misplaced them.

"Sweetheart, I promise to take you seriously if you'll talk to me." He framed her face. "Tell me what's going on."

She hesitated. She wanted to share everything, but he wouldn't understand. Not her need to protect her family. Not her need to solve this mystery and feel like a viable, sane, contributing member of society still.

"Tell me, Kate." His thumb caressed her cheek. "Worrying about you is making me—"

"I'm trapped," she said, cutting him off with the truth. At least part of it.

His hands lowered to her shoulders. "Because you're carrying our kid?"

"No." She sighed. "I mean yes, but not like that."

"Then like what?"

She poked him in the shoulder. "You are watching me all the time now."

"Not *all* the time." He had the decency to look sheepish.

"I have very little freedom anymore."

"Sweetheart," he started.

But she wasn't done yet. "And as soon as our child is born, I'm really going to have to give up my independence, at least for a while, since I'll be a mom. I'm not saying that parenthood is going to be a bad thing, it's just that the 'Kate' I have been for the first thirty-plus years of my life—the one you fell in love with—will go away. Maybe for good. And that scares me."

Heck, Kate's own mom was still struggling with the loss of her "self" due to motherhood, and Kate and her sisters were long grown. Was she going to end up in the same mental boat? There was no way he'd want to be married to an angry, depressed version of herself.

"Kate, we're in this together, remember."

"Yeah, but you're still going to go to car shows and do your man things out in the garage while I walk around with a baby attached to my boob."

"Lucky kid." He smiled down at her chest.

"Valentine."

His gaze returned to hers, steady and serious now. "I told you before, Kate, I'm not going to any car shows without you and the baby. Either we all go, or I send someone else to buy in my place."

"You say that now, but when the kid is teething and I'm pulling my hair out in frustration, ranting and swinging punches like a mad gorilla, you'll want to get far away from us."

He shook his head. "This baby is equal parts mine. We'll tag-team when the times are exhausting. We'll figure things out together."

Her heart warmed at the sincerity in his eyes. "Okay, but we need to figure out now how to let me do my own thing. This constant checking up on me is archaic and patriarchal, not to mention insulting."

He tore at his hair, leaving horns sticking up here and there. "Look at it from my perspective for a second. Two days ago you placed yourself in one of Grady's jail cells."

"That was for my own protection."

"It wasn't the first time. His deputy jokes about naming a cell after you."

"He's a clueless asshole."

"So, you've taken on the task of educating him?"

She shrugged. "I am a teacher by trade."

"Fine, Miss Teacher. But maybe you need to rework your lesson plan, keeping this particular pain-in-the-ass student in mind."

Hey, that was a good idea. Kate needed to stop thinking that Deputy Dipshit was going to be anything other than a spoiled, egocentric brat and come at him from another angle for her "schooling."

"I'll take that advice into consideration," she said. "Besides my problematic tactics of educating Grady's deputy, what other reasons do you have for confining me?"

"I don't like the word 'confining,' sweetheart."

"Fine. Why else are you so overly worried about me?"

"You fell on the sidewalk." He made it sound as if she'd fallen from a ten-story building into a pool full of hungry sharks.

"Dear Lord, Valentine. I'm not Humpty Dumpty." Not yet anyway. "I won't break that easily."

"Do you know what it does to a guy when he hears his five-months pregnant woman fell?"

"Did you just call me your *woman*?" She raised one eyebrow. "Are we going back to caveman days?"

"What should I call you, Kate? We are way beyond boyfriend and girlfriend." He huffed. "I'd like to call you my fiancée, but you won't accept any of my damned proposals."

"That's because you don't ask them right."

"Well, I'm sorry, but I'm new at this."

She rolled her eyes. "Valentine Carter, you haven't been seriously trying and you know it."

He blushed slightly. "It's nerve-racking."

"I would think that I've said 'No' enough times by now that it would be old hat for you."

"You would think," he grumbled, repeating her words. "Well, it's not, Kate." He walked away from her, flopping face-first onto the bed. "You're complicated," he told her in a muffled voice.

"Why do you want to get married so badly right now?" She moved closer, standing over him. "You know I'm not going anywhere."

"Because I want to take care of you and our child."

"You already are. Look how much you fret over every little thing."

"So, sue me. I love you and don't want anything to happen to you."

"It's one thing to worry. It's a whole other thing to suffocate someone."

He rolled onto his back. "You have to admit, Kate, you have a knack for landing in trouble."

"Only when it comes to Deputy Dipshit."

"Not only." He frowned. "You also seem to have taken quite an interest in Grady's ex-wife."

"Elizabeth is a selfish, infected canker that won't heal up and go away." When his eyebrows raised, she added, "That's only my medical opinion, of course. I'm sure she has some lovely qualities somewhere under all of those bitchy comments and spiky teeth."

He stared at her for a long time, his frown lines growing deeper by the second. "What would you have me do, Kate? You're asking me to back off and leave you alone to do what you want when you want, come what may. At the same time, Grady is in my other ear telling me that he can't keep covering for you when his deputy has legitimate claims of crimes you've committed."

"I only want a bit more breathing room before our child pokes its head out and takes over our lives."

The baby kicked right then. Or elbowed. Or just twitched. The fluttering, almost tickling feel took her breath away. Kate gasped, touching her stomach.

"What is it?" Butch shot to his feet. "Are you okay? We should stop arguing. It's not good for the baby."

"Valentine, I told you, I'm not a fragile egg." The fluttering continued, stronger. "And I have a feeling this kid won't be either."

"What do you mean?" His face paled. "What's going on? Do we need to go to the doctor?"

"No." She took his hand and placed it on the side of her belly where the fluttering was still happening. It was like she had a hummingbird trapped in there.

"Do you feel that?" she whispered, covering his hand with hers.

She'd told him about the fluttering the other day when it had first happened, but he couldn't feel anything at the time, or even later that night. Nor hear anything with the stethoscope he now kept in his nightstand.

When the baby moved again, Butch's eyes grew wide.

"There you go, big daddy," she teased. "We probably need to start thinking about names before Chester picks one for us."

He groaned, sounding sickly.

Kate stared at him, noticing the sweat lining his upper lip. "Valentine? Are you okay?"

"Feeling lightheaded," he mumbled, his face now a sickly, ashen color. "Little dizzy."

"Did you eat yet this morning?"

"No time." He swayed slightly, his hand slipping off her stomach. "Busy working on the Zephyr."

Damn it! Ever since he'd gotten that truckload of old clunkers in, he was forgoing sleep and food so he could spend time playing with his cars. The sooner Claire and Mac took over The Shaft, the better.

"How long have you been up?" she asked.

"Since five." His Adam's apple bobbed as he gulped several times. "I think I need to sit down."

"You look like you're about to …"

"Narg," he blurted and slumped to the floor.

Faint.

She squatted next to him. He was still breathing, his skin now flushed pink. "Valentine?"

He let out a gurgled groan.

"You know you have to eat in the morning, darn it!"

Kate raced toward the kitchen, yelling over her shoulder, "Between my hopped-up hormones and your low blood sugar, I'm going to wind up with an ulcer."

Chapter Twenty-Three

Ronnie didn't need the binoculars to see the frown on Grady's face, especially since he'd taken several steps out onto the porch to get a better view of her.

She didn't care much about Elizabeth catching her playing "I Spy." Grady's ex-wife had probably planned on telling a sordid tale around town about this morning's meetup to cement the whole we're-getting-back-together bullshit story she had going.

As for the passing jogger, he didn't have a clue who Ronnie was, and the same went vice versa. But it was a small town, so she'd undoubtedly run into the guy at the worst possible moment somewhere else. That was how her luck had gone ever since she'd arrived in Arizona. Actually, it was more like ever since Lyle had been busted by the FBI. Before that, ignorance had kept her lonely and miserable, but at least not consciously humbled on a daily basis.

But Grady knowing she'd been eavesdropping—well, paint her in mortified red. Now he'd want to talk about this, and with the way Ronnie's morning was going, she wasn't in the mood for any sort of relationship therapy. Not with her mom and not with her lover boy.

Nope.

The way Ronnie saw it, she now had two options. She could take the high road and ask Grady what in hades was going on; or she could flee the scene of the crime.

The choice was easy.

She started the Jeep and did a U-turn in the middle of the street, glancing in the rearview mirror as she drove off.

Grady stood on his porch steps, frowning after her.

Shit criminy. What had she been thinking? She should have

driven off as soon as she saw Elizabeth get out of her car and simply trusted Grady to fill her in later. That would have been smart, cool, and mature—what the woman Ronnie wanted to be would've done.

She blew out a breath. "Way to go, ding dong."

Her cell phone rang two blocks later. She glanced at the screen. "Now is not a good time, Sheriff Hardass." She sent Grady's call to voicemail, wondering if his ex had left yet, or if she were standing next to him, sneering while he tried to get Ronnie on the line.

"You had to go and make things awkward," she told the pale-faced broad staring back at her in the rearview mirror.

Her hands were sweating still as she pulled into the grocery store parking lot. There were only about half the cars as usual in the lot today, so getting a good parking spot was easy. Saturday mornings appeared to be sleep-in time for the locals after Friday night benders.

She looked at her phone before heading inside the store to make sure there wasn't another text from Butch with more to add to her grocery list. While she was checking, a text popped up from Grady: *Call me. PLEASE!*

Not yet. She needed to gather her wits first, so she didn't come across as some silly ninny or a jealous stalker. Currently, her wits were hiding in a toilet stall back at The Shaft. She turned her ringer to silent mode and pocketed her phone.

Inside the grocery store, the produce section was mostly empty. Besides Ronnie, there were only two younger girls wearing Yuccaville Copperstars school sweatshirts, plaid flannel pajama bottoms, and flip-flops. Next to them, Ronnie felt downright fancy in her cowboy boots and yoga pants, and the Santa Fe–style, thigh-length cardigan she'd borrowed from Ruby's closet earlier.

She grabbed a couple of heads of cabbage; some red, yellow, and orange bell peppers; and a bag of limes. Next on her list were four dozen eggs and paper towels. She pushed her cart along the back of the store toward the dairy section in the other corner. After grabbing four cartons of eggs, she paused by the flavored coffee creamer. If she were going to be spending some time at the RV park in the mornings, she should probably grab some of her favorite creamer to store in the fridge so she didn't drink all of

Ruby's stock.

As she opened the cooler door, movement on the other side of the glass made her glance toward the meat department. Her glance turned into a full-on stare at the sight of Sadie following close behind a big, beefy guy in khaki cargo pants and a camouflage jacket. He looked familiar, but Ronnie couldn't place where she'd seen him last. Probably at The Shaft.

Sadie wore her usual black ensemble, including a knit stocking hat and combat boots. Seriously, Ronnie needed to take her shopping. Sadie and she could both use some new clothes for spring.

As Ronnie watched through the glass in the cooler door, Sadie nudged the big guy toward an alcove that led into the stock room. When they disappeared from view, Ronnie let the cooler door close and slipped into the paper towel aisle, which was closer to the alcove. She dinked around in the aisle, waiting and watching for Sadie and the guy to return, thinking of things to say to Sadie when she came back out.

Hey, fancy meeting you here.

Are you stalking me again?

Hello. My name is Inigo Montoya. You killed my father. Prepare to die.

Ronnie chuckled to herself over that last one from the movie *The Princess Bride*. She needed to watch that again. It'd been too long.

Three minutes passed.

What were they doing back there? Ronnie had sneaked into the stock room once with Katie, who somehow knew there was a bathroom for employees there. At the time, Katie had told her some tale about pregnant women being able to sniff out bathrooms from a mile away. Anyway, all Ronnie remembered were stacks of boxed and crated dry goods and a big door leading into a built-in freezer.

Four more minutes passed in the paper towel aisle, during which time Grady tried calling again, as well as Deborah. Ronnie sent both to voicemail. Neither left a message.

Ronnie inched her cart closer to the alcove, parking near the very end of the aisle so she could peek through the shelves of various types and flavors of tortilla chips. One of the store employees walked into the alcove while chatting on his store walkie-talkie about a lost pricing gun. He disappeared through the doors into the back.

Six more minutes passed.

"What the hell are you doing back there, Sadie?"

Ronnie sucked in a breath as the doors opened. But it was only the employee, pushing a cart stacked with boxes. He headed the opposite way and then turned down one of the other aisles.

Something was wrong. Ronnie could feel it in her gut.

Or maybe Sadie and the big meathead were screwing around back amongst the crates and boxes, and what Ronnie was feeling was the results of sweetened canned coffee on an empty stomach. She should have grabbed some nuts on her rush out of the General Store.

No, it wasn't a sex romp. Ronnie was pretty sure of that. There hadn't really been any chemistry between the two of them when they went back there. No heated looks or flirty touching. Just the intensity, which Sadie seemed to carry wherever she went, times ten. Hell, for all Ronnie knew, that intensity *was* Sadie's flirting style.

Or it could be that Sadie was in trouble back there. The woman did have a history of near-death scrapes. Along with her mom. It must be a family trait—fatal clumsiness.

Her gut weighed in again on the "trouble" theory, wondering what Ronnie intended to do about Sadie's plight.

She checked her phone. Two more minutes ticked away as she waffled on what to do.

"Fuck it." She listened to her gut and headed for the doors, leaving her shopping cart off to the side in the paper towel aisle.

Easing through the heavy swinging doors, Ronnie paused inside to take in her surroundings. She watched for movement while listening for any sounds of talking or struggle. The temperature was cooler back here, and the place smelled like damp cardboard and slightly spoiled milk. The lighting was dimmer, with long fluorescent lights hanging overhead, some of the bulbs not working, others flickering.

The coast was clear.

Ronnie tiptoed forward, coming to an intersection.

To her left was the backside of the dairy coolers.

In front of her, the aisle narrowed with tall stacks of boxes lining either side of the path, veering out of sight.

To her right was a narrow walkway with a wall covered in notices about employee rights on one side and a bunch of lockers on the left. Ronnie remembered them from her trip with Katie to the bathroom, which was located at the far end of the walkway. Several feet before the bathroom had been a door leading into the meat butchering area according to the sign. Across from the bathroom was the wide freezer door that had been dented in several places. She remembered it well because it had taken Katie forever to empty her bladder, and her little sister had insisted Ronnie wait for her right outside the bathroom rather than return to filling their shopping cart.

Ronnie stared toward the bathroom, because today, that wide freezer door stood ajar. Had it been closed, she wouldn't have been able to see it from her current position. Had the employee left it open by accident? No, his cart hadn't been stacked with freezer goods, at least not that she'd been able to tell. So, why hadn't he noticed it?

Ronnie glanced in the other two directions again, seeing no sign of movement or anything that seemed suspicious. She looked behind her at the doors leading out into the main part of the store. Maybe she should return to her cart—and her normal life—and leave Sadie and the guy to their business. Actually, maybe they weren't even back here. They could have left via some back door for who knew what reason. For all Ronnie knew about Sadie, she could …

A loud *thud* came from the hallway to her right.

Followed by a *clunk*.

And then a *clatter*.

Then *crash*.

Someone grunted loudly. Not a sex-is-good kind of grunt, more like a pain-filled one.

Then another *crash* sounded, followed by a gargling noise and several more *thuds*.

The flight or fight urge kicked in again. This time, Ronnie charged into battle. Okay, more like tiptoed into battle, trying to pull off a sneak attack in case this wasn't a little tussle and turned out to be some bizarre style of rough and rowdy, subzero, polar bear sex.

When she peered around the freezer door, she saw the back of the big meathead leaning over the floor, down on his knees, straddling Sadie's writhing body. All clothes were still in place, so Ronnie crossed hanky-panky off the list.

She stepped over the freezer's threshold, standing in a blast of super cooled air that was trying to make up for the temperature rise due to the open door. The freezer smelled like meat packing paper and cardboard, which covered much of the metal floor.

Sadie started thrashing wildly, her combat boots kicking every which way. Steam clouded around them. Sadie's foot collided with a metal pan on one of the steel shelves, making another crashing sound.

Ronnie inched closer. Oh, Jesus! Meathead was strangling her.

Ronnie's pulse redlined. She needed to do something! Now! Get the brute off of Sadie somehow!

But he was even more huge up close. There was no way she could take him down with her body weight alone.

She glanced around the freezer. Several hunks of beef and pork dangled from the ceiling by steel hooks. No, too heavy. She tiptoed farther into the room as Sadie gasped and thrashed and landed punches to the guy's shoulders and chest and chin. He grunted but held her tight in his chokehold.

On the shelf to the right of the door were what Ronnie guessed were several legs of lamb wrapped in butcher paper. Or maybe they were some part of a cow. Whatever. It wasn't important. What did matter was that the size fit perfectly in Ronnie's hands and was weighted like a maple wood bat.

She gripped the frozen leg as tightly as she could, took several silent steps closer to the big guy, set her sights on the back of his head, and ... hesitated.

What the hell was she about to do? What if ...

Sadie's struggling waned.

But what if ...

The meathead grunted and then sat up straight.

Sadie wasn't moving anymore.

At all.

Ronnie raised the frozen leg, like she was standing over home plate, her sights on the back fence. Gripping the leg tightly, she swung.

* * *

Claire kept scanning the top of the ravine, looking for a sun flare reflecting from a pair of binoculars or a scope. Some sign that they were being watched by a man who was supposed to be dead. Her trip to Sophy's last night only doubled the shadows of dread hovering in her peripheral vision.

"What's going on, Claire?" Luke asked as he measured and marked several lengths of composite decking that were going to be cut and used to create a ramp up to the platform.

Gramps had decided last night that instead of two sets of steps, one side should have a ramp to accommodate those who struggled with stairs. When Claire had brought up the fact that the path out to the birding platform would be tough for those who had problems climbing up or down steps, Gramps started looking up how much an electric golf cart would cost to use as transportation for the disabled.

His goal was a vehicle that would be quiet yet easy to get in and out of, accommodating to both the birds and those who struggled with long walks across gravel. Claire's goal was to keep Gramps from returning to the idea of paving the path. That task would be another couple of weeks of hard work, and she didn't have the time or energy to spare much more.

"Nothing," she told her cousin, returning to her task of building the steps. "Some days I wish I still smoked is all."

He looked up, frowning around the pencil in his mouth. "That bad, huh?"

She shrugged. "I've had worse." Then again, if Joe was alive, he might top all the others who tried to take her out of commission before him.

Luke pulled the pencil from between his lips and pointed it behind her, toward the gravel path. "He looks like he could use a cigarette, too."

Claire turned to see who Luke was talking about, cringing in anticipation of it being Gramps with more absurd to-dos, until she remembered he and Ruby had left for Tucson.

Thankfully it was Mac. Although Luke was right, he didn't look happy to see her.

Maybe he was ticked about something else. Like a problem in Yuccaville this morning with finding all the hardware on the list she'd given him for the brewery addition. Or some issue about his upcoming meeting with Butch this morning. Wait, shouldn't he have left for The Shaft?

Claire wiped her brow with the back of her hand, and then double-checked the time. "He should be at the bar with Butch right now, looking over some of the transition paperwork," she said more to herself than Luke.

"Were you supposed to go with him and forgot?" Luke moved to the next board.

"No, I build. Mac uses his big brain for the paperwork. That's our deal."

"You did turn your ringer on after Ronnie came back and chewed us a new ass, right?"

"Yeah." She chuckled at the memory of Ronnie's frustrated rant while double-checking her phone. "There are no messages or missed calls."

Before anything else could be said, Mac joined them. His hazel eyes were as stormy as his brow.

"Luke," Mac said with a nod in her cousin's direction. "How are you doing this morning?"

Claire had introduced Mac to Luke last night at The Shaft, and then left them to get acquainted over a beer while she took care of a few customers.

"Better than last time we talked," Luke said, grinning as he marked another board.

"I warned you about Chester's new drinking game," Claire told her cousin. "But oh no, you thought you could outsmart the old goat."

Luke stood, sticking his pencil behind his ear. "You know, I think I want to be Chester when I grow up."

Mac and Claire groaned in unison.

"What?" When Luke smiled wide like he was at the moment, he reminded Claire of his sister. Natalie and he shared that same smartass glint in their eyes, along with the creases fanning from the corners.

"As much as I like Chester," Claire said, "he's not a good role model. His list of crimes is long and cringeworthy."

Luke waved off her censure. "Chester has it all—money, charm, and no woman trying to tie him down. That's the good life."

The "charm" part she wasn't buying, but the mention of a "woman" caught her attention. Claire thought back to Kate's theory on why Luke was visiting Arizona. Maybe her sister was right, and he was here due to trouble with a woman. Or maybe it was as simple as him being between jobs and missing his family. Time would tell.

For now, Claire needed to deal with whatever had Mac giving her a gunslinger glare. Was he still ticked about her communicating with Sophy behind his back? Claire thought they'd come to an understanding last night after returning to the RV park. Mac hadn't seemed to have a problem putting that subject aside after they'd crawled under the covers.

When Luke returned to measuring, Mac pointed at Claire, motioning for her to follow him back toward the tool shed.

Shit. Whatever had him ticked was bad enough that he didn't want an audience for the hashing-out part. Claire crossed her fingers it was something to do with her mother instead of her. Or even Jessica. Crazy Kate was good at lighting fires. Maybe she'd done something to piss Mac off. Kate was certainly good at pushing Grady's buttons. Hell, anyone besides Claire being on the receiving end of a tool shed talking-to would be nice. She'd already gotten reamed by Ronnie this morning.

"Hey, Luke," he said, his calm tone contradicting the

frustration lining his face. "I need to borrow Claire for a few minutes back at the tool shed. You need anything?"

"Yeah." Luke glanced up at Claire. "Bring the spare battery for my drill. I have it charging in the corner."

She nodded and then took off to catch up with Mac, who was crunching along the gravel trail at a fast pace.

"What's going on?" she asked as soon as they were out of earshot of Luke.

He glanced back toward the platform before leveling a scowl at her. "Rumor has it that you hired Luke to help build the brewery."

Oh! He'd caught wind of that. Claire wondered who spilled the beans already. Jess? Butch? Chester? It didn't matter really. It would have come out eventually. She was relieved they'd moved past the subject of Sophy. At least for the time being.

So, this thundercloud on Mac's horizon was about her hiring Luke. She shrugged. She'd meant to tell Mac herself, but had been waiting for a good time. Over the phone wouldn't do. This sort of news needed to be done face-to-face. Apparently, that moment had arrived.

"Yeah, I asked him to help with the build." She owned up to it.

Hiring Luke made complete sense. He built things for a living, whereas she did it on the side. Luke could be the general contractor and would do a better job, and Claire was happy to act as his crew. Hell, she might even catch a breather from working seven days a week and be able to visit Mac in Bisbee for a day or two before his consulting job was done.

They crunched along in silence for a few more steps.

"Did you even think to ask me how I felt about paying for more help?" Mac asked, his frustration coming through loud and clear.

Claire's own frustration spiked, matching his. As strung out as she was, it didn't take much to make her want to start yelling and punching the air. Instead, she took a breath and kept her voice level and calm. If they were going to live together on a more permanent basis eventually, she needed to practice filtering how and what she said, especially when things were tense.

"Sure," she told him. "I thought about asking you."

That was the truth. But then she'd considered how he'd made the decision about the consulting job without really listening to her concerns, so she'd made an executive decision. Hell, she'd signed on to build the damned brewery and she would own half of the business when all was said and done. She should get to have a little say here and there.

"How are we going to pay your cousin?"

"With money. Maybe some beer and food, too." Luke's family rate was very reasonable. Gramps and Ruby were letting him camp for free and he wasn't charging them anything for his time and expertise.

"What money?" Mac huffed. "Damn it, Claire, I'm already working this Bisbee job to cover the extra costs for the brewery."

The tool shed was just ahead. Claire picked up her pace to keep from snarling back at him.

"If you're going to hire your cousin," he continued, matching her faster stride, "I'm going to have to work even longer. Had you thought of that?"

If she didn't hire Luke, *she* was going to have to work even longer. Had Mac thought of that? Because she had, and she was getting real fucking tired of the long hours with plenty of hard, back-breaking labor thrown in for extra shits and giggles.

She pulled out her keys. "Of course I did," she said in a quiet voice as she unlocked the door, not wanting the campers in the area to hear their arguing. "I thought about it for a minute or so. About the same amount of time you spent thinking about me and what you taking that damned Bisbee job would mean to my level of stress and exhaustion here in Jackrabbit Junction."

"You and I discussed why I took the job. We agreed we needed the additional money to cover the extra brewery costs."

She yanked open the door and stepped inside, whirling on him when he followed. "No, Mac. That's *not* how it went. You informed me why you needed to take that job, ignoring my protests and blowing off my idea to borrow more money from Gramps instead."

"I don't want more of your grandfather's money."

"Why not?" She jammed her hands on her hips. "Is this a pride thing?"

"Yes, it's a pride thing." He frowned, but not really at Claire, more—it seemed—at the fact that she'd pulled the truth out of him. "Well, it's at least partly a pride thing. I want to be able to do this on my own."

"On *your* own?"

He sighed. "I meant *our* own."

"No, I don't think you did. Not deep down." And that was the root of the problem with this whole situation they were in now.

"Come on, Claire," he started.

"Don't." She put a stop to whatever he'd planned to say. "I'm not an idiot."

"I never said you were."

"I know what part of your underlying plan was with buying The Shaft."

"Really?" He crossed his arms. "Well, fill me in."

"It ties us to one another. Sort of like having a kid, but probably cheaper in the end. We'll be raising a business together, pouring our blood, sweat, and tears into it. We'll be committed to each other on a deeper level than simply sharing a bed."

He glanced to the side, shifting his weight to his heels.

"I'm right, aren't I?"

"Partly, but not entirely." His hazel eyes returned to her, a storm still swirling in them, but now a glimmer of emotion reflected in their depths. "I'm in love with you. Don't forget that part, because I certainly haven't."

"Here's something else I think I'm right about," she continued, ignoring the rush of affection his words had spurred. She needed to stay her course and get this all aired before she changed her mind. "You feel you're in this endeavor at a deeper level than I am, which gives you more ownership power."

"You're wrong. We're splitting the bill fifty–fifty."

"No. You put in fifty percent of your own money. Gramps forked out the money on my part."

He shrugged. "The terms are clear—we pay him back over time, and if something happens to him, then we continue to pay my aunt until it's all paid off. He's acting as a lender, that's all."

Mac wasn't addressing the part about *him* having to help pay back *her* portion of the money, which didn't make her stake in the business really equal when push came to shove. That fact was something that had weighed on Claire from the start, making her feel like she wasn't ponying up as a true fifty–fifty partner. It was also why she'd gone along with this brewery idea of Mac's even though she had no passion for that aspect of the business. She felt she owed it to him.

"Okay, if Gramps is only a 'lender,' then why not borrow more from him to finish what we need?"

"Because we've borrowed enough from him," he said, once again making a decision without considering her feelings.

"Or is it that if Gramps has more than half of the money into this, you're concerned he'll want to have a say in how you run *your* business?"

"Possibly." He grimaced. "But it's not how I run our business." He pointed at his chest. "It's how *we* run it."

"Hmm." She shook her head slowly. "I don't think you're fully on board in that 'we' part yet, Mac."

"I am, too."

"No, you're not, or *we* would have had more of a discussion about you continuing to do consulting work." She walked over to where Luke's spare battery was charging. "You see," she said, picking up the battery, frowning down at it rather than at Mac as she geared up to say what had been in the back of her mind since shortly after she'd agreed to go in on this business with him. "You have been running your own money show for a long time, and you've done very well for yourself. But I don't think you're ready to truly share that part of your life yet."

When he started to object, she interrupted. "And that's okay, Mac. I get it. You've worked really hard for everything you have. Just don't say things are 'ours' and that decisions are 'joint' when they're not."

"You've been running your own money show, too."

She laughed with a good dose of sarcasm mixed in. "I wouldn't call mine a profitable money show, though. It's more like a poor traveling circus that's barely scraping by with the help of some spare change tossed into the tips can after every act." She set the drill battery back down on the counter. "I think when you've lived most of your life without much money, it's easier to share it with others."

"You make me sound selfish, like some kind of miser."

"You're one of the last people I would call selfish. When it comes to helping and protecting others, you go out of your way. But you always maintain control, especially when it comes to spending the money you've worked hard to earn."

She took his hands in hers. "Mac, what you did by choosing to take the Bisbee job without considering my feelings on the matter is an example of this need to control. And the fact that you are pissed at me for hiring Luke without asking how you felt on that decision first—well, that doubly proves my point."

He sighed, pulling her in for a hug. "How many college psych classes did you take?"

"A few." She snuggled in closer, wrapping her arms around his waist. She'd missed him over the last week. And this. Always this.

"Are you going to be continually analyzing me for the rest of our lives?"

"No. Except for how you perform in bed. But don't worry. That analysis I'll share with only my sisters."

"Oh, Jesus."

"Maybe my mom, too. She's been going to therapy now and wants to rehash our past relationship woes. My scrutiny and assessment of *your* sexual performance will be a great distraction from dredging up my past horrors under Mom's watch."

He leaned back, looking down at her in mock horror. "Are you kidding?"

She grinned. "I wish I was, about both Mom and a psychoanalysis of our sex life." She traced the line of his smooth jaw. He must have shaved, because last night his scruff had tickled her in the best places. "So, what are we going to do about this brewery business?"

"Luke is going to help us build it and we pay him as you planned," Mac said with a nod. "It's a logical and good decision."

"That doesn't really fix our financial problem. I still don't want you to keep taking consulting jobs. I'm tired of working my ass off here and you being hours away. One of the reasons you quit your job in Tucson was so that we could be together."

"And we will be, once we have enough money."

She frowned up at him. "Mac, we'll never have enough money for this. It's like having a kid. Unless you're super rich, there's not enough money to cover the costs. You just have to jump in and adjust where you can to make it happen. That's all part of the ups and downs of running a business."

"Claire?" Kate hollered from outside the tool shed. "Are you in there?"

Mac glanced at the door. "We're busy," he called back.

"We seem to have reached our first partnership impasse," Claire said, patting him on the chest before stepping out of his arms. "Now we'll have to figure out a compromise that works for both of us. So, wrap your big brain around that puzzle, Garner."

"Claire?" Kate knocked on the door. "I need to talk to you, so stop having sex and come out here."

She grinned at Mac. "See, the sharing of sex stories for further examination has already begun."

"Shoot me now, please." He held the door for her.

She grabbed Luke's spare battery. "Mac and I were just planning our day," she said loudly for Kate's benefit. She winked at him as she passed.

Outside, Kate waited with her hand on her belly. "Your shirt is on backward."

"What?" Claire looked down. Her shirt hadn't been touched.

"Ha! Gotcha."

"Your sister thinks she's funny," Mac said.

Claire wrinkled her nose at Kate. "Funny looking, for sure."

"You two are dorks." Kate moved closer as Claire locked the tool shed door, whispering, "Did you guys get what you-know-who wants to make the deal for info on Joe?"

"We did." Reaching into her inner jacket pocket, Claire pulled out an envelope holding the sheets of paper Mac and she had found under Sophy's dresser.

She handed the envelope to Kate, who was practically salivating as she pulled out the papers.

Mac checked his phone. "Hey, Kate. Was Butch heading for The Shaft when you left home? He'd texted me earlier that he'd be running late for our meeting because he couldn't find his keys."

"Huh?" Kate stared down at the encrypted papers, frowning as she scanned them. "Oh, yeah. There was an issue with his keys this morning and then he fainted."

"What?" Claire said, exchanging a worried look with Mac. "Is Butch okay?"

Kate snorted. "Yeah. He forgets to eat when he's playing with his cars. He was just fine after I splashed him with water and then made him eat some orange slices." She thumbed toward the General Store, her focus still on the papers. "He dropped me off and headed back to the bar to meet up with Mac."

"I'd better go." Mac glanced at Claire, one eyebrow raised. "To be continued?"

She nodded. "Let me know if Butch is really okay. Doctor Frankenstein here doesn't have the best bedside manner."

"Will do." He leaned down and gave her a quick kiss on the lips. "Stay out of trouble, Slugger."

As he walked away, she turned back to Kate, who was taking a picture of the pieces of paper with her cell phone.

"Now what?" Claire asked the Mad Hatter.

Kate folded the pieces of paper, stuffing them back into the envelope. Her eyes were a little too wide and red-rimmed for Claire's comfort when they met hers. "Now we set up another phone call with Sophy."

Chapter Twenty-Four

Ronnie dropped the leg of lamb.

The sickening *thunk* of frozen meat and bone slamming into the big guy's skull resounded in her head.

He keeled over, face-first, like a falling redwood. Timber! He landed flat on Sadie, making her boot heels bounce on the freezer floor.

Ronnie covered her mouth. What had she done?

"Oh, shit." Was he still breathing? It was hard to tell under that bulky coat. She'd only wanted to knock him out, but she might have swung too hard.

There was no might *about it*, a voice scolded in her head.

"Shit, shit, shit." Her hand trembled as she pushed her hair out of her face. "Please don't be dead."

How was she was going to explain this to Grady? He'd want to know why she'd come back into the stock room in the first place. Why not call him first? After all, he'd been clearly waiting for her to ring him back, so there wasn't really a good excuse for Ronnie dragging her feet on that.

Maybe she should just take off. Run out the back door. Get in Claire's Jeep and go to work sans the groceries. Tell Butch she hadn't been feeling well and turned around after leaving Grady's. No, wait! Better yet, she'd caught her boyfriend with his ex-wife and had a fit of jealousy, so she'd gone back to Jackrabbit Junc ... *What about Sadie?!*

Oh, God! In the midst of panicking, she'd forgotten about Sadie! Maybe she was still alive under the dead guy's body.

Please don't let him be dead.

She nudged the guy's beefy shoulder with her boot, but he didn't move. She needed to figure out how to somehow roll him off Sadie so she could try to resuscitate her. Maybe if she …

The meathead's body shifted slightly.

Ronnie froze. Maybe he wasn't dead after all. Maybe he was alive. Right, and after he woke up fully, he'd start thinking about adding a second strangulation to his to-do list.

"Hey!" A muffled voice called out from under the guy.

The body shifted again.

"Get this fucker off me," Sadie said from somewhere underneath all the flesh and muscle.

"Sadie!"

Relief washed over Ronnie, spurring her into action. She tried to lift him, but he was too heavy. She changed her tactic, grabbing onto his coat at the scruff of his neck and tugging. He moved sideways a couple of inches, but then Ronnie's boots slipped on a piece of cardboard covering part of the floor and she landed hard on the left side of her ass. *Ouch!* She pushed onto her knees, rubbing her left cheek. That was going to leave a mark.

"Listen," came Sadie's voice from underneath the oaf. She sounded wheezy and winded. "I'm going to push up on his right shoulder while you tug on it. On three, ready?"

Ronnie scrambled to her feet and got a firm grip on his coat. "Okay."

"One. Two." Sadie coughed. "Jesus, he's heavy."

"Three!" Ronnie dug her heels in and pulled hard.

The guy flipped over just far enough from their joint effort that Sadie could wiggle out from under him. She scooted back against one of the shelves, breathing heavily. The bruises were already forming on her neck, dark red for now. Higher up, her stocking cap sat askew and her left eye had a crescent-shaped blood bruise around it. She must have taken a punch. Or maybe a head butt. That would be a black eye, for sure, even if she got some ice on it.

Ronnie looked back down at the meathead. His eyes were closed. Blood covered part of his face. Thanks to gravity, it had trickled down from the open wound on the back of his skull while he was facedown on top of Sadie. She could smell the copper scent of it along with the cardboard. Practically taste it, too. She gagged a little, stepping back so quickly that she almost fell again.

"Veronica, are you okay?" Sadie asked in a raspy voice,

wincing as she lightly tapped around her eye.

Was she okay? Yes. No. She needed a drink.

Ronnie looked down at her hands. A high-pitched cackle escaped from her throat. She quickly pinched her lips together, glancing wildly at the door. She needed to get out of here before someone came to grab some frozen stuff and found her guilty of attempted murder by leg of lamb.

"Veronica?" Sadie said again, coughing as she struggled to her feet.

"Is he dead?" The guy's eyes were closed. Weren't dead people's eyes usually open? Didn't morticians need to weight down their eyelids or sew them shut or something else horrifying?

"I don't know." Sadie limped over to the freezer door and peeked outside before pulling the door closed.

"What are you doing?" Ronnie asked, her breath coming out fast and hard now, steaming around her head. She was having trouble getting enough oxygen. They really needed to open that door again.

"Veronica, you need to calm down before you hyperventilate." Sadie limped back to Ronnie's side. "Breathe in through your nose and hold it for a few seconds."

"I was just getting some eggs and paper towels," she said, trying to catch her breath per Sadie's words. "And then I saw you and him come back here." She took another breath through her nose, following Sadie's lead. "But you didn't come back out."

"Things got out of control." Sadie frowned at the guy.

"He was strangling you!"

She shrugged. "We had a small disagreement."

A cackle-gobble-caw escaped from Ronnie. Apparently, there was a panicked chicken hawk inside of her chest anxious to escape this freezer. "Listen, Sadie. We need to do something before one of the employees comes." She pointed at the guy. "Or he wakes up—if he's not dead."

"You're right." Sadie took a couple of steps toward the far wall, reaching down behind a waist-high stack of boxes with "Sonoran Chicken Ranch" printed on the outside.

Ronnie continued her deep breathing, frowning at the boxes. Wasn't a chicken ranch another name for a brothel? Surely the owners of the Sonoran Chicken Ranch realized ...

Sadie pulled out a handgun from behind the boxes.

"What are you doing with *that*?" Ronnie asked.

"My job," Sadie said, fishing a long metal tube from her jacket pocket. She screwed the tube into the end of the barrel.

Oh, no.

Oh, no!

What had she done? Ronnie had walked right into a trap. Suddenly it all made sense—Sadie showing up wherever Ronnie had been this week, keeping an eye on her.

Sadie was a hired killer.

Christ, what an idiot she'd been. So naïve. Then again, she had been wary of Sadie from the start.

Mostly, anyway.

"You're going to kill me now, aren't you?" Ronnie raised her hands. "I'm going to die in a freezer in the back of a grocery store in Yuccaville, Arizona." She shouldn't have thrown that frozen leg on the floor. She looked down at the meathead bleeding out, nudging him with her toe. "Get up and help me, dammit. I didn't hit you that hard."

"It was a solid hit," Sadie said, moving up next to Ronnie to frown down at the guy. "But he deserved it."

"For trying to kill you?"

Sadie aimed the gun at his head. "For trying to kill *you*."

"Me?"

"Yeah." Sadie leaned closer. "It's a good thing they keep cardboard on the floor in here."

"You mean to keep it from being so slippery?"

"No. To keep this from being such a pain to clean up."

She pulled the trigger. Twice.

* * *

"So, I'm just supposed to shrug this off?" Penny asked her brother via the wireless microphone earbuds connected to her cell phone.

She was alone in the diner's kitchen at the moment, taking care of breakfast orders while her cook was on a break. When Grady's call came in, she'd answered it on the second ring. What she'd hoped to hear was that her brother had figured out a way to throw

Elizabeth behind bars for breaking Penny's front window; or at least, that he'd slapped her with a hefty fine and made it so she'd be forced to pay for the damages.

She should have known better than to dream too big when it came to that bitch's demise. Penny's horoscope for the day had warned her that an old hurt would resurface and she'd have to tackle a tough issue.

Boy, she'd sure love to tackle Elizabeth right about now. Penny the Pounder would put that "old hurt" out of everyone's misery with a solid sucker punch and throw in a good old black eye as a bonus.

Shaking off her oven mitts, she scowled down at the Shaker lemon pie she'd pulled from the oven. The crust was golden brown and perfectly flaky, but now that she'd heard Grady's answer to how she should proceed after Elizabeth's attack last night, she wanted to throw the pie at the wall. Better yet, she could nail up a damned picture of the backbiting strumpet and throw the pie at it.

"I didn't say you have to shrug it off." Grady sounded tired this morning, as if he'd been up through the middle of the night dealing with a vandalism crime at his sister's diner and trying to keep Penny calm when she wanted to gather a certain posse to go raid Elizabeth's house with pitchforks and torches. Which he had, of course, and he could thank his ex-wife for that.

"It sure sounded like that to me."

"What I said was to tap the brakes for right now and put things on cruise control for a little longer."

"To what end? So that she has time to burn this place down around my ears?"

"You have no hard evidence pointing directly at Liz yet." He yawned. "If you were to start blaming her publicly, she could sue you for slander."

"Oh, that's rich. She fucks with my business, literally throwing a damned brick through the window, and I could get sued for slander. Do you know how much fixing that freaking window is going to cost me?"

"You have insurance."

"Sure, and I have a deductible."

A weary sigh came through the line. "Penny, please."

"Don't 'Penny, please' me, dammit," she said as she finished plating up an order for a Mexican chorizo hash scramble, adding some sliced avocado, a dollop of sour cream, and some parsley on the top. "You need to get your ex-wife under control, *Sheriff*."

"I'm trying, for crissake."

"Did you meet with her this morning?" She set the plate in the order window and returned to the oven.

"Yeah."

"And how did that go?" Before he could get a word in, she said, "Let me guess. She blinked those long, fake eyelashes at you, shook her big bazongas a few times, and giggled at every other word you said. And in the meantime, your tiny caveman brain melted in the palm of her hand."

"Give me some credit. I'm nearly forty, not fourteen."

"Please, you're a male, and about the only thing Elizabeth has ever excelled at is turning somewhat intelligent men into goober pie."

"Is that even a real thing?"

"Yes, it is, but I'm not making it for you until you fix this fucked-up mess with your ex."

"Jesus, Penny. You need to off-gas some of that bitterness. Your face must be puckered clear to your chin."

"I'm going to add a definite pucker to yours, Grady, if you don't neutralize Elizabeth. I've put over twenty hours into cleaning this week because she made me contend with a nit-picking health inspector on top of her negative reviews and doctored pictures."

"I'm trying, but the days of driving someone to the county line and kicking them out of the car with a warning to 'Get out and stay out' are over."

Penny donned her oven mitts again. "So, what did the two-bit whore say when you asked her about throwing the brick through my window? Did she look to her upper left? Or did she stare down at her feet?"

Didn't one or both of those body gestures mean the suspect was lying?

"She smiled," Grady answered. "And she said it wasn't her and that her mother was her alibi for last night."

"Of course she didn't get her hands dirty doing this." Penny opened the oven and waited for the wave of heat to blast past her. "She wouldn't want to break a nail."

"If we give her enough rope and time," Grady said, "she'll hang herself."

"And in the meantime, she'll drive me out of business."

Penny pulled the cranberry-orange pie from the oven. The streusel crust was lightly browned. She took off her oven mitt and picked off a small morsel, blowing on it and then popping it in her mouth. It was crispy, yet buttery and sweet. The perfect counter for a slightly tart pie.

"I'll see if I can get a deputy to keep a closer eye on your place in the evenings," Grady told her.

A lot of good a periodic drive-by would do. Grady was placating her now. Besides, Penny had seen proof that Elizabeth was having drinks with Ernie. Who was to say some of Grady's other deputies weren't already in her pocket? Or even in her pants, knowing Elizabeth's history of being a tramp.

"Don't bother," she told him. "I'll figure out something myself."

"Penny," he said, sighing again. There was the weight of the world in that one. "Between you and Veronica, I'm pulling my hair out here."

"What's up with Ronnie?" She opened the fridge and grabbed one of the two uncooked cherry pies—the one with a glazed almond flour latticed crust. "Is Elizabeth throwing shit at her, too?" she asked as she slid the pie into the oven and set the timer.

"I screwed up."

She heard the sound of a microwave beeping on his end. "Grady, are you heating up one of those breakfast burritos?"

"Yeah."

"Dang it, you know I'll make you something much healthier without all of the sodium and by-products if you'd get your butt over here."

"I thought you were mad at me about my ex giving you problems." His voice had a teasing note in it.

"I am, but that doesn't mean I want to hear about you dying from a heart attack." Penny walked over to the order window and took a slip of paper from her assistant manager. Speaking of breakfast burritos—she grabbed some slices of raw brisket and diced pork belly from the fridge.

He guffawed. "I'll probably die from a severe case of the

Morgan sisters first."

She grinned. Those three had certainly turned Grady's world upside down since they'd come to town. "Don't let Kate hear you say that, or she'll gut you and leave you in a ditch for the scorpions and rattlesnakes to eat."

"I don't know how Butch handles her."

"There is no 'handling' involved with a woman, don't ya know. We need lots of sugar and love and respect." A little pie didn't hurt every now and then either, she thought with a coy smile. Lemon meringue pie with a side of Mississippi had tasted downright delicious last night. Stupid Elizabeth and her brick had screwed that up, too.

Penny laid the meat on the grill and grabbed some seasoning. "What happened with Veronica?"

"She found out I was meeting Elizabeth this morning before I had a chance to explain what was going on."

"So what? It's not like you had your ex-wife in your living room first thing in the morn ..." she trailed off, adding things up in her head—him yawning, coffee brewing, the microwave beeping. She grimaced. "Jesus, Grady, why would you invite that she-devil into your house."

"It used to be hers, too."

"That doesn't make it any better, you bozo." She grabbed some chopped orange and yellow bell peppers and caramelized onions, tossing them on the grill next to the meat. "Let me guess. Ronnie called while your ex was there, and Elizabeth conveniently said your name in a seductive, breathy voice."

"No. Veronica stopped by, only she didn't come inside."

"You mean she waited on the porch?" The spatula clanked on the grill as she stirred the veggies around, trying to get a nice sear on them.

"I mean she sat in Claire's Jeep a little way down the block and spied on us."

Oh, hell. Penny shook her head. "Note to Sheriff Featherbrains—don't use the word 'spy' when you are trying to patch things up with your girlfriend. You do realize your meeting with Elizabeth probably looked more like a clandestine breakfast-in-bed reunion."

"Of course." He cursed at length under his breath. "Veronica took off when I noticed her."

"Did you see her right away?"

"No, Elizabeth and I were finishing up on the porch when a horn honked. Veronica must have hit it by accident, because she did an illegal U-turn in the street and took off after that."

"Oh, God." Penny felt for Ronnie. That was like a double-tap on the mortification button. "When you say 'finishing up,' did that involve a good-bye kiss or some lovey-dovey petting?"

Silence came from his end of the line for a couple of beats. "When have you ever witnessed me doing any lovey-dovey petting?"

She shrugged, grinning in spite of the mess he'd made. "Maybe that's your problem with women. You need to add a teaspoon or two of kissy-face, lovey-doveyness. Actually, knowing what you look like in the morning light, make that a cup of it."

"Have I ever told you how funny you are … not?"

She made kissing sounds over the phone and then pretended to sound all sweety-pie like Elizabeth when she said, "Oh, Grady-bear!" She used one of the bitch's old endearments that used to grind on Penny's nerves. "Do you wanna pretend to be the daddy of my baby again, so I can screw up your life in front of everybody in the whole ding-dang county one more time?"

A snort-snicker-cough came from him. "I'm going to hurt you next time I see you, Penny, and I don't care if you tell Mom."

Penny laughed. "You love me and you know it, Grady-bear."

A tap on Penny's shoulder made her turn.

Her cook had returned from break and was holding up the paper with the food order on it, her eyebrows raised in question.

Nodding, Penny handed over the spatula and gave up control of the grill.

"So, what are you going to do to fix this with Ronnie?" she asked her brother.

"I was thinking about arresting her and locking her up in my bedroom."

"Oh, you mean a territorial Neanderthal abusing his power." She headed for the sink and the stack of dirty pie-making dishes waiting for her there. "That went out of sexiness several decades ago. Try again."

"I could shower her with roses and chocolate and jewelry and throw myself at her feet, begging for mercy."

Penny wrinkled her nose. "That only works in the movies. Real women want real apologies. The nitty-gritty kind that nearly costs a man his soul before all is said and done."

Grady groaned. "I'll think on it some more. Her birthday is coming up, so maybe I can combine the two."

"Are you serious?"

"Um, noooo." It almost sounded like there was supposed to be a question mark at the end of that last drawn out "o."

"Grady, don't fuck this up. Ronnie is the best thing to happen to you since I was born and brought all this amazing sunlight and love and laughter into your life."

"Please, Penny," he said, chuckling. "I'm trying to eat this nutritious burrito here."

"Think hard about what you would like from Ronnie if the situation were reversed, and then ask someone with more charm and wisdom their opinion on the matter."

"Fine. Okay. Stop making me feel bad about myself."

She turned on the water, washing her hands as she filled the sink with hot, soapy water. "You know I love you, ya big bonehead."

"Yeah, well, your love is like a jumping cholla cactus."

"You mean crafty and majestic with lovely pink and lavender blossoms?"

He snorted. "I mean it hooks stubbornly into your skin and won't let go without a modicum of pain involved."

Smiling, she dried her hands. "Oh, family bonding times are the best." She pulled her phone from her back pocket. "Now stop screwing around and fix this county."

She hung up before he could get in a comeback, setting her phone aside and then returning to the sink.

After splashing water around for ten minutes, she finished up at the sink and squirted some lotion on her hands. Somehow, she had to figure out a way to pay Elizabeth back for screwing with her livelihood without getting herself—or her brother—into trouble with the law.

"Good morning, Penelope," Mississippi said from behind her, making her jump.

The FBI gods must be eavesdropping on her thoughts. If

they'd tapped into her brain last night before the brick ruined her evening, they would have been able to have a stag film party starring one of their very own agents.

She turned, taking in his brown button-up shirt tucked into his crisp blue jeans. Cowboy boots and hat bookended him at the bottom and top, although he held the hat in his hand at the moment. His hair curled at the ends, looking damp. Was he fresh from the shower? Penny wanted to lean in close and sniff his neck to see if he smelled as good as he'd tasted last night.

"Good morning. How did you sleep?" she asked, and then resisted the urge to smack herself on the forehead. What was she? Hostess extraordinaire?

He shrugged, looking around her kitchen, nodding a "Hello" at her cook. "I've slept better."

"Was it the bed?"

His eyes took on a wicked gleam. "No," he said in a quiet voice, turning his back on the cook. "It was the lack of activity that I'd been led to believe was going to happen in that bed, but didn't."

Her cheeks warmed. "Well, there was that brick."

"Yeah."

"And then my brother showed up."

"Uh-huh."

"He's kind of a mood-killer."

"I can see that." He leaned against the baking table where their pie-tasting had happened last night. After a glance down at the pies cooling there, he raised one brow. "What flavors are on deck for today?"

She listed off the two that were cooling on the baking racks along with what were already in her pie display out front. "Oh, and a couple of different cherry pies."

"Damn." His gaze dropped to her lips. "I'd like to try a few of those."

She knew without question that he meant try them on her, but because they had an audience, she offered, "I could get you some slices right now, if you'd like."

"I can't. I need to head over to the grocery store."

"If you're looking for some breakfast, I can throw something together on the grill really quick. You get room and board, remember?" she added, noticing the cook peeking their way.

He hesitated, glancing at his watch. "I need to see if I can cross paths with Ronnie when she makes her morning run to the store."

"Is something wrong?" she asked in a quiet voice.

"Isn't there always when it comes to her situation?" His smile was grim. He turned his back to the cook again while pulling on his coat, speaking so low that Penny had to lean closer to hear. "I was sent word from one of our sources of a definite lead on a hired killer, picture included. I'm going to need to up my game."

"Which means more surveillance?"

"From your brother and me."

Christ, as if Grady didn't have enough shit to deal with at the moment.

Mississippi pulled out his cell phone, pretending to check something on it in case her cook was watching. "I've been giving Ronnie a little leeway, hanging back a block or so when she does her store runs, just making sure she's not being followed. But with the information that came in this morning, that might need to stop for a while. Either the sheriff plays doting loverboy, or I'm her number-one best friend. Unfortunately, she doesn't have much choice."

Poor Ronnie—not only because she was going to have a constant babysitter, but because someone was actively going to have her in their sights. Penny shivered. That put her troubles with Elizabeth in perspective. Grady's ex was an annoying gnat. Ronnie's killers were like tarantula hawk wasps, with bullets for stingers. Or worse, since Grady had mentioned before that they might not have instructions to kill initially. Kidnap. Torture. Maim. Then, if that didn't work to their benefit, they might take mercy on Ronnie and put an end to her life.

"Yeah, you definitely need to go." She touched his arm in what could be read as a friendly landlady way. "But give me one minute to throw together something for you to eat along the way."

"I have a breakfast bar."

"Mine is better." She hurried to her refrigerator. "I make these myself and pack them full of protein and just the right amount of carbs to taste great. I keep a supply in the fridge for when Grady swings through needing a quick snack. Grab a coffee to go and I'll have them ready for you when you come back through."

While he was out front, Penny grabbed a few of her

homemade breakfast bars, wrapped them in parchment paper, and threw in a couple of slices of sharp white cheddar cheese that paired well with the sweet fruit and roasted nuts in the bars, along with a few napkins.

She held out the sack when he returned. "Happy trails."

His hand touched hers as he took the sack and lingered, clearly on purpose. "Thanks, landlady." His gaze fixed on her lips for a couple of seconds before returning north. "I'll see you later."

She followed him to the back door. "Take care of yourself, Special Agent Brown. Ronnie isn't the only one whose life is on the line these days."

"All in the line of duty." He started outside, but then stopped and turned back. "I'm going to be thinking about those pies all day, Penelope. If you have a bite of one, let me know." With a grin and wink, he left.

Penny closed the door and leaned against it for good measure. That man was a problem. The question was, would sleeping with him again make it better or worse?

Chapter Twenty-Five

"Jesus, Sadie!" Ronnie said, her back turned on the now-for-sure dead guy. "What did you do that for?"

"I was making sure." Sadie cleared her throat, her voice still gravelly from nearly being strangled to death.

Ronnie gulped down a wave of nausea, frowning at her accomplice. "Making sure of what?"

"That you'd killed him."

"I don't think I'd killed him fully before you shot him."

"Okay, I was making sure that one of us had definitely killed him." Sadie unscrewed the long tube, which Ronnie now realized was some sort of suppressor.

"But he might have lived."

"You delivered a major blow to the back of his head, Veronica. There was a good chance he would have had severe brain swelling and not come out of that well."

"Yeah, but he had a big head."

Sadie smirked. "And a small brain."

"That was probably surrounded by a very hard skull."

"Oh, he had a hard skull all right. Trust me." Sadie pointed at the bruise next to her eye. She slipped the gun inside her coat. "Come on, we need to hide the body for now."

"Hide the body?" Ronnie glanced at the door. "Shouldn't we run?"

"No. Running is for victims." Sadie started sliding boxes of frozen chicken away from the wall. "Remember that for next time."

"Next time?"

"Yeah. Now help me make some room for him over here."

Fifteen minutes later, they'd tucked the big dead brute behind several stacks of boxes. Sadie had done most of the hard work. She was far stronger than Ronnie, able to lug the meathead mostly on her own.

Ronnie stood shivering in the freezing cold, trying not to think about the smell of blood or the sight of bullet holes, while Sadie made some final adjustments to their hiding place and then scraped up the small amount of blood left behind.

Sadie opened the freezer door a crack and peeked out into the hallway. "Come on. It's clear." She led the way out and opened the bathroom door across from the freezer. "Why don't you go wash your hands and slap some color back into your cheeks, while I take care of one more thing. I'll knock five times when I'm done. After you hear the knocks, count to thirty before coming out. Finish your shopping and then meet me in the parking lot."

Ronnie nodded numbly.

"What did you drive? The sheriff's rig?"

"No." What had she driven here today? It all seemed like another lifetime ago.

"Claire's Jeep?"

Oh, yeah, that was it. Ronnie nodded.

Wait. How did Sadie know the Jeep was Claire's?

"I'll find you out in the lot," Sadie said, making pointed eye contact with Ronnie. "Do not leave until we have a chance to talk, okay?"

Ronnie nodded again.

Sadie pushed Ronnie into the bathroom. "Everything is going to be okay, Veronica. Trust me. Just do as I said." She closed the door in Ronnie's face.

The woman in the mirror looked like she'd seen a dead man. "Fuck me."

Ronnie washed her hands for a solid minute, letting the hot water warm her up. Then she splashed her face with the water, pinched her cheeks a couple of times, and combed her hair with her fingers.

"Everything is going to be okay," she repeated Sadie's words, trying not to think about what had happened in the freezer.

By the time Sadie gave her five-knocks signal, Ronnie was ready to get the hell out of the tiny, claustrophobic bathroom and drive all of the way to Patagonia. She'd read they had some beautiful scenery down that way, and cute cousins to the llama called *guanaco*. Maybe she could ride off on one into the South American sunset.

She counted to thirty, flushed the toilet for sound effects, pretended to wash her hands, and then opened the door.

The stockroom was empty.

Thank God.

After one last glance at the closed freezer door, she forced herself to stroll casually toward the doors leading out to the main part of the store. Her cart was still where she'd left it, which made the last hour feel even more surreal. She headed to the front of the store, paid, and walked on wobbly legs to the Jeep.

After packing the bags into the back end, she crawled behind the wheel. Now what?

Ronnie stared at the front of the grocery store where people were entering and exiting, going about their daily lives, clueless there was a dead man in the freezer.

The passenger door opened and Sadie joined her inside. "You okay to drive?" she asked, buckling her seat belt.

"I think so."

"Good. Turn left out of the lot."

Ronnie did as told. When she got onto the street, she glanced at the woman sitting next to her. "Who are you?"

"Who I am isn't important. It's what I am that matters."

"Fine. *What* are you?"

"Take another left here."

Ronnie followed her order.

"Three blocks up, I want you to pull up next to the curb and let me out, as if you were simply giving me a ride home."

Ronnie drove the three blocks, checking her rearview mirror several times to make sure they weren't being followed.

She pulled up next to the curb as told, shifting into park. "Are you here because of me?" Ronnie asked her.

Sadie flipped down the visor, checking out her reflection in the small, lighted mirror. "Officially, yes."

"To kill me?"

"No."

Ronnie blew out a breath of relief. "Then why?"

Flipping the visor closed, Sadie turned to Ronnie. "I'm a

cleaner."

"What does that mean?"

"I was hired to clean up and remove all evidence after the job was done."

"And killing me was this 'job' you're talking about?"

Sadie nodded.

"So that meathead back there at the store ..."

"He was hired to kill you." Sadie checked the side mirror. "He'd been tracking you for days and knew you'd be coming to the store this morning. But you were early."

"Yeah, I had some stuff come up." The whole Grady and Elizabeth deal flitted through her thoughts, seeming so trivial now after what had happened in that freezer.

"I noticed him tracking you a couple of days ago in the store parking lot," Sadie told her.

A memory popped into her head. "The day you almost got backed into?"

"Exactly."

That was where Ronnie had seen that guy before. He'd been in that blue truck she'd zipped behind. "So, he was here at the store today to kill me?"

"Or at least try." Sadie chuckled. "But you're a wily one, Veronica Jefferson."

Ha! Sadie didn't know the half of it. Then again, maybe she did.

"So, you went into the back of the store with him to help kill me?"

"That's what he thought. He recognized me. I'd cleaned up after him before. The big oaf thought he was all that and a bag of jerky, but he made a real mess when he closed an account."

Hmm. There was that accounting vernacular again. Sadie's comments about things not being "balanced" made more sense.

"You mean when he'd killed someone." At Sadie's nod, Ronnie asked, "But when I came up on you two, he was strangling you."

"Yeah, I'd kicked him pretty hard, trying to drop him, but that guy was as solid as a safe. Then I tripped over a cardboard box and my gun flew behind the chicken boxes. During the tussle that followed, he'd gotten the better of me thanks to his lard ass. I was lucky you showed up when you did. Fighting with that fucker was like wrestling a rhino."

Yes, a rhino was a fitting description of what Ronnie had hit with that leg of lamb.

"So, now what?" Ronnie was still trying to process everything, but she needed a point on the horizon or she might just head south and not stop. Once again, Patagonia was calling.

"Now, you go back to The Shaft and do your job."

"And pretend nothing happened?"

"Exactly."

"What about the dead guy in the freezer?"

"I'm a cleaner, and I'm damned good at my job." Sadie patted Ronnie's arm. "Nobody will know anything happened when I'm finished."

"You can just make that whole thing go away?"

"I certainly can. And will."

"What about his family or friends?"

Sadie laughed. "He's a hitman, Veronica. The only person who will miss him is the fucker who hired the hit on you."

"So, the person who hired you didn't hire him, too?"

"Nope. This guy worked for someone else. But I have an idea who did. She's one merciless asshole, and she doesn't care about cleaning up her messes afterward."

So two different "bosses" had hired a hit on her? Christ.

Ronnie was getting really tired of assholes in general, hired killers or FBI higher-ups or ex-wives.

She stared at Sadie, realization washing over her. "It was you that morning at the diner, wasn't it? Not your mother. You were in disguise."

"I like to learn about my accounts ahead of time—their habits, where they live, places they like to eat. It helps me get a feel for the lay of the land so I can make cleanup go smoother and quicker." Sadie smirked. "And then I choked on that damned grape and nearly gave my cover away. Luckily, you were quick on the draw and saved me."

Raking her hand through her hair, Ronnie said, "I think today proved that saving you was far luckier for me in the long run."

"Maybe." Sadie opened the passenger door. "You can't say a word about this or what I am to your boyfriend. Or to your FBI shadow or anyone else. This is between you and me only. Got it?"

Ronnie nodded slowly.

"If anyone else finds out who I am and what I do, my cover will be completely blown and I'll have to leave. And if I leave, I won't be here to give you a heads-up when the killer arrives who I've been hired to clean up after."

"Right," Ronnie said, seeing the whole picture clearly. The question was, whose side would Sadie be on when that day arrived? Her boss's or Ronnie's?

"You saved my life again, Veronica."

"I did?" It felt the other way around now that Ronnie knew the nuts and bolts of it all.

Sadie stared at her, her expression unreadable. "Yes, damn it. I was on my way out and then you clunked that idiot on the head. When he fell on me, it kickstarted everything on the inside again with gusto."

Actually, the leg of lamb was the star of the freezer show. Without it, Ronnie would probably be sprawled out dead next to Sadie.

"Aren't you going to offer me any money this time?" she asked with a small smile, trying to make light of the whole mess.

Sadie laughed. "That's my girl. Way to swing hard today, Veronica Jefferson. You're a real ass kicker."

"Call me Ronnie," she told Sadie. "Ronnie Morgan. Veronica Jefferson is dead."

"Ronnie it is."

"Is your name really Sadie?"

"Partly."

"Will I see you again?" Ronnie asked, confirming her guardian goon wasn't going to be leaving town anytime soon.

"Of course you will. My ledger remains unbalanced." Sadie closed the door and waved through the window.

Ronnie felt unbalanced, too, but she shifted into gear and rolled down the road toward Jackrabbit Junction.

Gripping the wheel hard to keep from trembling, she tried to make sense of this morning while breathing her way back to a calm, slightly more sane state. She needed to make it through the rest of the day without having to be muffled and carted off to a loony bin.

Her cell phone pinged with an incoming text as she passed the

Yuccaville city limits sign and reached the open desert. Mississippi's name was on her phone's screen when she checked it. He was apparently thinking about her earlier than usual.

She slowed, easing onto the side of the road in a gravel pullout so she could read what he'd written.

Where are you? I'm at the grocery store and don't see any of your usual vehicles.

Why was he at the store looking for her? That was new.

She wrote back: *I'm on my way out of town. Already been to the store.*

She skipped the part about whacking the killer with a leg of lamb. That really wasn't texting material.

Shit-criminy. What was she going to do about Sadie when it came to Grady and Mississippi? Nothing, as Sadie had directed? Could Ronnie really keep that big of a secret from the man she loved and the FBI agent here to help protect her? Well, officially, the feds were interested in using Ronnie as bait more than keeping her alive, but Mississippi was running rogue. Oh hey, it turned out she was doing her job on the FBI front—being bait, at least. She deserved a reward for her troubles.

Mississippi wrote: *Need you to keep an eye out for trouble.*

She laughed—it was loud and crackly and borderline manic. Her eye might have twitched, too. She checked it in the mirror. Nope. She hadn't reached Katie's level of temporary insanity yet.

She typed: *What sort of trouble?*

A picture popped up on her screen. She stared down at it, her heart pounding in her ears.

He added: *He goes by the name Blue Hornet.*

She stared at the picture of the dead man back in the freezer. It was slightly blurry, obviously from long range, but it was definitely the guy she'd clobbered.

Mississippi added: *I'm on my way to join you. We need to talk about surveillance plans.*

Ronnie stared out the windshield at the wide-open desert dotted with creosote bushes, groupings of cholla and prickly pear cacti, and the occasional tall and spindly ocotillo. With Sadie in town, Ronnie had already upped her surveillance game a level, it seemed.

See you soon, she texted back to Mississippi and pulled back onto the road. She cranked up the radio, humming along with Gordon

Lightfoot, envious of the carefree highway he was singing about as she rolled along.

Ronnie was almost to The Shaft when her phone rang. She glanced down at the screen. Grady was calling again.

Her thumb hovered over the button to accept the call. Maybe she should talk to him.

On second thought, she sent it to voicemail.

She was going to need a little longer before she could look him in the eye and pretend she hadn't been an accessory to murder today in the freezer of a grocery store in his county.

* * *

"Mirror, mirror on the wall," Mac said under his breath as he scowled at himself in the mirror behind the bar. "Who's the most Scrooge-like of them all?"

Mirrors didn't lie, unfortunately. And now, after having some time to think about what Claire had said this morning, he could see how inconsiderate he'd been when it came to the brewery.

You have been running your own money show for a long time, and you've done very well for yourself. But I don't think you're ready to truly share that part of your life yet.

Claire was right.

Add to that the fact the brewing aspect of the business was his passion, not hers. He was the one who'd brewed beer off and on during college, and then experimented with different lagers, ales, and meads in his basement in Tucson throughout the years.

Claire hadn't brewed a day in her life. But she'd supported his idea to have a brewery from the first mention of it, volunteering to build it. Even after her grandfather added the birding platform to her plate, she'd still planned to do the build, trying to figure out how to balance it along with helping out at the bar.

When Mac had realized they'd need more money, he'd done the same as he had prior to Claire being in his life. He'd decided how *he* would secure more money, not thinking about her feelings or limitations on both time and endurance.

Mirror, mirror, who was the biggest idiot of them all?

He growled at the mirror. Maybe he'd take it down after Butch handed off the keys. Who needed this much introspection when sitting in a bar anyway?

"Shit," he said, shoving his hand through his hair. Maybe it was time to swallow some of his pride and ask Harley for more capital. This job in Bisbee could be his last, and he would be here to help Claire and Luke with the build.

"Hey, sweet buns!" Chester peered out through the kitchen order window. "Why are you sitting out there looking like a sad, wrinkly sack of moldy potato salad sandwiches that somebody tossed into the ditch?"

That seemed oddly specific. "I'd prefer you thought of me as a Philly cheesesteak sandwich." Mac reached for the bottle of beer that Butch had given him to try. It was from a microbrewery in Yuccaville.

Chester shrugged. "It's your sack. You can be whatever sort of sandwich tickles your fanny."

"You mean 'fancy,' don't you?"

"I dated a woman once who liked to have her fanny tickled with feathers to warm her up, if you know what I mean." He wiggled his bushy eyebrows at Mac. "Ever since then, I preferred 'fanny' over 'fancy' when talking about ticklin'." He pointed at the bottle in Mac's hand. "You drinking your problems away already?"

"Actually, I'm taste testing to see if I want to continue contracting with the brewer after Claire and I take over."

Correction—make that he and Claire needed to make the decision to continue contracting with the brewer or not.

He sighed. Damn it. He'd operated on his own for years. Financially single. He might say he wanted Claire to think of the wealth he'd accumulated as "theirs," but there was a part of him that was uneasy about sharing decisions when it came to that hard-earned money.

"Oh, hey!" Chester clapped his hands together. "That sounds like a fun part of the job. I'm coming out to help." Chester disappeared from the order window, hurrying out through the batwing doors.

He joined Mac, reaching for the bottle of beer. "What is this?"

"An IPA."

"You gonna brew some IPAs?"

Mac shrugged. "Sure. Porters and stouts, too."

"This is a good thing you're doing here. Butch is burned out and Jackrabbit Junction needs a quality watering hole or it might dry up and blow away in the spring winds." Chester glanced over his shoulder as if somebody might be listening in, lowering his voice to add, "It's also good that Claire finally figured out something else she can do well besides taking all of those college classes and building stuff."

Mac rubbed his ear. It seemed to him that intelligence and craftsmanship were high qualities on their own. Why would she need something more?

"Mind if I take a drink?" Chester's question was apparently rhetorical, because he wiped the rim of the bottle with his T-shirt, going forth no matter Mac's answer. "I don't want to get your loverboy cooties," he explained with a grin. "I have a good thing going with the ladies. Wouldn't want to mess that up with too much of that sappy romance crap I see you using on Claire. It might ruin my reputation as a sexy rogue pirate coming 'round to plunder the ladies' chests."

"We wouldn't want that," Mac said dryly.

Chester took a drink, audibly swished the beer around in his mouth, and then swallowed. "Well, the hops start out biting you, but it finishes nice and smooth." He slapped the bar. "I'd keep this one."

"I like it, too. We need to try the other two Butch carries." Mac went around the back of the bar, pulling out a bottle of ale and a hard cider. He grabbed four glasses and poured two for Chester and two for himself.

They both sipped, swilled, swallowed, and then had some more. Both were good, but not as good as the first.

"I think I can do better," he told Chester.

"You think or you know?" Chester finished the ale.

"I know. At least when it comes to IPAs and stouts." Mac leaned on the bar. "If you were in my shoes and had your five-plus decades of experience under your belt, what beers would you carry?"

Chester rubbed his whiskered jaw. "Well, I'd want to keep the basics, of course. You know, the big name, boring brands, and a well-known Mexican brew or two since we're this close to the border. And maybe a few specialties from someplace else, like this local guy's product. Then that opens up the opportunity for you to do a larger variety of craft brews here on site. I might start with four and then expand from there, testing out ingredients on customers." He picked up the glass of remaining hard cider, taking a swallow. "Are you getting smaller tanks or a few big ones?"

"I was thinking of a few smaller tanks to start with," Mac told him. "And then one or two big ones when I see what goes over well. Maybe building up over time to a sizable variety, trying out seasonal flavors."

"I had a coffee-flavored brew once that surprised me," Chester told him. "It was almost like a stout. Dark, rich, good body. I think you could do well with serving flights with four or five different flavors. Expand the folks' palates around here."

He liked the way Chester thought on this, which surprised him. "I thought you liked cheap, generic beer."

"Sure, when I'm paying for it. But if it's free, I like to expand my fermented barley horizons." He pointed down at the bar. "This venture here is exciting. It's a good thing I'm sticking around to be an official taste-tester after you're up and running."

Mac chuckled. "I see how you are. You start out in the kitchen, learning the art of Butch's signature sandwiches, and next you move into the brewery business. You're a cunning businessman."

"How do you think I made enough money to coast through the rest of my days chasing skirts and wrestling in the mud with bikini babes?"

Mac hadn't ever thought about Chester's financial state. The guy usually seemed like he was a tightwad, but now that he thought about it, Chester did drive a newer pickup and never complained about losing money at the euchre table.

Chester took another draw of hard cider. "You know, you could sell your craft beers to other venues in the area. Put some in the General Store. Maybe even push it clear to Tucson."

They were on the same page, it seemed. "I was scouting out the bar and grill scene down around Bisbee," Mac told Chester. "I might be able to play on the mining theme around these parts and create a new niche. Maybe try some varieties of a miner's grog to go with Bisbee's and Yuccaville's historical theme."

"Good thinking." Chester nodded. "How about a cowboy theme for some, too. Tombstone is a big hit with tourists and that ain't too far from here. They'd drink up that cowboy beer in a hiccup. You could try a sage or chili bean brew and brand it as 'Something to drink around the campfire.' That might get the campers and hikers coming through this way, too. Double your audience with a single marketing message."

"Damn." Mac gaped at the guy. "I like the way you think, Chester."

"What can I say? I know beer inside and out. Hell, I should have an honorary degree in beer drinking after all of these years of working so hard at it."

An idea struck Mac as Chester finished his drink.

No, he shouldn't, should he?

Maybe, though.

With the right parameters set ahead of time it could work.

But how would Claire feel about it?

Before he found that out, he decided to see if there was any interest on this end.

"Chester, how would you feel about investing in a local brewery, if that option were available?"

One bushy eyebrow raised. "You talking about my money, Mac? Or my time and know-how?"

Mac shrugged. "Maybe all three."

The other bushy eyebrow rose to line up with the first. "Are you asking what I think you're asking?"

"Well, I need to talk to Claire before making it an official 'ask,' but we need some additional capital to cover some of the brewery costs, and I'm tired of working elsewhere to come up with the cash." He crossed his arms. "I'm only talking about the brewery part of the business, not The Shaft itself. If Claire agrees, we could form a separate business entity for the brewery, and then purchase the beer we brew for the restaurant to keep things separate on the books."

Chester drummed his fingers on the bar. "I'll tell you what. You talk to your partner. If Claire is willing to take on a third for the brewery, we'll put our heads together and hash out the particulars."

"Sounds good. I'll bring it up to her this afternoon after she finishes at the RV park."

Mac's attention shifted to the batwing doors as Ronnie pushed into the bar. She looked different this morning, roughed up and tumbled. Like she'd just rolled out of bed after a long night of hitting the bottle.

"Hey, Mac." Her quick smile seemed forced. "Is this customer bothering you?" She came over and rested her arm on Chester's shoulder, trying to act casual, but her movements were stiff and jerky. "If you want, I can call the county sheriff and have the troublemaker thrown in the slammer."

When Ronnie finally met Mac's gaze, she looked away quickly. Oh yeah, something was definitely up with her. Something that was making her evasive as hell.

Her unwillingness to hold eye contact reminded him of how she'd acted when she first moved down to Arizona and lived with him and Claire. Back when she was wearing colored contacts and changing her image, which Mac later found out was Ronnie's way of trying to hide in plain sight in order to evade the avalanche of shit her ex-husband had brought down on her head.

"Which slammer are you talking about?" Chester asked her, grinning wide. "The cell you and your sisters are practically paying rent for down at the county lockup?"

She poked Chester in the ribs, making him wince and snicker. "She's got itchy fangs today, Mac. Watch your backside."

Frazzled. That fit her better, in Mac's eyes. Like she'd gotten her tail caught in a wringer earlier and managed to escape, but at a cost. Was she fighting with Grady? They'd seemed to be doing fine last night.

Maybe it was Deborah who had Ronnie off her game. What had Claire said earlier? Something about their mother wanting to talk about their mother–daughter relationship? That would probably cause a lot of frustration and some loss of sleep for all of Deborah's girls, not only Claire.

"I'm going to go check the restrooms," Ronnie said, still avoiding looking at Mac. "You two quit sitting around drinking and get to work."

They both watched her walk away.

"Something ain't right there," Chester said in a low voice.

Mac played dumb. "What makes you say that?"

"She's twitching."

What? Mac had been watching her face almost the whole time. "I didn't see any twitches."

"I mean on the inside. I could feel it here." Chester tapped his shoulder where she'd been leaning. "Small waves of tremors rolling through. That isn't normal for her. Katie? Sure. She's one big lightning bolt most days, zapping the shit out of everything in her path. But Ronnie hasn't been strung out like this for a while now."

"You think it's her mother being back in town?"

Chester shrugged. "Could be. Medusa can certainly make a weaker soul turn to stone." He pushed off the bar stool. "We'll need to keep an eye on Ronnie today. She's been known to make a run for it when she feels cornered, and with all the trouble she has with gunslingers sneaking into town thanks to her ex-husband, we need to keep her tucked into the middle of the herd nice and safe."

The sound of tires on gravel outside made them both look at the door. Chester hobbled over, peeking out the window. "Should I let Mr. FBI in early or make him wait until we're officially open?"

Mac shrugged. "Might as well get the party started."

Chapter Twenty-Six

Sunday, Feb 3rd

K ate was going to kick Butch's sexy buns all the way to Mexico. Maybe even to the South Pole.

Earlier this morning while eating breakfast together, he'd asked Kate to run to the store in place of Ronnie, who, according to Mississippi, was now on high alert for incoming assholes. Kate had practically bounced off her chair with excitement.

"Yes! Yes! Yes!" She'd hopped up and kissed him like she'd just landed back on Earth after a long, lonely trip to the moon and back. Finally, she had a chance to take care of a few extracurricular activities without having to sneak and plot behind Butch's back.

A trip to the store meant Kate could meet with Millie, who'd called this morning while Butch was in the shower and mentioned that she had a "top-priority" pickup for Kate. And "top secret," too. The sheriff was not to hear about it, nor Ronnie or Penny. Claire wasn't mentioned, but Kate assumed Millie had forgotten about her other sister.

After having secretly hired Millie last week to dig up some dirt on Elizabeth, Kate couldn't wait to get her hands on whatever the Geritol Gangster and her girls had found.

But when Butch and Kate pulled into the parking lot at The Shaft an hour later, Chester was waiting, his truck idling. It didn't take someone with an IQ even half of hers to see the big picture.

"Really?" she snapped, giving Butch not just one evil eye, but two. The son of a gun was lucky she wasn't a black widow spider with eight evil eyes in her arsenal, along with fangs and venom. "I thought we'd reached an understanding yesterday morning about my lack of freedom."

"We did." Butch caught her hand, holding onto it when she tried to pull away. "But things are different today."

"I don't need a babysitter, Valentine."

"Chester isn't a babysitter, sweetheart. He's a bodyguard. You think that Ronnie is the only one in the high-risk category now? You're her sister *and* you're pregnant. If someone wanted to get to Ronnie, taking you hostage is a sure way to lure her out of hiding."

Good point. "I need to start packing heat."

He winced. "How about you start packing Chester instead. He's licensed for concealed carry in Arizona."

"He is? Since when?"

"According to him, since he established residency here last month."

"But his license plate isn't an Arizona one."

"Grady pointed that out, too. Chester promised to have that fixed before the end of the month when his old tags expire."

Kate guffawed. "Between the sheriff and Mac, nobody can get away with anything shady around here."

"So, Chester offered ..." Butch started to speak and then changed course. "What kind of shady things, Kate?"

Oops. She shrugged, avoiding his searching gaze, focusing on Chester's pickup instead. "Just the general, harmless, slightly dodgy sort of stuff." She needed to get the spotlight off her and fast. "I didn't realize Chester planned to stick around for good."

Although it made sense since Gramps and Manny, his two best buddies, had both settled here. Kate understood the pull of someone you love drawing you in and holding you in place. As soon as Claire had made it clear last spring that she wasn't returning to South Dakota, Kate had started planning on joining her some way or another. Falling for Butch while she was here visiting had sealed the deal.

She'd only gone back north once since, and that was with Claire to grab more of their things. And, unfortunately, their mom's, who'd decided to stay here in Arizona, too.

Shit, her mom. Kate frowned.

"Kate." Butch tugged on her hand. "What sort of dodgy stuff? More crap that will land you in Grady's jail cell if you're caught?"

"No." Which was the truth, because she was changing her tactics and wouldn't be caught the next time.

Now that Kate knew Deputy Dipshit had been spying on her while she was at the library, she was going to turn the tables on him. She was ninety-nine percent certain he was the asshole who'd tucked the anonymous, threatening notes under the windshield wiper on Gramps's Winnebago where Ronnie had been temporarily living. Before catching Ernie with Grady's ex at that bar, Kate had been wondering why he was leaving the notes. What his motivation was. If it were some kind of small-town version of a hate crime, or if someone were paying him to harass her sister. But now, Kate was pretty sure she had it figured out, and she simply needed to prove it. Or maybe not so simply. Time would tell.

"Kate, if you're going to—"

"Valentine." She needed a distraction, and she had a real doozy. "I have a problem that I'm not sure you or Chester can help me fix."

Butch loved trying to fix her problems, whether she wanted him to or not. Some days it made her want to throw fruit at his head during breakfast. Right now, though, she would be happy to have his help with this newest issue.

"What's wrong?"

"Mom called me yesterday."

He grimaced at the mere mention of her mother. Kate couldn't blame him. The poor guy had been stung enough by Deborah's pointed tail.

In her mother's eyes, it was bad enough that Butch had made her daughter fall in love with him and give up Deborah's lofty career dreams for her youngest child to end up a school district superintendent by age thirty-five. Add to that a pregnancy without a sparkling diamond on Kate's ring finger, and poor Butch currently ranked near the top of Deborah's shit list, in line behind Kate's dad and Grady. Mac was on that list somewhere, too, but lower since her mom had pretty much given up on "fixing" Claire a while ago.

"She wants to meet somewhere private to talk about our mother–daughter relationship struggles over the years and come up with a plan for going forward. She said that according to her therapist, this is a necessity, so that she can put the past behind her for good and move toward a healthier, sober future."

"So, the demon Lamashtu has not only returned," Butch said. "But she wants to have tea and crumpets, too."

Kate knew that name from one of her literature classes back in college. "Was Lamashtu the Greek monster demon who would devour children if they disobeyed?"

"No, that was Lamia. Lamashtu was Mesopotamian. She menaced women during childbirth, and then tried to kidnap the kids so she could gnaw on their bones and suck some of their blood. You know, all of that fun demon goddess stuff." Butch held up his fingers to make a cross. "You're going to need a priest to perform this exorcism, mama jama."

"How do you know so much about demons? Is there a dark side of you I don't know about yet?"

"Sure, but not as dark as your mother's heart, so no worries."

She chuckled, but then groaned. The thought alone of having that conversation with her mom ... Crudballs.

To make matters with her mom worse, her father had sent a message last night saying that his house was now up for sale in South Dakota. Randy Morgan was following through with his plans to move south and join his girls, no matter if his ex-wife were living close by or not. Kate and her sisters needed to do what they could to help Manny make sure their mom was as stable as possible before their dad arrived and set up camp in the same county.

"Did you agree to meet with her?" Butch asked. "If so, I could kidnap you for a few weeks and take you to a secret tropical island where she can't find us."

That sounded lovely ... and boring. There was too much happening around here with Elizabeth pulling her shenanigans and Ronnie needing Kate's help keeping a lookout for hitmen. Not to mention working with Claire to figure out the mystery behind the ancient knife and Joe's death.

"I put her off for now." She sighed, staring out the windshield without really seeing anything, her thoughts stuck somewhere back in long-ago. "The past is full of emotional land mines and buried frustrations that are better not trespassed, but she's determined to find a shovel."

"How'd she take your rain check request?"

"I don't know. She didn't text back."

"No response, huh? That makes me nervous."

"Me too." She frowned his way. "I'm all for her being sober. But if we start digging up the past, I might need to lock myself in Grady's jail for a whole new set of crimes."

Chester honked the horn. When she looked his way, he held up his arm and tapped his watch.

She flipped off Mr. Impatient, then turned back to Butch. "Okay, give me the damned grocery list."

Ten minutes later, she was on her way to Yuccaville in Chester's rig, singing about counting flowers on the wall along with the Statler Brothers on the radio.

"You should've let me drive, slowpoke," Kate said when the song was over. She'd been waiting for Chester to put the hammer down for the last five miles. He could at least go the speed limit.

He snickered. "And risk you trying to run down one of Grady's deputies with my rig? No way. I'm no tenderfoot when it comes to wild and whacky women."

"Yeah, well I sure wish you had a lead foot when it comes to driving. At this rate, I'm going to deliver my kid before we make it to the store and back."

"What's your big rush? You heard Butch. We have an hour to kill before opening time. My ol' granddad used to always tell me to be the tortoise, not the hare. Hell, you even look like you're wearing a tortoise shell backward in that plaid shirt."

Kate smoothed the brown and green flannel shirt she'd borrowed from Butch over her round belly. She needed some new prettier maternity clothes, but Yuccaville's pickings for expectant mothers were slim.

"I'm not in a big rush, Chester. But I do have an errand I need to run."

"What kind of errand? The baby sort? I can help you pick out a crib for Chester Jr."

An errand that she'd rather do on her own, but if Chester were going to be her bodyguard for the time being, she might as well knight him so he was prepared to go into battle alongside her.

"A secret errand."

He grinned. "Those are my favorite kind. Where are we going? Does it involve women's underwear?"

"Before I tell you, I need you to pinky promise that you'll keep your lips zipped if anyone asks where we've been. And if you go back on that promise …"

"You'll cut off my pinky?"

"Worse. I'll pay one of the girls at Dirty Gerties to put the squeeze on you so hard that your days of wrestling in the mud with bikini babes will be history."

Chester's grin flipped upside down. "Don't go ruining a good thing."

She held out her pinky. "Do we have a deal?"

He pursed his lips. "I promised Butch I'd keep you and the baby safe."

"What I have in mind won't hurt either of us."

"What about me?"

Kate thought about her and Claire's experiences with Millie and her gang. "You might end up with a few scratches."

"Will this be illegal?"

Kate wasn't about to ask Millie how she went about getting whatever information she had. "Maybe."

He laughed, taking her pinky in his for a short squeeze. "Deal. So, where to?"

"Behind the library."

"I thought you were banned from that place."

"Only for six months, but my business isn't in the library. It's in the parking lot behind it."

"How many orders of business do we have scheduled for this morning?"

"Only one today. But as far as anyone else is concerned, we went to the supermarket, dilly-dallied in the produce department, and then returned to The Shaft." She pointed at the stoplight up ahead. "Turn left there."

Chester followed her order. "You know what I think, Katie?"

"That I'm crazy?"

So what? Maybe she was hovering just this side of deranged, but better to be a little cracked and enjoying life rather than be tediously sane. Life was meant to be a fun, slightly bumpy, and sometimes hair-raising adventure, not a tethered walk on a smooth path under a temperature-regulated bubble.

"There's nothing wrong with a little craziness." Chester shot her a wild-eyed grin. "My first wife was chock full of it. Every other time we'd fight, she'd chase me around the house with wire snippers, threatening to castrate me."

"That's more than a 'little' crazy, Chester."

"Yeah, but we were *really* good at making up." He winked.

Before they traveled any farther down this R-rated version of memory lane, she returned to his original question. "What do you think, Chester?"

"I think that you and I are going to make great partners in crime."

She liked the sound of that. "And I think having a bodyguard isn't such a bad idea after all."

"Darn tootin'!" He pulled into the lot behind the library. "Now, how about you try to stay out of jail this morning, so that I don't get fired my first day on the job."

* * *

This wasn't working for Ronnie. This whole normal, mundane, bookkeeping shit. Not today. Not after what happened yesterday in that freezer.

She sat alone in Ruby's basement, closed away from the world, but she couldn't focus on the numbers in front of her no matter how much she pounded her head on the antique Queen Anne–style desk. And pounding her head on the desk only reminded her of the sickening *thunk* when she'd clocked the guy with the leg of lamb. Not to mention what followed after that.

Burying her face in her hands, she wondered what to do about Sadie. She didn't want to hide things from Grady. Nor Mississippi. Not telling them the truth meant not warning them about why Sadie was in town—to clean up after Ronnie's demise. Not to mention that if they listened to the FBI's latest advice, they were going to be focused on finding the wrong man. One who was already dead.

But telling them the truth threw Sadie under the bus with both the feds *and* maybe whoever hired her. While Sadie might have started out playing for an opposing team, she seemed to have changed sides thanks to Ronnie saving her life multiple times. With her access to inside information, Sadie also had a leg up on Grady and Mississippi. Ronnie couldn't risk losing Sadie's eyes and ears "out there," could she?

Lowering her hands, she stared down at the column of numbers. It was basic accounting, just a matter of adding. Easy-peasy. Time to get back to work.

She started in again, punching the numbers into the calculator. A third of the way down the list, she jumped when someone knocked on the door.

"Jessica," she said with a frustrated growl in her voice. "I asked you to stop interrupting me while I'm working on your mom's books."

"It's not Jessica."

Grady!

Ronnie looked up in surprise. What was he doing here right now? He was supposed to be at work.

Uh-oh! This wasn't about Katie doing the run to the store in Ronnie's place, was it?

"It's unlocked," she said, rising as he stepped inside and closed the door behind him, locking it.

Her heart sank at the sight of his khaki uniform and sheriff's badge, his hat in hand. "What did Katie do now?"

He pulled back the chair across from her, placing his hat on the floor next to the desk as he sat down. "Nothing." He made a wry face. "At least nothing I've heard about yet."

"Oh. Good." She lowered back into her chair. "Is there something else wrong?"

"Why would you ask that?"

"Because you're on duty."

His whiskey-colored eyes watched her from behind narrowed lids. "Actually, I'm here because of you."

A panicked voice shrieked in her head.

Had he found out about the dead guy? Or about Sadie? Or about the dead guy and Sadie, along with Ronnie's participation in yesterday's kill?

She licked her suddenly dry lips. "What did I do?"

"It's what you *didn't* do."

He almost sounded like he was teasing her now.

Ronnie was too strung out to play a game of suspicious cops and secretly guilty suspects with him.

"Grady." She picked up the calculator, threatening to throw it at him. "Don't mess with me. I'm not in the mood."

"That's the exact reason why I'm here." He crossed his arms and took a slow breath. Released it even slower. "You're still upset about Elizabeth being at my place yesterday."

"No, I'm not." And that was no lie.

Grady's ex-wife and her petty bullshit were the last things weighing on her mind, especially after Ronnie had finally calmed down enough yesterday afternoon to call Grady back and learn the truth of his ex's visit. He'd explained the whole situation to her, about how he was trying to help his sister and derail Elizabeth before she struck again.

Ronnie was pissed on Penny's behalf, but that was it. She had bigger problems at the moment. Problems that resulted in people dying. That might result in her own death.

Besides, if Elizabeth thought she could win back the man she'd hurt and thoroughly humiliated with a coy smile and a few blinks of her long lashes, then her biscuit was clearly not done in the middle.

Grady shifted in his chair. "Then why did you spend last night here instead of coming home with me?"

She waved her hand at the paperwork surrounding her. "I told you, I wanted to get up early and make some progress on this bookwork for Ruby."

That held an element of truth to it. Waking up in Jessica's room, heading down to the kitchen to grab a yogurt and a cup of coffee (since Gramps and Ruby brought home a replacement carafe from Tucson), and then walking down a few more stairs to go to work was a lot easier than commuting from Grady's bedroom.

But there was more to it than that.

She loved Grady, and she wasn't sure she could hide all of her angst and fears from him first thing in the morning. It was one thing to sit on the other side of a desk and assure him all was sunny and fine with their relationship, and another to wake up curled into him and stare into those all-seeing eyes before she had time to raise her shields.

"I think there is something more going on here," he said, still watching her closely.

Ronnie bristled under his searching gaze. "Are you here to interrogate me, Sheriff Hardass? Or is this a visit from the guy I'm sleeping with on a regular basis?"

"Not regular enough." He leaned forward, resting his elbows on his knees. "This is not an interrogation, and I don't like sleeping alone anymore, which is your fault."

"I would think you'd enjoy a break from all of the females who are making your life hell lately."

One dark eyebrow lifted. "There is only one female giving me grief at the moment."

"You mean your sister?"

He blinked. "Make that two females."

"What about Katie locking horns with your deputy?"

"Three females, then."

"And then there's your ex, telling everyone around town that you two are an item again."

He shook his head. "I was already counting Elizabeth in that list."

"Oh, I thought I was the first female."

"You're not giving me grief, Veronica. A little heartburn every now and then from worry, but that's not your doing."

"So, to clarify, you're only here right now because you think I'm still upset about finding Elizabeth at your house?"

"No. I'm here because I'm nuts about you, and there is something going on in that beautiful head of yours that keeps making you scowl at the woodwork when you think nobody is looking."

Criminy, he was too good at his job. Which was the exact reason why she'd avoided being alone with him yesterday.

"I'm just scared," she said.

And she was. Yesterday's adventures at the grocery store had made this whole crazy hitman business real. As for knowing the purpose behind Sadie's presence in town—well, that had knocked the wind clean out of her.

"Then let me take care of you. Let me protect you."

The angst edging his voice tugged on her heart. "You already take care of me as much as you can, Grady. You can't keep me locked up in your jail day and night."

"Maybe not, but if you'd move in with me, we might both sleep better at night."

"You think someone can't get to me at your place?"

He sighed, glancing around the room. "It's a lot safer than here, where you have strangers coming and going every day."

That was true, but a killer could find out where Grady lived with ease and wait for her to take the trash out or go for a jog or any other mundane task. He—or she—could park down the street, waiting for Grady to leave for work and then ...

The gray pickup!

The one on Grady's street with the hulking shadow waiting inside.

That was the morning when Ronnie had been reading Butch's grocery list on the way out to Grady's rig. Sadie had jogged up to Ronnie and scared the daylights out of her.

Who ran in combat boots? Sadie did, that was who. Someone who was trained to fight to the death, apparently, and clean up the mess afterward.

Sadie had needed a lift to the store that morning, and when Ronnie had passed by that gray pickup, trying to get a look inside, Sadie had distracted her. Something about a lizard crossing the road, of all things. Ronnie should have known something was off right then. Too many things hadn't felt right in that scene.

Had there been someone in that pickup waiting for Ronnie? Someone scoping out where she was staying? Or someone waiting to kidnap her and start cutting pieces off her to send to Lyle? She needed to ask Sadie about that, and see if Ms. Combat Boots had removed a threat that day.

That gray pickup showed that living with Grady wouldn't solve Ronnie's problems, only add to his, most likely.

"Grady, I don't want to move in with you." Not yet, anyway. Not until sleeping in bed next to him every night didn't put his life in danger. "It's too risky."

He raked his hand through his hair, his fingers leaving a rumpled mess of waves in their wake. "I'm not afraid of risk, Veronica. It's part of my job."

"That's what worries me. You'll go and do something wonderfully heroic to save me and end up being a name on a sign along one of the highways around here. Or on a park bench. Or on something else dedicated in your memory." Ronnie shook her head. "I can't live with that. I like you alive way too much."

He stared down at his palms for several seconds as if studying the lines on them. When he looked up at her, his face was etched with uncertainty. "What if I asked you to marry me?" His voice was barely above whisper level. "Would you move in with me then?"

It took a moment for his words to register. When they finally sank in, her heart stumbled to its knees. She'd daydreamed about a future with him so many times. Pictured a life at the new place he was building, filling it with laughter, pets, maybe a kid or two, and love. Lots of love.

But this felt wrong. Forced. Blackmailed into marriage. Offering himself as a sacrifice.

"You don't really want that," she whispered back.

His gaze hardened in a blink, his cheeks darkening a shade. "You don't know what I want, Veronica," he charged in a clipped tone.

She recognized his self-preservation tactic. She'd used something similar herself many times, especially when the FBI was trying to tear away her last remnants of dignity so she'd squeal on Lyle. Unfortunately, she'd had nothing to tell.

"I have an inkling, Grady."

"Oh, really? Tell *me* then."

She shrugged. "A big house in the country, a law-abiding wife, a couple of dogs, and no worries about having to watch over your shoulder all of the time because a dickhead holing up in a South Dakota prison rolled over on some really vicious criminals."

His eyes stayed narrowed. "One dog is enough."

"My mistake."

"And you forgot about cats. I'd like a passel of them to help keep the vermin away."

So, she was nearly on target. "What about kids?"

"What about them?"

His question didn't really answer what she'd been wondering about off and on since they'd taken their relationship to the next level. But his expression had softened enough for her to make offspring part of this equation.

"Think how much you'd worry about children if I were involved in their making."

He looked at his hat, a frown settling in on his forehead. "I'd worry a hell of a lot more about your mother wanting to move in with us."

A laugh erupted from her before she could contain it. "We could put her out back in a tiny house."

"I'd rather she live with Butch and Kate in that huge house of his."

"Good idea. I'll suggest it to Butch when I head over to The Shaft later."

He looked back at her, frown still in place. "Veronica, I'm serious here about you and me. I love you."

"I love you, too, Grady. But we need to face reality. I won't make a good, wholesome county sheriff's wife."

There was a time in her past she might have, but she didn't want to go back to being Veronica Jefferson, the hostess with the most-est, with a tray of champagne glasses in one hand and a dust mop in the other.

"I don't care if you're law-abiding all of the time or not."

"That's not true and you know it."

"Okay, so it would make my job a hell of lot easier if you were, but I'm not looking for some 1950s television housewife."

Had he been reading her mind?

"Good, because I'm more like Daisy Duke in the 1980s, trying to run under the radar at all times."

His grin was fleeting. "Stop trying to distract me with an image of you in short-shorts and a tank top."

"We could play that fantasy out some night, Sheriff Hardass." She wiggled her eyebrows at him. "I might like being arrested under the right circumstances."

He stared at her for a minute, then took a breath and grunted. "Damn."

"We have a good thing going here, Grady. It's fun and flirty. Nobody gets hurt in the end."

"Too late. I'm in way over my head."

That made two of them.

"Live with me," he pressed. "Even if you don't want to marry me."

But she did want to marry him. Just not yet.

"What would your constituents say to that? I'm a tarnished woman with a stained past, and Elizabeth has done her best lately to make sure local folks know that."

"I don't give a damn what anyone else thinks about you. About us."

"You're up for re-election this fall," she reminded him.

"Maybe I'll drop out of the race."

She leaned across the desk. "Don't say that. Don't make it as if I'm forcing you to choose, because I'm not."

He shrugged. "I choose you."

"No." She hit the desk with her fist, a makeshift gavel. "You can't."

"It's my choice in the end."

She pointed at him. "You're a good man, Grady Harrison. The people of this county need you at the helm, serving and protecting."

This time both of his hands raked through his hair, leaving it as chaotic as the torment in his eyes. "Let me serve you, Veronica. Let me keep *you* safe. Especially with this Blue Hornet killer coming to town."

"Damn it!" She pushed out of her chair. He was making it nearly impossible to hold her ground, blowing her defenses to smithereens. She walked over to the bookcase and rested her head against the cool wood.

And now this business about that freakin' dead asshole in the freezer—or wherever Sadie had buried him. If she hadn't cut him into pieces and scattered him to the four corners of the state. Actually, maybe if she … never mind!

Ronnie sniffed, knowing what she needed to do. She had to tell Grady that the Blue Hornet was no longer a threat. Not to waste his time watching for the bastard. She couldn't let him hunt the wrong killer. She would have to warn Sadie later and deal with the repercussions of that in turn.

Before she could get a word out, someone knocked on the door.

"Ronnie?" Deborah called through the wood. "Are you in there?" The doorknob twisted. "Open the door, please."

Grady cringed. "Shit," he said under his breath, sliding lower into his chair.

Ronnie would have laughed at the big, tough sheriff's reaction to her mom if she hadn't been on the verge of spilling her guts seconds before. "I'm busy, Mom."

"I know you're working on Ruby's bookkeeping with some help from a certain sheriff—wink wink—but your grandfather is looking for you, and he's in a bit of a huff. If you're not in the kitchen ASAP, he'll be down here to get you and probably even more grumpy." Deborah snorted. "If that's possible."

Now what? Was this something about Kate or Claire? Because Ronnie hadn't done anything of late, had she?

"So, get your clothes back on and get up here," Deborah added.

"Mom, our clothes are on. Grady's on duty, for crissake."

"Ohhhh, kinky. Maybe Manny and I should do some role playing, too. Does the sheriff have any extra handcuffs or badges?"

Was her mom drinking again? She certainly sounded sober, but normally any talk about the sheriff was through gritted teeth and involved a swear word or two.

"Dear Lord," Grady whispered, looking a little green around the gills. "I think I liked it better when she hated me outright."

"Mom!" Ronnie moved closer to the door. "Go away, please."

"Okay, but I'm not kidding about your grandfather. He's got a bee up his ass, and he's looking for someone to sting."

After her mom left, Grady picked up his hat and stood. "I'll let you deal with that."

"Chicken."

"Damned straight."

She closed the distance between them. "Grady," she started and then hesitated.

Maybe there was a way to give him everything else he wanted from her *except* for Sadie. At least not yet. Ronnie could help lead him in the right direction, using Sadie's inside knowledge. Somehow.

He waited, brow raised, eyes wary.

Taking his face in her hands, she went up on her toes and kissed him. He held back for a second, but then let out a low groan and kissed her back. His free hand slid down her side, rounding her hip, squeezing while drawing her closer.

"Can I spend the night with you?" she asked when he leaned back to catch his breath.

His smile was half-hearted. "You know that answer."

"Can I spend the next many nights with you?"

The smile widened, reaching his eyes. "And that one, too." He wrapped her in his arms, resting his chin on her head. "But bring your own underwear. I'm tired of you borrowing mine."

She laughed into his chest. "Who needs underwear?"

A growl came from his throat. "You're right. Just bring your birthday suit."

Chapter Twenty-Seven

Mac didn't want to drive to Bisbee in the morning.
So many hours wasted on the road. On the job. On
something that wasn't what he wanted for his future.
The money would be good, though. He had to keep that in mind.

It was only going to be two more weeks of work according to
the latest call he'd received from his old boss. Then the other
project manager would be back on his feet and able to return to
work, and Mac could come back home to Jackrabbit Junction and
stay put. He'd already turned down a second consulting job offer,
no longer needing the extra funds thanks to Claire agreeing to the
idea of bringing Chester on board.

"I need a pitcher of lager, handsome."

Speak of the devil—the sexy, toolbelt-wearing one; not the old
bowlegged one who was flipping burgers back in the kitchen with
Butch.

Claire sidled up to the bar, looking soft and entirely too
tempting tonight with her hair loose, curling around her face and
over her shoulders. She glanced around at the small crowd
scattered throughout the place before turning her brown eyes his
way.

"Looks like we might be able to leave early tonight," she told
him. "Let Kate and Butch close 'er up, so you can get some shuteye
before hitting the road."

Damn, he really wished he'd listened to her and tried to come
up with a different solution before signing on for this Bisbee job.
Right now, getting a root canal sounded better than leaving in the
morning.

Mac grabbed an empty pitcher, taking it over to the taps.
"Who wants to sleep when there's a naked babe in my bed?"

One dark eyebrow raised. "Who are you sleeping with tonight, McStudly?"

"A long-legged brunette who looks hot in a toolbelt."

"You're sharing a bed with Luke?" she teased. "I'm not sure you'll like his hairy legs, but he can get hot and sweaty with the best of us."

"You're adorable when you're being obtuse."

Her grin slipped a little, edged with a hint of melancholy. "I wish you didn't have to leave already."

"Two more weeks, Slugger." He sounded more upbeat than he felt. "Then I'm all yours to tie up and torture."

"Good. I'll have the battery charger and nipple clamps at the ready."

He sat the pitcher of beer on the bar in front of her. "No more electric shock therapy," he said, playing along. "You crank the dial too far every time, and then I keep finding stray socks stuck to me all the next day."

She laughed. "Fine, take the fun out of sex, why don't you?"

He glanced over her shoulder at Kate, who was helping Mindy Lou deliver a couple of trays of sandwiches and fries to a table of young guys who looked like they'd spent the day playing in the dirt. Mac had a feeling they were part of that group of campers who'd pulled into the RV park this afternoon towing several mud-crusted four-wheelers.

"You have to promise me that you won't do anything crazy with your sister if Sophy gets back to you with this surefire evidence of hers that supposedly proves Joe is alive."

She took his hand, rubbing her thumb over his knuckles. "I promise I'll wait for you to join me on my next daring deed."

"And I want you to call me as soon as you hear from Sophy." He pulled Claire toward him, so she was leaning partway over the bar. "Even if I'm on the road or busy on the jobsite. Especially if Kate wants you to promise to not tell me."

"Even if and especially." She nodded, her gaze solemn. "I'll call you."

"And if I don't answer, leave me a message about what Sophy said." He hit her with a stern glare. "And don't be cryptic."

"Okay, I'll be like Jess—long-winded and annoyingly detailed." She lifted his hand to her lips, kissing the same knuckles she'd rubbed a moment ago, one at a time. "Thank you, Mac."

He watched her lips as she delivered her appreciative kisses, wishing they were alone somewhere else so that she could continue thanking him all over. "For what?"

"For coming up with a good fix to our money problem with the brewery." She finished with her kisses, lacing her fingers into his. "Something that keeps you at home."

"You sure you don't mind going into business with Chester?" he asked yet again, even though the verbal deal was pretty much set now and the papers would be drawn up this week.

"As sure as I can be at this point." She glanced toward the order window. "I think this will be good for him and us. If anyone knows beer, it's Chester. According to Gramps, the guy has great business sense. It's his lady-sense that's been broken since they returned from active duty."

"I can relate on the malfunctioning lady-sense," he joked.

She stuck her tongue out at him. "Careful, or I'll take my pliers and hammer to you. A little pinching and pounding will fix you and your lady-sense right up."

"I love it when you work me over, Slugger."

"You're warped."

"Then you should grind on me some, too."

Her laughter made him homesick already, and he hadn't even hit the road yet.

He snagged her by the shirt front. "Come here."

She leaned over the bar, her focus on his mouth, apparently reading his mind. "Is this how it's going to go when we take over the place and you have to run the bar during Gary's days off?" she asked for his ears only. "You flirting with me every time I come to pick up an order, expecting kisses as payment?"

"Most definitely. And not only kisses. Other stuff, too."

"Kisses are good. Other stuff is even better." She angled closer and brushed her lips over his, soft and sweet, tasting like everything he wanted in life and more.

"Order up, lovebirds," Chester hollered from the kitchen window.

Mac groaned, pulling away. "Get back to work, you saucy barmaid."

"You're not the boss of me," she quipped.

"I will be later tonight."

"Promises, promises." With a wink, she headed off, pitcher of beer in hand.

Mac wiped down the taps, his mind shifting from Claire and their immediate future to The Shaft and his pipe dreams.

At the moment, Butch had four taps, using three of them for well-known brands. The craft beer Mac and Chester had tried out was bottled. But if they brewed in-house, they could use a couple of the taps for their own stock. Draft beer almost always tasted better than canned or bottled. Matter of fact, maybe they should look into adding some more taps, all for their own brews. With Chester coming on board, that would be doable financially.

"Hey, Mac," Ronnie said, taking the place on the other side of the bar that Claire had vacated. "I need two bottles of Corona, one bottle of pale ale, and a root beer."

Mac looked over at her, studying her. Her hair was messier than normal tonight, like she'd tried to corral a wind-blown mop with a couple of barrettes and a worn-out rubber band. On top of that, her eyes had dark half-circles under them, making her face appear borderline haunted, and her forehead was a tangled fence line of creases.

What the hell was going on with her?

"Mac." Ronnie moved closer. "Stop thinking about brewing beer."

"I wasn't thinking about beer."

"Then stop thinking about my sister in the raw."

"I wasn't thinking about ..." Well, now he was.

"I need two bottles of—"

"I heard you the first time," he interrupted, reaching into the mini fridges below the bar for the drinks.

She leaned her elbows on the bar, frowning at him. "What's wrong with you tonight?"

"Nothing." He sat the bottles on the bar.

More interestingly, what was wrong with *her*? Because she appeared to have gone off the rails recently and was heading for a cliff.

"You're full of shit," she said. "You keep staring off into outer space." She made a spiral motion with her hand that made no sense to him. "Come on, Mac. Out with it."

He shook his head. Maybe she'd picked up on his early onset of homesickness. "It's nothing. I don't want to drive clear to Bisbee tomorrow." He set a small tray on the bar next to her, moving her drink order onto it. "I'd rather stick around and daydream about the brewery." He smiled. "And your sister in the raw."

She wrinkled her nose at him, and for a moment, the old Ronnie was there—cocky and teasing, sparking with verve. But then the dark clouds returned and she closed the shutters again. "It could be worse, you know."

"That's true. I could have to take your mother with me for the week."

"Exactly." She picked up the tray, hitting him with a smile that looked slippery, like she was having trouble holding it in place on her face. "Or you could have to bash someone over the head with a leg of lamb and leave him dead in a freezer." She shrugged. "Six of one, half dozen of the other."

Before he could fully process what Ronnie said, she took the tray of drinks and left.

He was still standing there almost a minute later, watching Ronnie deliver drinks and take another order, when Kate joined him at the bar.

"Hey Venus, you trying to catch flies?"

He frowned at her. "Venus?"

"Yeah, Venus. You're standing there with your jaw hanging wide, like a Venus fly trap waiting for its prey." She rolled her eyes. "Sheesh, Mac. You're usually Johnny on the spot with this kind of stuff. What's wrong with you tonight?"

"What's wrong with *me*?" She should be focusing on what the hell was going on with Ronnie.

"Are you hard of hearing now, too?" Kate reached over the bar and grabbed the bottle of disinfectant and a clean rag from the stack next to it.

Now if Kate were to say something about a leg of lamb and a dead guy, Mac wouldn't think twice.

No, that wasn't true. He'd be three times as concerned, because she would probably be cooking up a plan to use one to cause the other.

Shoving aside his unease, he returned to cleaning the beer taps.

"What do you need, Kate?" If she had a drink order, she'd have given it to him already.

"A favor." The left side of her face twitched.

If Mac had blinked, he would've missed it.

"Is this going to be about Sophy or Joe or both of them?" He eyed her closely, watching for any more twitches or tics.

"No." She was quick to answer. Maybe too quick?

"I'm all ears."

She glanced around, and then scooted down the bar closer to him, leaning in. "Butch told me that according to his accountant, the paperwork for the sale of this place will be ready for signing by the end of the week."

Mac nodded. Butch had informed him of the same thing, which was another reason he really didn't want to leave. He and Claire needed to celebrate. Chester, too.

"I need you to distract Ronnie tonight."

"I think she's already distracted."

"You noticed that, too?" Kate frowned toward her oldest sister. "Claire figures it's probably due to her turning another year older tomorrow, inching closer to forty. But I don't."

The weight Ronnie was carrying seemed heavier than just another year of life under her belt, but some people really loathed birthdays.

"Why do I need to distract her and what's that have to do with the sale of this place wrapping up?"

"The second has nothing to do with the first." Another twitch, quick as a blink. But a twitch nonetheless.

"Then why did you …" Mac shook his head, frowning.

"Stay focused here, Mac." Kate tapped her index finger on the bar. "We're going to throw a little surprise pre-birthday party tonight. One without Mom."

"Ah, isn't that sweet," he said, tongue in cheek. "You wanted to make sure I was here to party with you."

"Yeah. That's it." She matched his tone. "But if anyone in particular asks, it has nothing to do with the fact that Mom keeps trying to have these big heart-to-heart therapy sessions with the three of us."

"Or the fact that your mom doesn't like Grady, Butch, or me very much?"

She smiled a little too wide. Somebody seemed to have wound her up too tight tonight. How long until she sprung a sprocket? "If it's any consolation, my stepfather thinks you have a sweet pair of buns."

Mac chuckled. "It's too bad we couldn't invite Manny to join tonight's celebration without your mom finding out."

"He's the one who suggested we have a pre-birthday party. He's keeping Mom busy elsewhere, so she doesn't try to crash the party."

Manny was a good man. A good *crazy* man, considering the fact that he'd married Claire's mother without coercion of any sort.

"When do I need to begin this distraction?" Mac asked.

"Grady and Penny will be here in an hour. As soon as they show up, we'll officially close the bar and start the party. I'll give you a signal as soon as Penny texts me that they pulled into the parking lot. Then you convince Ronnie to join you in the office, so she doesn't know they're here, and we can set things up quick. Maybe tell her it's a bookkeeping thing and make her run through some figures. She has numbers on the brain a lot these days. Too much, I'd say, considering the dark circles under her eyes."

Mac didn't think that the extra bookkeeping work was what had Ronnie looking like the sky was about to fall, but maybe tax season deadlines along with the FBI's news about an increased risk of trouble were tag-teaming up on her. Those two problems would certainly toss Mac's ability to sleep out the window.

"Will do," he told Kate, wondering what figures he could have Ronnie double-check that would kill enough time.

"Penny made some kind of special pie for Ronnie."

Just about any pie Penny made was good for Mac, special or not. That woman could give Betty Crocker a run for her money.

"I wonder what Grady is going to give her for a birthday gift," Kate continued, staring in her sister's direction. "After Ronnie caught him hanging out with his ex-wife yesterday morning, he'd better go big or stay home."

Mac did a double-take. "What do you mean, she caught him with his ex?"

"You know, Ronnie went to his house and found Elizabeth and him together there." She leaned closer. "And they weren't having breakfast."

"At his house?" What the hell? How come Mac was just hearing about this now?

"Jeez, Mac. You're back to catching flies again." Kate looked around suddenly, let out a squeak, and then turned back to Mac with wide eyes. And another twitch. "Here comes Ronnie. Play it cool for now, and I'll give you a signal when it's time."

"What signal?"

"I'll wink a couple of times." She took off, saying something to Ronnie as she passed that made her older sister frown after her.

Mac frowned, too. With the way Kate's face kept twitching, how in the hell was he going to tell if she was winking?

Chapter Twenty-Eight

Later that night …

It was cold. It was dark. And Penny was alone once again.
She sat in her SUV outside The Shaft, letting the cab warm up before heading home.

Ronnie's pre-birthday party had gone well with lots of revelry, some good-natured ribbing for the birthday girl by her sisters and cousin, and plenty of tasty food and drinks. Grady had sat near the head of the group of tables pushed together, smiling and laughing with everyone else. He'd been dressed in jeans and a flannel shirt, but after years of being a lawman, the badge still showed through no matter the clothing. Several times, Penny had caught him studying Ronnie when her attention was focused elsewhere, his brow crunched up with deep grooves.

What was behind those grooves? Work? Ronnie's recent bad news from the FBI? Or the fallout from Elizabeth's attempts to rekindle the past?

When Penny and her brother had arrived at the bar earlier, he'd told her that the "situation" with his ex-wife had been smoothed over. Knowing Grady, though, he'd probably used a heavy hand when it came to sanding off any rough edges.

He'd better not blow it with Ronnie. Penny liked the Morgan sisters. They'd made her feel like family already by including her in their posse. Having grown up only with brothers, it was nice to have fellow female compadres.

But enough about Grady's struggles. Penny had her own alligators to wrestle.

She held her hands over the vents, enjoying the hot air now baking her fingers while peering up at the stars.

According to her daily horoscope, now was the opportune time to take risks that would reap remarkable rewards. But what sort of risks?

Something to do with her diner?

With Grady's pain-in-the-ass ex-wife?

With her heart?

No, not that silly organ. Not again. Once bitten, twice shy, and all that crapola.

Take risks …

She looked down at her phone. The glow of her SUV's dash lights along with the phone's screen lit the cab in a warm glow. Or maybe it was the text message she'd received from Mississippi in the midst of Ronnie's party that had Penny running hot.

Need to talk to you tonight. Mule Train Diner at 11.

Talk about what? About why Penny hadn't been waiting for him at the diner last night when he'd finished working? About how taking things any further than a one-night stand could backfire, leaving a certain Scorpio female feeling pissed and betrayed, wanting to torture another FBI bastard?

Her sigh turned into a yawn. Eleven was past her bedtime, especially when she had pies to bake in the morning.

Take risks …

The only way Penny was going to find out answers to her questions was to talk with the man.

"Dang it." Shifting into gear, she rolled away from The Shaft, her headlights lighting the wide open road.

Overhead, the Milky Way lit a trail toward the horizon, same as it had for billions of years. There was something calming about the steadfast, systematic movement of the heavens. As if the consistency of the stars moored her mentally, while the chaotic dust devils of life twisted and raged around her, pelting her with grit and debris.

Up ahead, the orange streetlights of Yuccaville came into view. She yawned again. Her bed called to her. But so did Mississippi's text.

As she neared the city limits sign, a coyote stood at the edge of the road. Its eyes glowed in her headlights. She tapped her brakes and hit the horn, scaring him back into the shadow-filled desert.

Crap. A coyote. At least it hadn't crossed her path. According to the book of omens Aunt Millie had given her at Christmas, that would have meant Penny would be facing off with danger soon. A mere coyote sighting, on the other hand, simply meant it was time to start fresh and let go of her fears, enjoy life, and laugh more. She could do with more pleasure and jollity, that was for sure. But wasn't there also something written about being aware of the consequences of her actions?

Penny slowed to the town's posted speed limit even though the streets were empty. The sheriff's sister could get speeding tickets like everyone else, but the ramifications weren't worth the few minutes of journey spared.

Need to talk to you ...

Mississippi could have talked to her at the party, since he'd been sitting across the table when he'd sent the text message. Then again, everyone else had been sitting there, too, including Mac, who had a knack for noticing details others didn't, according to Kate. As it was, Penny had been having a hell of a time not leering at Mississippi whenever she'd glanced his way. The last thing she needed was Mac catching on to this ridiculous crush she had for yet another FBI agent and then mentioning it to her brother.

By the time she rolled into the parking lot behind her diner, her stomach felt like it was full of grasshoppers. She parked next to Mississippi's rig and killed the engine, taking a couple of slow, deep breaths in preparation for whatever waited for her inside the diner. No sooner had she stepped out of her SUV, Mississippi was standing next to her in the semi-darkness. Turned out he was waiting outside the diner, not in.

"What do you need to talk about?" she asked, trying not to sound as breathless as she felt.

He ushered her toward the back door of the diner. "How about we go inside to your office in case your brick-throwing nemesis is in a voyeuristic mood tonight?"

Penny hesitated, partly because it was late and her Monday would come way too early, but mostly because she wasn't sure being alone with him was a good idea for her dignity or her libido—both for the same reason. She wanted him, of course, and the last time she'd acted on that notion, she'd made a colossal fool of herself.

"I promise to keep my hands to myself," he said, misreading her hesitation.

That was all fine and swell, but she didn't want him to make that promise, and therein lay the problem. However, like a moth drawn to a blowtorch, Penny led the way inside the back door of the diner anyway and prepared to be burned to a crisp.

He closed the door behind them and locked it. She decided not to read anything into being locked inside with him and moved deeper into the building.

The kitchen was dark except for the light over the sink area, which she liked to leave on for when she came in before dawn to make pies. He followed her through the kitchen and into her office, which smelled like the lemon-scented furniture cleaner she'd used to polish her desktop and wipe down the chair legs earlier. She didn't trust the health inspector not to extend the white-glove treatment to her office during the next visit.

Mississippi settled onto the couch with a sigh that sounded more than simply tired, making her wonder how much keeping an eye out for Ronnie's enemies wore on him. Constant vigilance had to be exhausting. She searched his face, spotting signs of fatigue around his eyes especially.

The urge to make him something sweet and comforting swelled within her. Something that would make him smile again with that flirting sparkle in his eyes. Maybe a piece of pie … Then again, pie had gotten her into trouble last time.

She sat on the edge of her desk, keeping a safe distance between them. "So, what do you want to talk about?"

He scrubbed his hand across his eyes, blinking in its aftermath. "I'm not sleeping for shit."

Oh. She hadn't expected this "talk" to be about his sleeping accommodations. That was a bit of a letdown. "Is there something wrong with the bed upstairs?"

He shook his head. "The bed is fine."

"You can adjust the temperature on the wall next to the bathroom if it's too cold or hot." Last time Penny was up there, the heat from the diner below had the apartment comfortable with help from the wall furnace.

"The temperature isn't the problem." He leaned back against the cushions, staring at her with an unreadable expression. "The problem is you."

She touched her chest. *Her?*

"Sorry. Was I too noisy this morning?" She'd tried to be quieter than usual, thinking about him in bed far more often than a landlady should.

"It's not about you being down here. It's about you *not* being up there." He glanced toward the ceiling. "With me." When he focused back on her, his intent was crystal clear in his gaze. "With or without pie. I don't care."

She shrugged out of her down vest, the upper half of her body suddenly much too warm. "I see."

"I don't think you do," he said in a low, serious voice. "Which is why I wanted to talk to you alone tonight without any possibility of interruptions."

Penny wasn't sure what to make of his body language or tone, because they didn't match the words coming out of his mouth. "Okay, explain what I'm not understanding here."

Did he want her as much as she did him? Or not?

He stared at her for several seconds, his expression flat, unreadable. "You're really pretty, Penelope."

He put about as much emotion into that sentence as he would a weather report calling for a week of drizzle.

She opened her mouth to retort with something smartass, but she held back at the last moment. If her history around Mississippi had taught her anything, it was to keep her pie-hole shut and smile instead.

"Thanks," she said, playing it cool with a polite smile.

"And I like the unorthodox way you kiss."

The smile flatlined. Her brow tightened. *Unorthodox?*

Don't ask, said the voice of logic in her head.

What did he mean by *unorthodox*? Was he referring back to when they were screwing around in his pickup last week?

Don't ask, her pride spoke up, louder yet.

Jeez, how bad had her kisses been compared to others?

Don't ask! Logic and pride begged in unison.

"What do you mean the 'unorthodox' way I kiss? Do I move my lips weird or something? Is there an abundant amount of saliva in my mouth?" She crossed her arms. "Listen, if this is about my tongue high-diving down your throat last week, keep in mind that I was a tad schnockered at the time and had some trouble with my depth perception."

His one raised eyebrow was maddeningly ambiguous. After a few seconds of awkward silence—at least awkward for Penny—he suggested, "How about I show you?"

She thought on that for a moment. "How are *you* going to show me how *I* kiss?"

He held out his hand, palm up, summoning her. "Come here." When she nailed him with a hard squint instead, he amended his request. "Please, come here."

She pushed off her desk, edging closer. "I think we're getting off subject. We came in here to talk, didn't we?"

"Yes on talking and no on getting off subject." His hand snaked out and caught hers. "A few details need clarification, this one included."

"Clarified how exactly?" She stood at his knees, frowning down at him.

He continued to recline against the cushions, as if the sexual tension in the room hadn't ratcheted with every step she had taken to reduce the distance between them. As if he weren't fighting any urges to strip away clothing and touch skin to skin, unlike Penny's current internal battle.

"Closer." He tugged on her hand. "You're too far away."

"If I come any closer, I'll be sitting on your lap."

"Yep." He let go of her hand and caught her behind the knees, pulling her down, positioning her so she straddled his thighs. "There, that's better." His hands fell away, giving her the freedom to leave if she wanted.

But she didn't want that at all. Her earlier intentions of not continuing to feed the flames were going up in smoke. Good ol' Coyote, the clever trickster, had wanted her to let go of her fears and enjoy life. So, why not start here tonight?

She settled onto him so that they were eye to eye, feeling the heat of him through her jeans. "Now what?"

He shrugged, his gaze lowering to her mouth. As he stared, his eyes darkened, reminding her of a shadowed rain forest in the mist, full of vibrant, verdant greens. He shifted under her, lining her body up better with his. Two puzzle pieces fitting perfectly together. Penny had forgotten how right this could feel.

She tried to keep her breathing smooth and level, not wanting to let him see that he had her cogwheels spinning too fast, wobbling and sparking. But damn it, he smelled absolutely scrumptious. The scent of his skin and cologne was heady, blending to give off a sweet and spicy aroma that made her mouth water. The union of citrus and exotic spices reminded her of a d'Anjou pear pie she liked to make in the fall with craisins, orange zest, and a blend of cinnamon and muscovado sugar. She was tempted to taste him. If only she had some homemade whipped cream left over in the fridge.

His focus returned to her eyes. "Now, you kiss me."

Okay, but … "How is *that* going to show me how my kisses are unorthodox?"

"Just try it." He flirted, looking downright devilish. "Trust me."

She cocked her head. "This sounds like some kind of FBI bait-and-switch bamboozlement."

"No bamboozling, I swear." He held up his right hand. "You wanted a demonstration. I'm going to give you one. Plain and simple."

There was nothing "plain and simple" about her sitting on his lap. It felt way too good to be anything other than complicated, and she had no doubt that this would be hazardous to her mental well-being.

Let go of your fears, Coyote whispered in her ear.

Her hands moved to his shoulders to keep her from toppling into him as she closed the distance between them. It would be her luck to give him a split lip when going in for a kiss. Her reputation was already well tattered when it came to heated moments with him.

She paused, licking her lips. "I still don't get how my kissing you is going to—"

"Penelope, hush up and kiss me."

She did as told, easing into him, wanting to take this slow so she didn't screw it up this time. No stumbling body slams. No bumbled, octopus-inspired attempts at seduction. No electrifying reenactments of getting zapped while kissing.

She began with casual brushes of lips on lips, her thoughts centered on keeping control.

"Relax," he said after several of her starter kisses.

"I can't." She brushed her lips over his again. "I feel like I'm on that old amateur talent show." She touched her tongue to his lower lip and followed it with another grazing kiss. "Where the judges might gong me at any time." She shifted in his lap, her knees now bracketing his hips. "And I'll have to exit the stage before I'm finished with my act." She swept her lips over his again. "Then I'll be thoroughly humiliated and have to run on home with my tail between my legs."

His chest rumbled with laughter. Sliding his hands down her ribs, he palmed her hips. "This is it, Penelope."

"This is what?"

"This is why I like your unorthodox kisses best." He rocked against her, making it clear his body wanted more.

Pulling back, she frowned. "Because I'm afraid of being gonged off the stage?"

He leaned forward, stealing a kiss from her. "Because they're not boring or typical." He stole another, deepening it with a stroke of his tongue. "They don't follow the textbook." One of his hands slipped under her shirt, his fingers tickling their way up her back. "Never tame." He unsnapped her bra with a deft flick. "And I can't stop thinking about them in the middle of the night." His hand slid around front, leaving a trail of goose bumps in its wake. His eyes drilled into hers. "I can't stop thinking about _you_."

She arched into him, encouraging him to explore further. "I want you." She covered his hand with hers, showing him where and how.

"Kiss me again, Penelope," he ordered. "And no holding back this time."

"Yes," she breathed and finally let loose, framing his face, showing him how wild he made her feel.

He returned her ardor, stroke for stroke, groaning. When she pulled back enough to tear off her shirt and bra, he watched with lust-rimmed eyes. His jacket and shirt came next, several seams ripping in Penny's rush to reach skin.

"My turn," he said and took over, rolling to the side and pressing her down into the cushions. He kissed her forehead, the underside of her chin, the line of her jaw, and everything she'd bared below her collarbone.

She moaned, her body arcing as he slid farther south. She reached for his zipper, wanting to feel more. To explore and inflame. To bewitch him as much as he was bewitching her.

"Not yet, darlin'," he said, staring up at her with an intensity that made her ache for him sink even deeper. "I didn't get to enjoy this in the light last time, and I'm not foolish enough to make that mistake twice."

"Please," she said, gripping his forearms, trying to pull him closer. "You can enjoy it after the show is over. I'll give you an extended encore."

"Did I just hear you say 'Please'?"

She nodded, wetting her lips in anticipation.

One eyebrow quirked. "Penelope Harrison, you're not really a beggar when it comes to sex, are you?"

"Not usually." But tonight she'd make an exception. Hell, she'd even drop to her knees in front of him.

"I didn't think so."

He lowered his half-clad body onto hers, pressing her into the cushions. His chest pressed into her, hard where she was soft. Finally, she had skin on skin, like she'd wanted from the start.

"But I'll beg if you'd like," she offered, wrapping her arms and legs around him, randy octopus be damned.

"No." He nibbled his way down the tendon below her ear. "I like it better when you take without asking."

"You need to let me on top then."

"Tempting," he said in the crook of her neck. "But I have a better idea." He rose slightly above her, staring down into her eyes. "A game of power that you might enjoy."

She smiled, liking the sound of it already. "What are the rules?"

"No rules."

Even better. "How do we play?"

"Tell me what you want, how you like it, and where you want me to do it, and I'll comply."

Her mouth went dry. "You'll obey me?"

"I'll do my best to toe the line," he returned with a wicked glint in his eyes. "If you want me to stop at any point, I will. But it won't be easy."

What, how, and where.

She shivered in anticipation. "I'm not sure where to start this game."

"Liar. What do you want?"

Her laugh was husky, edged with longing. "You to lick me."

His grin turned feral. "How? Light and playful, or like I want to taste every inch of you."

"Like I'm made of sugar and spice."

"You are." His gaze slid to her bare chest. "Where do you want me to start?"

She lifted her chin. "My neck."

He did as ordered while her body strained to hold still.

"Now my earlobe."

Again, he licked, and then he nipped her, as if he couldn't resist the temptation.

"I didn't say you could bite me."

"But you liked it," he countered.

God, yes! And then some. She trailed her finger down the valley between her breasts. "Now here."

"My pleasure."

He took his time about it, too, straying off course, tickling her with his beard stubble as an added treat.

"You took liberties," she chastised when he finished, panting now.

"Guilty as charged," he said with a smug, sexy smile. "Where to next?"

"Here." She pointed at her stomach above her navel.

He slid onto the floor to do her bidding, his tongue drawing circles. Teasing, tickling, tempting, but not straying lower in spite of her devious attempts to lure him south.

When he paused and looked up at her, eyebrows raised, she lifted her leg, pointing at her knee.

"Your jeans are in the way."

Shrugging, she commanded, "Take them off."

"Yes, ma'am." He pulled the fabric down inch by inch, his gaze wolfish when he glanced up. "Black lace. For me?"

She could lie to save face, but she wanted him, so why deny it. "For you."

The sound of him sucking air through his teeth, made her

body tingle deep and low. He tugged her jeans off and dropped them on the floor, pausing to stare down at her.

"We're not done here," she said, lifting her leg and resting it on his shoulder.

"Of course not." He gripped her ankle and forced her to hold still.

His tongue was nearly her undoing, stroking up to her thigh, when he finished with the back of her knee. His lips grazed over her tender skin, tantalizingly close to the epicenter of the quakes now pulsing through her muscles. He moved to her other leg then, teasing her some more.

"Next?" he asked when he'd finished. His breathing was ragged, matching hers.

"You went one leg too far," she scolded, leveraging up on her elbows to nail him with a mock glare.

His fingers inched upward along her inner thigh, his thumb brushing over the black lace with a practiced touch.

She closed her eyes and moaned.

"Open your eyes, Penelope," he said, his touch glancing over her again. When she obeyed, he slid his thumb inside the black lace. "Don't pretend you didn't like my disobedience."

She gasped, but tried to remain playfully stern. "You're too rebellious for an FBI agent."

"That's what they keep telling me," Mississippi returned, pulling his hand away along with her underwear. He tossed the scrap of black lace over his shoulder. "Next?"

She hesitated, under no illusion about who was really in control here. It turned out she liked being dominated by him. A lot. It was a new sensation, one she wanted to savor for a few breaths.

But the time had come for her to take back some power.

"Remove your pants," she ordered.

"I'm not done licking you."

She sat up. "Remove your pants," she repeated. "Now."

After holding her stare for several heartbeats, he stood and unfastened his jeans.

"Boots, too, cowboy." She leaned back against the cushions to enjoy the show.

He did as commanded, moving confidently, as if he undressed

in front of an audience daily.

"Everything," she said after he'd shed his socks and stood in front of her in only his boxer briefs.

Naked men weren't anything new for her, but she still took her time admiring Mississippi from top to bottom.

"Am I up to snuff?" he asked after she'd looked her fill.

Shrugging, she teased, "I guess you'll do."

He growled, dropping onto the cushions next to her and then tugging her onto him, helping her straddle his hips again. He looked up at her, tucking a wisp of hair behind her ear. "Now what, Penelope?"

"Just this." She shifted and lowered her hips, taking all of him before he realized her intent.

His eyes widened in surprise at her power play. "Penelope!" His gasp held an emotional charge that shocked her.

She kissed him, but wanted more. More of him. More of the satisfaction only he could offer. More of the pleasure of being wanted in return.

Mississippi took over the game, threading one hand through her hair at the nape of her neck while gripping her hip with the other. He guided her, gasping her name as she moved right along with him, as if she'd done this dance with him many times before, not just once in the dark while half-drunk.

Finally, she was doing everything right, and it felt *sooo* good. Too good, damn it! She beat him to the punch, her release making her whole body rock and roll.

When the tremors stopped, he flipped her so that she lay under him again on the couch. He moved faster now, winding her up all over again, following the demands she whispered in his ear about how, what, and where. It wasn't long until she arched against him, pulsing with pleasure again, only this time he joined her, his body going rigid as he groaned her name.

Then there was silence, broken only by the whir of the furnace kicking to life. Penny sighed and smiled at the ceiling, stroking her fingers down his back as he rested his head in the crook of her neck. Coyote was right. Enjoy life. She'd deal with the consequences later.

His breath warmed her skin.

"Is this what you wanted to talk to me about?" she jested. "Per your text during the party?"

"Sort of." He rolled half off her, leaning into the back cushions, and rested his head on his hand. His unreadable expression was back as he stared down at her. "I like you, Penelope."

"You said that already."

He traced her cheekbone, circling around to include her jaw. "But you and I have a lot of obstacles in our path."

Which particular path? She wasn't on this journey for anything more than great sex.

Liar.

"We do," she agreed, ignoring the inner know-it-all voice.

"I don't know where I'll end up next."

She did. "Wherever the FBI sends you, most likely."

"And you'll still be here in Yuccaville." His tone left her uncertain about his feelings about that.

She opted to keep things light. "Sure."

Although life was short. Maybe she would leave the diner after a time and let someone else run the diner for her. Or sell it. Not that she was going to follow Mississippi like a lovesick puppy. She didn't need somebody in her life to find her happiness, but a good bedmate didn't hurt.

Liar. The voice said again.

She needed some duct tape to shut the freaking thing up.

"You can see where I'm going with this," he said, his brow tightening.

"I'm a big girl, Mississippi. I think I can juggle sex with you and the reality of our situation."

His eyebrows lifted. "Okay, but who says I can?"

She laughed. "Please, the Bureau implants indifference microchips in you agents during training."

He didn't laugh along with her. "Maybe I've gone rogue."

"Maybe you're just trying to soften the blow of you leaving long before the time comes."

She wondered if this was normal etiquette for him when taking a lover. Lay the groundwork and lay the woman at the same time.

His gaze narrowed. "Don't confuse me for your ex."

"I'm not. You're a lot better at giving pleasure before taking your own." She turned toward him, entwining her leg with his.

"Multiple orgasms during sex only happened when I kick-started things on my own before he joined me."

"Then he was a selfish bastard."

She nodded. "To the bitter end."

"Penelope?" He leaned closer, kissing along the curve of her ear, his lips rousing her libido back to life.

"Yes?"

He pulled back, eyes hooded. "Do you like me, too?"

While she hadn't said as much, she was pretty certain she'd shown it. But something in his gaze showed a hint of uncertainty, surprisingly.

"I really do, Mississippi. Especially your tongue."

A rumble came from his chest—a chuckle or a growl, or both. He kissed her, his tongue tangling with hers as his hand slid down over her hip.

"It's my turn to give the orders now," he said, lifting her enough to shift onto his back on the cushions below before settling her on top of him.

"I suppose I can let you be in charge this time." She leaned over him, rubbing skin against skin with a tantalizing amount of friction. "If you want to weird it up a bit, I have some pie in the fridge."

He stilled. "What kind?"

"Another prickly pear chocolate chip, for starters. Like the one I made for Ronnie's party."

"Sweet and tart, like you." His grin would have given Lucifer a run for his money. "Can I lick it off you?"

A shiver of excitement rushed over her. "It's your turn to rule."

"That's right." He pulled her down and kissed her. "We're going to take Pie with Penelope to an all-new level tonight, darlin'."

Chapter Twenty-Nine

Monday, Feb 4th
The Mule Train Diner

H ear ye, hear ye! I, Kathryn Morgan, officially call to order
today's meeting of the Prickly Pear Posse to discuss ..." Kate
paused, frowning at Claire. "Why are we having this
meeting?"

Claire yawned, covering it with the back of her hand. She'd
much rather be back in bed at the RV park with Mac, but he'd left
for Bisbee before she'd even dragged her carcass out of bed. Her
fingers were crossed that he was right about having only two more
weeks of work there, because she really wanted him home for
good.

"More important, why so damned early?" Ronnie asked,
sitting across the table from Claire with her hair a tousled mess.
She looked about ten years old in Grady's big, brown flannel shirt
that fit like an oversized dress, half covering her yoga pants. "And
on my birthday to boot."

Claire and Kate had stopped at Grady's to pick up Ronnie on
the way to The Mule Train Diner, enduring the birthday girl's
grousing ever since. The multiple glasses of gin and tonic Ronnie
had slammed the previous evening in celebration of another year
around the sun had certainly not done her any favors.

Although, thinking back to last night, Ronnie's extra drinks,
along with a handful of fake smiles and too-loud laughs, had Claire
wondering what was really going on in Grumpy Dwarf's head. Was
it only a birthday thing, or was it the maelstrom of trouble
darkening Ronnie's horizon?

Hell, maybe the extra drinks were spurred by Grady's ex, who seemed to think she could waltz back into town and choreograph her own musical, starring herself as the tragically wronged heroine and Ronnie as the villainous femme fatale. If that were the reason for her sister's worries, it was time to let Ronnie know that Claire had dropped the curtain on that shitshow. Nobody kicked her sister while she was down—not while Claire was still on her feet and able to throw punches.

"Have a seat, Pregosaurus," Claire said, grabbing Kate by the arm. "I'm running this meeting." She pulled her down into the chair next to her. "We are here because I have some information that the four of you need to hear."

"Four? There are only two of us here besides you." Kate aimed a confused glance at Ronnie and then returned to Claire—or, rather, Claire's forehead. "Did you accidentally hit your head with a hammer again?"

"Make that three besides you," Penny called out, joining them from the kitchen with a plate full of steaming rolls along with a small stack of dessert dishes. She set her load down on the table, smiling at Ronnie as she wiped her hands off on a corner of her flour-splattered apron. "Maple-glazed pecan cinnamon rolls on the house in honor of the woman who has upended my brother's dull, saintly life for the better."

"I'll eat to that," Kate said, reaching for a plate and a roll.

Claire's mouth watered. "Oh man, Penny. With friends like you, who needs a waistline?"

Penny dashed behind the diner's counter, stacked a few mugs on a serving tray and grabbed a fresh pot of coffee and some creamer. She returned, passing mugs around and filling them with coffee as Claire took a bite of a warm roll. The glazed sweet bread blended perfectly with the crunchy, nutty bits and spicy cinnamon.

One bite alone made up for Kate's non-stop conspiracy theorizing about Deputy Dipshit all of the way from Jackrabbit Junction to Yuccaville at the butt crack of dawn. The second bite was worth the last quarter hour of Ronnie's bellyaching about having to get up so early. Claire reached for another roll before she'd even finished the first.

"Holy sticky buns!" Kate licked her lips. "This glaze is downright sinful. What's your secret, Penny?" She leaned across the table and whispered, "Are you really a cannibalistic witch who lives in a house made of gingerbread, cake, and candy?"

"A witch for certain, according to my brother's ex-wife." Penny sat next to Ronnie and grabbed a roll for herself. "Pure maple syrup from Vermont is the key." She licked some frosting off her index finger. "Plus a zest for sinfully sweet acts of rebellion."

Penny took a big bite, her eyes bright and sunshiny this morning. For someone who'd been on the receiving end of Elizabeth's vindictiveness for the last week, Penny seemed pretty happy at the moment. And a bit distracted, judging from the way she kept glancing back toward the kitchen as if she couldn't remember if she'd left the oven on. Then again, she probably had something else baking, like a cherry pie or more scrumptious rolls.

Claire could get nice and plump hanging around Penny too much. It was a good thing Mac liked her curvy.

"How long have you been awake?" she asked Penny. These cinnamon rolls were clearly made from scratch, so she must have been at the diner for an hour or more.

Penny glanced toward the kitchen again with a grin that bordered on mischievous, like a self-satisfied Cheshire cat. "Most of the night. I was playing with pie and experimenting with other sweet treats."

"I, for one, am grateful for your diligence when it comes to pie." Kate crammed the last of her roll in her mouth and moaned.

"Thank you." Penny returned her focus to her roll, her cheeks suddenly a tad flushed. "That's the second compliment recently about my expertise with pie."

"So, who's the fourth?" Ronnie tore a small piece from her roll. The poor cube of sweet bread looked as if it had been pecked at by a bored chicken. Apparently, Ronnie was off her feed this morning. Was it due to too much gin last night? Or something else?

More likely it was *someone* else.

Claire finished off the second roll, wiping any remaining glaze from her lips with a napkin. "The fourth attendee is a 'maybe.' We'll see if she makes it or not."

The meeting's early hour had earned Claire an earful of complaints from that particular possible attendee, too. But since she had a bird watching platform to finish building and the property behind The Shaft to clear and level for the brewery, everyone else would have to suck it up and deal with having to wake before the sun along with her.

Reaching for some creamer for her coffee, Claire asked Penny, "Do you have the knife I texted you about this morning?" No need to beat around the bush.

"Oh, yeah. One minute." Penny pushed away from the table and headed back into the kitchen.

"What knife?" Ronnie asked.

Kate kneed Claire under the table, then nudged her head toward Ronnie. "Ixnay on the ifenay."

"Ronnie knows pig Latin, knucklehead. Who do you think taught it to us?" Claire kneed Kate back, earning a sharp elbow in return. "Keep it up, brat, and I'll retaliate. I'm not very virtuous and won't hesitate to elbow and pinch a pregnant woman."

"What knife?" their oldest sister asked, picking another morsel off her tattered roll.

Penny returned to the table, holding a small wooden box out toward Claire. Kate tried to snatch the box away before Claire could get it, but Ronnie beat them both to it since she was closer. She lifted the lid and extracted the tissue paper–wrapped knife, carefully withdrawing it.

Her brow furrowed, then she looked up at Kate. "You took this from Mom that night at Dirty Gerties." It wasn't a question, more of an indictment.

Kate whirled on Claire, her left eye twitching like a blinker light on a ship sending out SOS flashes. "Why are you bringing this out now? Here of all places!"

"Get hold of yourself, Kate. The *Titanic* isn't sinking. Penny doesn't open for another half-hour, so there's only the four of us in the building."

"Officially," Penny said, pointing toward the ceiling. "There's an FBI agent right above us, but I'm pretty sure he's still asleep." Her Cheshire cat smile back in place, Penny lifted her roll and licked a row of glaze off the top.

Oh, yeah. Claire had forgotten that Mississippi had moved in upstairs recently, forced to extend his stay due to Ronnie's ongoing and ever-growing predicament.

Claire held out her hand toward Ronnie. "May I have the knife, please?"

"Should you guys be touching that without gloves?" Penny asked as Claire inspected the knife.

Claire focused on the binding where the jade hilt met the obsidian blade. "If we were in a museum, then gloves would be required," she answered. "But I don't think this is as rare an artifact as it appears." She turned to Ronnie. "You have a pair of nail clippers in your purse?"

"Sure." She fished out a pair, handing them over.

Claire admired the pink rhinestone-studded clippers. "Fancy."

Ronnie shrugged. "I found them at Grady's. They were probably left over from when Elizabeth lived there."

"And you didn't burn them?" Kate asked.

"Metal doesn't burn that easily, Katie." Ronnie lifted her coffee. "You have to really mean it to melt most metallic pieces."

Ronnie said that as if she knew that from experience. Claire wondered if her sister had tried to burn something of her ex-husband's after finding out about his long list of crimes.

"You could have pulverized them with a sledgehammer," Penny said, taking a second lick off the roll's glazed top. "That's what I did with some of Liz's favorite trinkets that she left behind."

"Nice work, Scorpio," Kate said, giving Penny two thumbs-up. "I like that vein of wickedness in you. You and I would make great partners in crime. It's too bad your brother had to be such an overachiever and land that sheriff job. It sucks to have to toe the line because of family relationships."

"Hear, hear," Penny said, raising her pastry roll in a toast.

Ronnie swallowed a sip of coffee, lowering her mug. "Bite me, Katie."

"Speaking of Elizabeth," Claire said, looking at her older sister while flipping the little metal arm around on the clippers so she could cut with them. "She has grudgingly acquiesced to stop messing with Penny and you."

The diner went silent, all eyes on Claire.

Kate, the chatterbox, spoke first, which was no surprise this morning. "Since when?"

"Since I made a quick stop at her house yesterday for a little game of show-and-tell."

Someone pounded on the diner's glass door.

Claire looked over and smiled. "And there's our fourth."

"You invited Grady's aunt?" Ronnie asked as Penny stood to head over and unlock the door.

"No, I invited Penny's aunt. It's not Millie's fault that her nephew insists on being the pure and dutiful sheriff of the county."

"He wasn't very 'pure' last night," Ronnie said under her breath for her sisters' ears only. "Although he did his duty particularly well and delivered an extremely satisfying early birthday present with promises of more to come today."

Claire chuckled. "Did he spank you hard, birthday girl?"

"Not hard enough," Ronnie said, playing along, her corrupt grin reminding Claire of Chester's.

Kate pretended to gag. "Gross, stop it. Don't make me think about Grady and you fornicating. It's bad enough that Mom and Manny show their love even more now that she's sober."

Ronnie made a face. "And here I thought that was a cognac-inspired act. Turns out she really does have the hots for Manny's body."

"Who knew Mom was so lecherous?" Kate groaned.

"You're one to talk," Claire said to Kate.

"What?"

"You and your pet names for Butch's southern anatomy."

Kate beamed. "Leave Captain Reamus of the Lusty Womb Raiders out of this."

"See, that's the shit I'm talking about right there," Claire said, cringing.

"Katie, you haven't been right in the head since you met Butch."

In response, Kate lovingly patted her pregnant belly under her green overalls. "It's all Valentine's fault, but I wouldn't change a single thing."

"What's Valentine's fault?" Millie asked, setting her walker off to the side and taking the seat at the head of the table. Her steely curls looked lopsided this morning, the left side battered and half-flattened, but her focus was as sharp as ever.

"Katie's plight of temporary insanity," Ronnie said, pushing the plate of remaining rolls toward Millie. "I'm surprised you're up this early after last night's fun at the senior center."

"Well, bingo doesn't last much past eight," Millie said with a huff. "Besides, those geriatric flumpnuggets can't keep their eyes open or dentures in much past nine."

"What time did you go to bed?" Penny asked, settling in next to her aunt.

"Ten-thirty. All of that 'Bingo!' bellowing wore me out early, not to mention the dancing."

"You were dancing?" Kate asked.

"Hell, yes. They were playing lots of disco tunes and my moneymaker needed to shake it up a bit." She squinted at Claire. "Did you tell them yet?"

"I was just getting to it, but now that you're here, how about you do the honors."

That would free Claire up to figure out where to start clipping on what she believed was a fake prop of Joe's from his arsenal of fenced goods, albeit a realistic-looking replica.

Millie pointed at Penny. "Those low-down reviews Elizabeth left should've been taken off the internet by now."

Penny did a double take. "What?"

"Me and this crazy cookie here." Millie nodded in Claire's direction as she grabbed a cinnamon roll. "We paid Elizabeth a neighborly visit yesterday."

"You went to see Elizabeth without me?" Kate whined to Claire. "I thought we were partners in crime detecting."

Ronnie turned on Claire next. "You took Millie with you? Jesus, Grady is going to be pissed when he hears about this."

"Calm down, Chicken Little. Millie stayed in the Jeep."

"But still," Ronnie continued.

Millie harrumphed. "I slid down in the seat so that two-timing hussy couldn't see me."

"Such language, Aunt Millie." Penny pretended to be shocked and then ruined it by laughing.

"You ain't heard nothin' yet." Millie bit into the roll. "This is really good, sweetie. Better than the last time you made them."

"I've been doing some hands-on practicing lately."

She stared at Penny for a minute as she chewed, leaning closer. "What's going on?"

"Nothing." Penny smiled wide. Too wide, in Claire's opinion, especially at this hour after so little sleep. "Why?"

"There's a sparkle in your eyes that I haven't seen in a long time."

Penny shrugged. "It's called good friends."

Millie snorted. "Looks more like good sex to me."

"Ha! I wish." Penny reached for the penultimate roll on the plate, avoiding her aunt's gaze. "Anyone want more rolls? I have another tray in the kitchen." She looked around the table, getting no takers.

Kate cleared her throat. "So, Claire. What did you two do to shut down Elizabeth?" Judging from Kate's tone, she was still pouting about being left out. "Is this about that envelope from Millie I picked up for you behind the library?"

Claire nodded.

"We dug up some of her dirty laundry," Millie supplied. "And then showed her the stains."

"Holy crap," Penny said, frowning down at her phone. "You guys aren't kidding. The reviews are gone." She looked from Millie to Claire. "I can't believe you got her to pull them down so quickly."

Claire shrugged. "We just provided some motivation."

"The floozy promised to back off from Grady, too," Millie said, looking at Ronnie as she took another bite.

"She'll retaliate, though," Claire said, repeating the prediction she gave Millie yesterday after returning to the Jeep. She was almost as certain of that as she was that this Maya knife was fake, especially after taking a closer look at it under the bright diner lights. "But when she does return fire, she'll aim at me instead of Ronnie and Penny."

"Why you?" Ronnie asked.

"Because I told her nobody else knows besides me that her boyfriend left her and took their kid with him because of her gambling addiction."

"Oh," Penny said, frowning at Millie as she chewed. "I forgot that she used to sneak over to the casino and blow Grady's paychecks sometimes."

"I didn't," Millie said, smirking.

But Claire wasn't finished. "When Elizabeth tried to shrug off my knowledge about her gambling problem, claiming she was bored with being a mom and tired of that asshole with whom she'd left town when she dumped Grady, I explained that I also knew about Sunny Blaze."

"What's Sunny Blaze?" Ronnie asked while topping off her coffee.

"It sounds like a color of rouge," Kate said.

Penny looked at her aunt. "Didn't Elizabeth have a couple of cocker spaniels named Sunny and Blaze when she was growing up?"

Millie nodded, grinning at Claire. "I told you that two-timer had no imagination."

"Sunny Blaze," Claire continued, "is the fake name Elizabeth used while working at a brothel about thirty miles north of Vegas."

Gasps filled the room, with Ronnie's being the loudest since she also managed to spill coffee in her lap at the same time.

Penny shot out of her chair and grabbed a hand towel from the counter, tossing it to Ronnie. "Go on," she said, sitting back down next to her aunt.

"It turns out that Elizabeth owed a good chunk of money to a cutthroat bookie in Vegas," Claire said. "After her boyfriend left her, she got desperate for cash and invented Sunny Blaze. But daily mattress workouts are not for wimps, so she left the brothel and scuttled home to live with her parents. Of course, Millie and I don't know what lies she's told her family, but judging from the way she's back to her old song and dance when it comes to Grady, apparently the old slogan still applies in this case—what happened in Vegas stayed in Vegas."

"What about the money she owed?" Penny asked.

"Your aunt seems to think she's paid back her bookie."

"She'd be more nervous otherwise, jumping at shadows," Millie said, indicating toward Ronnie. "Like this one here."

Ronnie frowned but didn't deny Millie's charge, looking down at the coffee-stained towel on the table next to her.

"Anyway," Claire said, "After I laid out the facts for Elizabeth and backed her into a corner, she agreed to deliver on my demands or risk me sharing what I had on her with that hoity-toity grandmother of hers, among others."

"Hot damn," Kate said. "You two have been busy this week."

"Here and there," Claire admitted, focusing her attentions back on the knife. She lined up the nail clippers and snipped one of the hardened strips of leather holding the obsidian blade to the sheath.

"Claire!" Kate cried out, reaching for the knife. "What are you doing?"

Claire moved out of her sister's reach and snipped several more strips of the leather binding. "I'm going to see if this is what I think it is."

"You're destroying it!" Kate turned to Ronnie. "Do something."

Ronnie didn't move a muscle. "Isn't that illegal?"

"Not if it's a fake." Claire clipped twice more and then peeled away the last of the leather strips.

Penny rested her elbows on the table, leaning closer. "What makes you so sure it's a fake?"

"Because Joe Martino would have done a better job at hiding a real historical artifact."

The blade sat loose in the sheath now. Claire tugged on it, separating the two with relative ease. Something clattered onto the table.

Kate reached out and snagged the small key that had fallen out of the fake knife's sheath, holding it up for all of them to see. "Holy shit."

"I knew it!" Claire set down the knife pieces. "The binding was wrong."

"How in the world would you know about that?" Ronnie asked. "Did you take a class on ancient weaponry in college?"

"Millie and her crew scoured the internet and found several pictures of legitimate, ancient Maya knives from some museums south of the border. I studied those, especially the symbolism on them and the binding. Joe did a decent job making it look legit, but it was too polished. The bindings weren't ragged enough."

"So, what's that key open?" Penny asked. "It's too small for a door, don't you think?"

"Who knows with Joe." Claire rolled her eyes. "That's another mystery to solve." Then again, if the son of a bitch was still alive, maybe she could ask him in person, preferably through the bars of one of Grady's jail cells.

"I can do it!" Kate said, holding up her hand like she was back in elementary school volunteering to be hall monitor. "Let me work with Millie and her gang on this one. You're too busy building stuff and Ronnie needs to keep on the down low for a while."

"Katie," Ronnie said. "I hate to be a killjoy, but Butch isn't going to like you trying to dig up one of Joe's old treasures. Maybe we should give the key to Grady and wash our hands of this." She looked at Claire, her gaze earnest. "Along with this business about Sophy having proof that Joe is still alive."

"No way." Kate closed her fist around the key and clutched it to her heart. "Grady doesn't need to know about this. He has his nose in enough of our business." She shot an apologetic look in Penny's direction. "Sorry."

"No need to apologize for my brother's tendency to meddle," Penny said, taking a sip of her coffee. She grinned around the table. "Things are a lot more exciting since you three came to town. Wouldn't you agree, Aunt Millie?"

"Yes sirree. People are dying now for reasons other than old age and boredom. I'm all in for tearing up the place and painting the town red."

Kate's phone rang, muffled some by her purse. "I still want to know how you two figured all of that out about Elizabeth," she told Claire and Millie as she fished it out. When she checked the screen, she let out a squeak of surprise. "I think it might be Sophy," she whispered, looking up at Claire with wide eyes.

Claire's heart picked up speed. There was only one reason why Sophy would be calling Kate. She must have gotten the email Kate had sent with pictures of the cryptic lists Claire and Mac had found under the dresser, along with a post office receipt showing the lists were on the way to her.

"Well, answer it already," Millie said. "Some of us are getting on in years and don't want to die before we find out what that old floozy has to say."

"Put it on speakerphone," Claire ordered.

"Hello?" Kate said, holding the microphone end of the phone up to her mouth. Her hand was trembling.

"Kate Morgan," Sophy said, sounding like a hostess calling out names to announce a table was ready for them.

"Yeah, it's me, Sophy."

"I received your email."

"Good. Now it's your turn. What proof do you have that Joe

is still alive?"

There was a pause, maybe a hesitation even. Then she cleared her throat. "I have two words for you—Horatio Hornedadder."

"What is Horatio Hornedadder?"

"A name. My tit for your tat."

"Let's leave all tits off the table," Millie grumbled.

"What was that?" Sophy asked.

Kate scowled at Millie. "Nothing. I have the TV on in the other room." She returned her focus to the phone's screen. "What does Horatio Hornedadder have to do with Joe?"

Sophy's laugh was like a frigid wind, the sort of thing that left a person with chills and windburned cheeks. "I'm not your gal Friday, Kate. I delivered on my part of the bargain, it's up to you to figure out what to do with the information. After all, weren't you tellin' me you were the smart one of the bunch?"

Under the weight of Claire's and Ronnie's glares, Kate had the decency to blush. "Uh, yeah."

Ronnie flipped off Kate. Claire seconded it.

"Well, then, you should be able to figure it out. And if Lady Luck is on your side, in plenty of time."

"In time for what?" Kate frowned at the phone and then Claire.

"In time to keep from pushing up daisies. Since you're carryin' Butch's baby and he's done me well over the years, I'll leave you with a warning. As soon as you start askin' around about that name, the clock will start ticking."

"What clock?" Kate asked, but the line was dead.

"I think 'whose clock' was the better question in this case," Millie spoke up, interrupting the silence that hovered around the table.

Kate worried her lower lip. "What do we do now?"

Claire didn't know about the others, but first she needed to call Mac, as she'd promised last night, and tell him what Sophy had said, warning and all.

"You and Claire need to decide if pursuing this is worth more trouble," Ronnie weighed in, clearly still not wanting to touch this "Joe's alive" business herself.

Millie snorted. "You girls know what they say about trouble, don't you?"

"Double double, toil and trouble," Kate said, using a cackly, witch voice. "Fire burn, and cauldron bubble."

"I'm not talking about Shakespeare, smarty-pants."

"Trouble never comes alone," Ronnie tossed out. "I think that's an old proverb I read somewhere. Might have been German or Russian. Or I might have picked it up from the damned FBI."

"While that's true," Millie said, "it's a tad boring."

"Life is worth every bit of the trouble," Penny added.

"No, Penelope Sue." Millie patted her niece on the forearm. "That's actually what they say about Scorpio females, not about life. And it's as true about you as the sky is blue here in Arizona."

"What do they say about trouble, Millie?" Claire asked, not bothering with the guessing game.

"The saying goes, 'The trouble with trouble is that it starts out as fun.' " Millie clapped her hands together, grinning at each of them in turn. "Now, who wants to have some fun?"

"I do! I do!" Kate blurted, raising her hand again.

Ronnie and Penny exchanged worried frowns.

Claire groaned and reached for the last cinnamon roll. "Here we go again."

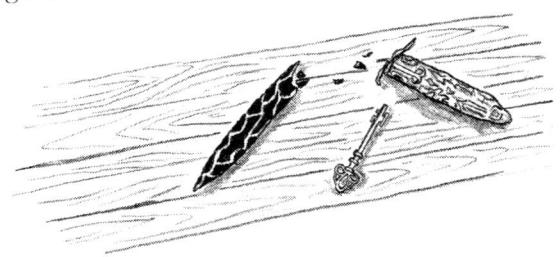

Claire's Epilogue

Author Note: For those of you who are like me and crave a bit more at the end of a story, enjoy this peek behind the scenes with Claire and Millie.
~*Ann*

Seven days ago … (Monday, Jan 28th)

Hey, Ronnie," Claire said as she followed her sister out of The Mule Train Diner. "Can I borrow your phone for a minute?" She needed a phone number that Ronnie and Kate both had, but there was no way she was going to ask Cuckoo Kate for it. She didn't need to know Claire's intentions, or she'd insist on taking part. Neither did Ronnie need to know, for that matter. This was something Claire was going to take care of without her sisters' help.

Ronnie paused, shivering in the cool morning breeze as she fished her phone out of her purse and handed it over. "Where's yours?"

"I left it back at the RV park," Claire lied as she quickly pulled up the phone number and memorized it while Ronnie was busy frowning back toward the diner, probably reliving Elizabeth's venomous threats. Claire's own phone was tucked away in her coat pocket, and she hoped like hell it didn't ring before she could escape her sister's company.

"What are you doing?" Ronnie asked, turning back to Claire.

"I wanted to check the weather quick." She handed the phone back to Ronnie, repeating the number in her head again. "Gramps wants me to clear some brush in the ravine behind the tool shed today, and I was wondering how thick of a coat I'd need."

Part of that was true. Gramps had mentioned something as

Claire had headed out the door earlier about wanting her to meet him back in the ravine after she returned for a job he had in mind. Claire figured he'd tell her to clear out some of the dead brush before the coming spring fire season or maybe build a picnic table down near Jackrabbit Creek. Ever since Jess had put together that website for the RV park, Gramps had also been on a clean-up-the-park campaign.

"Sunny and dry," Ronnie said. "Same as it's been since October."

"Right." Claire took a longer look at her sister in the morning sunlight. "You okay?"

"Sure. Why do you ask?"

Because ever since Elizabeth's visit to the diner this morning, Ronnie had looked far from "okay," but Claire wasn't going to lean on her sister if Ronnie didn't want to talk about her feelings.

"Just checking." She thumbed toward her Jeep. "I'm going to head back to the RV park. You need a ride? Kate can sit in the back."

"No, Grady is letting me borrow his pickup. Butch asked me to pick up some stuff from the store before heading to The Shaft."

"I thought today was your day off." The bar was now closed on Mondays, so Ronnie shouldn't have to go into work beyond dropping off whatever Butch needed.

"I'm just going to do some bookkeeping, and then I think I'll go over to the RV park and see if Ruby needs any help around the place. Grady has to work, so I might as well keep busy."

"Okay. I'll see you later then."

While waiting in her Jeep for Kate, who was using the restroom before their trip back to Jackrabbit Junction, Claire typed the phone number into the text messaging screen and wrote:

Going to teach Grady's ex-wife a lesson. You want in on this?
Claire Morgan

She hit send and then switched the phone to silent mode, pocketing it as the passenger door opened.

"Someone needs to do something about that bully," Kate said as she hopped in and fastened her seat belt.

"You mean Elizabeth?" Claire asked, playing dumb. She

started the Jeep.

"Yes. Ronnie has enough stress these days without that two-timing tyrant taking potshots at her."

Claire's phone vibrated in her pocket. She pulled it partway out, peeking down at the two-word response from Grady's aunt, Millie:

Hell, yes!

Good. Now it was just a matter of digging deep enough into Elizabeth's world to find the rotten spots.

"Yeah, someone should teach her a lesson." Claire pocketed her phone again. "But not you, Kate."

"Why not me?"

"Because you don't need to end up in jail again."

Kate crossed her arms. "You're not the boss of me, Claire."

Claire rolled her eyes and shifted into gear. "Not yet, but after Mac and I purchase The Shaft from your baby daddy, I might be."

* * *

Six days ago … (Tuesday, Jan 29th)

The midday sunshine warmed Claire's shoulders through her light jacket. She watched Kate's back as her sister hurried along the trail toward the campground restroom, glad for another chance to sneak in a phone call.

Claire pulled out her cell phone, moving to higher ground to try and get a decent signal. She hoped like hell the call would actually go through this time. She didn't think she could keep sending Kate to the tool shed for random useless items without her sister becoming suspicious that Claire was up to something.

Millie answered on the fourth ring. "Who is this?"

"Claire Morgan."

"Yeah, I know."

"Then why did you ask?"

"Just making sure. It pays to be cautious in my business."

"What business is that?" Claire asked, wondering how much her nephew, the sheriff, knew about Millie's affairs.

"That's none of *your* business. Now what can I do for you today?"

"I was thinking about the price you sent for your time and services, and I want to know if you offer some kind of guarantee."

"You want a guarantee?"

"Yeah. You're not cheap."

"I had to up the price because you want me to drag my feet when it comes to helping your sister, and Kate's money is going to sponsor a trip to the casino for me and my girls. I need extra cash in case she gets frustrated with how long I'm taking to deliver what she wants and decides to not pay up. We already booked a night in the casino's hotel suite."

"So, you're basically milking me for insurance money."

"There's no need to take that tone. I'm old and could die before long, so I have to make hay while the sun is shining."

Claire scoffed. "You're not giving me a lot of faith in your abilities."

"I'll deliver, don't you worry."

"Fine. I'll pay your price, and for starters, I want to know where Elizabeth lived prior to returning to Yuccaville."

A harrumph came through the line. "What is it with you Morgan girls and addresses?"

"What do you mean?"

"Yesterday Kate wanted the address of Elizabeth's parents' house, where she's living at the moment."

"Did you give it to her?"

"Sure. That was before you said to start dragging my feet."

Ah-ha. That was probably where Kate had been hanging out last night instead of attending the mini-meeting at the bar with Butch and Mac.

"From now on," Claire said, "let me know what information Kate wants before you make any moves. I need to stay at least one step ahead of her, so she doesn't end up in jail again."

"Does that include information about that Maya knife?" Millie asked.

Claire frowned toward the restroom where her busybody sister was still emptying her bladder. "She hired you to help with that knife?"

"Yep."

"When?"

"A couple of weeks ago."

Kate should have kept the knife a secret, dang it. "What have you found out?"

"That information will cost you extra."

Claire sighed. This was going to end up costing her a pretty penny to stay ahead of Kate. "Fine, add it to my bill with the same treatment as the other."

"So, you want me to give you the information on the knife before I give it to Kate?"

"Yes."

"Consider it done. Although I had Penny deliver some information about that knife yesterday."

Ah, the gift bag from Millie that Penny had handed off during Kate's posse meeting at the diner. *Baby gift, my ass.* It was no wonder Kate tucked it away. "What sort of info?"

"A few articles and some pictures that came with them."

"Can you send those pictures to me?"

"Sure. I can get you the links to the articles, too."

"I'll take whatever you have on the knife."

Some papers rustled on Millie's end. "Okay, I have a pen handy now. So, you want to know where Elizabeth was in Nevada since leaving Grady, and what she was up to while there, right?"

"Yep, everything you can find out about her life during that time."

"We'll get on it."

"Good. We need to strike back before Elizabeth can do too much damage to Ronnie's reputation."

"It might be too late already."

"What do you mean?"

"Elizabeth was overheard talking on the phone somewhat recently, asking about Lyle Jefferson."

Shit! "If that fire she's lighting gets out of control, it could split up Ronnie and Grady."

"That isn't going to happen on my watch," Millie said. "I'll get you the information you need pronto."

"Let me guess. This rush service will cost extra, too?"

"Nope. I'll give you a family discount this time."

Claire hung up, frowning at the blue sky. It wasn't going to be easy to stay ahead of Elizabeth. Or Kate, either.

* * *

Five days ago … (Wednesday, Jan 30th)

Everything about Arizona was dusty, including Claire this afternoon. Especially after spending most of the morning mixing cement. She headed for the campground restroom to clean up, figuring she'd take a quick shower to rinse off rather than traipse through Ruby's rec room and make a dusty mess.

Her phone rang as she neared the building. She pulled it out of her pocket, hoping it was Mac. She could use the calming sound of his voice in her ear after spending too much time today worrying about Joe still being alive and what that would mean for Ruby and the rest of the family.

It wasn't Mac, though. It was Millie.

Claire answered in a quiet voice. "You have something for me?"

"Yep. You have company?"

"Not at the moment. Let 'er rip."

"It turns out that Elizabeth didn't leave her man. He left her, and he took the kid with him. They're living up near Reno now according to his driver's license. His address matches his mom's."

"So, they must have had some sort of falling out, and she let him take the kid with him." That was interesting, but not enough to shut down Elizabeth's crusade to get Grady back. "Any clues about what spurred the breakup?"

"We're still digging. She moved to Vegas after the split, and the place she rented is in a not-so-nice part of town."

"Makes you wonder if she got messed up with drugs or the wrong sort of folks somewhere along the way." With her family's money, why live in a seedy part of town?

"I'll let you know more soon. We're going to check out police records next." Millie cleared her throat. "Did you get my text yesterday with those articles and pictures?"

"Yep."

"What do you think? Is it the same knife?"

"I don't know. My memory from the night I first saw it is

blurred with alcohol. I'm going to have to see if I can somehow get Kate to let me look at it again without making her suspicious."

"Good luck on that. Your sister has some loose wires."

Claire chuckled. "That's one way of putting it."

* * *

Four days ago … (Thursday, Jan 31st)

After dropping Kate the jailbird off at The Shaft, Claire headed back to the RV park. When Gramps had told her to go get Kate out of jail again, she'd been in the tool shed figuring out what she'd need for tomorrow's work back at the birding platform. She needed to finish that task and then jump in the shower.

She drove past the General Store, parking in front of the tool shed. Before hopping out, she pulled out her phone and dialed Millie's number.

"You have good timing," Millie said in lieu of an answer.

"Why's that?"

"I was just getting ready to text you." There was a rustling sound on the other end of the line. "Ruth found something in the public police records about our little floozy."

"I'm all ears."

"Turns out Elizabeth wasn't paying her bills. She was turned in to collections by a couple of doctors, a hospital, and the power company."

"So, she ran into money trouble."

"Yeah. Within about six months of moving to the city."

"Any idea why she was in the hospital?"

"According to what we could find, she got into some sort of physical altercation and had a possible concussion."

"I wonder who she was fighting with," Claire said. "A bill collector?"

"Or some thugs sent by a bookie. They don't like it when you don't pay back gambling debts, and that girl was always loose with her cash at the casino."

Christ, what had Grady's ex gotten herself into in Nevada?

"I think we're on to something juicy here," Millie said. "I've been wanting to take down that no-good hussy for years after what she did to my nephew."

"Well, I'm certainly glad I'm on your side in this battle."

"Your sister is good for Grady. We need to keep him happy. He's so busy chasing her tail these days that he doesn't come snooping around the library much anymore."

Claire had a feeling it wasn't Ronnie keeping him out of their way as much as Lyle and his shenanigans.

"You need anything else from me?" Millie asked.

"Yeah, one more thing. Watch it when you're out spying on Elizabeth. Kate was doing some shadowing of her own and took a picture of Elizabeth and Deputy Ernie at a bar over by Roadrunner Auto Parts. Your walker was partially visible in the picture."

Millie cursed. "I told that waitress to leave my walker where it was, but she insisted on moving it to the side of the booth."

"Did Elizabeth know you were listening in on her conversation?"

"I don't think so. She didn't even look our way. As far as she could tell, we were a bunch of old ladies having a few beers. I kept my head low when she passed, though, same as with Grady's deputy."

"Could you hear what they were talking about?"

"No. It was too loud and echoey in there. I don't understand the appeal of metal roofs and concrete floors. Drunks fall down the same as old people. They're just asking for a lawsuit."

Claire needed to remember that when it came to the floor at The Shaft.

"Oh, one more thing," Millie said. "Elizabeth married her baby daddy after she left Grady."

"It must have been true love, huh?"

Millie snickered. "Right. Nothing to do with her baby daddy winning a settlement around that time from a trucking company for an accident that left him with a permanent limp."

"Money makes people do stupid shit."

"Amen, sister. But what's even more interesting is that we can't find any evidence of her divorcing Mr. Big Money Settlement. Not even separation papers."

"You're kidding."

"Nope. It appears that Elizabeth is still married."

"Well, that's certainly going to make it tough to renew those wedding vows with Grady anytime soon."

Millie chuckled and hung up.

* * *

Three days ago … (Friday, Feb 1st)

Claire had just pulled into the parking lot at The Shaft when her phone pinged. She parked around back, crossing her fingers Mac was texting to say he was coming home early, but it was Millie instead.

She read Millie's text: *Struck gold!*

Claire glanced around to make sure nobody was nosing around the parking lot, such as her little sister, or even Butch, who seemed to have upped his watchdog routine since Kate put herself in jail.

She texted back to Millie: *How much extra for this gold?*

With all of the time the Geritol Gangsters—as Kate called them—were putting in to help Claire take down Elizabeth, she was going to have to ask Gramps for a loan.

Millie wrote: *This one is free, but I need $20 for additional fees.*

"It's not free then, is it?" Claire muttered and typed: *What additional fees?*

Millie returned: *I have to pay Greta for extra leg work.*

Claire rolled her eyes and typed: *Fine. Add it to my bill. What did you find?*

A link appeared on her screen.

Claire tapped it and watched the video that started playing. It appeared to be a segment from some television reality show set in Las Vegas called *Hot Cops on Street Patrol.* As Claire watched, a good-looking cop leaned down to talk to a blonde, who was sitting on a curb with her hands cuffed behind her back. It was hard to see the blonde's face clearly, though. Claire leaned closer to her phone right as the woman looked straight at the camera.

She gasped and hit the pause button. "Gotcha!"

There was no doubt about it, that was Elizabeth. However, written at the bottom of the screen were the words: *Sunny B. arrested for public intoxication and solicitation.*

Claire finished watching the short clip before replying to Millie with: *Sunny B? An alias?*

Millie sent back: *We're tracking that name down. Stay tuned!*

Claire typed: *Well worth the extra $20! Thank Greta for me.*

She pocketed her phone, chuckling under her breath. Damn, Grady needed to contract out to the Geritol Gangsters. Those women didn't mess around.

What in the hell had gone on in Las Vegas? Elizabeth had been hurting for cash, that was clear, but why not write home to her family and ask for help? They certainly seemed to have plenty of cash to spare, judging from the fancy mini-mansion of theirs.

As Claire headed for the back door of The Shaft, she stared out across the open desert, watching a narrow dust devil in the distance swirl lazily along the valley floor. It appeared there were a lot of layers to the rotten onion that used to be Mrs. Elizabeth Harrison.

* * *

Two days ago ... (Saturday, Feb 2nd)

Claire stepped out of the shower and reached for a towel. As she was drying off, her thoughts once again returned to this morning and her talk with Mac. He'd seemed to listen to her this time about compromise and finances, but she was prepared to stand her ground if he were to change his mind about hiring Luke to help with the brewery addition.

There had to be some other way to make this work that didn't involve Mac having to drive to Timbuktu and back for another six months. Or more.

Her phone rang while she was buttoning her shirt.

"Hey, Millie," she answered after seeing who was on the other end of the line. "What's going on?"

"We figured out the mystery behind Sunny B."

"Is it something more than just a fake name used on that reality cop show to cover their asses legally?"

"Oh, this is way better than that." Millie snickered. "The B stands for 'Blaze,' as in Sunny Blaze, who tried her hand at working in a brothel north of Vegas to pay for her debts, including the gambling ones."

Claire coughed in surprise. "You're kidding me."

"It's all right here in front of me in color pictures."

"Pictures?"

"Yep, the brothel tried some creative marketing, making a website showcasing their girls. She may have a few layers of makeup caked on her face, but there is no doubt that I'm looking at Elizabeth."

"Wow." Claire's brain was struggling to get back onto its feet. This was blowing up bigger than she'd ever imagined.

"Yeah, and you should see the list of services she offers."

"Is that website even legal?"

"Probably not, being that we found it on the dark web using a top-secret browser."

The dark web? A top-secret browser? Holy crap! How did Millie and her pals know about all of this deep investigation shit? Maybe Grady was right to check up on them at the library.

"Oh God, please tell me you didn't use the library's computers for this. Your nephew will sniff that out in a heartbeat."

"You think this is our first time around the horn, child?" Millie scoffed. "We have resources outside the library."

"Remind me to stay off your shit list, Millie."

"I could say the same when it comes to you Morgan sisters, especially Kate."

Claire smiled at her reflection in the bathroom mirror. Finally, something was going her way. "I need a printout of those web pages in my hands by tomorrow."

"Why tomorrow?" Millie asked.

"Because that's when I'm going to take them to Elizabeth and tell her to back the fuck off or we'll go public."

Millie whistled. "I like the starch in your girdle."

"Is that even a saying?" Claire asked.

"I just said it, didn't I? I want to go with you when you meet her."

"You can't. Elizabeth knows you. I need to go alone. That way any retaliation is focused on me."

"I can ride along and lay low in the car."

"I don't know."

"Come on. How about this deal—if you let me come and watch the show, I'll remove all costs for my services."

Now she was talking! But wait … "I thought you needed funding to cover your casino trip."

"Don't you worry about my money matters, girlie."

Claire hesitated still. "If Grady finds out you're involved with any of this—"

"He won't. Ronnie has him running in circles right now anyway with her new problems."

"How do you know about Ronnie's new problems?"

"Kate told me earlier about the FBI warning when she was inviting me to your sister's pre-birthday shindig."

Claire sighed. Kate and her bucket mouth. "Are you coming to the party?"

"I can't. I promised Ruth that I'd be her partner during Bingo Night at the senior center. They have some pretty big pots on the line, not to mention a good buffet sponsored by the local fried-chicken joint up the road."

Claire's stomach rumbled. There was nothing like good fried chicken.

"So, can I tag along on the takedown?" Millie asked.

"Fine," she conceded. "You can come with me."

"Oh, this is gonna be good. So, when are you coming to get these pictures?"

"Well, I can't get over that way today or tomorrow morning." With Mac home and the work with Luke planned for the birding platform, it would be hard for her to find an excuse to head to Yuccaville. Maybe if … Wait! "I have an idea. Contact Kate and let her know you have some information for her to pick up."

"But you said not to let her know about what you and I have been up to."

"Pretend it's for her, but when she comes to pick it up, make sure it's sealed and tell her the package is for me."

"She's not that easy to fool, you know."

"Okay, maybe tell her that bit you told me the other day about the knife."

"That the stolen one we read about last week in that article was reported found?"

"Yeah, that will give her something more to chew on." Claire finger-combed her hair in the mirror. "If she pouts about wanting to know what's in the envelope, tell her it was something I wanted for Ronnie's birthday and I made you swear to secrecy."

"Okay. One more question."

"What's that?" Claire shut off the bathroom light and opened the door.

"What time are we going to Elizabeth's place to drop the bomb on that opportunistic hussy? I want to make sure I have popcorn popped and ready for the big show."

* * *

One day ago ... (Sunday, Feb 3rd)

Clutching the envelope with the copies Millie had made and sent through Kate, who had been like a dog with a bone about the unopened envelope, Claire climbed the steps of Elizabeth's parents' fancy-schmancy house.

She paused on the veranda, casting a glance back at her Jeep. True to her word, Millie was hiding low in the seat, completely out of sight.

Claire took a deep breath, lifted her chin, and rang the doorbell. She didn't love confrontations, but enough was enough. Elizabeth's assaults on Penny's business needed to stop, along with the two-timer's attempts to convince everyone in town that Grady and she were reconciling.

The door opened and a woman looking like an older version of Elizabeth stared down her nose at Claire. "Can I help you?"

"I need to talk to Elizabeth."

The woman's penciled-in, dark blond brows pinched together as her gaze took in Claire from head to toe and apparently found her wanting. "Are you a friend of hers?"

"We know many of the same people." Claire held up the envelope. "I have a delivery for her."

The woman held out her hand with perfectly manicured peach fingernails. "I can take that for her."

"No, I need to speak with Elizabeth to explain what this is." Claire smiled. "Trust me, she'll want to handle this herself."

The woman's lips tightened along with her eyes. "Fine. Give me a moment. I'll send her down." She closed the door in Claire's face, clicking the lock behind her.

Well, wasn't she just sweet as sugar-laced arsenic? And Claire had even showered before coming today. It appeared her fresh jeans and black sweater were too low-level for Elizabeth's typical cohorts.

She glanced back at her Jeep. Millie was still slouched low. Claire hoped the old tiger hadn't gotten stuck. There wasn't a lot of leg and foot room in the cab.

She was turning back toward the door when it opened. Elizabeth stood there in silver spandex workout gear with her hair pulled back and her cheeks pink. It appeared Claire had interrupted the Barbie doll during her workout routine.

"Who are you?" Elizabeth asked, her eyes hard and suspicious.

"You should close the door," Claire said, seeing the older version of Grady's ex hovering in the background.

"Why?"

"Because you have an audience." Claire smiled without meaning it. "And from what I've learned," she said in a low voice, "you prefer to give only private lap dances to your clients."

Elizabeth's nostrils flared and her whole body jerked as if she'd been zapped. She recovered quickly, though, glancing over her shoulder. "Give us a minute, Mother." She stepped out and closed the door, whirling on Claire with a mixture of fury and panic battling for control on her face, coming together in a snarl. "Who are you and what in the hell do you want from me?"

Claire opened the envelope and pulled out the copies Millie had made. "I'm Claire, Veronica Morgan's sister," she said and held up the first piece of evidence showcasing Elizabeth's very checkered recent past. "And I'm here to shut you down."

* * *

Today ... (Monday, Feb 4ᵗʰ—Ronnie's Birthday)

Claire stepped out of The Mule Train Diner, looking east at the warm glow of the rising sun in the sky. Another day of work awaited her back at the RV park, but for a moment, she paused to breathe in the cool, desert air and enjoy some quiet calm while she waited for Kate to go to the bathroom for the fifth time in the last hour.

"Hey, Claire," Ronnie said, joining her on the sidewalk in front of the diner. "Hold on a minute. I need to talk to you."

Ronnie was supposed to be catching a ride back to Grady's with his aunt. She'd told Claire she planned to head to The Shaft later, claiming the need to do more bookkeeping there even though it was her birthday. Crazy woman. In the meantime, Claire would take Kate back to the RV park and plant the pregnant princess in her chair in the ravine to keep her out of trouble.

"What do you need?" Claire asked, jamming her hands in her coat pocket.

"Since you fixed my problem with Elizabeth," Ronnie said, frowning down the street, "I need your help with another situation."

"If this is about the hitmen on your tail, I'm not sure I can be any more help than Mississippi and Grady already are." Especially now that she and Luke needed to get started on the brewery.

"It's not about that." Ronnie scrunched up half of her face. "Maybe it sort of is."

"Are you finally going to tell me what's had you twitching and fussing for the last couple of days?"

"You noticed that, huh?"

Claire snorted. "You're short-circuiting worse than Kate lately." She stepped closer, lowering her voice. "Out with it."

"Well," Ronnie licked her lips. "I sort of killed a guy."

Knocked speechless, Claire managed a single blink.

"You have to pinkie promise not to tell anyone what I'm going to tell you."

Claire was still working her way through that previous part about killing a guy. "You mean there's more?"

Ronnie nodded, holding her pinkie in front of Claire's face. "Pinkie swear."

"I'm not sure I want in on this," Claire said, but she locked pinkies with her sister anyway.

"Too bad. I need your help."

"Why me?" She had enough stress with Joe being alive and undoubtedly wanting to get even with Claire for his missing treasures.

"Because you're my sister."

"So is Kate. You should confide in her instead."

"Let me rephrase that—you're my only rational sister."

This had to be some kind of game Ronnie was playing. A birthday prank, that was it! Only in reverse, using Claire as the sucker. She couldn't be serious about having killed a man.

"So what do you need from me? Help burying the body?" she joked half-heartedly.

Her sister didn't laugh.

"Oh, Jesus, Ronnie," Claire whispered, struggling to breathe all of a sudden. "What kind of trouble are we in now?"

The End ... for now

Ann Charles is a USA Today bestselling author who writes award-winning, character-driven stories full of mystery, humor, adventure, suspense, romance, and supernatural mayhem. When she is not dabbling in fiction, arm-wrestling with her children, attempting to seduce her husband, or arguing with her sassy cats, she is daydreaming of lounging poolside at a fancy resort with a blended margarita in one hand and a great book in the other.

Facebook (Personal Page):
http://www.facebook.com/ann.charles.author

Facebook (Author Page):
http://www.facebook.com/pages/Ann-Charles/37302789804?ref=share

Instagram:
https://www.instagram.com/ann_charles

YouTube Channel:
https://www.youtube.com/user/AnnCharlesAuthor

Twitter (as Ann W. Charles):
http://twitter.com/AnnWCharles

Ann Charles Website:

More Books by Ann

The Jackrabbit Junction Mystery Series

Bestseller in Women Sleuth Mystery and Romantic Suspense

Welcome to the Dancing Winnebagos RV Park. Down here in Jackrabbit Junction, Arizona, Claire Morgan and her rabble-rousing sisters are really good at getting into trouble—BIG trouble (the land your butt in jail kind of trouble). This rowdy, laugh out loud mystery series is packed with action, suspense, adventure, and relationship snafus. Full of colorful characters and twisted-up plots, the stories of the Morgan sisters will keep you wondering what kind of a screwball mess they are going to land in next.

The Deadwood Mystery Series

WINNER of the 2010 Daphne du Maurier Award for Excellence in Mystery/Suspense

WINNER of the 2011 Romance Writers of America® Golden Heart Award for Best Novel with Strong Romantic Elements

Welcome to Deadwood—the Ann Charles version. The world I have created is a blend of present day and past, of fiction and non-fiction. What's real and what isn't is for you to determine as the series develops, the characters evolve, and I write the stories line by line. I will tell you one thing about the series—it's going to run on for quite a while, and Violet Parker will have to hang on and persevere through the crazy adventures I have planned for her. Poor, poor Violet. It's a good thing she has a lot of gumption to keep her going!

The Deadwood Shorts Series

The Deadwood Shorts collection includes short stories featuring the characters of the Deadwood Mystery series. Each tale not only explains more of Violet's history, but also gives a little history of the other characters you know and love from the series. Rather than filling the main novels in the series with these short side stories, I've put them into a growing Deadwood Shorts collection for more reading fun.

The Deadwood Undertaker Series

From the bestselling, multiple award-winning, humorous Deadwood Mystery series comes a herd of tales set in the same Deadwood stomping grounds, only back in the days when the Old West town was young.

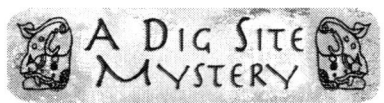

The Dig Site Mystery Series

Welcome to the jungle—the steamy Maya jungle that is, filled with ancient ruins, deadly secrets, and quirky characters. Quint Parker, renowned photojournalist (and lousy amateur detective), is in for a whirlwind of adventure and suspense as he and archaeologist Dr. Angélica García get tangled up in mysteries from the past and present in exotic dig sites. Loaded with action and laughs, along with all sorts of steamy heat, these books will keep you sweating along with the characters as they do their best to make it out of the jungle alive.

The AC Silly Circus Series

From AC Silly Circus Co. comes a series of paranormal mystery novellas chock-full of oddball shapeshifters, dangerous secrets, spicy steam, and loads of laughs.

Made in the USA
Las Vegas, NV
30 November 2025

35386296R00226